DEADLY

WATERS

OTHER TITLES BY DOT HUTCHISON

A Wounded Name

THE COLLECTOR SERIES

The Butterfly Garden
The Roses of May
The Summer Children
The Vanishing Season

DEADLY WATERS

DOT HUTCHISON

Published by Thomas & Mercer, Seattle
www.apub.com

Amazon, the Amazon logo, and Thomas & Mercer are trademarks of Amazon.com, Inc., or its affiliates.

ISBN-13: 9781542005579
ISBN-10: 1542005574

Cover design by Caroline Teagle Johnson

Printed in the United States of America

To the girls who whisper and the girls who scream,
and the ones made of rage who burn in between

1

When I was younger, my grandmother used to swear that lightning bugs knew when storms were coming. The more lightning bugs there were, the more they flickered and glowed, the worse the storm was going to be. I was never sure if she actually believed that or if she just liked telling me.

There are certainly worse things to believe.

It's hard not to think of that right now, though: my grandmother slowly rocking on her back porch, a wispy cloud of smoke around her as she steadily worked her way through two packs a day, her voice creaking as we looked out into muggy summer evenings and she told me to count the lightning bugs. There is a storm coming tonight—a proper gully washer, according to my phone—and the air is thick with moisture and fireflies. A warmer-than-usual spring brought the fireflies out early this year.

I take a deep breath, feeling the heavy moisture creep into my lungs. Sweat-damp clothes cling unpleasantly. It's going to be a long, miserably hot summer if this spring is any indication. This late at night the rest stop is deserted. We're just close enough to town that travelers would rather press on to someplace more populated before stopping, and even the truckers are largely off the road. Many of them are probably an exit or two south at Café Risqué, and they'll wander up here in the early hours of the morning looking for the prostitutes who know where to wait for easy marks. For now, however, there's precisely one car in the parking lot, a two-door sports car that looks too expensive for its current location.

It's parked a good distance away from the buildings, out of range of the diffuse yellow lights. A couple of smaller lights are posted at intervals to at least make people aware the pavilions are here, that the grassy stretch of picnic space is broken up by concrete and wood from time to time, but they're not meant for evening use. They're meant to indicate, not illuminate.

Fortunately for me—unfortunately for general safety—that also means that the pavilions have no security cameras.

I lean against the wooden post, looking out at the trees that loom behind the rest stop. The stop was built near the crest of a hill, but not far at all into the wood, the ground is broken by a jagged gully. There are signs posted around not to go into the forest because of poor visibility and uncertain ground. Some of the signs have additions tacked on below: **BEWARE OF ALLIGATORS.**

"Why we here again?"

I turn to the voice and see the young man swaying drunkenly down the path. It seems to take him extraordinary effort to stay relatively upright. Then again, he was blisteringly drunk even before I picked him up with a bottle of paint-thinner vodka. "We've still got a bit of a drive, baby," I tell him. "You said you needed to stop on the way."

"Yeah." He blinks at me in the moonlight, mostly shadow. "Yeah, I need a piss. But why we down here?"

"The bathrooms are closed for maintenance." I wave out at the woods. "You're a guy. You can get away with plan B."

"Hell, yeah, I can piss in the woods!" He kind of sounds like he's cheering. It's almost funny, but more sad; this is the best conversation I've gotten from him.

Jordan stumbles down the path. Where the sidewalk gives way to marshy grass, he falls to his hands and knees and starts laughing. "Oh, man, my dick is gonna get muddy. You gonna be okay with that?"

"I think we can manage to wash the mud off at my place," I say. "You don't want to take care of it now?"

"Do I want mud and piss in my mouth? Not so much. Come on, baby, do your business in the trees, and we can get on with the rest of the night."

He starts laughing again, but he does push himself back to his feet and meander into the woods, past the tree line and into the shadows. Stray bits of light gleam demonic red off eyes close to the ground, there and gone and there again. Around his crashing footsteps and the snaps of twigs, I can hear deep-throated croaks and singing crickets and the occasional grumble of a car passing on the interstate down the hill. In that relative silence the jangle of his belt is surprisingly loud.

Thankfully, thunder booms and rolls overhead to drown out the sound of his pissing, the bass rumbling through my bones to make my toes tingle in my sneakers. There's still time before the rain hits, the clouds congregating to the southwest and gradually shifting to cover more of the sky.

Suddenly there's a dull roar, a crunch of breaking bone, and a pained, panicked scream. After pulling the mini-flashlight out of my pocket, I click it on and train it toward the trees. The light is just barely strong enough to see Jordan falling to the ground, and it reflects red off a pair of eyes. The gator lumbers backward, dragging Jordan with it out of sight. His screams get hiccupy and strained as alcohol and shock combine to temper his reaction.

Normally people aren't in very much danger from alligators; the four-legged suitcases are at least as scared of us as we are of them. Humans are far more likely to be bitten by a shark than an alligator. But it's April, and the gators are starting to get frisky and hungry ahead of mating season, throwing off the sluggishness of the winter months. There were problems with alligators in the gully last year, too, but the winter convinced people that the danger had passed.

People, as a rule, aren't very bright.

More growls and a few bellows join the chorus of Jordan's screams before a sickening thump and squelch silence the screaming. Maybe Jordan's head hit a rock? I'm certainly not going to go over and find out.

As hot as the spring has been, it's also been wet—days and days of rain that keep the humidity soaring and make some of the meteorologists look nervously ahead to hurricane season. The creek in the gully should be a good depth, deep enough for the gators to stash Jordan's body under the water to age for a while.

Fun fact: alligators can bite, but they can't chew. They rely on decomposition in water to soften their food enough that they can bite off chunks and swallow.

I keep the flashlight trained on where Jordan disappeared, not because I think it'll do anything to frighten off other alligators but because I'd like to see them coming if they start moving my way. No eye flash, no sign of scales. Probably safe to move.

Pushing off the post, I walk back along the sidewalk to the main path and stumble over something on the concrete: Jordan's keys.

I was the one to drive us here, given his inebriation. We're close enough to the same height that I didn't need to adjust the seat or the mirrors, and I carefully removed all signs of myself from the vehicle before I gave him back the keys. My hair is tucked up into a hat, and even this late at night, the metal on cars is hot enough to hurt and burn; gloves may not be a popular fashion choice, but they're a practical one. In more than one respect, as a matter of fact. Even the vodka bottle is back in my bag for later disposal so an intrepid officer doesn't try to find out who bought that specific brand of vodka in the past few days. (Not that it would much assist an investigation; UF may not be one of the top-ten party schools anymore, but it is absolutely still a drinking school, and this is one of the cheapest bottles on the shelf.)

The keys, though . . . there's a reason I gave them back to Jordan. It's important that it looks like he drove himself. I even made sure to park worse than he usually does. That wasn't easy. Jordan routinely gets ticketed for taking up two spaces in permit lots because he's an asshole and overprotective of his stupidly expensive car. That's not a reason to kill him, of course, but it's certainly not a reason to spare him.

I pick the keys up by the main ring, careful not to let any of the teeth bite into my thin leather gloves. I could toss them into the woods, I guess, and hope it looks like they fell out of his pocket when he was attacked. The problem with that is making the location of the keys match up with the path of carnage. That means getting closer to the alligators and the gully than I'd like to be at the moment. The keys jingle as I bounce them in my hand, weighing my options.

After a moment I head back to the car and stand at the driver's door as if I've just gotten out and locked it. The keys fall with a clink and a clatter to the asphalt, and with an almost accidental kick they're half under the car. Drunk boy drops his keys. Perfect.

Resisting the urge to whistle, I walk along the far edge of the parking lot to the ramp that leads back to the interstate, keeping a safe distance from the cameras mounted on the main building. I wait for a lone car to pass, then sprint across all three lanes of highway to the median. Luck is with me, and there are no northbound cars, which means I can cross the rest of the way to the shoulder. Safely tucked away in the shadows of the opposite rest stop—and still out of range of the cameras—I crouch down and shrug out of the straps of my bag.

When I got accepted to college, my dad and I sat and went over the pros and cons of trying to get me a car. My scholarships would cover pretty much all of my actual school costs, but cars were expensive. Even a junker would add up with repairs, maintenance, and gas. Eventually we decided that Gainesville had a decent enough bus system that I could make it work, and I bought a bike instead. Not just any bike, though; this one is designed to get routinely folded down and stored, making it perfect for students with limited space. Two and a half years later, I can unfold it and set it to rights nearly in my sleep.

In less than five minutes I'm off, riding along the shoulder of the highway until I can get to the next exit and the back roads that will take me home, thunder shivering down my ribs with each new rumble. When I look behind me, back to the quiet rest stops, I can see lightning flash within a cloud, a brilliant glow of rose and lilac that's almost more the memory of the colors than the colors themselves, fading away as quickly as sunspots through your eyelids.

Beautiful.

My grandmother always said the lightning bugs knew when it was going to storm. I know it isn't true, but on a night like tonight, it's easy to believe it anyway.

2

Fidgeting with the pair of thin coasters, Rebecca watches the bartender make her drinks. The woman who was there an hour ago didn't give her any grief for getting virgins, and she actually gave Rebecca one of them for free when she saw the large purple *DD* written on the back of her hand. The current bartender leered at her when she walked up, mocked her for not getting boozy, and then tried to badger her into adding alcohol, as if she were somehow less of a person for not wanting to get plastered.

Sometimes she wonders if there are certain words men are genetically hardwired not to understand—*no* being the most significant of them.

So she watches his hands, and he scowls when he realizes it. "Relax, Princess," he tells her, almost shouting over the music. "I'm not adding booze."

"Less worried about the booze than the roofies," she replies, "seeing as one of your coworkers drugged one of my classmates last week. And given that we have no word as yet that he's been fired or arrested, I'm going to go ahead and watch."

He blinks at her. Then, carefully keeping his hands and the glasses in her view the entire time, he finishes making the drinks. When he plunks the glasses on the bar, liquid slops up the sides, some of it splashing over. "He hasn't been fired."

"Shocking," she says deadpan.

"There's no proof."

"Sure. Only witnesses who came forward to police and a picture of his stash behind the bar." She balances the coasters on the rims to prevent both spilling and dosing as she walks. His scowl, she notices, has disappeared, leaving his furrowed brows as a mark of concern rather than anger. Did he really think stories wouldn't spread across campus? Picking up the drinks, she eases back into the crowd.

People press in all around her, yelling and laughing—in a few cases crying—and while this is a bar, not a club, there are a handful trying to dance to the combination of pulsing music and shrieking televisions. Mostly college students, she thinks, or people still drinking like they're college students. This close to campus, especially in a bar this cheap and this prone to skipping ID checks, the students have pushed out nearly everyone else who might come.

Rebecca weaves through the dancers and shifts around the knot of frat boys chanting and egging on two of their brothers competing to see who can chug a pitcher of beer the fastest. The corner she and her friends managed to stake out can't really be called *quiet*, but it's a bubble of something at least less chaotic. She slides into her chair near the walls and hands the second drink to her roommate.

"You were watching him pretty closely," Hafsah notes. She pulls away the coaster lid and sniffs at the drink.

"It should be safe." But it doesn't stop her from studying the way the liquid moves against the glass and looking for any shifts in color or undissolved particles. Rebecca's always careful about her drinks, but she can acknowledge that what happened to her classmate has her more paranoid than usual. She wishes they'd gone to a different bar, one without a recent history of roofies, but Ellie wanted this one.

Ellie, she thinks, eyeing her friend, wants a fight.

There are five of them around the table. Ellie's two suitemates, Luz and Keiko, begged off in order to work on a group project. There should be a third suitemate—specifically Ellie's roommate—but Kacey's been in a coma since she was attacked the first week of fall semester. None of them want to replace her in their suite, but Ellie is the one to terrorize her newly assigned roommates until they run away and Housing surrenders. Rebecca mostly disapproves of bullying.

She's never tried to stop Ellie from keeping Kacey's space sacrosanct, though.

Susanna and Delia share a study space with Rebecca and Hafsah, and all seven of them share the bathroom, God help them all.

In fact, Susanna and Delia are the ones who wanted to come and drink, self-medicating after stressful presentations, but Ellie is the one who decided where. Ellie, who poured herself into leather pants and a clingy, plunging top, who slapped on makeup as bright as any mating call. Ellie, who's already on her third drink because she threw the first one in the face of a man who grabbed her ass at the bar. Ellie, who's glowering over the rim of her glass at a couple a few tables over, the man leaning too far into the space of a woman inching so far away from him she's barely still in the chair.

"Ellie."

"He's harassing her," her friend snaps.

"Yes," agrees Rebecca.

"And you're just going to watch?"

"I'm not going to go break his nose, if that's what you mean," she says evenly.

Delia props her chin up on her fist—or tries to. It takes her a second attempt before she manages it. She's not always a lightweight, but when Delia gets stressed, she forgets to eat. "His nose could use breaking," she announces a little too loudly. "It's so thin and twitchy. It needs character."

"Certainly Ellie has character to spare," Hafsah replies, and Delia breaks down into giggles.

Rebecca gently elbows her roommate. "Do not encourage her. The last thing we need is to get thrown out of another bar."

9

"You know, technically—" Susanna starts, and the others groan. "Technically," she continues unabashed, "we've never been thrown out of a bar. Only Ellie has. We just leave with her because we're nice."

Rebecca cants her head. "I thought it was to keep her from shanking people on the street."

"Only catcallers," Ellie says with a shrug.

Delia shakes her head. "Have you seen your ass in those pants? I'm pretty sure the pope would rip a whistle at the sight."

Closing her eyes, Hafsah mutters under her breath. Rebecca can't actually make it out, but knowing Hafsah as she does, she's pretty sure it's a plea for forgiveness. It's Hafsah's usual response to all their little blasphemies.

Glancing back at the target of Ellie's ire, Rebecca sees that the man has an arm slung around his companion, trying to pull her back onto the chair and closer to him. The woman is unenthused, eyes darting around the bar. "I've got it," Rebecca says.

"You sure?"

"There's this thing you may or may not have heard of: It's called discretion?"

"You mean cowardice? Yeah, I've heard of it."

Rebecca rolls her eyes and slides out of the corner. "I'll be back."

She doesn't head straight to the other table, though. Instead, she eases into the shadows along the wall toward the bathrooms. When she reaches the hallway, she walks normally to the table, squinting slightly to convey a mild sense of panic. She taps a nervous knock on the table, near the woman's hand, to get their attention. "I'm sorry, but by any chance do you have a tampon I could have? I'm early, and I don't have my purse, but the machine in the bathroom is out."

The man—and up close she can see that he's older than she thought, too old for the girl he's hitting on—looks grossed out, but the girl looks relieved at the interruption. "Do you have a pocket?" she asks.

Rebecca holds out her hands, showing the front of her flimsy skirt. There are actually pockets there, but they're almost impossible to see if they're empty. "Sorry."

"No worries; I'll just come with you," the girl says, yanking away from the man's grasping hands. "That way you don't have to wave a tampon around."

"Thanks so much. I could kick myself for not having something."

"We've all been there, right?" Hiking her purse over one shoulder, the young woman manages to kick the chair, jostling the man a little farther away. "Just through there?"

Together they walk to the bathroom, stepping around the long line. There are a few protests, but as long as they don't skip into a stall, it's not like they're actually cutting in line. At the sinks, the other girl props her purse on the counter and starts to dig through it.

"That's okay," Rebecca tells her. "I don't actually need anything."

"Oh, God." The girl wilts against the counter, brown eyes filled with chagrin. "Was I that obvious?"

"You looked like you were counting exit signs."

"Oh, God," she says again.

"Hey, if I overstepped, I apologize. You just looked like you needed the out."

"I did." She straightens, taking advantage of the mirror to fluff partially curled blonde hair. She wears a lumpy cardigan over a slinky dress and knee-high Doc Martens. "My fucking friends. They were supposed to meet me here more than half an hour ago, but the only one who's showed up so far ditched me to give a guy a blow job by the dumpster." She pulls out her phone, checking it for texts, then shakes her head. "I didn't even want to come out tonight. I have a test tomorrow morning."

"So why not go home? They're not here. They can't complain."

"There's a thought." She opens a rideshare app but hesitates. "What if he follows me outside?"

"We'll wait in here until your ride is closer. With any luck you won't even see him on your way out."

"Okay." She clicks through her request and sends her phone to sleep but doesn't tuck it back into her purse. "Thanks for the save."

"Anytime. Maybe some century we won't need to rescue each other anymore."

"God, wouldn't that be nice."

Nice, yes, but regrettably unlikely. Not if past experiences hold true.

Rebecca and the girl, who belatedly introduces herself as Ashton, stay near the sinks, chatting comfortably about nothing in particular. Ashton helps a few girls fix their makeup if they need it while she waits for the text from her driver. Fortunately, rideshare drivers tend to hang near the bars downtown if they aren't already driving. The girls don't see the guy as they walk back through the bar—or outside—and Rebecca waves goodbye as Ashton settles into the back seat of the car.

She stays outside for a couple of minutes, breathing in air that doesn't reek of cheap beer and too many bodies. It isn't fresh, exactly, heavy and thick with humidity and the fetid swampiness that clings to the city after a rain. Half the city is marshy from the amount of rain the spring has brought.

She walks back inside to a sudden sharp increase in volume, the sound of breaking wood, and the sight of a tall redhead kicking a man in the junk.

Oh, Ellie. Must be Tuesday.

3

At least, Rebecca thinks ruefully, this isn't one of their usual places. It would suck more to be barred from someplace they like. She sticks Delia's clutch into Susanna's purse and shrugs into the cross-body strap, following it with her own purse. Hafsah has her purse and Ellie's card case. Hafsah doesn't drink ever, and Rebecca only drinks in safety, so somehow they're always the only responsible ones when they go out.

Hafsah is blushing fiercely, mortified by getting thrown out. It's amazing she isn't used to that already. Or maybe she is, and she's just that optimistic. Her hand keeps twitching to the edges of her hijab the way it does when she's embarrassed and wants to hide her burning cheeks with the excess fabric.

They help Susanna and Delia stumble out in the wake of their friend, who's ranting and punching the air from over the bartender's shoulder. Despite his earlier dickishness, he's careful about where he touches her, one arm banded about the middle of her back, the other hooked around her knees to keep her legs in place. It's a good call on his part; she will absolutely kick him if given the chance and not care that she'd fall six feet to the floor.

Rebecca ignores the laughter and drunken insults that surround them. It happens too often to really faze her anymore, and it's not like Ellie is the only one to ever get thrown out of a Gainesville bar. If she were the type to get embarrassed by what her friends do, she wouldn't be friends with Ellie. Though that was admittedly easier when Kacey was there to be a calming influence.

Outside, the bartender sets Ellie down hard on her feet, giving her a small shove so she's leaning against the wall rather than him in order to regain her balance. "One month," he tells her, his finger up in her face. Perilously close to her mouth, really. "You don't come back for one month, and don't think we won't have your picture up."

Her teeth snap, barely missing the finger he jerks away. "Do you put up the rapists' pictures too?" she snarls. "The ones who drug the drinks and grope the girls?"

"One month," he says again. "Break that, and there'll be charges."

He doesn't say if those charges would be of a law enforcement kind or the monetary kind. She did break three chairs, several glasses, and possibly a table. Ellie starts with the dick punch, always, and the brawls sort of sprawl out from there.

After the bartender stalks back inside, Rebecca adjusts the two purses against her hip and studies her friend. She'd be a lot less tired of the brawls if they ever seemed to accomplish anything. "Feeling better?"

"He shoved his hand up her dress! After she specifically told him she wasn't interested!"

"The friends she came with retrieved her," Hafsah says quietly. "Hopefully they won't be bothered by his friends."

Ellie growls and stomps off.

"That's the wrong way, tipsy!" Susanna calls and trails off into giggles.

Pot. Kettle.

Hafsah jogs after Ellie and turns her around. "Back to the dorms?" Hafsah asks hopefully.

"More booze!" yells Delia. The yellow-tinted lights outside cast strange shadows on her dark skin.

"Back to the dorms," Rebecca confirms and hooks her arms through Susanna's and Delia's to get them moving in the right direction. She agreed to three hours, no more, and if they haven't hit that, she'll consider the brawl as added time. "Giggles and Chuckles here wanted to drink—they drank, and we all have classes in the morning. That and getting thrown out of one place a night is my limit."

"You girls have limits?" asks a male voice. "Nice to know."

Delia growls and lifts her pepper spray. The man standing in the streetlight edging the parking lot raises his empty hands in response, holding them out from his body to look as nonthreatening as possible.

"Det Corby!" Rebecca greets him cheerfully, fighting back a blush. "Who'd you piss off to be on patrol?"

Ellie spins around. And then around again when the momentum proves stronger than her spatial awareness. "Det Corby!"

The man grins at them. "Can I put my arms down?"

Delia glances at Rebecca, who nods.

Detective Patrick Corby of the Gainesville Police Department is still smiling as he puts his hands in the pockets of his black slacks. He's one of the younger detectives on the force, barely thirty, and, according to three informal Twitter polls, by far the best looking. In deference to the heat and humidity, both still staggeringly high even now that the sun is down, he's not wearing a blazer, his sleeves rolled to his elbows, and the collar unbuttoned above his loosened tie in hope of some relief. His gun and badge hang heavy on his belt.

Ellie and Rebecca met him through a class the fall of their sophomore year, when an injury confined him to a desk for a few months and he agreed to teach an undergrad seminar for criminology majors. The class is long done, but a handful of the students keep in touch with him, especially with regard to other classes and projects. Somewhere along the line he traded *hot professor* for *hot friend*, at least for Rebecca and her incredibly inconvenient crush. Even setting aside the question of whether he's interested in her or not, she's fairly sure that he's the type of guy who stopped dating undergrads as soon as he wasn't one anymore.

She approves of that, in principle. In practice, in this specific instance, it's a little depressing.

"What brings you out?" Ellie asks, leaning over Rebecca's back. Her chin digs into Rebecca's shoulder because she can't quite support her own weight. "I thought you were scared of the dark."

"UPD is having a meeting, and they asked if we could help cover downtown."

"A meeting?" Digging her phone out of her purse, Rebecca pulls up her email. "Oh, my. University hit up the LISTSERV."

"What? What is it?" demands Susanna. She drapes across Delia's shoulders, but since Delia is five inches shorter and about a hundred pounds heavier, it's only Hafsah shoving them toward the wall that keeps them reasonably upright. Susanna doesn't even seem to notice. "Oh, God, please tell me we're not having a fire drill tonight. Do. Not. Want."

"No, there was another alligator death."

"Oh, no." Delia looks up at them, lower lip quivering. Delia is an emotional drunk; whatever she feels, she feels three thousand percent. "Oh! They can turn into shoes! They'll live again!" Whatever she feels also changes rapidly.

"A UF student died out at the hooker stop," Rebecca reports, skimming the email.

"Rest stop," the detective corrects with a grimace. "It's a rest stop."

"It's a hooker stop," chorus four of the girls. Hafsah doesn't, but she does nod along with the others. When the stop opened back up after a complete remodel, the arrests for prostitution soared because of its proximity to Café Risqué down in Micanopy, and the well-lit, clean restrooms made a lot of the prostitutes feel safer. Arrests dropped over time, but even the state troopers don't like to say if it was because prostitution and solicitation declined or if the troopers just got tired. It's a topic the criminal justice students tend to discuss a fair amount, largely because it makes their professors uncomfortable.

"UF student ID, release of the name pending verified identification and notification of the family," Rebecca continues. "They . . . huh."

"What is it?" Ellie squints at the bright screen of the phone. "Come on, read faster."

"The car has been there since Friday or Saturday," she says. "That prompted a search of the woods behind the stop. No one was actually reported missing."

"But it's Wednesday."

"Tuesday."

"But it's Tuesday."

Both of them look up at Det Corby, who for all his efforts over almost two years can't convince them to call him Patrick or even just Corby. He shrugs. "That's state trooper territory, and they only found the body this afternoon. We just got called in to cover tonight so that the campus cops can go over safety guidelines and new patrols."

"Right, they had that floater in the lake two weeks ago."

Rebecca elbows her in the gut. Ellie oofs but doesn't otherwise react.

"There have been over half a dozen deaths by alligators this spring, at least that we know of." He rubs at his forehead, running his fingers back through sweat-darkened auburn hair. "Until the last few years the state has looked at maybe three in a year."

"Well, what does anyone expect?" Susanna says with a snort. "The past couple years have seen habitat encroachment on an almost unparalleled level. When the gators are forced into urban areas, of course deaths are going to jump."

"Hell of a jump."

"Hell of a habitat loss," she retorts, sounding remarkably steady for someone as drunk as she is. "I'm amazed there haven't been more deaths along the St. Johns, given how dirty parts of that river have gotten."

"Crystal River and the Santa Fe both have larger gator populations this year," adds Delia. She ducks under Ellie's flailing arm, stumbling back into her roommate and fellow environmental science major. Also the wall. "Lake Alice has a lot more too."

"Oh!" Susanna blinks at the detective. "Oh, that's why they're meeting! Because of Lake Alice!"

"And the smaller lakes, which might equally attract alligators," he agrees mildly. He glances behind them to the bar. "None of you are driving, right?"

Ellie gropes along Rebecca's arm until she can lift her friend's hand, showing the large letters on the back. "Designated driver," she announces, overenunciating the words.

"Also, no one's driving," Rebecca says. "We walked. Servers are a lot less twitchy if they know at least one person per group won't be swaying."

Det Corby gives a dubious look to the street, busy with bar traffic despite the late hour, and at the intermittent lights on the campus beyond. "Want me to call you a ride?"

"We're good." Rebecca smiles, hoping that her blush doesn't look as bad as it feels. Or, if it does, that it can be explained away as a by-product of the heat and humidity. "We just need to make sure Ellie doesn't get in any more fights."

With a deep groan, Det Corby shakes his head. "Another one? Ellie."

"He deserved it."

"Did the table?" mutters Hafsah.

"It was in the way."

"Everything's in the way when you're on your fi—"

"Don't!" Det Corby lifts his hands, palms out. "Do not tell me how many drinks you've had when I know damn well that none of you are twenty-one."

"My ID would beg to differ." Ellie sniffs.

"Please don't continue."

Rebecca grimaces. Fake IDs and underage drinking are an inescapable part of the college experience. Even the police seem to acknowledge that. If you make it very obvious or force the point, they'll make the arrest, but otherwise they seem to rely on a few random checks to keep the fear of God in the students and hope that will keep the alcohol poisoning to a minimum.

Meeting the one law enforcement officer who knows for absolute fact that Ellie is not yet twenty-one because he taught them a year ago how to tell a good fake ID from a real one is already a problem. Given that they're still in the parking lot of the bar . . . ?

It's a good thing he likes them, Rebecca decides and refuses to think more deeply about that. She scrolls through the rest of the email and puts her phone away. The university has been compulsive about sending out alligator-safety-and-awareness messages throughout the semester, and the past couple of weeks have been particularly saturated. Then again, that's what happens when you find what's left of an alligator's dinner bobbing on the campus's most popular lake a few hours after a storm churns up the shallows.

Det Corby studies them all and sighs. "Come on, I'll walk with you partway."

"We are just fine!" Ellie says too loudly.

"Humor the cop, and let me help. I'd feel bad if you splattered all over University Avenue. Besides, it works best to have a one-to-one sober-to-drunk ratio." He bows and offers Susanna his arm, and he catches her when her drunken curtsy starts to tip into a face-plant. In order to keep her balance as they start walking, she winds around his arm and presses her cheek into his biceps, humming happily in a way she probably doesn't intend to sound as suggestive as it does. A moment later the humming ticks up into a wobbling off-key rendition of "Nessun dorma."

Susanna's older brother is an aspiring operatic tenor; they can always tell what show he's rehearsing for by what Susanna sings (badly) when she's drunk.

Rebecca's more impressed that despite the muffled snorts of laughter from Det Corby, the shoulder supporting Susanna doesn't move at all.

They make their way slowly down to the crosswalk, which they honestly wouldn't have done if the detective wasn't with them. Backtracking sucks. Delia and Hafsah put their arms around each other's waists, close enough in height that it provides balance without a lot of wrestling. Delia tends to list left when she's been drinking, and they've all learned to stay on that side to make steering her easier. At the rear of the group, Rebecca draws Ellie's closer arm over her shoulders, firmly grasping the other one just over the elbow to keep her from launching herself at the catcalling, laughing boys loitering outside the bars they pass. Ellie loudly complains about chauvinism and patriarchy and damsels in distress and only succeeds in kicking someone once. The brawl has her in a good mood.

After the crosswalk, a grinning Det Corby gently extricates himself from Susanna and hands her off to Hafsah. "Ladies. You're sure you're good from here?"

"We're always good," Ellie retorts.

"We'll be fine," Rebecca says. "We're not that far in."

"All right. The UPD meeting should be letting out pretty soon, so if you need to call them for help back, please do so." He holds a hand out to Rebecca, but both of hers are occupied with Ellie. With a grin, he gently tweaks the tip of her nose, making her eyes cross. He gives the rest of them a little wave and jogs back across the road before the light changes.

Nose twitching, Rebecca looks after him until he disappears into one of the bars. When she turns back around, she jumps at Ellie's face nearly pressed up against her own. "Personal space. That's still a thing, even when you can't walk on your own."

"You liiiiiike him," crows Ellie. "You have a crush on Det Cooooorby."

"Hush."

"You really liiiiike him."

"I can drop you."

"I think it's cute," she announces. "I can be your wingman. Wingwoman. Person?"

Rebecca grits her teeth and tries not to blush. Again. Still? "Tell me the last time you flirted with someone that didn't end with their getting stitches, and I'll consider it."

"Who needs boys? You don't need boys. You're good."

Susanna and Delia cackle. Hafsah sighs. Hafsah sighs a lot when the others have been drinking.

"Let's just go back to the dorms," Rebecca says. "And keep an eye out for alligators, I guess. University is certainly worried."

Ellie lurches forward, dragging Rebecca with her the first few feet until Ellie breaks away. "Heeeeere, alligators! Come eat all the stupid boys!"

Swearing, Rebecca chases after her suitemate so Ellie doesn't crash headfirst into a sign. Or a tree. Or a building.

Again.

4

Rebecca scrolls slowly down the latest email from the university, one hand shading both her eyes and the phone screen. Her sunglasses, currently pushed up to keep her orange-red hair out of her eyes, would make it hard to read the screen, but the glare from the sun isn't much better. On the increasingly rare occasions they can get Ellie to agree to drink in the dorm instead of going out, the usual snarls mellow out into silliness. On one such night, Ellie spent hours arguing that they were both redheads. Just to keep her arguing and laughing, Rebecca insisted that *ginger* was separate from *redhead*—because freckles—and ever since then it's become a kind of shorthand within their suite for the kinds of conversation that can only happen when Ellie is surrounded by girls.

Rebecca frequently wonders what happened to Ellie to make her so constantly enraged. It got worse after Kacey, but that wasn't what started it. She's never asked. Some things can only be shared by choice, and Ellie doesn't owe the rest of them an explanation for her traumas. It just means that Rebecca tries harder to find those bubbles of silliness, to spark the laughter without that furious edge to it. It'll probably help her friend live longer.

Ellie managed to struggle through her hangover to attend her morning classes but gave up after lunch and returned to her room to take a nap instead of going to History of Criminal Justice in America. Which means that despite her interest, she probably hasn't seen the newest LISTSERV.

"Are you reading porn on your phone again?" asks Hafsah, coming up beside her.

"That's Delia," she answers automatically. She finishes the email and puts her phone in her pocket, mulling over the information. "Ready?"

"Where's Ellie?"

"Sleeping."

Her shorter friend rolls her eyes, adjusting the strap of her bag on one shoulder. "I don't understand how she keeps the grades she does when she misses this many classes."

"She tracks which classes factor attendance and participation into the final grades and attends those."

Hafsah blinks, then shakes her head. "So what were you looking at?"

"New email blast; they released the name of the student they found out at the hooker stop."

"Do I want to ask how much of him they found?"

"Probably not," Rebecca admits. "They also didn't give that information. His name was Jordan Pierce, a senior in the accounting program."

"Why wasn't he reported missing?"

Pushing off the brick wall, Rebecca starts walking. The AC in the dorms may be anemic, but even that's better than this oppressive heat. After a moment, Hafsah falls in step beside her. "It says he lives on Fraternity Row; maybe they're used to him being gone at all hours. Or maybe he's in a single, no roommate. Some of the houses have those rooms, right?"

"Not really," Hafsah tells her. "Do you know how many people live in those houses? He almost certainly shares a room, and still no one reported him missing. That's frightening—that someone can be missing for days, and no one notices."

"It was a weekend."

"Part of it was a weekend. Then we started the week, and no one missed him."

"Or they missed him and didn't think it was a bad thing."

"Is that better?"

"No," answers Rebecca. "Just different." She carefully pulls her sunglasses out of her hair and shakes out the chin-length curls, feeling the itch of sweat along her scalp. Removing a stray hair from the joint where the earpiece meets the frame, she slides them back on properly. The amber-tinted world relieves a little of the building heat headache behind her eyes. "If you were ever missing, it wouldn't take me days; I promise."

"Same. So does this mean you'll finally tell me where you've been sneaking off to at night?"

"Oh my God!" She walks faster, her longer legs swiftly putting some distance between her and her entirely too-pleased roommate.

Hafsah just laughs and jogs to catch up. "I think it's cute you're being discreet."

"I am not secretly dating Det Corby."

"Seriously?" Hafsah plants herself directly in front of Rebecca, forcing her to stop, spin around her, or run her over. Rebecca doesn't think she'd be a bad person for being tempted by the last option. Briefly. Fleetingly tempted. Hafsah pokes her stomach with a strong finger, making her yelp. "Then where do you go?"

"For a walk if it's cool enough. For a bike ride if I need to make the breeze."

"And you feel the need to hide this?" she asks, crossing her arms over her chest. For someone eight inches shorter than Rebecca, Hafsah is weirdly intimidating.

Rebecca sighs. There probably isn't a way out of this. "I don't sleep well. Like, ever. And I realize you generally sleep like the dead, but I can't just spin in circles in the room or suite. It would bother Susanna and Delia, even if you didn't notice. And it bothers me to pace the hall or the lounge. I go for a walk or take my bike, and I come back when I can either sleep or sit still."

"But why keep it secret?"

"Because I didn't want you to yell at me for not taking a buddy at night."

Rolling her eyes, Hafsah shakes her head and turns around so they can get moving. "You could have just told me, you know. I mean, there's an RA on night duty at the desk; I'd feel okay knowing you were checking in with them. It is a shame, though," she continues. "All this time, we thought you were sneaking out to see the detective. Insomnia is much less sexy."

"Especially when you're the one living it."

"Any chance your nocturnal ramblings cross his—"

"Stop."

"Are you blushing or heatstroking?"

"Yes," Rebecca grumbles.

"Why are you so touchy about him anyway? He's cute. He's young. He actually seems like one of the good ones. What's wrong with enjoying your crush?"

"Because y'all tease me about it?"

"Barely. Well, except for Ellie."

Rebecca sighs. "You have no idea how much of it I get from Gemma."

Hafsah giggles. "Okay, that's fair. Family trumps. Heavens, I want to be there when Ellie and Gemma finally meet."

"No! They are never, ever, never to meet!" Christ, her heart is pounding at the mere thought of it.

"Why not? They'd get along like a house on fire."

"Yes, because they'd *set the fire!*"

Rebecca loves Gemma more than anyone else in the world—which is saying something in their very large close-knit family—but she's also aware that whenever she gets in trouble, her parents turn to look at Gemma to find out how it's probably her fault. Ellie has more than enough bad habits of her own already; as shitty as the world seems to be on a regular basis, Rebecca's fairly sure it doesn't deserve whatever Ellie and Gemma could cook up between them.

Hafsah erupts into giggles so strong she nearly falls over. Muttering under her breath, Rebecca grabs her friend by the elbow and steers her around a boy kneeling in the middle of the sidewalk to pick up his scattered papers. The giggles gradually fade despite a couple of relapses.

"So the Det Corby conversation is done now, yes?" Rebecca asks eventually.

"Agreed. Sourpuss."

Rebecca sticks out her tongue. Maybe if there was an actual chance of something with Det Corby in the near future, she wouldn't want to keep her crush so private. It's not enough, though, that she likes him or even that he likes her—if he does in that way; her age and his job take the possibility out the window. She doesn't think it's unreasonable to not want to be teased for a relationship that can't happen.

They walk around clusters of talking students in Turlington Plaza, giving a wide berth to an aggressive hate preacher and someone posing in sweat-streaked body paint that may be intended as performance art. Midterms are almost a month gone, and final exams/papers/projects are not quite a month out, which means the barely restrained sense of panic that grips the campus at those times is mostly absent. Here and there, though, Rebecca can hear groups discussing the news email.

Waiting at a crosswalk, they watch a knot of girls cluster around a crying freshman. They're all wearing Greek letters somewhere—if not on their shirts, then on their large quilted tote bags—and the girl in the middle is laughing hysterically through her tears. Hafsah reaches for one of the girls on the edge of the group, lightly touching her elbow to get her attention. "Is she okay?" she whispers.

"Mostly?" the other girl answers. "It's just a shock, is all."

"The alligator?"

"The asshole."

Before Rebecca can ask what that means—or decide if she wants to know—the crying girl gives them a huge smile. "He's dead. I just . . . he's dead! He can't hurt anyone anymore!"

Hafsah and Rebecca trade an alarmed look before turning back to the girl. "Hurt anyone?" Rebecca asks cautiously.

"Jordan is an absolute dick," one of the other girls tells them.

"Was!" corrects the crying one. She laughs giddily, but it hiccups into a sob.

"Was," the first girl agrees, petting her friend's braided hair. "He started a pantie scoreboard in his frat house, and he and his brothers like to put names and pictures up with them, sometimes even phone numbers. They don't care if the girl doesn't like it."

"*It* meaning the board?" asks Rebecca. "Or how the panties get earned?"

A lopsided smile is the unsettling answer. Rebecca scowls and studies her toes. She can imagine more than a few ways that girls might lose their underwear without wanting to. It sounds like some of these girls don't have to imagine.

"I called the police from the party," the crying girl tells them. "I went with friends from class, not my sisters, and I needed help to get to the hospital. And then the, you know, the exam and kit. They told me they responded to crimes, not to drunk sorority girls who feel guilty about their promise rings."

"And it was Jordan?" asks Rebecca. It could have been one of his fraternity brothers, she supposes, but the strength of the girl's reaction suggests it was probably Jordan himself.

The girl nods. "And it wasn't just me. Some of my sisters, some girls in my classes, and they've told me about others. He just . . . he hurts people, just because he wants to, and he never gets punished for it. He always gets away with it."

"Well, he can't do it anymore," Hafsah says soothingly. "He can't hurt anyone anymore."

Rebecca gives her friend a sideways look. The asshole doesn't have to be around or even alive to keep hurting the girl—her own memories will do that. Society will do that.

"No." The laughter is losing to the sobs. "No, but he won't ever be held accountable either. What about us? What kind of justice do we get?"

"It's more than you would ever get with him alive," one of her sisters points out. "You don't get justice from guys like him. They join the Supreme Court or get elected president."

All the girls grumble at that, Rebecca right along with them. As someone studying criminology and journalism, she'd like to believe things are better than that. Hell, as a member of a large sprawling family with more than half its members in some form of law enforcement, she used to believe it was better than that. She learned otherwise the hard way.

One of her cousins learned it worse.

Reflexively, she checks her ankle to make sure the knotted thread bracelet is still there. Not everyone gets justice or even the pretense of it.

"I don't know what he was doing out there," says one of the sorority girls, "but thank God. I never realized a blessing could be shaped like a reptile."

"Alligators eat man?" suggests one of her sisters.

"Woman inherits the earth!" they chorus and burst into laughter. There's still an edge to it—serrations of fear and pain, rage and bitterness. After a moment the one starts crying again.

Rebecca glances around, not wanting to intrude further. The light changes. She nudges Hafsah, and with nods of farewell they step into the road. The Greek girls stay in a tight knot on the sidewalk, supporting their distraught sister. The sound of her gasping sobs follows Rebecca through the crosswalk.

"That's definitely not in the obituary the university threw together," Rebecca notes, glaring at her shoes.

"Quelle surprise."

Rebecca kicks a fallen palm frond off the sidewalk to where people are less likely to trip over it. "Wonder how many other girls are feeling that kind of relief."

"And that misery?"

"That too." Kacey won't get either, she thinks and sees a similar thought in Hafsah's pained smile.

A trio of young men with a large alligator-shaped pool float roar and run at a pair of girls, who shriek with surprise and stumble into the grass. Laughing, the young men run off to find their next victim.

"You know, it's weird," Rebecca says abruptly.

"What is?"

"The university set up a hotline for alligator sightings, and they've been swamped. For two weeks we've been deluged with warnings and safety tips, and professors largely gave up marking people tardy for taking alternative routes to classes so they wouldn't have to go near any body of water larger than a puddle. Now someone is dead, and they're . . ." She trails off, groping for the words to convey a feeling she hasn't fully identified. "An alligator just killed someone, but those girls aren't scared—they're angry. And not at the gator. That's a weird reaction, right?"

"Right," Hafsah says slowly. "It could be shock."

"Sure." Partly, maybe. When the shocks wears off, will the celebration still be greater than the fear? She resolves to pay attention to the people she passes, see how they're reacting. Somewhere, someone has to be sad. Somewhere there are people who are more afraid of the gator than the man.

Right?

By the time they get to their dorm, Rebecca can feel the sweat dripping down her spine, her shirt clinging unpleasantly. It's only April, she reminds herself, and only early April at that. It's going to get a lot worse in the months to come. She digs out her wallet and slips her student

ID out of its pocket so she can scan into the building. The door opens with a beep and a flash of green light, releasing a blast of cold dry air. Sometimes she wonders how anyone has a functioning immune system with the constant shift of extremes.

Even as they trudge up to the third floor, most of the bursts of conversation that drift into the stairwell from the halls center around Jordan Pierce and the public service alligator. There's something sad about that, she thinks. She's sure it must be a different story in his fraternity house—she assumes his brothers will mourn him, and his family as well—but what a wasted life if your death is met largely with relief. Sad and, well . . . horrible.

Hafsah is the one to dig out her keys so they can get into their suite. Both girls drop their bags on the bench desk with a groan. The study area is cluttered, which is no surprise when it has to be shared between four students. Now that their presentation is done, Rebecca thinks it wouldn't be unreasonable to ask Susanna and Delia to tidy things up. She doesn't mind navigable clutter as a general rule, but trash should be collected, and dishes should be clean. Florida bugs are already keen trespassers; there's no need to issue an invitation.

Hafsah plucks at her lightweight tunic. "I am going to take a cool shower. This is terrible."

"Just wait for July."

"Sure, but by then I'll be back in Minnesota, with a different hellscape of heat, humidity, and mosquitoes."

"Way to sell it." Grabbing two bottles of water from the minifridge that Delia contributed to their side of the suite, Rebecca salutes Hafsah with one of them, leaving a delightfully cold trail of drops on her forehead. "I'm going to check on Ellie, make sure she's hydrated."

"Better you than me. I can't deal with her when she's hungover."

"It can be rough," she agrees. "But at least we don't have dicks. Then she'd really be intolerable."

Hafsah gives her a look, but whether it's reproach for the crassness or a reminder that Ellie is generally intolerable is anyone's guess.

Grinning, Rebecca heads through the bathroom, which smells faintly of mildew and mold despite the janitors that come through every Friday morning. The girls are pretty careful to keep it clean, spraying down the stalls after showering and hanging their towels to dry. She has a feeling that smell has been there for a few decades, and even the best care can't lift it out of the tiles.

In the connected suite, Luz's and Keiko's sections of the study space are covered in project detritus and a frankly alarming number of Pop-Tarts wrappers. Ellie's, on the other hand, is perfectly organized and tidy. Even the books from her classes this morning are up on the overhead shelf, arranged by class and then by size. Her room looks much the same, not even a stray sock marring the view.

At least until you looked at the walls. Articles printed off from digital newspapers, e-zines, and blogs fill the wall space, bits of tape or blue adhesive gum peeking out from the corners. A handful of pages are glossy with ragged edges from where they were torn out of print magazines. Highlighted lines jump out between furious scrawls of bleeding red ink. The headlines, especially, show these angry corrections.

WOMAN SHOT BY PINING EX WILL RECOVER has been written over to read **CLINGY, VIOLENT MAN SHOOTS WOMAN IN FACE; SCARS WILL BE PERMANENT.**

COMPETITIVE SWIMMER LOSES SCHOLARSHIP, SENTENCED TO THREE MONTHS has become **CONVICTED RAPIST SENTENCED TO SLAP ON WRIST AND DISAPPOINTED HEAD SHAKES.**

As far as journalism goes, the "new" headlines aren't great, but they're more honest.

Aside from the windows and the closet sliding doors, the only break in the morbid, infuriating decor is over the bed on the right side, where a poster-size photo hangs above a tiny Plexiglas shelf with two LED candles. The girl in the photo has a brilliant smile, her eyes crinkled at the edges, and a crown of orange blossoms rests askew on a cloud of sunset-orange hair spilling over one shoulder.

Kacey Montrose.

The bed is filled with Kacey's mountain of throw pillows. Kacey used to come home from classes and simply collapse on the cushions, and if she got cold, she'd just burrow under them like she was burying herself in sand at the beach. After the attack that left Kacey in a care facility, Ellie took the cushions home with her over winter break and brought them back when the new semester started, to preserve Kacey's space. Several of the girls in the suite were nice—or nice enough—but Kacey was the one who was kind. Kacey was good.

The yearbook of national assaults wasn't here when Kacey was still with them. Rebecca touches the edges of the framed photo and closes her eyes, praying for Kacey and her family. *Please let her wake up. Please let her recover.* Letting out a slow, deep breath, she turns away from the photo to look at Ellie.

Ellie is sprawled in the bed on the left side of the room, under a pale-blue sheet with the blanket shoved down around her feet. Judging from the clothes neatly folded on the nearby chair, Rebecca's pretty sure that her friend is some degree of naked she'd rather not think about just now. She sets both water bottles down on one of the nightstands and, passing the sleeping girl, rifles through the closet and baskets of clothes.

The wonderful thing about being the same height and general build as Ellie is the ability to borrow clothes from each other. The terrible thing about being the same height and general build as Ellie is the ability to steal clothes from each other. While Rebecca feels guilty if she doesn't get borrowed clothing returned as soon as it's clean, Ellie has a habit of putting things away with her own stuff. It means Rebecca has gotten used to staging periodic raids in order to reclaim her clothes. Somewhat to her surprise, it's not too bad: four shirts, two pairs of shorts, one pair of jeans, seven socks, a lightweight hoodie, and two pairs of underwear she's going to write off because that's not actually something she shares back and forth. Piling her clothes on the end of Kacey's bed, Rebecca turns back to her friend.

Her hair is a mess around her, tangled and frizzy and thankfully a few shades too bold to look like blood where it spills across her bare back and the bottom sheet. The top sheet drapes around her waist, one arm flung out over her head, the other tucked in close against her side and cradling a nearly empty bottle. Frowning, Rebecca carefully tugs the bottle away, reading the label that's sweating away from the glass.

Rebecca's never been thrilled about keeping booze in the rooms. Bringing it in for immediate consumption is one thing. Still against both the rules and the law but unlikely to have longer repercussions because inspections, as rare as they are, happen during the day. Keeping it, though, is just asking for trouble. She'd rather not risk expulsion from the school or dorms just because a suitemate is experimenting with alcohol. She grimaces at the label and sets it on the nightstand. She's pretty sure gasoline would taste better. If Ellie's going to risk getting caught, she could at least get something that tastes good.

Opening one of the water bottles, Rebecca pours some of the cold liquid into the cap, then sprinkles it over Ellie's bare back.

Ellie comes up swinging and swearing and gets so twisted up in the sheet that she falls back to the bed before she can manage to open her eyes. She blinks blearily at Rebecca, her eyes slowly focusing. "Baby, that was mean," she whines.

"I know," Rebecca says with a satisfied smile, "but you've napped long enough, and you're almost definitely dehydrated." Rebecca holds out the bottle.

Shoving herself up to sitting, Ellie huffs but takes it, sipping carefully.

There's a part of Rebecca that marvels at Ellie's complete lack of self-consciousness. She might even be a little bit envious. Not enough to ever want to hang out naked, but she does admire the confidence.

Being that secure in your own skin is a very different kind of confidence than knowing you have the answer in class. Retrieving the other water bottle, she drops back onto Kacey's bed and takes a long drink. The water's cold enough to hurt her throat and stomach, sloshing painfully for a moment. "You ever heard of a guy named Jordan Pierce?" she asks once Ellie looks a little more awake.

"He's one of the fucknut pantie thieves," she answers with a scowl. "You remember the September pantie raid?"

"No, given that I wasn't there, but I remember picking you up from the police station for trespassing in one of the Row houses."

"We got caught dismantling their scoreboard. You've heard about the scoreboard?"

She thinks about the mingled shock, guilt, relief, joy, and fury of the crying sorority sister. "Yes," she says grimly, "I've heard of it. I'll ask you what I wasn't going to ask the girl crying: What gets the panties on the board?"

Ellie's scowl deepens. Rebecca braces herself for an answer she knows she's not going to like. "The board is arranged in rows by rank, which earns the boys different points. Just hooking up normally with someone earns the least points. Girl's a virgin? More points. In public? More points. Threesomes or groups? More points. Disgusting, but potentially consensual."

"But?" asks Rebecca, stomach knotting.

"There's a row for underage girls. Anything above that rank is scumlord and/or illegal. Drugging a girl or getting her drunk. Taking pictures or videos. Having an audience. Rape. Other things."

Rebecca doesn't want to ask what she means by other things.

"Then they take a Sharpie and write their name on the panties, plus the girl's name, phone number, and sometimes even their addresses. A lot of times they staple on a picture of their victim too. At the end of the semester, whoever has the most points gets some kind of prize. They built a pocket door or whatever to hide it whenever people are over, but word got around anyway." The plastic bottle crinkles as Ellie's fingers tighten. Not quite a fist, but it would be if the bottle weren't in the way.

Rebecca watches the water level in the bottle rise with the force of Ellie's grip. "So Jordan was one of the ones playing the game."

Ellie snorts. "Jordan started the game when he came back for second year. Guess he figured not being a freshman meant he had enough sway in the house."

"Did he need sway in the house for that?"

"From the old guard, yeah. For a few years, the chapter here was trying to keep a low profile. Most of the chapters in the state have had serious issues. But the careful ones graduated, and the current ones are stupid assholes. You ever get invited to a party there, don't go."

Rebecca nods. She's not really one for parties anyway, especially not on the Row. She knows that many, maybe even most, of the Greeks are decent enough but also very prone to group influence and pressure. It only takes a few bad apples to make the whole house a toxic and dangerous place for outsiders. Especially in the fraternities. There's just something about testosterone and patriarchy.

"Why are you asking about Jordan anyway?"

"He's the corpse at the hooker stop."

"Really?" Ellie laughs and leans back against the wall, holding the cold bottle to her breastbone. "Wonder what he was doing all the way out there?"

"Well, not to guess the obvious, but . . . hooker stop?"

But Ellie shakes her head. "I doubt it. We've got a couple of his frat brothers in Crim. Theory, and according to them, Jordan likes his prostitutes like he likes his cars: flashy, pricey, and in your face."

"Can't say I've seen his car."

"You've definitely seen his car," says Ellie. "It's that tomato piece of boxy shit that's always double-parked at Gerson Hall."

Rebecca doesn't tend to pay much attention to cars, purely for the satisfaction of infuriating several of her car-obsessed cousins. She shrugs and takes another drink, smaller this time, and holds it in her mouth until it's warm enough to swallow painlessly. "Well, he's dead now. Any particular reason you were drinking in the middle of the day?"

"Hangover was being a bitch."

"That's what water is for," she says reprovingly.

"Sure. And while I'm waiting for the water to have an effect, I'll have some hair of the dog." She scratches her scalp, leaning forward just enough to shake her hair behind her shoulders. "Admittedly, that works better when I don't fall asleep before I drink the water."

"Also probably helps if you drink something that doesn't double as pesticide."

Ellie glances at the nearly empty bottle on the nightstand and snickers. "Taste sucks, but you can't beat the price." She smothers a yawn behind her hand. "If you're not doing anything tonight, we could get something better."

"We have a test tomorrow."

"So?"

"So I'm studying tonight," Rebecca says firmly. "You're welcome to join me at the library."

"I study better with tequila."

"I've seen you on tequila. You don't do anything better with tequila."

Ellie just flaps a hand dismissively.

"You enjoy that, then," says Rebecca. "I'm taking back my clothing and doing some reading before I head to the library. If you change your mind, you're still welcome to join me later." She stands and gathers the pile of clothing. One of the socks makes a break for freedom as she stands. When she crouches down to retrieve it, Ellie's hand wraps around her wrist. She looks up to see her friend leaning forward across the narrow bed. "What?"

"Why do you do it?"

"Do what?"

"Obsess so much about homework and tests and things. Once you finish the class, no one cares."

"Yes, but first you have to finish the class." She rests her chin on the edge of the mattress near Ellie's knee. "How you do in one class affects your ability to get into others. The work you do or do not put in affects your relationships with professors, affects recommendations and references and internships. But more than that . . ." She licks her lips and gathers the words she wants. "I signed up for these classes," she says eventually. "I agreed that they were necessary steps toward what I want to do, and I paid good money for the opportunity."

"Please, you've got scholarships," Ellie says. "You're spending other people's money."

"All the more reason to take it seriously. If I'm not going to do the work—if I'm not going to give my best—then that money would have been better put to someone else's goals. By accepting that money, I pledged to be worthy of it."

"Ever thought that you're working harder instead of smarter?"

"If I'm not willing to do it right, I shouldn't be here." She rocks forward to nudge Ellie's knee with her nose. "So why are you here, then?"

"Because my parents didn't give me a choice." Ellie laughs. "What else was I going to do?"

"Get a job, go to trade school, get married, go traveling . . ."

"I'd get arrested if I went traveling without a keeper, and for the rest? Pass."

"So you don't care at all?"

"Only about the important things, which excludes most of what they prattle on about in class."

Rebecca blinks, trying to wrap her head around that. School is so expensive and time consuming, and she can understand not wanting or being able to go, but to be here and waste it? Her family cares less about grades than about effort; whatever the result, you do your best. They'd skin her alive if she routinely skipped class or did the bare minimum. Frowning, she pulls her wrist away from Ellie and reaches for her sock. Her pinkie tangles through a shoelace, dragging the shoe out from under the bed.

Rust-brown splotches stain the pointed toe of the gray suede boot. Rebecca stares at it.

"Oh, right." Ellie grabs the boot and launches it through the door into the study area. "I tripped over some asshole's nose at Kentaya's birthday party."

"And I'm sure you were innocently walking at the time."

"Just like he was innocently shoving his hand down a girl's shirt."

Rebecca sighs and glances in the direction of the footwear. "Did you stop at breaking his nose?"

"Close enough."

Despite the number of times this school year Rebecca has been called to the police station to pick up her friend, she's still amazed that Ellie's never actually been arrested. But all she says is "Please clean the boot before it attracts bugs."

"Fussy, fussy."

Bit rich for someone who organizes her DVD collection by director's last name. "All bugs I find will be humanely relocated to your pillowcase. Drink your water."

"Yes, Mama."

With a grin, Rebecca stands, kisses Ellie's forehead, and fixes her grip on the armful of clothes. "And eat your vegetables."

But as she returns to her room, Rebecca can't help but wonder: Given how much trouble Ellie gets into when she's there to see it, what the hell does she get up to when Rebecca isn't there?

5

Gainesville is a town that blooms and fades in cycles. An area dies as other parts of the city develop and thrive and flourish; in time, revitalization efforts come back to transform the strip of barely open stores and empty restaurants, and the cycle begins again. Tonight's party is in one of those dying areas, a cracked and weed-pitted parking lot between what used to be the big-box store anchoring a shopping strip and a four-screen movie theater. The far end of the strip still has some stores and offices that open late and close early, not able to afford the payroll for better hours, but this side has been empty for years. A gym briefly tried to make a go of it in the cinema, but it died with barely a gasp; neighborhoods that can barely keep a grocery store alive don't have the disposable income for fancy fitness centers.

It's made the parking lot a popular place for driving practice during the day and parties at night, even during the week. Trees on the street side of the lot filter out most of the ambient light, so the party is a mass of writhing shadows backlit by a handful of older-model cars and trucks willing to risk battery drainage by keeping their headlights on. It's not a rave, but there are hundreds of glow sticks being worn as bracelets and necklaces and belts and as crowns over synthetic, improbably colored wigs. It's something close to anonymity.

With a neon-blue wig cut with a long bang and heavy fringe along the sides, plus a glow-stick coronet set far enough back on my head to cast more shadow across my face, I could be literally anyone. I guess it's the appeal of parties like this. Hard to know who you're dancing with, who you're kissing, who you're disappearing off into cars with, and in the morning you have a mystery to regret with your hangover. Maybe it's courage.

Or stupidity.

It's probably stupidity.

I weave easily through the crowd, keeping an eye on a handful of bobbing shapes. Glowing stars hang from their belts; they may or may not be aware of them yet. You don't really notice people touching you at a party like this, the way hands skate up waists and ribs, press down against hips and asses to dance. Almost impossible to notice someone clipping a carabiner through a belt loop, and even if you do, they left a present. Who could protest more glow-stick designs?

The uneven asphalt is sticky with slowly drying beer. The squeak and pop of shoes pulling away almost sounds like part of the music throbbing through speakers in the bed of three pickup trucks parked near the wall of the big-box store's carcass. Extension cords snake up through a broken window to disappear into the building, where the property owner is required to keep power running for emergencies.

Two of the star-wearers converge on a heavily made-up girl who looks too young. Not just for the beer spilling out of her red plastic cup as she sways, but too young to be here at all—too young for college and this kind of party. She looks between the two larger shapes with confusion as they both lean in to talk to her. One of them puts his hand over her cup, as if to keep it steady; in the piss-yellow light of his glowing bracelets, the powder he drops in seems to glitter like fresh snow as it falls. He leans in closer, and she shifts away, which brings her up against the other boy.

She may be young and drunk, but she's not entirely stupid; she starts to look a little scared. Like scenting blood in the water, the boys move even closer, their shoulders nearly touching to block the view of her face from others.

I shove through the boys and drape an arm around the girl, her cup falling to the ground to splash across our ankles and shoes. "Never go for two boys," I tell her, almost yelling over the music. "If they have to pair up to get the job done, they're both going to be terrible in bed."

"Hey!" one of the boys protests. "I don't need this asshole to get laid!"

His companion sniggers. "You chickenshit. You know if anyone compares, they'll know how pathetic your dick is."

"You're a pathetic dick!"

"You take that back!"

As they start shoving each other in a prelude to punches getting thrown, I ease the girl away to a better-lit patch in front of a semi-circle of cars with their headlights on. She keeps throwing looks over her shoulder at the fighting boys, and she's shivering despite the muggy heat. When we stop, I step back and put my hands on her shoulders. "Do you have anyone with you?"

"What?"

Very drunk. "Did you come with anyone? Someone who can get you home safe?"

She stares at me.

I pull her phone out of her pocket and dial 911, putting it in her hand. After a second I put her hand up to her ear. The tinny voice of the dispatcher asks a question, and she answers by reflex. Good enough.

I walk away, looking for the glowing stars. Most of the boys wearing them have been fairly innocuous this evening. Maybe they're not always assholes—not that that matters in any real way. But the pair . . . they were the main reason to come to this party. They haven't successfully drugged or assaulted anyone at the parties where I've been observing them, but that is not for lack of trying. Once they make the attempt—prove the intent—I'd be a terrible person if I didn't interfere on their victims' behalves.

They're still brawling in the shadows. That's fine. The police will be here soon enough to break up the party and hopefully take that girl home to her parents. It's time for me to leave so I don't get caught up in all of that. One last look at the boys, and I'm off, mind spinning through possibilities. I know who they are, where they live, what they drive. They go almost everywhere together; whatever I do, I'll have to factor that in.

As I jog through the darkness, I can hear the sudden shriek of sirens, and the panicked chorus of yells drifts through the night from the direction of the party. I reach my bike, locked to a post beside a defunct Dairy Queen that's between reincarnations that never succeed in looking like anything but a barely renovated Dairy Queen. I toss the glow sticks and wig in the dumpster behind the building, mount the bike, and ride off, building plans in the peace of my mind. Rumor isn't enough, but I've now lost count of how many times I've seen these particular boys tanking girls' drinks.

No more chances.

6

Despite her wish for a quiet Friday night in—something that requires nothing more than cookies and maybe a pizza delivery to rest her brain after a big test—Rebecca finds herself smashed into a booth at a sports bar with all of her suitemates except Hafsah, who stayed at the dorm to call home for her grandmother's birthday. She feels intensely jealous of her roommate. Hafsah can go to bed whenever she wants. Hafsah doesn't have to try to decipher bellowed conversation over the roar of half a dozen baseball games on television, a blisteringly loud music selection, and the chatter of another hundred or so people.

Rebecca's father is fond of saying that his little girl was born old. Nights like this make her think he might be right. She'd rather be a fuddy-duddy comfortable in pajamas than be "enjoying her youth" in, well . . . she's in one of Ellie's dresses, less by choice than by resignation. When Rebecca tried to get to her own clothing, Ellie plastered herself in front of the closet and refused to move until Rebecca put on the dress laid across her bed. She tugs at it now, desperately trying to pull the hem down to a more comfortable length.

It rides up as soon as she lets go of the fabric.

She sighs and crosses her arms on the table, letting her forehead drop down to rest on them. If she'd known she would be at risk for flashing her underwear every time she fidgets, she would have prepared. Moisturized, maybe. Shaved higher. Gone to the library after class and not come home until Ellie was gone. A hand rubs soothingly against her unsettlingly bare back. The hand is small enough that it has to be Delia, who pets and comforts even when she doesn't know what's wrong but always seems a little surprised when anyone reciprocates.

Luz and Keiko are giddy over the successful completion of their semester project in one of their mixed-media art classes. Every so often, the realization that it's really done and presented and nothing she has to worry about ever again strikes Keiko anew, and she bursts into tears. The girls have mostly stopped noticing except for Luz, who at least gives her girlfriend a napkin even as she keeps talking.

She can feel someone else—probably Susanna, judging from the angle—pick at the edge of the large sticker covering the back of her hand. "Hello, my name is Sober," the other girl reads aloud. And it is in fact Susanna. "Was something wrong with just writing DD like you usually do?"

"I'm a little worried about ink permanence," Rebecca says into her arms. She shifts to rest her cheek there instead, blinking up at Susanna. "And I'm kind of sick of all the breast jokes."

"I don't think men really have any idea what breast sizes actually mean," Susanna says with a sigh.

"That does not keep them from making the jokes and crass comments."

"That's because men are nothing but jokes and crass comments," Ellie informs them, each word very carefully and precisely formed, which is a good indication that she hasn't eaten, hasn't hydrated, and possibly that she pregamed with another of her bottles of paint-thinner vodka. Given that Ellie takes her drinking so seriously, Rebecca has never understood why she is willing to consume alcohol that costs less per gallon than gasoline.

"You promised me food," Rebecca reminds her.

"We ordered food. Unless you want me to invade the kitchen, I've done as much as I can."

Grumbling, Rebecca looks out over the bar. Nobody seems particularly invested in the games, but basketball is done, football has been done, and people tend to forget how many years UF has a decent base-ball team. Then again, she also has no idea if this is one of those years. There's a bachelor party clustered around some of the high-tops—or at least the first stage of a bachelor party. Holding court over the rest of the high-tops, a bunch of fraternity brothers in matching shirts surround what look to be their youngest members, the boys racing to chug entire pitchers of pale-gold beer. She doesn't try to identify the Greek letters on their shirts; she never remembers which ones are which anyway.

Ellie scowls at them. "How do they not get arrested for that?" she asks with disgust.

Sitting up partially, Rebecca lifts one hand to indicate a circle around their own booth. "Everyone at this table. Underage."

The others hush her frantically, looking around in a definitely not-suspicious way to make sure no one else heard her.

Ellie just transfers the scowl to Rebecca. "That's different. We're not making anyone drink. That could make them really sick."

"You have clearly never met hungover you," she answers, "or you would not be discussing anyone else getting sick from drinking."

"Killjoy teetotaler."

"Judgmental alcoholic."

Keiko bursts out laughing, then looks faintly embarrassed by it.

A server comes to hover at the end of the table, carefully unloading a tray of appetizer baskets. Luz whoops and drags one of the baskets in front of her. "Mozzarella!" she cheers, pronouncing the *z*'s as *s*'s and the *l*'s as a *y*. She's had just enough to drink that it's hard to tell if she's joking or not.

After the waiter dashes off, Rebecca takes a wedge of quesadilla and shoves it in her mouth to chew on as she loads a small plate with selec-tions from the baskets Luz hasn't claimed, including the second order of mozzarella sticks.

"Hungry much?" Ellie asks with a laugh.

Rebecca just nods and takes a second wedge of quesadilla. She skipped both breakfast and lunch to study for the test, and she's about ready to mug someone if it'll make her stomach stop clinging to her spine.

They don't stay at the sports bar much longer than it takes to demolish the appetizers. Most of the girls are looking to flirt as well as drink, and the men there are a little too focused on their own friends to allow for that. Now that she's got some food in her, Rebecca isn't as grumpy at the change in location as she thought she'd be. She'd still rather go home and watch Netflix, but at least the outlook is a little brighter now that she's not hangry anymore.

At least until they arrive at Ellie's chosen destination.

"No," Rebecca says, leaning back on her heels to keep Delia and Susanna from dragging her forward to follow the others into Tom and Tabby's.

"What do you mean, *no?*" the redhead demands.

"You got kicked out with a month's ban, remember?"

"That was forever ago."

"That was Tuesday!"

"But the asshole bartender isn't working tonight! I already checked." She digs her phone out of her purse and waves it, like that's supposed to mean anything.

"They have your picture on the banned board," says Rebecca, hands on her hips. The stern effect is somewhat ruined when the dress rides up, and she twitches to yank it back down.

Ellie just shrugs. "Yeah, but who checks that?"

The employees. The employees check that.

Rebecca checks it, too, when the others succeed in getting her inside. Best to make sure it's only Ellie up there, not the whole group. She finds Ellie's photo and snorts. The second bartender took it at a beautiful moment—when the male bartender had Ellie thrown over his shoulder, and Ellie braced herself against his back so she could keep

46

arguing. Pulling out her phone, she carefully frames the shot and snaps the picture to text Hafsah. Hafsah sends back a picture of herself in pajamas.

Unlike the sports bar, which had something of a mix of ages, this place is almost entirely undergrads tonight and is filled with more people than the fire marshal would approve. Rebecca has to weave through a crowd to catch up with her friends. A hand from behind her grabs her ass and squeezes. She growls but hesitates, then pushes forward rather than lash out and risk hitting the wrong person. She doesn't want her picture up there next to Ellie's.

Over the next hour, it takes the combined effort of all five of them to keep Ellie from getting in three different fights, including with the server, who leers at them a little too long while delivering their drinks. Ellie's been angry longer than Rebecca's known her—and yes, violent too—but she didn't used to be so wild. So reckless. Not until Kacey. Rebecca sometimes thinks that if this version of Ellie had been the one they met freshman year, their group would be fundamentally different now. And probably Ellie-less. Still, loyalty is a hell of a drug, as is shared pain in a friendship. All too often Ellie utterly exhausts her, but she's not going to walk away.

Rebecca studies her drink, sniffs at it, balances its seemingly innocuous appearance with the familiarity of the man's leer, and decides not to risk it.

"Coward," Ellie says.

"You have clearly never been roofied."

"You have?"

She nods, keeping her eyes on the drifting particles in the drink. They could just be undissolved sugar or powdered fruit from whatever flavoring they used, but better to be safe. "High school. I played soccer, and there was a big party for both varsity teams. Boys' team talked one of their fangirls into tanking our drinks."

The group abruptly falls silent. She can feel their attention like a living thing—a crawling, uncomfortable thing despite the warm familiarity of her friends. This, she thinks, the precursor to pity, is why she's never brought it up before. Well, this and not wanting to get into the broader fallout from that night.

"What happened to you?"

"She didn't manage to get the whole group. My friends helped the rest of us back to the house where we'd planned to spend the night." She crosses her legs at the knees, slumping against the table until she can hook her fingertips around the knotted thread anklet. It's not quite enough to stop her hands from shaking.

"What happened to her?"

"We spread the word of what she'd done, and not a single other girl trusted her for the rest of high school." Sighing, she drapes a cocktail napkin over the glass so she doesn't accidentally drink it. "When you come out of it, disoriented and with a gap in your memory . . . it's an awful feeling. And I was safe. I woke up around friends, in a place I recognized, with the promise that they'd been with me the entire time and nothing had happened. It was still terrifying to know that gap was there, when anything could have happened."

Ellie's silent for a long moment, her brow furrowed in a fierce frown. The noise of the bar presses against the solemn bubble of the conversation. "What happened to the guys?"

Rebecca gives her a lopsided smile. "What do you think?"

"Nothing," says Ellie, sounding disgusted.

"Exactly. The guys called it a prank at first. When they realized they weren't going to get punished for it, they said they didn't have anything to do with it. The juniors and seniors knew to be extra careful if they were at parties with them, but there are always freshmen and sophomores ready to learn things the hard way. It's hard to protect everyone. Also hard to get proof. Just because everyone knows doesn't mean that anyone can prove it."

Holding her glass up to the light bulb swaying nearly to the beat of the music, Ellie peers at the liquid. She ordered it straight and neat, so there shouldn't be anything in it. Rebecca's not sure her friend actually knows what to look for anyway. Rebecca and her cousins had the advantage of growing up in a law enforcement family keen to show them, using confiscated material. Without seeing the real thing in person, YouTube tutorials and lectures only help so much.

The conversation kills what little enjoyment the appetizers afforded, and it doesn't take long before being the only sober person at the table grows more irritating than entertaining. This is why she and Hafsah are usually sober together. Tucking the clip with her cash, ID, and debit card into her bra—the opposite cup from her phone—she pushes her stool back. "I'm getting some air," she tells the others.

Susanna blinks at her. "What flavor?" she asks.

"Swampy, humid, tinged with gasoline fumes, and, if there's a bit of a breeze, maybe some *eau de* dumpster."

"Oh. None for me, then, thanks."

Rebecca rolls her eyes and makes her way slowly out of the crowded bar. Despite the whistling air conditioner, the constantly opening door and the sheer press of people mean there's not much of a difference between inside and outside. Even so, she at least feels like she can breathe in the parking lot. She carefully picks a spot against the side of the building, illuminated by both the entrance and the softly lit cone from a lamppost in the lot. The rough brick catches at her curls as she leans her head back, letting whatever breeze might come by wick the sweat sticking to her throat and chest. She closes her eyes and takes a shaky breath, letting it out slowly.

She doesn't like thinking about that party. Doesn't like remembering waking up in a confused fog, trying to cut through to clarity and memory and failing to find either. Her friends were with her the entire time, and that helped a little, to get the recounting. It didn't really remove the panic of those missing hours. Because there'd been beer and spiked punch at the party, because they'd all had alcohol even if not all of them had been drugged, her friends had been too scared to call her family or take her to the hospital.

If they had, if police had gone to the party and found the booze and the roofies, they also would have found Rebecca's cousin Daphne, who arrived a little while after Rebecca's group left. Daphne was a freshman on the JV team and showed strong signs of joining Rebecca on the varsity team the next year. As a player, Rebecca was solid and dependable, but Daphne was the kind of good that heralded athletic scholarships. She and her friends on the team decided to crash the varsity party, which was supposed to be restricted to the players and their dates but more realistically was the same free-for-all the sports parties always became.

Rebecca presses a hand against her stomach, against the anxious tangle of feelings that always bubbles up when she thinks about that night. Or, more important, the next day.

Daphne's friends weren't as protective as Rebecca's were. Most of them were sophomores, torn between admiration for and resentment of the rising star. They wanted to be noticed by the junior and senior boys, wanted to be invited to prom. They got to the party and scattered, and none of them were paying attention when Daphne started stumbling. One of the senior girls, not realizing that Daphne's drink had been drugged, thought she'd had too much punch and settled her on a heap of hay in a stall of the barn where the party was held, according to what the senior later told Rebecca.

No one's ever come forward with the truth about what happened after that. Rebecca called her parents from her friend's house to ask them to take her to the hospital. An hour after they got her there, her aunt—Daphne's mother—called to say that Daphne had been out all night. The doctor had already taken a blood sample, for whatever good that could do, so Rebecca left the hospital with her father and gave him directions to the farm. The gravelly lot that had been so crammed with cars the night before was empty save for the few pieces of heavy equipment in one corner. They went into the barn, accompanied by deputies who weren't related to them, just in case. It was still trashed from the party, cans and red plastic cups strewn everywhere. Bags and boxes and paper plates sprawled around half-collapsed folding tables, and one of the mousers slept on a mostly empty platter of cheese, its greasy muzzle and bulging belly a good sign of what had happened to the leftover cheese.

A deputy found Daphne's purse in the stall, with her phone and wallet still intact. They called her name again and again, and as the minutes passed, Rebecca stood beside her father and twisted her fingers through the yellow plastic hospital bracelet. Then they heard a groan that silenced them all, straining to hear, and Daphne's head emerged from the loft that had been off limits for the party. The deputy down in the stall called out her name; Daphne twisted to try to see them . . .
. . . and fell.

Rebecca can still hear the scream sometimes, the crash as Daphne landed on the table with the punch bowls. She can still see the deputies racing across the barn to her cousin, her dad's voice choked and quavering as he called for an ambulance. She knows it isn't fair, but Rebecca's never quite forgiven her old teammates for their selfishness. Hardly anyone would have cared about the underage drinking, but they knew there were other dangers at that party. If they'd just told someone, anyone, the cops or parents would have found Daphne before she was taken to the loft. Before she was raped. Before she was left there like so much trash so close to the edge.

Before she fell. Before the doctors had to tell her that the damage to her spine had left her paralyzed, that the rape—with cans and bottles and farm tools, anything that came to hand that wouldn't leave the DNA of her attacker or attackers—had injured her so badly that they had to do a full hysterectomy. Daphne spent the rest of the school year in the hospital. When it came time to go back to school in the fall, both Daphne and Rebecca were homeschooled by one of their aunts.

Nothing ever happened to Daphne's attackers. The investigation stalled because the boys' varsity team stuck together. Everyone knew, and no one could prove it, and Daphne is never going to see any justice for what was done to her.

She thinks about the sorority girl with her sisters, laughing and crying and feeling every emotion at once because the action that left her and other girls that little bit safer also cheated her, stole from her. It's easy to think of her as Daphne, sitting up through the night and knotting jewelry when the nightmares keep her from sleeping; everyone in the family wears something she made. There's no good solution, Rebecca realizes. Even prison won't erase the harm that was done. Fines, imprisonment, death—there's no possible consequence that matches the harm. So what's justice, then?

"Well, aren't you a pretty—"

"No," she interrupts. A flash of fury spikes through her; it takes more effort than she'd like to bite it back. That kind of anger isn't safe for a girl on her own, Ellie to the contrary.

"Huh?"

"Whatever you were about to say," she tells the male voice. "No interest in hearing it."

"You don't have to be a bitch about it."

"Seeing as you're not walking away, clearly I do." She opens her eyes and stands straight, forcing herself not to wince as the brick tries to keep some of her hair.

The boy standing a little too close is alone, at least, no friends crowding around him to outnumber her. His blond hair is slicked back, some kind of cologne or body spray wafting too heavy in the thick air. If he weren't sneering at her, he might be some kind of good looking. A small petty voice in the back of her mind says it's the kind that won't last. "I was just trying to compliment you," he complains.

"I came outside to be alone and enjoy some silence. Whatever your intention, you're bothering me."

"Listen, bitch, you should be—"

"Grateful?" She snorts derisively. "Hardly."

"Not everyone is as nice as I am, you know."

"Nice, yes. You've called me a bitch twice already."

His face twists further, turning into something ugly rather than just spoiled arrogance. Maybe she should have played along until she could get back inside, let him pretend his attentions were flattering. It might have been safer. But she's tired and restless with memory and just wants to be home in her pajamas—and all in all in no mood to give him anything he wants. She shouldn't have to. The fury bubbles back up, splashing through the fear and irritation that have become her standard response to too many college boys who think their dicks give them an all-access pass to the world. She studies the toe of her pink Doc Martens as she tries to figure a good way out of this confrontation.

She flinches from the hand that suddenly fills her peripheral vision, and it closes around the strap and surrounding neckline of the dress rather than her throat as intended. "Let go," she snaps.

"You need to be more appreciative of people taking the time to compliment you," he growls, yanking on the dress to pull her closer.

"Let go of me!" she yells, trying to get the attention of anyone else outside the building. She can hear the dress start to tear as she digs her heels in against his tugs. She braces one hand against the bricks, shifting her weight. Past the heartbeat thudding in her ears, she can hear footsteps hurrying across the lot, but who knows if they mean to help. Or who they mean to help. Does he have a gun? Will protecting herself put her in more danger?

"I'm gonna teach you—"

Her foot swings up, the steel-toed boot landing with a muffled thump in his crotch. He wheezes, his face turning somewhat purple as he bends, but he doesn't let go of her dress. The long rip is terrifyingly loud even against the spill of music from the bar. His fingers dig painfully into her skin as his hand drops with the rest of him. She presses her free arm against her chest to keep her bra covered. She tries to back away, but her steps just bring him stumbling with her, hand still clutching the fabric.

"Bitch, you're gonna regret that."

Regaining her balance, she hauls her foot back to kick him again.

"Let go of her," orders a new voice, male and stern.

Rebecca risks looking away from the boy to find Det Corby side by side with a uniformed UPD officer. Neither has his gun drawn, but the officer has his left hand on the baton hanging from his belt, behind his gun.

"This bitch attacked me!"

"Save it for someone who didn't see it. Let go of her."

He still seems reluctant, but he does open his hand to release the torn dress.

She immediately steps away, closer to Det Corby and the safety he represents, and she holds the fabric together from neck to waist. She can see Det Corby's shoulders roll back like he's trying to take off a blazer he isn't wearing to offer it to her. The detective gently curls his hand around her elbow to lead her even farther away, letting the UPD officer continue the conversation. "Are you okay?" he asks quietly.

She looks down at the dress, at the lace-trimmed paisley bra that's peeking through despite her best attempts and at her shaking hands trying to fix it. "Ellie's going to kill me. This is her dress." She blinks in surprise, fairly sure that's not what she intended to say. She hates the adrenaline crash, the falling apart when the danger is past. Hates the sense of weakness and relief when, goddammit, she was strong, and she's safe now.

He chuckles and lets go of her elbow, keeping his eyes on her face. "Is it just the dress?"

"Yes, the bra is mine." It's only at the pink in his cheeks that she realizes that's not at all what he meant. "Oh. Um, yes. He was going for my throat but got the dress instead. He didn't touch me otherwise."

Glancing over at his colleague, who has the boy's ID in one hand and a phone in the other, Det Corby sighs and shakes his head. "I'm glad you're okay, but . . ."

"But it means there's nothing to arrest him for," she finishes bitterly. "Yeah."

Because why would it ever be different? Why punish someone for the harm they intend to cause if you can just wag your finger at them a few times? Closing her eyes, she presses her forehead against Det Corby's shoulder. His hand is warm and solid at her elbow, supporting without gripping. It's not his fault he can't haul the boy away. The problems are so much bigger than that. She focuses on slowing her galloping breaths, timing them to the soft brush of his thumb against her arm.

She suspects that may be the reason he's doing it. He doesn't move closer, doesn't try to touch her more than that, just lets her use his shoulder to brace herself and breathe, and she's pathetically grateful.

She recognizes the UPD officer, she thinks, hearing his calm questions and the boy's truculent responses. Officer Kevin, as he's known around campus, can always be relied on to walk students, especially girls, back to their cars or dorms after dark. He always seems so pleased to be asked.

"Nice kick, though," Det Corby murmurs. "Ellie will be proud. Might even be enough to get forgiveness for the dress."

She smiles slightly, about as much as she's capable of at the moment. "She's inside."

"Thought she must be," he says. "This isn't someplace you come on your own. Do you want me to go find her?"

She shakes her head and reluctantly straightens up. It would be nice, but she would rather he not be directly confronted with the sight of her friends drinking underage. He's generally willing to overlook things he can reasonably ignore, but actually seeing them drinking or buying alcohol would probably stretch that kindness past its limits. "I'll text them."

Then she remembers where her phone is. A scalding, painful blush heats her cheeks.

"I'm going to look at Kevin and the asshole," he says cheerfully and immediately does so.

She quickly fishes out her phone, wiping the sweat-slick screen on the dress, and texts Hafsah to ignore the next few messages. Then she pulls up the group thread. Rather than sending a single text, she breaks it up into several messages. Hopefully the repeated alerts will get somebody's notice, when just one would be easily missed.

I'm outside.

I need to head home.

Asshole attacked me.

Please take me home.

Please.

Please.

Please.

Please.

Hey, I kicked someone in the junk.

That's the one that gets the response. From Ellie, which doesn't really surprise her.

That's awesome! Not the asshole part. The part where you kicked him. Good job.

And then, from Delia:

2sec we go

Good enough. She tucks the phone back into her bra, glances at Det Corby, and casts about for something to say, some kind of distraction from the boy who just attacked her. "Your hours have been kind of weird lately; are they changing your shift?"

"Had a meeting," he replies, not dismissively or curtly, but there's something in the tone that says not to ask more about it. She hums and shifts her weight, not sure where to go from there, really. A second later he sighs and shakes his head. "Sorry. It's been a long day."

"It really has."

"It's going out in the morning," he says quietly, "but we finally have an ID for the body in Lake Alice."

Rebecca folds one arm under her chest to anchor that part of the dress and splays her other hand across the pieces of neckline to keep herself marginally decent. "You got a hit on DNA? Or you finally found the head?"

"Both, in fact," he says with a grimace. "Though the head was secondary confirmation. Missing person report mentioned that the family had done one of those ancestry kits, in case we needed to compare samples."

The asshole with Officer Kevin suddenly drops a loud f-bomb, and Rebecca flinches. Even as she castigates herself, Det Corby's hand returns to her elbow with just enough pressure to be reassuring.

"Missing person?" she asks, because it's easier to focus on that than on the warmth of his touch or the asshole still too close for comfort. "Was the report filed before or after the body was found?"

"After." He sounds grim. "He never returned to classes after spring break, but he was seen out and about in the week and a half after that. Apparently his family and friends thought he was just lying low."

Which begs the question: "From what?"

"He incurred some legal difficulties over spring break."

She recognizes the careful phrasing from hundreds of conversations with her law enforcement family members. She can think of two possible reasons for it. First, whatever trouble he got into could have a bearing on his death, so the police can't talk about it. Second, the family is litigious as hell and ready to sue the pants off whoever casts aspersions on their darling. Or both.

Either way, there's no point in pursuing the question. Not without more information in general. "He was a student, then?" she asks instead.

"Sorry?"

"The deceased. He was a student?" She starts to shrug at his curious look, then decides she'd rather not find out if that imperils the already precarious positioning of the dress. "Spring break. If a professor didn't come back, the whole campus would be talking about it. If a high schooler didn't come back, the whole damn city would be buzzing."

"True. He could be in admin."

"Administration and support get spring break?"

He chuckles and runs a hand through his hair. Some of it promptly swings back into his face. "I don't even know. Yes, he's a student. Or was, I suppose. They'll release his name in the morning."

"So you were meeting with his family?"

"No, with my captain, trying to convince him to open an investigation." Her surprise must show on her face, because he gives her a look equal parts sheepish and defiant. "Statistically speaking, the fact that two male UF students, roughly the same age, were apparently killed by alligators within two weeks of each other is more than passing strange. I know what the environmental theory is, but it's still unlikely."

"Environmental theory," she repeats slowly. "You mean the encroachment?"

Det Corby nods. "The habitat loss has been happening over years. If that were the only factor, we'd have seen an increase each year, not a sudden spike."

"So you think . . . what?"

"Honestly I don't even know yet. Maybe there's a new frat challenge running around—take a picture with a gator or something stupid like that. Maybe they're just drunk and stupid."

"And maybe?" she asks cautiously.

"And maybe it's not coincidence or stupidity." He almost looks like he's bracing himself against her response, which gives her a fair idea of how his captain took his hypothesis.

She turns the idea over in her head, poking at it thoughtfully. "That seems . . . complicated," she says finally.

"That's the kinder portion of the consensus." He isn't frowning, but he doesn't look happy either. "Any other year this state averages three deaths by alligator. In a *year*. Even nonfatal alligator attacks aren't much more common. And somehow this year we have half a dozen across the state with the mating season just starting, and two of them happen to be very similar people at the same school? Statistical anomalies exist, but there's usually an explanation for them."

"And your explanation is a serial killer." Despite the subject matter, she can't quite hold back a small smile. It just sounds so ludicrous. Murder by alligator seems more like something from a Bond film than a real-life problem.

"Don't forget accident and stupidity," he says ruefully. "I have them about equally weighted right now."

"Does that make you feel a little less silly?"

"Yes," he says with a laugh, "but that might be wishful thinking."

Her suitemates burst out the door in an explosion of noise, clustering so tightly around Rebecca that they push Det Corby to the side. He grins and holds up his hands in surrender, stepping back toward Officer Kevin and the belligerent boy.

As Delia and Susanna tut over the torn dress, Ellie crouches down to examine her shoes. "No blood," she notes.

Why would there be . . .

"I got him in the crotch, not the nose or mouth," Rebecca tells her "Still."

Rebecca stares at her, trying not to visualize how that would work. "I'm a little unnerved by how hard you must be kicking them if they're bleeding."

"Do it hard enough, and they can't come after you again."

"Do it hard enough, and you could get the bill for their ruptured testicle."

Ellie waves that off as unimportant. "Bills aren't enforceable without a court order. Come on. We'll get you home so you can change before we come back out. Don't let the bastards get you down."

"I am changing into pajamas and staying home," Rebecca says firmly. "No arguments, no compromises, no begging. I am not leaving the room once I'm in it."

"I can give you ladies a ride home if you'd like," offers Det Corby, returning to the girls. "Kevin is going to stay and try to put the fear into Mountebanks there."

All six girls stare at him, then swivel to stare at the increasingly cowed attacker. "Mountebanks?" Delia asks eventually. Rebecca bites her bottom lip. A giggle slips out anyway.

"According to his license, that's his name."

She dissolves into giggles, which sets the other girls off as well. If Rebecca's laughter is somewhat tinged with hysteria, well, that's understandable, isn't it? It's on the tip of her tongue to ask if it's his real license, but she doesn't. That would invite too much attention to her friends' licenses.

Ellie, of course, has no such compunction. "Jesus, it's so bad it almost has to be real, right? How does a polo-and-highball name like that not buy its way into the Ivy League?"

Rather than try to answer, Rebecca swallows the giggles, thanks the detective, and accepts the ride. None of the girls have jackets or sweaters, and she really doesn't want to walk back to the dorm clutching her dress closed. She also doesn't have quite enough confidence—or foolishness, perhaps—to let it flap open to the waist and pretend she isn't bothered by it. Ellie would. Hell, Ellie would see it as a badge of honor. *If you think I look bad, you should see what I did to him.* Rebecca is more used to de-escalating situations than learning how to wear the shreds with pride. She just wants to get home, where she can lock at least one door between her and the outside world and let go of the hyperawareness that has her cataloging every shadow and movement in the parking lot.

"My car is two blocks away," says the detective, "so give me a couple of minutes."

When he comes back, driving a dark-blue sedan that could be his or the department's, Rebecca settles into the front seat while the others pour into the back. Ellie immediately starts complaining that there's no perp gate between them.

Rolling his eyes, Det Corby hands Rebecca a bold-blue hoodie, the Royals logo swiped across the front in baby blue and white. "I promise it's clean. Just washed a few days ago."

Rebecca eases into it, not letting go of the dress until her front is covered. "Suffering loyalist or bandwagon?"

He laughs and puts the car into gear. "Neither. Corby Family rule is that the home team is wherever our parents are. They moved to Kansas City a couple years ago."

She adjusts the hood against her back, pulling her hair free, and curls her fingers into the cuffs. Strange that a hoodie that smells only of laundry detergent can hold the same sense of safety as the dorm. Or maybe, she thinks, sneaking a sideways look at his soft smile, less strange than satisfying.

7

With Rebecca refusing to go back out and Hafsah refusing to go out at all, the other five have no one sober to make sure they don't end up dead in a ditch somewhere. None of them are precisely happy about that, but they seem resigned once Ellie remembers she has another bottle of rotgut tucked away under the spare bed. They cheer and stumble off to her room to keep drinking.

Hafsah shakes her head. "Are you okay?"

"Little shaken, but otherwise okay, yes." She pulls off the dress and examines it. A good seamstress could probably make it wearable again, she thinks, but it'll never look anything but mended. She tosses it down on the bed with a huff. She didn't even want to wear the damn thing, and now she'll be buying a replacement with money she'd really rather not spend. Her scholarships cover pretty much everything she actually needs, and her parents can usually send her a small allowance each month to help with other necessities and a social life, but she doesn't like risking her safety net to replace a dress someone else forced her to wear. "I'm going to shower."

"I'll make some hot chocolate when you're out."

She gives her roommate a grateful smile and shuffles to the bathroom, bringing her pajamas with her. The water is cool and refreshing but brings into sharp relief the pink marks on her chest from where his fingers dug in before curling into the dress. She frowns down at them and gives them a careful poke. Are they going to bruise? Then again, maybe that's something of a relief. With a physical reminder of the attack, maybe she won't feel as embarrassed about being jumpy in the days to come. If the attack leaves visible marks, people are less likely to tell her to get over it already because she wasn't *really* hurt.

She's never believed that assaults need to meet a minimum limit to be deserving of sympathy, but she's found herself to be in the minority in that.

With no one waiting for the stall, no one to yell at her for using hot water, she leans against the wall and lets the water rinse away the sweat and the smell of whatever he was wearing. The water pressure is a little better than usual, probably because not many other people are showering this late at night.

There's a part of her that wants to yell and rage at the unfairness of the evening, at the wretchedness of not being able to punish the asshole in any way. She can't press charges, and even if she could, they wouldn't stick. Who'd bother to prosecute over an assault that ended with nothing more than fear and a torn dress? Especially if he tried to ignore the fact that she has two police officers as witnesses and claimed she assaulted him first. She was smart, she was careful, she was sober, and none of it made any difference when a man decided he was entitled to her time and attention.

She can't stay in the shower forever, though. When she's toweled off and in her comfortable cotton shorts and long-sleeved tee, she walks back to the study area, rubbing the towel carefully through her wet curls.

Her chair wheezes as she plops onto it. Det Corby's hoodie is folded on her desk, next to the nonanatomical contents of her bra. She reaches for her phone, wakes it up, and hesitates, her thumb floating over the screen.

Who does she contact first? Her gut says Gemma, who will absolutely want to be told by Rebecca rather than the Sorley Family grapevine, but Gemma is also a morning person. She's been in bed a couple of hours already with her phone turned off like a heathen. Rebecca should definitely call her parents, even as late as it is. Before that, though, she pulls up her text thread with Daphne.

Her cousin is up in Pennsylvania in her second semester at Bryn Mawr, studying social work and advocacy. A solid eighty percent of her communication since October has been baffled complaints about the cold and snow. Hard enough for a Florida girl to navigate, but learning how to handle icy sidewalks in her wheelchair has been the subject of more than a few rants. She should definitely not be told about the incident by the grapevine.

First of all, I'm okay, Rebecca types. *I was attacked by a boy in a parking lot while I was out with the girls, but I promise you, aside from a bruise on my chest, I'm not injured and I'm okay.*

You promise? comes the swift response.

I do. There were cops nearby who heard me yell, they interceded. I'm safely back in the dorm.

Have you told the family yet?

You're the first.

Before Gemma?

At this time of night?

True. Thanks for worrying about me.

They chat for a few minutes—apparently Pennsylvania is skipping spring to go straight from winter to summer, which means Daphne is finally feeling right at home—before Daphne's roommates nag her back to a game they're playing. Rebecca calls her parents, but her mom's phone rings through to voice mail, and her dad's goes directly to voice mail, so she ends up leaving both of them messages. Strictly speaking, she doesn't *need* to talk to them, but it leaves her feeling somewhat disgruntled regardless. So she calls Gemma, knowing she'll get voice mail, and leaves a similar message for her and a promise that Gemma can call her back at whatever ungodly hour of the morning she hears it.

Keeping the phone in her hand, Rebecca pushes back from the desk and crosses to her room. She stops in the doorway and sighs at the sight of Ellie sprawled across her narrow bed. "You have your own bed," she says. "Apparently it even has booze."

"It does not have booze," the redhead replies with a pout. "I drank the bottle I thought I had. All that's there is terrible beer."

"Why do you have terrible beer?"

"Because it was cheap, and they weren't checking IDs."

"Have you ever thought that maybe they don't check the IDs on the really godawful stuff so you'll drink it and think everything tastes that bad and stop drinking?"

"But if I get drunk on the good stuff, I can stay drunk on the awful stuff once I can't taste it anymore."

Rebecca gives up. Ellie is hard enough to argue with sober; drunk, it's just spinning in circles, and tonight's not a night she can be entertained by it. She sits on the foot of Hafsah's bed rather than trying to shift Ellie, roughly drying her ears and neck.

Hafsah hands her a mug of powdered hot chocolate, steam rising from the thick surface and curling around the handle of the spoon. Here in the room, with two lockable doors between her and non-*mahram*, her hijab is put away, and her many thin braids hang down past her shoulders, some of them wrapped at intervals with neon cords.

Ellie has a strength that everyone can see, one of snarls and insults and flailing fists. Rebecca has always been more impressed by Hafsah's strength, navigating campus life—and life in general—in a time that is often unkind or flat-out dangerous for Black and Muslim women. Hafsah's strength is quieter but every bit as stubborn. It's harder, Rebecca thinks, to be brave than to not give a shit.

Rebecca holds her mug steady as Hafsah settles on the bed next to her. "Ellie, do you remember where you bought the dress?"

"Yes. Why?"

"So I can replace it?"

Ellie snorts and kicks the dress off the bed into a puddle of brightly patterned fabric on the thin carpet. "No."

"But I ruined it."

"Mountebanks the Asshole ruined it. You wore it after I forced you." She rolls onto her back, her arms flopping with just enough inco-ordination to tell the others the real reason she's not drinking anymore. As much as Ellie loves the feeling of being tipsy, she doesn't like being blackout or falling-down drunk and nearly always stops herself before she reaches that point. "Hey, if his name really is Mountebanks, he should be pretty easy to find. He can replace my dress."

"He's not going to."

"I could prolly make him."

"Is it worth it?" asks Hafsah.

Ellie blinks at her. "I paid eighty dollars for that dress. Eighty dollars, Hafsah, and that was on sale!"

"What do you think he's going to do? Cut you a check?"

"He might not, but his daddy's lawyer probably would. Men like that cut a lot of checks, right?"

Rebecca and Hafsah trade a look and roll their eyes. Part of Rebecca marvels at Ellie's ability to say *daddy* without a trace of self-consciousness. She remembers calling her father that once upon a time, but she's fairly sure she switched to *dad* around her first period. She's southern, but she's not *Southern*, not like Ellie. Draping the towel over her head, she leans back against the wall and sips her cocoa.

"I'm sorry I wasn't out there with you," Ellie says after a few minutes of silence, her voice unexpectedly soft.

"Why should you have been?"

"Because we shouldn't have let you go alone. It's not safe, and we know that, and we should have been there for you."

"I chose to go out alone. I chose to get some air."

"That shouldn't be dangerous."

"I know," she says with a sigh, "but it is, and that isn't your fault." It's his fault and society's fault. Too aware of her own misplaced guilt from the assault on Daphne, Rebecca's careful about assigning guilt to others.

Ellie rolls onto her side again, hugging a pillow to her chest. "You were being such a good sport, coming out with us when you didn't want to. We should have been taking better care of you."

"So next time, we agree to go back to a buddy system," Rebecca offers. "We're supposed to be doing it anyway." She really hopes Ellie doesn't start crying. She's rarely a weepy drunk, but it happens occasionally and unnerves everybody who sees it.

"You mean it? You'll go out with us again?"

"We have a year and change left of school; I'm reasonably sure we will find our way out again. Besides," she continues with a laugh, "*illegitimi non carborundum*, right?"

Ellie giggles and buries her face in the pillow. "Hey, that was my line!" comes the muffled protest.

Hafsah shakes her head. "Not only is that not the actual quote, that's not even real Latin."

"My aunt doesn't like the word *bastard*," says Rebecca.

Hafsah rolls her eyes.

As Rebecca and Hafsah slowly work their way through their hot chocolate—Ellie, the philistine, doesn't like chocolate in any form—conversation turns to Hafsah's classes in geology and oceanography. Hafsah's goal is to get to NASA and hopefully to Mars, if they can manage that before she ages out of candidacy. For Hafsah's last birthday, Rebecca got her the NASA astronaut teddy bear and spray-painted its boots from a distance so they would look like they were stained with Martian dust. It sits on Hafsah's nightstand, holding the embroidered Mars stuffie that Susanna found for her.

Every now and then, Rebecca finds her hand drifting up to her collarbone and the tender skin just below it. Peeking under her shirt, she can see the pink shapes darkening. She's pretty sure that means she'll wake up to bruises. There's a part of her that's pissed off, but mostly she's grateful it wasn't worse. Which, weirdly, serves to piss her off more. Come tomorrow, Mountebanks the Asshole will probably forget all about her. Why does she have to remember? Why does she have to carry the weight of how much worse it could have been?

When Hafsah starts yawning, Rebecca slides off the bed and takes their mugs to the bathroom to wash. She probably should have done it an hour ago, before the dregs had a chance to dry, but she didn't want to walk out in the middle of the conversation. While she's in there, she brushes her teeth and thinks about brushing her hair before the sight of the mostly dried curls makes her reconsider. Hafsah is already under the covers and almost asleep when she returns to the room. She sleeps more deeply than anyone Rebecca knows; she might be jealous.

Ellie, still clutching the pillow to her chest, perches on the edge of Rebecca's bed and looks up at her, her hair in a wild tangle all around her. "Can I stay?" she asks quietly. This is an echo of the Ellie who lived with Kacey—the Ellie who had daily exposure to someone so genuinely kind and full of light it was nearly impossible to be around her and not try to find some of that light within yourself. They all miss Kacey. Rebecca's fairly sure Ellie misses her the most—or at least needed her the most.

"You want the wall or the edge?"

Beaming, Ellie tucks her legs under the Captain Marvel sheet and scoots back until she bumps the wall. Rebecca flicks out the light, plugs in her phone by feel, and climbs into bed. Ellie slumps forward, a too-warm weight against her back, but she doesn't tell her to move. The bed is barely wide enough to be a twin; it isn't meant for two people. Accepting that means accepting that she's going to wake up hot and sweaty and probably cranky in the anemic air-conditioning because she could have told her no. She's not sure which of them needs the comfort—both, probably—but it brings with it the familiarity of a lifetime of sharing beds and air mattresses and sleeping bags with her horde of cousins and extended cousins, just because they could. Because it made the world a little less lonely.

A little less frightening.

"I hate this," Ellie whispers.

"You asked to do this," Rebecca replies, half into her pillow.

"No, not this; I mean *this*."

"Right. What?"

Ellie's frustrated huff hits Rebecca's ear and makes her squirm. "What happened tonight, I mean. I hate that we're not safe. I hate that even when we're fine, when nothing happens, it never *feels* safe, because it isn't. I hate that we have to pay attention to every man around us, that we can't always trust our drinks, that you couldn't go outside for a couple of minutes without being attacked. I hate that we spend half our nights trying to protect other girls from how we were all raised."

"And how's that?"

"Polite." She spits out the word like a curse. "You do it too; we're all taught to do it. Be polite, even when you want to run as far away as you can. Try to deflect the attention while balancing the need to seem flattered without seeming interested. Try not to hurt their egos so they don't hurt you. I hate men. I hate what they're taught and how they're raised and why they get away with everything."

"Not everything," Rebecca protests, feeling unaccountably defensive. Of her family, maybe, or of her own foolish dream of a more just world.

"Too much, then. Nothing's going to happen to Mountebanks the Asshole, but you have a ripped dress and another bad memory, and it's just . . ." Her arms wrap around Rebecca's waist, her words mumbled into skin. "I hate them all. So many of them do terrible, terrible things and get away with them, and they all benefit from the privilege. All of them. How have we not risen up and killed them all?"

Prickles of dread creep down Rebecca's spine. "Because it's against the law?"

"The law isn't always right."

"No," she agrees carefully, "but there's a difference between breaking unjust laws and committing wholesale slaughter."

"Sometimes it's hard to care about that."

Harder not to, in the long run. Ellie's never been good at looking that far.

They fall silent. Hearing the deep, even breaths of Hafsah across the narrow room, Rebecca can feel her mind drifting off, not quite to sleep but to something less than awake.

Then Ellie speaks again, her voice soft but no less bitter. "I'm sick of everyone eulogizing Jordan fucking Pierce. He was a predator. He hurt people, again and again and again, and crafted an easy way for his friends to hurt people for points, but no one's talking about that."

"They're talking about it," Rebecca says. She wonders how long she'll be haunted by the sorority girl's sobbing laughs. She doesn't even know her name. "They may not be writing it down, but they are talking about him."

"And which lasts longer? Whispering stories around doesn't matter for shit if no one makes a record of it. The things people see, the things strangers learn about him, are coming from his family and fraternity, and places print their words without bothering to learn if they're true or not. Five years from now, what will people know? No one's on the record about the girls he hurt. It's all just lost potential and terrible tragedy and grief, like he was someone worth mourning. Like a world without him in it is somehow less, when the truth is we're safer because he's dead. We're all safer when boys like him are dead."

Some things are easier to say in the dark, but there are things that still shouldn't be said. Rebecca lays her hand on Ellie's arm, feels the fury that makes the muscles quiver and twitch under her fingers. "What happened to you?" she whispers, breaking her own rule. "Before college. Who hurt you?"

Ellie's silent for so long Rebecca thinks she's not going to answer. She doesn't expect the broken-off laugh that hangs in the scant space between them. "We're pretty girls, Rebecca; what always happens to us?" She buries her face in Rebecca's hair and starts snoring, the loud, ostentatiously fake snoring that lets her pretend she can't hear anything being said to her.

That's fine. Rebecca doesn't know what to say anyway.

Maybe there just isn't anything to say.

8

She really does mean to be studying.

But then, Ellie has the amazing ability to disrupt things even when she's not there, so perhaps it's not entirely surprising that Rebecca has spent the past hour staring at a stack of books, wishing she could study like she intended but instead thinking of the unique Problem that is Ellie.

"If you're not being productive, would you like to go get some dinner instead?" asks Hafsah.

Rebecca blinks and looks away from her books. It takes her eyes a little too long to focus on her roommate. "What?"

"Dinner? And maybe conversation?"

She sighs and pokes at the books. "I need to study." And if she could put her thoughts into words, they probably wouldn't have her so preoccupied anymore.

"You're not going to be able to study until you talk through whatever's bothering you."

"Don't you need to study?"

"I've been studying." Hafsah stands and starts putting her things into her backpack, fussing over the order as she does. "Also, unlike you, I don't have tests next week. Where are we going for dinner?"

Rebecca gives up. She's starting to think it may be her lot in life to be constantly surrounded by people a hell of a lot more stubborn than she is. Sometimes that's a good thing; away from her family and her pack of cousins, she sometimes has to be reminded to let her hair down a bit. School is an obligation, and she takes that maybe a little too seriously. Far too seriously, according to Ellie. But then other times, she runs into Hafsah the imperturbable wall and Ellie the immovable object and wonders what happens to her spine.

She puts away her books and notebooks and shrugs into her backpack, bouncing twice in place to settle it into a better position. Her umbrella is not the small one she usually keeps in the side pocket of her backpack, but rather one of the large ones that feels like a club when she's carrying it. She can admit that last night still has her a little rattled. If that happens to come out in defensiveness and a greater propensity for violence . . . well. It is what it is, isn't it? Light as the umbrella may be, the weight is comforting.

The library isn't silent so much as hushed, the murmur of conversations almost at the same volume as the hum and hiss of the air conditioner. The difference between the main library and the entryway is palpable, like an air lock filtering out humidity and heat. The girls stop at one of the water fountains to refill their steel bottles. It sometimes feels impossible to win in Florida. Inside is cool and desiccated from the air-conditioning; outside is miserably hot and swampy, so you're in a constant state of dehydration for opposite reasons.

It wasn't that long ago that Rebecca spent summers running around the ranch at all hours with her cousins and friends, barely noticing the heat, even though they were a couple of hours south and still squarely inland. What happened in the last decade to make her so much less suited to it?

Hafsah takes a deep breath as they walk outside. "I miss winter."

"What winter?"

"My winter. That thing where I return to my family, and we have cold and snow and ice and livable temperatures."

"You mean that thing where you have to plug in your car to keep your engine block from freezing?"

"Minnesota does have summer, too, you know, just as hot and humid as here."

"Yes, but then the other nine months are snow," she teases.

"I can layer on more clothing when I'm cold. If you're naked and still overheated, you're just stuck in hell." Digging awkwardly through her bag, Hafsah pulls out a plastic-ribbed fan with brightly painted cabbage roses. It unfurls with a sharp snap of nylon. It doesn't create much of a breeze between them, but it's hot enough that any movement of the air feels better.

Rebecca smiles, remembering the hours and hours one of her cousins spent trying to learn old-fashioned fan language with a very similar fan. The attempts ended when the cheap plastic broke over the head of another cousin, and the first cousin decided fencing was a much more direct sort of language. "What kind of food are you thinking?"

"Moe's is easy and not too far out of the way."

"And open?"

"That too."

It's quiet for a Saturday evening, at least for their section of campus. There's always something happening, but some events are decidedly more low key than others. They pass a redbrick building with a large sandwich board at the top of the stairs. Flowers and candles surround the legs, and a couple of Sharpies hang on strings so people can scribble messages around the giant picture of Harrison Mayne, the boy who was found in Lake Alice. They released the name this morning, as Det Corby had said would happen, and less than an hour later this was up. In enormous red letters across his face, someone has written **RAPIST AND SCUMBAG**.

Apparently his family and friends weren't the only ones aware of his spring break legal difficulties. Or, if the campus rumor mill is at all accurate, perhaps it's more a general state of his life. After a morning spent balancing chores, errands, and reassuring family members,

Rebecca's spent the rest of the day in the library; the details haven't floated her way yet.

She wonders about the person who wrote across the picture. Were they hurt by him? Was someone they loved hurt by him? Even on a Saturday, that part of campus is well traversed, especially in the last few weeks of term. Whoever defaced the memorial was seen. Seen but not stopped. The picture hasn't been replaced; there's no one standing guard or loitering nearby to keep a more unobtrusive eye on it.

On the whole, the student body can be rude, irreverent, and even profane, with a collective sense of humor most commonly found in fourteen-year-old boys, but they generally respect memorials. Or at least leave them alone; there have been disagreements in the past, especially with controversial public figures, but Rebecca can't think of another on-campus memorial she's seen defaced like this.

Would it be weird to stop and read the rest of the notes on the poster? Probably. She's curious, though. Once someone was brave enough—pissed enough, *aching* enough—to say something in a big way, smaller comments must have followed.

She and Hafsah walk in comfortable silence. It's only as they get closer to Moe's that they start seeing more than the occasional person. A lot of the food places on campus close early, especially on weekends, which means the ones that do stay open tend to attract crowds. It isn't until they've got their food and are settled at a table in a reasonably quiet corner that Hafsah restarts the conversation.

"So what is it that's had you so distracted?"

Rebecca takes a larger-than-polite bite of her quesadilla to give herself time to collect her thoughts. She probably should have been doing it on the way here, but then, half the distraction was trying to convince herself not to think about all this. At some point, though, she can't keep chewing. "Do you ever worry about Ellie?"

"Constantly" is Hafsah's prompt answer. "Or do you mean something specific?"

Dipping a chip into the queso, Rebecca takes a deep breath and lets it out slowly. "Do you ever worry that one day she's going to snap and murder us all?"

"No."

The queso drips off the chip as her hand freezes over the cup. "Seriously?" It would be nice if Hafsah's response had brought only relief, but there's a healthy dose of incredulity there as well.

"Sure. When she snaps, she's only going to kill the men. Mostly only going to kill the men," Hafsah says. "There might be a few women who fall for willfully propping up the patriarchy. But the rest of us should be pretty safe. Eat your chip."

Rebecca obeys, but she feels a little wild eyed as she watches Hafsah calmly bite into her burrito.

"The thing about Ellie," Hafsah continues once she's swallowed, "is that her anger is focused."

"She hates all men."

"Exactly. All men. It's not ambiguous; it's not arbitrary. She hates all men, and therefore, when she snaps—"

"I notice you keep saying *when*, not *if*."

"—she's going to go after the men. As long as the women get out of the way, they'll be fine."

"At least until all the men are dead and the patriarchy-propping women take the same toxic place in the new hierarchies," she points out.

"Well, yes. But that's a future problem. She'd have to finish killing all the men first, and with something over three and a half billion of them in the world at the moment, that will take her a while."

Rebecca props her chin on her greasy palm, then makes a face and reaches for a napkin. "You are disturbingly calm about this."

"I've had most of a school year to think about it," she admits. She scoops up some queso and drizzles it over the end of her burrito. "I know we've always joked about Ellie going postal, but it's really only been this year that it's felt inevitable."

Since Kacey? Rebecca examines her friend's face for any sign of humor, any trace of a joke, but Hafsah has the same expression of serene attention she gives any of her friends in conversation. "And that doesn't bother you?"

Hafsah doesn't answer immediately, and Rebecca doesn't push. Serious conversations with Hafsah have a rhythm to them: a ripple of words followed by a retreat as inexorable as the ride. When what she's saying matters, Hafsah will not be rushed. They eat in silence, sharing the chips and queso. There's a long line at the counter, the tables filling up as students ready themselves for drinking and dancing. Most of the ones intent on studying know to grab their food and go at this time of day; it's too loud and too crowded to make camping out a reasonable thing.

"I think almost everyone is capable of murder under the right circumstances," Hafsah says eventually. She scrubs at her fingers with a thin napkin. "The right person, the right reason, the right triggers . . . we're all capable of it. And I don't mean just killing someone; I mean out-and-out murder."

Rebecca ponders that distinction, the intent of it, and nods.

"There's a line, though, between being capable of an act and being likely to perform it. Most of us are pretty far back from that line, I feel. For example, it would take a lot for either of us to cross it."

Rebecca grins and lifts her drink in a toast that Hafsah returns.

"It doesn't make us less capable," Hafsah continues, "simply less likely. Ellie's constant fury and outrage keep her a lot closer to that line than most. She's already violent. She's perfectly willing to beat the crap out of someone who pisses her off, and that frankly doesn't take much. She's even more violent if she feels she's protecting someone other than herself."

"Is she?"

"Remember the guy who grabbed Keiko last year?"

Rebecca can hardly remember one night to the next. Passing grabs and gropes in a bar are just an inescapable element—the societal transaction of going out. If she made the effort to remember every time some jackwagon palmed her ass, she wouldn't have room in her brain for classwork. But the way Hafsah says it, the weight of significance in her tone, tells her this one should be memorable. "When we went out after watching the Georgia game in the lounge?" she asks uncertainly. "The one who ended up in the hospital with a broken hand. Kacey called his mom and ratted him out when he tried to press charges against Ellie."

Hafsah nods. "Ellie got grabbed, too, a little earlier—so hard she had a handprint bruise on her hip, but she just kicked him."

Given how hard Ellie kicks and where she kicks, Rebecca's not sure any guy would classify that experience as "just," but she supposes that's not really the point. Fetal position aside, it's miles apart from slamming someone's hand in a door, saying whoops, and immediately doing it twice more.

"Ellie's everyday violence combined with her general prickliness and attitude are easy to dismiss. Because it's in your face and restrained from true consequence, it's easy to think that's all it is. It's when Ellie is calm in her rage that she gets frightening."

"How so?"

"Because that's when she starts thinking. When she's just reacting to something, she can be satisfied pretty easily. Boy grabs girl, Ellie stomps boy, boy is in no condition to grab anyone, Ellie goes back to drinking and dancing and having fun. End of issue. She'll remember it, sure, but it'll tack on to the incredibly long list of such occurrences and won't retain any particular significance. It's like a parking ticket. Minor infraction, pay your fee, and more or less forget about it except for the people who tease you. Hardly life or death."

Rebecca grimaces but doesn't argue the metaphor.

"But. Last night was a little different, wasn't it?"

"She never touched the guy last night, never even spoke to him," Rebecca says. "She was focused on me."

"She brought you home."

"Yes."

"She calmed down."

"Yes?"

"And how long did it take her to whisper that she wanted to kill all the men?"

"Goddammit." Rebecca groans and folds her arms on the table, thumping her forehead against her wrist a few times. She sighs and rolls her head so she can still see her friend. "I was really hoping that apparent sincerity was a fluke."

"Not so much." Hafsah sips from her drink and places it back on the pile of folded napkins with a precision that's almost fussy. "You spent a lot of time with Kacey's family after she was . . . after she . . ." She falters, then takes a deep breath and exhales slowly through her nose. "After she was attacked," she continues firmly. "Between your classes and the hospital and then the care facility, it felt like we hardly saw you last semester. None of us, not even Ellie, were angry about that—the Montroses were leaning on you pretty heavily for emotional labor."

She spent most of winter break in a haze of acute emotional collapse. Her mom, her dad, and Gemma rotated through the end of the couch so she could huddle under the handmade quilts and cry into their laps, and when Daphne got home from Pennsylvania, they clung together for comfort, both of them struggling with refreshed memories of Daphne's attack. Before that, though, she'd taken responsibility for Kacey's parents, chivying them into eating, sleeping, showering, and generally taking care of themselves. It was only as they started getting better—or at least better adjusted to their terrible new reality—that she felt she could give herself permission to fall apart.

Come to think of it, that was when Ellie got more stubborn about dragging Rebecca out with them more often. Maybe Rebecca still needs that sometimes, even if she doesn't always appreciate it.

"Kacey's family needed you," Hafsah says, "so none of us were going to resent your absence, but it was hard, feeling like we'd lost both of you. And it meant you weren't there for the great unraveling."

"By context, I'm guessing this is not one of Luz's knitting projects." She says it in hopes of making Hafsah smile, but her friend just looks at her until she has to swallow back the urge to apologize.

"It was genuinely frightening," Hafsah says softly. "Ellie was completely out of control. And yes, I do mean that in comparison to how she is now. However effective you may or may not be, you're a good influence on her, but you weren't here to restrain her, and Kacey wasn't there to make her want to be a better person, and she was . . ." She fidgets with the baskets of food, the napkins, the curling receipts—her brow furrowed with worry. "If she'd ever shown the slightest indication of turning that rage inward, we'd have checked her in somewhere for suicide watch. But it was always spiraling outward, so we did our best to haul her back from out-and-out killing anyone, and I think we were all grateful to go home for winter break. I know for me it felt like I could breathe for the first time since Kacey was attacked. Then we came back, and Ellie was, well, pretty much as she is now. Angrier and more reckless, more prone to start fights than she used to be, but still better. More stable. That's a good thing, right?"

Rebecca frowns, testing the tone. "You don't sound like you think so."

"I really wanted to. Maybe I did, at first."

"So what changed your mind?"

"The week before finals you spent more time in the dorm so you could study and work on papers. Do you remember the day she walked into the dorm without a shirt? Just her bra and shorts?"

"Sure. She said she lost a bet."

"I got attacked by the hate preacher in Turlington Plaza. Not the one there now who keeps trying to pull down the Potato because he thinks it's obscene, but the old man who was there until this year. He yanked off my hijab and set it on fire. Ellie whipped off her shirt and gave it to me so I could get my hair covered again. Instead of going after him, she made sure I got safely back to the dorm. She stayed with me and checked me over to make sure I hadn't been stabbed or scratched by any of the pins as they got snatched away, and while I was shaking and crying with the adrenaline drop, she was so calm and steady and reassuring." Rebecca starts to smile, but Hafsah shakes her head. "At least until I listened to what she was saying rather than just the sound of her voice."

Rebecca can feel her dinner turning into an uncomfortable weight in her stomach. She waits, though. Whatever this feeling is, Hafsah's been carrying it a lot longer than she has.

"She kept saying that he wasn't going to hurt me again; he wasn't going to get the chance to hurt anyone again. She was going to make sure of that. I was going to be safe, and no one would ever remember him."

That definitely sounds likes Ellie, and maybe it would be easy to dismiss it as empty comfort, except . . . she takes in Hafsah's solemn expression, her dark-brown eyes steady in their contact, and thinks she probably doesn't want to ask the question. She also knows she's going to because Hafsah is her friend, and so is Ellie, and it feels important in a way most things don't. "There was a new preacher yelling at everyone after winter break," she says slowly.

"Yes."

"What happened to the old one?"

Hafsah shrugs. It's not a casual gesture, though, and Rebecca's not sure if it's because of the subject or because of her personal stake in it. "He disappeared. No one I've ever talked to knew his name or where he lived. He was just a fixture, pacing through Turlington with his posters and microphone and vitriol. He was there, and then he wasn't, and he didn't come back. After a few days of peace and quiet, the current one came and set up shop."

"And Ellie?"

"The first time we passed the new preacher together, she smiled."

"A lot of people smiled. Everyone hated the old guy. He said females are inherently damned because we bleed and birth sin. He once chased Luz and Keiko out of the plaza, swatting at them with his sign, because they had the nerve to hold hands in public."

"All true."

But it's different because context is a thing that exists and matters, and they both know that.

"Are you saying you think Ellie . . ." She doesn't finish the statement. It's one thing to talk around it, another thing entirely to say it out loud. There are a lot of things that are safer understood but unsaid.

Hafsah shrugs again. "To be honest, I try not to think about it too much. I know she's capable. I . . . she's my friend. I don't want to know if it's more than that. Not for sure."

Rebecca bites her lip and considers the girl across the table. "Do you think I'm capable?"

"Like I said, I think we're all capable."

"And you haven't mentioned this to anyone." She leans forward, more of her weight on the table than the bench, it feels like. "Why not?"

"As far as I know, she hasn't done anything. Until she does . . . capability doesn't mean culpability. Surely that's something they teach you criminology majors."

It is, but she's having a hard time getting over one of the layers in what Hafsah's saying. *Until* she snaps, *when* she does . . . not *if*. Like it's a foregone conclusion that one day their friend and suitemate will absolutely become a murderer if she isn't one already. She thinks of all the interviews she's read, the documentaries she's watched for classes, where someone goes on a murder spree or turns out to be a decades-active serial killer, and all their friends and family, all the neighbors and coworkers, are shown sadly shaking their heads, confused and alarmed. "We never knew," they always say. "We never even suspected." She has to admit that even before this conversation, she couldn't have said that with a straight face about Ellie.

"You're still friends with her," she says finally, trying to piece together too many sharp-edged bits in her mind.

"There's no proof."

"No, this isn't about proof; this is about friendship." She holds up a finger to silence Hafsah's protest. "You are at least fifty-one percent sure she killed the preacher, or you never would have brought it up as an example." Her eyes dart around, assessing the tables nearest them. No one seems to be paying attention. She lowers her voice anyway. "For three months you've been reasonably certain she murdered a guy, but you're still friends with her. Not just tolerating her. You're not keeping her at arm's length, you're not afraid of her, you haven't told anyone. You're protecting her. Why?"

"She could have just threatened him, you know. Scared him off."

Sitting back, Rebecca drops her hands to her lap, worrying at her thumb. "Could have," she concedes, "but you don't believe that."

Hafsah carefully gathers all the trash into one basket, stacking the others neatly beneath it. Rather than argue with such a clear signal, Rebecca takes the drinks to refill. When they leave, their steel bottles swaying heavily against their thighs, the paper cups sweating profusely down their hands to splash against their clothing, it's full dark. They walk out into the humid night, away from the light and noise of the restaurant.

Finally, when it's just the two of them in a stretch between street-lights, Hafsah stops and turns to Rebecca, most of her face lost to shadow. "Because I feel safer with the man gone. I do. The new one is a creep, but he's so focused on sex and masturbation that he doesn't seem to care if a woman is hijabi or not. He's an annoyance, not a threat."

"Hafsah . . ."

"How do I condemn Ellie for taking a terrible action—*maybe* taking an action—when I'm so damn *grateful* for the results?"

9

There are certain things, Rebecca thinks, that invariably summon the end of a conversation with a thoughtful silence. A moment of memorial, for example, or the confession of a mortifying event. Asking the other members of a group project if they've got their parts ready.

Finding out one of your friends might be a murderer.

Or, more precisely, finding out your roommate thinks one of your friends might be a murderer.

Neither girl tries to speak as they make their way back to their dorm, automatically walking faster in the darker stretches between streetlights. Ahead of them, a small light about waist high on Rebecca approaches them too steadily to be a handheld flashlight and too low to be a helmet light of any kind. "Bicycle?" she murmurs.

Hafsah slows so they can dawdle in an illuminated area. "Probably. No scooter sounds."

Reaching behind her, Rebecca curls her free hand around the handle of her umbrella. A few seconds later reflective strips on the bike, helmet, and rider's clothing throw the light back at them in haphazard flashes. It's almost a minute before the rider enters the outer edge of the streetlight's cone and becomes recognizable.

"Officer Kevin," Rebecca greets him. She's rather glad he didn't come upon them a few minutes ago, when the conversation was firmly in the camp of Things Not To Say Around Law Enforcement.

He coasts the bike rather than braking, waiting for it to slow enough that he can safely plant his feet. "Becky, right?"

"Rebecca."

"How are you doing? Okay after last night?"

"I'm fine," she says. "Little rattled, but it wasn't the first time—probably won't be the last."

"That's unfortunate."

She nods along with Hafsah, who's standing much closer to her than she was before the rider came into view. Realizing that makes her notice that there's no one else in view, and a shiver jolts down her spine. They're overtrained, perhaps, by society and their own experiences; there's a reflexive fear in being alone with any man they don't know well.

Officer Kevin is a tall thin beanpole of a man in the dark-blue short-sleeved shirt and shorts of the mounted campus police. Strips of reflective plastic run down the sides of the shorts and near the sides of his shirt, framing his chest rather than marking the seams. An inch or two of black bicycle shorts peeks out underneath the uniform shorts, showing a long stretch of tanned leg until his heavy-duty black sneakers. Rebecca stares for a moment at the sneakers, then grants that it's probably somewhat difficult to ride a bike in boots. She's done it in slinky heels more than once, but women are generally asked to do more ridiculous things in the name of fashion than men are. His badge and nameplate are shiny on his breast pocket, and just above them a tiny red light blinks from his body cam.

"Has he bothered you today?" the officer asks Rebecca.

"No. Last night was the first time I've ever seen him, and I doubt I'll ever see him again."

"Where are you ladies headed?"

Rebecca and Hafsah trade a look. "I think we're calling it a night," Rebecca says after a hesitation just slightly too long to go unnoticed. Hopefully it comes off as diplomatic rather than evasive. She didn't even tell Det Corby where she lived until this fall, when he gave her a ride home through the rain from Kacey's care facility. He'd known her for a little over a year before he knew which building was home.

"Either of you have a flashlight?"

"We have flashlight apps on our phones."

"They don't give much light," he says with a frown. "If you live on campus, I can walk you to your building."

"We've been pretty safe on campus," Hafsah replies neutrally. "It's just the bars that offer trouble."

"Still. It's not exactly safe for two such pretty ladies to be out on their own this late. If the boys don't get you, the gators might think you look good enough to eat."

Rebecca's hand tightens on her umbrella, and the plastic handle creaks, startlingly loud in this quiet section of campus. As she uncurls each finger, she gives herself another stern instruction to let the irritation go. Some men just can't help being paternalistic. "Thank you for the offer, but we're good. We've got each other."

"You know where the call boxes are? In case you need help?"

"Yes, sir."

"And if you see a gator?"

"Run away," they chorus.

"In a zigzag," he adds, and if he feels ridiculous saying it, it doesn't show on his face. "Gators are fast, a lot faster than you think, and climbing up something isn't going to help you. You're not going to be faster, so be more agile."

"Yes, sir," says Rebecca. "The school's been sending out emails."

"All right." He folds his arms over his chest, one hand tapping against his ribs, the other cupping his shoulder. Rebecca can't help but notice that the gesture blocks the view of his body cam. "You ladies be safe."

"Yes, sir. Have a good night." They stand in place, watching him, and they can actually see the moment it occurs to him that they're waiting for him to leave first. With a smile, he touches two fingers to the front of his helmet in a kind of salute, kicks off, and pedals away.

"Is he always that pushy?" whispers Rebecca.

"That was Officer Kevin."

". . . that's an answer?"

"Not everyone in law enforcement is Det Corby, Rebecca."

Rebecca grew up surrounded by law enforcement—several uncles and cousins on her mother's side with a sheriff's office, and more uncles, a couple of aunts, and even more cousins with the city police back home—and every family gathering is full of friends and colleagues and mostly good-natured bragging about which force is better until everyone piles on the handful of relatives who went federal. Her uncle Mattes always told her to never blindly trust a uniform and a badge, that pretty girls will always have to be a little bit careful even around people meant to protect them.

It's only now that she realizes that care has never translated to fear for her. Not as it clearly and understandably does for Hafsah.

"Let's go home," she says and keeps her hand on her umbrella.

She's not sure exactly when the feeling starts, that prickling along her spine that could be the beginning of heat rash and sweat irritation but feels somehow heavier, more. A couple of minutes, maybe. She slides behind Hafsah as they hurry to the next streetlight and notices a smaller light reflecting off the stop sign on the corner. Turning her head, she sees the bicycle and rider matching their pace from a little way back.

"Officer Kevin?" Hafsah asks in an undertone.

"Yes."

The girls are standing so close that Rebecca can feel Hafsah suck in a deep breath, then slowly let it out. They stop and wait under the light. The bike halts, remaining motionless long enough to feel like a stalemate. Then they hear a huff, and a minute later Officer Kevin walks the bike into the cone of light. His expression hovers between sheepish and defiant.

"It's just not safe," he says plaintively, his friendly smile pleading with them to understand.

With a speculative glance up at Rebecca, Hafsah looks back to the officer with a strained but pleasant enough smile. "We're just at Thomas," she says. "Not far at all."

Rebecca blinks.

"Then it won't be any problem for me to escort you there."

Without a better option, the girls mumble thank-yous. Rebecca makes sure to walk between Hafsah and Officer Kevin.

"So what are you ladies studying? Becky?"

"Rebecca," she corrects automatically.

"You look like . . . let me guess. Education?"

She barely resists the urge to roll her eyes. If she weren't aware of the tension screaming off her roommate, she might have. "Criminology and journalism." And he has to know at least part of that already if he knew her as one of Det Corby's former students.

"Huh. So you're going to be one of those people writing think pieces against police."

Wary of his tone, Rebecca carefully picks her way through possible answers. "I'm already one of those people praising the police for what they do well and correctly and calling for correction of what's done in error or malice. I have a lot of family in law enforcement, and I respect the hell out of them, but that doesn't mean there's no room to improve the system."

He doesn't look convinced. She's not sure she cares. She's spent the past two summers volunteering with reception and records for both the GPD and the ACSO, and she's gotten praise from the chief and sheriff directly. She's confident in what she does and wants to do.

"And you?" he asks, craning around her to peer at Hafsah. "I don't think I got your name."

"Oh, I'm in earth science," Hafsah answers cheerfully.

Rebecca winces. The cheeriness is probably somewhat overdone and definitely a distraction.

"It's just incredible, you know?" she continues in a babble. "Like, did you know that Mount Etna started erupting last year, and it's still going? Nothing huge or shattering, just sort of a . . . oh, what's the word . . . like a persistent dribble of lava, and a year later it's still happening! It's amazing to think how many cultures and civilizations have been shaped or even completely wiped out by volcanoes. We know about Pompeii, of course, and then the eruption on Santorini that brought about the collapse of the Minoans on Crete, and there are a number of people who think the tsunami purported to have destroyed the city of Atlantis was likely caused by an eruption-triggered earthquake. Just think about how many cultures we might find trace of if we can ever excavate through hardened lava!"

Biting her lip to keep from laughing, Rebecca listens to her friend burble on in a dizzying monologue. She sneaks a glance at Officer Kevin, who looks both startled and confused. Everyone in their suite can speak extensively about their areas of interest, but no one can weaponize it quite like Hafsah.

The lights get brighter, more clustered together as they draw near several of the historic-register dormitories, the dull grumble of cars moving along University Avenue growing louder. At one of the doors to Thomas Hall, Hafsah stops with a laugh and holds her hand out to Rebecca. "Here, I'll hold your drink if you get out my wallet."

She hands over the sweating cup and obediently unzips the front pocket of her friend's backpack, only to find two wallets. Well, that's . . . odd. "Got distracted switching wallets?" she asks after a moment.

"Whoops," Hafsah says casually. "It's the pink one."

Drawing the wallet out—baby pink with a white Gator logo stitched onto the quilted fabric—she sidles closer to the door before pulling out the student ID. She runs the card through, hears the door unlock with a clunk, and quickly opens it for Hafsah. "Thank you, Officer Kevin. We're safely home now." She holds it until Hafsah is inside, then follows, the door shutting just after the officer wishes them a good night.

Then she looks down at the ID in her hand. "Who the hell is Yasmin al-Nasir, and why do you have her wallet?"

Hafsah trades her the wallet for her drink, tucking the ID card back in its place. "Yasmin is in a couple of my classes, and she left it on a table in the library yesterday after we finished studying. She's gone for the weekend, so I told her I would hold on to it."

"And the reason we're in Thomas?" she asks, one eyebrow twitching up toward her hairline. "Or did we move over from Sledd while I was in the library?"

"Rebecca, I am young, female, Black, and Muslim; in what world do you think I am comfortable being virtually alone with a cop after dark?" She shakes her head and shoves the pink wallet back into her bag. "Thomas was closer, that's all."

"And Officer Kevin is annoying?"

"There's that too."

They wave at the RA, who sits at the desk slurping from a Big Gulp; he doesn't seem to care that there are strangers in his building. Slipping out the door at the far end of the lobby, they walk the short distance to the side door to Sledd Hall. Rebecca's pretty sure she can spit watermelon seeds farther than that. If she can't, Gemma definitely can.

When they get upstairs, Susanna and Delia are in their room, playing a driving game on Delia's console that has them both in gales of laughter. Rebecca heads into the bathroom to dampen a cloth, scrubbing it against her overheated skin to remove the itchy layer of stickiness that comes of living in Florida. Luz is in the study space on the opposite side, a single light on overhead as she reads from a textbook, her cheek propped on one fist, a highlighter slowly twirling in her other hand. She smiles up at Rebecca, then holds a finger to her lips.

"Keiko's asleep," she whispers.

"It's barely nine o'clock."

"It's been a long week."

Nodding, Rebecca glances at the other door. "And Ellie?"

Luz shrugs. "Haven't seen her since lunch. She's not there, though. I checked because it was weird she didn't start bitching when Keiko was crying."

"That's still from the stress being over, right?"

"Right. No tragedies, I promise. I don't know where Ellie is. She hasn't texted anything."

"As long as I don't get called to the police station again."

Luz laughs softly, and they chat for another minute or two before Rebecca lets her get back to her reading.

Returning to her own room, Rebecca sinks down on the edge of her bed. Hafsah sits across from her, hijab across her lap, gently rubbing a cloth against her scalp. Rebecca hesitates, bites her lip. "Ellie isn't here."

"We don't know anything, Rebecca."

"Is that enough?"

Hafsah tosses the cloth in the direction of her laundry bag. It lands with a barely there thump, just one corner trailing out of the mesh bag. "It has to be. For now. She's our friend."

"And Mountebanks?"

Hafsah freezes. It takes a visible effort for her to relax again, and even then Rebecca can still see the tension in her. "We don't know anything," she says eventually.

It isn't enough.

Rebecca knows what she can live with. It took a long time, a very patient therapist, and a rather less patient Gemma to work through layers of guilt over Daphne's attack and understand what things were reasonable for her to carry and what she needed to let go. She repeated many of those lessons when Kerry, the third-floor RA, woke them up in September to tell them Kacey was in the hospital.

If something happens to Mountebanks and they were in a position to prevent that, can Hafsah live with it? Can Rebecca?

She touches the finger-shaped bruises on her chest, feels the muscles tight beneath the skin from the strength of his grip. Twenty-four hours ago, that answer would have been a lot clearer.

10

It's hard to laugh when the car fishtails through the parking lot, sliding just on the wrong side of out of control. Forrest is entirely too drunk to be driving, but when his cousin Nathan challenged him to a race, he insisted he had to be the one to drive, and I let him. Nathan is at least as drunk and a good two car lengths behind us. His little Pontiac isn't doing as well with the poorly maintained lot as Forrest's sturdy Corolla.

I make myself laugh, though, because Forrest is cackling triumphantly as one final donut brings us to a stop near a wall, the car facing the rest of the lot. It's amazing to me how little it takes—just a smile and a filthy suggestion—for boys to be so eager to go out in the middle of nowhere with a stranger. I lean into him, one hand high on his thigh, but he's too busy leaning out his open window to notice that.

"You drive like Grandma!" Forrest crows.

After parking perpendicular to the front of the Corolla, Nathan scowls and cuts the engine. "You're a cheating bastard!"

"My parents married before yours did!"

Nathan turns a blotchy red.

Family drama.

The boys spill out of their cars, lurching toward each other. I take a little more time, making sure there are no stray hairs on the seat or in the seat belt, that my shoes haven't left any prints on the floor mat. Forrest doesn't keep his car tidy enough that I can just wipe down the seat, but I don't see anything. I check the treads of my shoes for anything I might be tracking out with me—Cheeto dust and weed, to guess from the rest of the car—but the plastic grocery bags littering the well provided a good barrier. I adjust my gloves and resist the urge to touch my hair, all of it tucked into one of those felt caps that strives for something between vintage and ironic but stumbles into an ignominious landing on ugly. A handful of clips and pins do the rest, taming stray wisps up into the cap and away from pesky things like headrests, seat belts, and air vents.

The gloves are easier. Mention the fear of burns from metal and vinyl that's been baking all day in the Florida sun, and no one thinks twice about you pulling on cycling gloves to protect your fingers and palms. It's only practical, even if most don't bother with it. And if it leaves no fingerprints behind, well, that is a perk, isn't it?

Before closing the door, I reach over and pull the keys from the ignition, bouncing them in my palm once or twice to feel the weight of them. For as much crap is on the rings, they're surprisingly light. I pinch one of the dozens of tags and fold it over so I can see what it is.

Huh. It's a laminated concert ticket. Skimming through some of the other tags, I can see other ticket stubs from other concerts, movies, music festivals, clubs, even a couple of ballets. That's . . . that's kind of . . .

Jesus, I can't believe I'm thinking this, but that's actually kind of sweet.

The boys are shoving each other now, Forrest still laughing but Nathan looking genuinely pissed, both of them clearly forgetting there's a girl they were trying to impress. They did the same thing at the parking lot party and a club before that and a field party before that. They were raised more like brothers than cousins, and they're going to fight more like brothers than cousins. Which is, thankfully, about as useful as it is irritating.

Smoothing my skirt out, I sit on the back of the car, on the driver's side so I can see them better. "Boys," I chide them with a laugh. "Aren't you forgetting about someone?"

They both look at me, startled.

Idiots.

I'm honestly amazed we got down here in one piece with how drunk they are.

Forrest is the one to walk toward me, less invested in the argument and however much history they have behind it. His hands are hot and sweaty on my hips, even through my skirt and bike shorts. "Baby, you going to reward the victey . . . the vixey . . . the winner?"

"Ah ah ah. This is only half the race," I remind him. I hold his keys up and out, jangling them just past his ear. "Remember, the way back is part of it too."

"Please," he snorts. "Everyone knows Nathan ain't shit for driving cars or pleasing women."

I am mildly impressed that he managed to say that so clearly.

Nathan darts forward and snatches the keys out of my grasp. He sways a bit as he backs up, but then he plants himself and hurls the keys over the wall. They land in the darkness beyond with a small splash and a waft of fetid water. It's what I was planning to do myself, only I was going to make it look less like a fit of pique. I was leaning toward squealing, "Snake!" and tossing my arms up in the air, conveniently and "accidentally" losing the keys in the process.

This works, though. I can roll with this.

Forrest immediately lets go of me and turns on his cousin, fists clenched tightly at his sides. "Nathan! The hell you do that for, you little asshole?"

"You cheated!" the other boy snaps. "You stuck me behind those old farts, and don't say you didn't 'cause you had to slow down to do it!"

"Couldn't have done it without being ahead of you!"

"That's not a fair race!"

"How the fuck we going to get home, asshole?" demands Forrest. "We can't all fit in your piece of shit!"

Nathan turns and blinks at his Pontiac, realization slowly blooming across his face that this might have been a bad idea. The closest light in the lot is a ways away, but enough reflects off the white wall beside us to show his chagrin. "Fine," he says after some thought. "We'll just go over the wall and get your keys. Where are we, anyway?"

"Some kind of farm," I tell them, attempting to look indifferent. "I just remembered it was a good drive and a lot big enough to finish in."

Forrest stands in front of the wall, head tilted back to see the top. It's maybe nine or ten feet tall, not insurmountable but requiring some effort.

Or some teamwork.

"Get over here," he tells his cousin. "This is gonna take both of us."

"Want to give me your keys, baby?" I ask Nathan. "Last thing we need is for them to fall out while you're climbing and leave us looking for both of them."

"Yeah, thanks, that's a good idea." Nathan fishes his keys out from his pocket and tosses them to me. Like his cousin, he also has a bunch of laminated tags on the biggest ring. His, however, turn out to be Bible verses, with "in bed" scribbled on the plastic after each one. Fortune cookie Bible verses are a thing now—who knew?

Hooking a finger through the ring so I don't drop the keys, I watch the boys argue over which one should climb up first and why, and I try not to giggle at their reasons crossing over each other. They are both arguing for both positions, and neither one seems to realize that. I egg them both on impartially. Eventually, Forrest manages to convince his cousin that since Nathan was the one to throw the keys over in the first place, Nathan should be the one doing more work. Nathan doesn't seem happy about it, but he does brace himself against the wall so his cousin can awkwardly climb up to his shoulders and grab the top of the wall.

The wall isn't wide enough to straddle comfortably, which means it's also really hard to get any sort of a good stance. Forrest successfully pulls Nathan up to join him, but they both overbalance and fall back, landing on the other side of the wall with thumps and groans and a few choice insults for each other.

I have to bite my tongue to keep from laughing. I mean, I was pretty sure tonight was going to go well, but this is amazing.

They swear some more at the sight of another barrier inside, but if I'm remembering it correctly from other visits, that wall shouldn't be more than about waist high on them. I tilt my head, listening as they hop it and cry out in surprise at the way their feet slip on the slimy algae permanently lining the deep bowl that descends a lot farther than either of them thought. They land in the water with splashes and curses.

Low rumbles fill the air, followed by more splashes, then by screaming. It's the first time I've heard it as a duet.

I like it. One of the screams is higher pitched but held steadily, almost ululating with terror and pain. The other is a little deeper but more staccato, with ragged breathing between the bursts. Under them both, of course, is the chorus of disturbed alligators. The screams stop before the chorus does, though I can hear one of the boys still whimpering for a couple minutes more. Then that, too, dies away.

Shaking out Nathan's keys until I can find the one for his car, I head to the little Pontiac, and oh, sweet Jesus, if I wasn't already intending to shower away the sweat, the pungent reek of weed and flavored vape smoke would force the point anyway. Fuck, how can he breathe in this thing?

Well, I guess that's not really his problem anymore.

I pull out of the lot, passing the sign for Ole Suwannee Y'all Gator Farm and Bait Shop. It's an easy drive back to town and to campus. I don't pass any marked police cars, and given that I'm doing things like driving the speed limit and obeying traffic laws, if there are unmarked ones hanging out along the route, I present an uninteresting target.

Parking in Nathan's permit lot, I double-check that I've left nothing of myself behind, lock the car, and walk up toward the building.

Murphree Hall is beautiful, all stately red brick and pale trim. As I pass it, I drop the keys on the grass right at the edge of the sidewalk so the brightly colored tags spill onto the cement. No one will notice them tonight, I don't think, unless they trip over them by pure chance, but that's fine. Nathan has a habit of missing his pocket when he's driving drunk. It isn't at all uncommon for Murphree residents to find his keys and turn them in.

It's a good thing they aren't all this easy; I'd hate to get bored into carelessness.

11

"Hey, wake up; you've gotta come see this!"

"Come to the lounge; you want to see this!"

"Wake up, wake up! You've gotta see this!"

Rebecca sits up in bed, wrestling her tangled curls out of her face, and stares blearily at the door. The closed door, beyond which is a good six feet of open space before another closed door, all of which should add up to not hearing the pounding on the hallway door and the student gleefully pounding on what sounds like *every* door in the hall.

She doesn't really know many of the other girls on the floor, not outside their suite, aside from a nodding acquaintance down in the laundry room, but none of them have so far seemed the kind to wake everyone up as a practical joke. One of the boys on the second floor did that early in the term, pulling the fire alarm at three in the morning and forcing everyone to evacuate, but he got arrested and politely evicted from the dorm, and this doesn't sound like the same kind of thing.

Kicking free of her sheet, Rebecca yawns and rolls out of bed, lurching across the gap to shake Hafsah's shoulder. "Wake up; something's happening."

Hafsah opens one eye and glares. "What's happening?" she mumbles.

"I don't know. They want us in the lounge, I guess." She pulls her friend's long hooded yellow bathrobe off its hook and holds it out. "Come on. Don't make me go alone if it's another safety lecture."

Still grumbling, Hafsah sits up and takes the bathrobe. "Boys?"

"Maybe. Never know who's spent the night or come from another floor."

Hafsah pulls on one of the cotton caps she usually wears under her hijab, then shrugs into the bathrobe and tugs the hood up over the cap. Once she's covered up, they open the door and nearly fall over Susanna and Delia, both still in their pajamas. Susanna looks the unsettling kind of awake that suggests she was up the whole night mainlining Red Bull. Neither of them seems to have any more information than Rebecca does, though, so the quartet heads out into the hall to join the parade of shuffling, sleepy zombies to the lounge at one end of the building. The room of couches and televisions is attached to the kitchen that few people know how to use and even fewer people know how to clean. It was probably meant to foster floor unity or something but finds most of its use during the Olympics, on election nights, and when an attempted pantie raid requires creative retribution—or at least communal venting.

Now it's full of confused undergrads, many in pajamas, but a few already dressed for eight o'clock classes or still in towels from the showers. All three televisions are tuned to the same channel, showing the morning edition of the local news. When it switches from the anchors to a field reporter, a small cheer goes up from a handful of journalism students; Anike Moss is an alum of the program, only two years graduated—many of them know her.

"Holy shit," Rebecca says, staring wide eyed at the screen. "That's a gator farm."

A sharp burst of sound pounds around her at the word *gator*. Most seem to make the same connection she did, though one poor girl with a thick Boston accent plaintively asks the purpose of "fahming alligatahs." In one of Rebecca's first-year journalism courses, the grad student teaching his first semester of classes decided there should be a field trip to the gator farm to give the students a feel for reporting on local color. Even after the clusterfuck of having to arrange transport and manage other classes, the trip was an unmitigated disaster as three lecture halls of eighteen-year-olds discovering the first vestiges of independence and problems with authority descended on the kitschy, touristy farm. Some of the students still aren't welcome back there.

The grad student has been banned for life for bringing them.

"It's been an unusual morning for the owners of Ole Suwannee Y'all Gator Farm today," Anike announces, holding her microphone comfortably in front of her. The part of Rebecca's mind that's possibly overtrained by a class she loathed notes that the reporter has her eyes focused properly at the lens of the camera rather than on the camera's operator as so many new reporters do. "When they arrived a little over two hours ago, they found an unfamiliar car in the parking lot. Despite their best attempts at prevention, the gator farm has a long history of trespassers and daredevils; at first there was no reason to think this was anything different. The car, however, was empty, with no trace of its occupant. That's when Mike Wallace, the farm's founder and co-owner, noticed signs that someone might have gone over the boundary wall."

She stands at the entrance to the farm's main building, a squat single-story structure that houses a gift shop, mini-museum, ticket office, and bait shop, all indicated by cartoonish, overeager signs. Sheriff's deputies mill about in the background, several of them speaking to an older couple. The man looks pale, one arm around his wife's shoulders and his other hand shaking in front of him as he tries to gesture. Her face is buried in his chest, fingers on her cheek, as if she's covering her mouth. Rebecca feels a pang of sympathy for them. She knows what it's like to stumble into something terrible, as they clearly have.

"The gator farm is an educational tourism attraction," continues Anike, "and most of its resident alligators are born and raised right here on the farm. While no alligator can truly be considered tame, there has never been an incident at Ole Suwannee Y'all. Given the recent spate of alligator attacks and deaths, however, the Wallaces called the Alachua County Sheriff's Office before going in, where they found a truly shocking scene. Although no identification has been released, deputies have said they believe at least two people were attacked last night. They also said they'll be making an official statement once"—here Anika falters slightly, looking a little sick, but regains herself quickly enough most won't notice—"they're able to locate and retrieve all body parts from the main alligator pool."

The room explodes into a roar of student chatter, bellowed back into silence from those standing farther from the televisions. Rebecca thinks of Harrison Mayne, of how long it took to find his head in Lake Alice. What did Anike see? The screens split, one side fixed on the professionally concerned pair of anchors, the other rotating between shots of Anike and a few background shots, including one where deputies are examining the stretch of wall behind a dark-blue Toyota Corolla. A vanity plate on the front end of the car says **EAT MY DUST**, surrounded by a heavy metal frame of chain links surmounted by devil's horns.

"Holy shit, that's Forrest's car!" cries one of the eleven girls crammed on the three-person couch.

It's impossible to make out individual statements in the flurry of responses, but all attention is on her now rather than the television. One of the seniors lets out a piercing whistle to calm everyone down. "Are you sure?"

"I mean, that's definitely his car," the first girl answers. "He's from my hometown, him and his cousin Nathan. We kept telling him it would make a better bumper sticker than plate, and he'd get so mad."

The decorations do make it a very distinctive car.

"They said two bodies," a thin boy crammed in a corner of the room points out. Rebecca squints at him but can't tell if he lives on one of the male floors or if he's someone's overnight guest.

"I've got Nathan's number," another girl offers. "We had a group project a few weeks ago, and I haven't deleted it yet." She whips out her phone and brings up the contact, fingers pressed against her opposite ear to help her hear. "Voice mail," she says a moment later.

"Know where they live?" asks someone else.

The girl from Nathan's class nods. "Murphree. Don't know which room. But I remember Murphree because Nathan can't say it right. Always says Murphy and gets mad when anyone corrects him."

"So what I'm hearing is that they get mad at everything," Ellie drawls, draping herself across Rebecca's back. She's one of the people in a towel, her hair dripping down Rebecca's shirt. Rebecca grimaces and pushes her away a little, at least out of the splash zone. She's not sure Ellie of all people gets to laugh at other people having a short fuse.

A girl with hair dyed in a neon rainbow and giant hipster glasses raises her hand. "I live in Murphree. It's just across Fletcher."

"Then go find out, you moron, and come back and tell us!" orders the girl next to her. She kisses the Lisa Frank girl before literally shoving her back toward the hall.

"Anyone else know them?" asks the senior.

Some hands raise, but not many.

"They're freshmen, both of them," says the girl who identified Forrest's car. "They rushed in the fall and were nearly accepted, except . . ."

"Except?" pushes someone else in the room.

Rebecca knows what comes after an *except* like that. What always comes after a hesitation like that.

Next to the first girl, a brunette hunched nearly in two straightens up. Her arms are still tightly folded around her, though, and her face looks nearly gray with shock. "Except they drugged me, took me back to their dorm room, and when I fought back, they pushed me out of Murphree Hall naked," she says, her voice shaking. "Campus cops picked me up after someone nearly hit me on Fletcher, but by the time I was clear enough to insist on anything and then convince them to take me to a hospital, the drugs weren't going to show up on a tox screen."

"Did you press charges?" someone asks in a hushed voice.

She shakes her head. "They said there were no charges to make, that I'd just run up legal bills without making anything stick."

"They also told her she shouldn't try to ruin boys' lives just because she had regrets about her behavior," another girl adds tartly, pulling her friend into a hug. "They made it clear that if she tried to pursue charges anyway, they'd get in her way, so she didn't make a formal report."

"Nathan and Forrest have an uncle who was on the force here," says the girl from their hometown. "He was well liked before he got booted for excessive force. Turns out that's not okay against a congressman's kid. The boys bragged that their uncle's friends would look out for them."

"So I just had bad luck getting those particular officers?" asks the brunette.

"I'd say you had bad luck the whole night," Rebecca says, and a murmur of agreement ripples out.

"And the fraternity?" asks one of the seniors.

"Has a bad enough reputation already. This chapter's at risk of getting banned here. They decided to do the smart thing and not take a chance on assholes who will absolutely get them in more trouble."

"What would they even be doing out on a gator farm?"

"Drinking?" The first girl shrugs. "Those two get into the most stupid, inane, bullshit competitions with each other. One will dare the other to shimmy up a flagpole; the other will insist on doing it naked, so the other will insist on doing it naked and covered in glitter."

There's a contemplative hush in the room, just for a moment. It's a strangely specific example.

The televisions are largely ignored now that they have insider information, and the screens are showing alligator safety tips and animal control numbers anyway. Anyone still watching it at this point is just hoping to see body parts. Rebecca has no desire to see that.

Lisa Frank's girlfriend goggles at her phone screen. "Shay just found Nathan's keys on the ground."

"How does she know they're his?" asks Rebecca.

"He loses them so often after drinking everyone in Murphree knows they're his," she says dismissively. "She says they were on the sidewalk up to the building, and the RA is making her stay there to talk to police."

"What, they're there already?"

"No. So, wait—why does the RA think the police are coming? If they haven't identified the bodies, and all."

Ellie clears her throat and, given her somewhat terrifying reputation, gets immediate silence. "Crim. major speaking; she just walked in with keys and said she thinks they belong to the newest gator bait. Anyone with a lick of sense is going to assume that cops will want to talk to her."

A girl with a severe caffeine twitch and streaks of highlighter all over one side of her face looks around. "Do you think they'll be okay?" When everyone turns to stare at her, she glares back. "It didn't say they were dead, just that they're having trouble locating parts! They could have taken them to a hospital and come back to look for missing limbs!"

"I'm pretty sure if they were still alive, they'd feel more comfortable releasing their names," Rebecca says eventually, fighting back an inappropriate laugh.

"Oh. That makes sense."

Kerry, the third-floor RA, joins them, clutching a steaming mug of coffee like a lifeline. She holds her other hand up to stop the flood of noise. "I didn't miss it; I watched it while the coffee was brewing," she says, her voice rough from sleep.

"You missed some things," one of the other girls says helpfully.

Kerry sips her coffee as the others fill her in relatively quickly. There are a couple of tangents or points where too many people are talking at once to understand them, but she gets the gist soon enough. "I'll put a call in to the housing coordinator's office," she tells them. "I'm sure somewhere in the day they'll have information they want out. Read your emails. Don't just skip over the LISTSERV because it's the LISTSERV, and I'll send one out if we need to have a hall meeting."

"Kerry?" asks the highlighter girl. "Do you think this is an accident?"

"I know literally as much as you do about it," answers the RA. "Is it hella weird? Yes. Have there been a lot of alligator-related bodies contributing to the mortality rate? Undeniably. Is it an accident? Who knows? Clearly we should all count ourselves lucky that these two have been removed from the gene pool, but I doubt we'll know the actual circumstances for a while. Something for you all to keep in mind: There'll be reporters and bloggers and whatever bullshit lurking around campus today hoping for a scoop. Whatever your personal theory, remember that the names have not been confirmed or released yet, and you could be causing families a lot of pain by speculating. I'm not going to tell you not to talk about it. I don't have that right. But think about what your own families would be feeling if they heard on the news that people think you're dead. Whether it's true or not, that's not how anyone should find out. Let the police do the actual informing."

"Yes, Kerry," mumbles most of the room.

"One more thing: don't be stupid. Don't think that the gators won't eat you, too, if you do something fucking dumb. If you need to read back through the safety tips, they're posted on the boards and on the website. Obviously it's a fucking tragedy for anyone to die, but I sure as shit don't want the next one to be any of you. Pay attention. Don't be stupid."

Some of the girls look so shocked that Rebecca wonders if it's honestly never occurred to them that alligators don't choose victims based on anything more than availability. The Boston girl, in particular, looks close to panic.

Ellie snorts. "Rapists, assholes, more rapists and assholes," she says a little too loudly. "Sounds like the gators are doing us a favor."

Enough people nod along, albeit in varying degrees of enthusiasm, that no one feels comfortable replying.

Rebecca glances at the brunette still in the arms of her friends. She doesn't look like anyone's done her a favor.

12

Around midmorning, an email blast goes out confirming that student IDs were found on the scene but that identification of the victims is still pending. Between classes—and even during classes, for those brave enough or those rooms where the professors have given up trying to keep them on topic—all anyone can talk about is Forrest and Nathan Cooper. Rebecca hears more stories like the scared girl's this morning. Not exactly the same, but they speak to a behavior in the boys that wasn't a rush-week fluke.

She thinks about Det Corby and strange coincidences, wonders what he thinks about these new deaths. How many people agree with Ellie's "good riddance"?

The entire dining hall is buzzing about it, and in the absence of official information, the rumors are flying. Rather than stay and listen to wilder and wilder speculation, Rebecca scoops her lunch into the off-brand Tupperware she keeps in her bag, drops off her dishes and tray, and retreats outside, where it may be hot and humid, but at least there's enough space that the conversation doesn't press in so. Her mouth is actually open to take the first bite when her phone rings.

Groaning, she puts down both bowl and fork to dig out her phone. "Hafsah?"

"Detective Corby just came by the dorm," her roommate says. "He's hoping to speak with you if you have a moment."

She's a little confused that he didn't just text her; he has her number. Unless he's asking in a professional capacity. If he's on the clock, he might not want to insert that in the middle of more casual conversation. She looks down at the bowl that's supposed to be a taco salad—it looks unappetizing enough to explain why that option had the shortest line—and shrugs. As hungry as she is, it's not worth trying to scarf down something unappealing. "Is he still there?"

"Yes. Do you need him to meet you somewhere?"

"No, I'll grab something from the fridge in the room. I spent meal points on something I think has been there a few days."

"You know that's not true."

"I know, but Hafsah, this looks gross."

"Then why did you get it?" the other girl asks practically.

"Because no one in that line was talking about gator bait."

"Then you'll probably be disappointed in the detective's conversation," she points out. Even expecting that, Rebecca feels a brief pang of dismay. Stupid bloody crush. There's a muffled male voice in the background, and when Hafsah speaks again, she sounds rather amused. "He's promised to feed you in exchange for making you listen to more of it."

"I accept," she says happily. "I'll be there in a few minutes."

She feels guilty about wasting both food and meal points for the approximately eleven seconds it takes to empty the Tupperware into the nearest trash can and then puts it out of her mind. Settling her backpack more comfortably, she jogs around the stadium toward the historical-register dorms that line the front edge of campus proper.

And promptly regrets it, but that's what jogging in the middle of the day in a Florida April will do.

She sees Det Corby before she's within polite hailing distance, standing outside of Sledd. He's in dark-gray slacks and a vest today, with a blue-gray shirt with the sleeves rolled up near his elbows. She takes a moment to admire the view before shoving that admiration, and its constant companion of general appreciation, into a locked corner of her mind, where it hopefully can't come out in conversation and embarrass her.

He laughs when he sees her, his eyes hidden behind his sunglasses. "Why are you running in this?" he calls.

"Because you promised me food!"

He laughs again and strolls away from the shaded overhang to join her. "How do you feel about subs?"

"I could eat a sub," she replies, slowing to a walk. There's a decent place just across University Avenue, so they won't have to go too far. As an added bonus, it isn't exactly a date destination, so her imagination should have less to run away with. "Oh, I should have gone up to the room," she realizes abruptly. "I still have your hoodie."

"There's no rush," he tells her. "It's yours as long as you need it."

Stupid. Bloody. Crush.

"I'm assuming you heard about this morning's excitement," he says after a minute.

Rebecca nods. "It's all anyone can talk about, it seems. Anike looked like she was going to hurl as soon as the camera was off."

"Anike?"

"The reporter. She mentored some of us as freshies."

"Didn't realize she was local."

"Well, she is now, anyway. I think this might have been her first big story."

"Is that where you're headed someday? Suit and microphone?"

"In front of a camera? Hell no." She shakes her head, reaching up to fluff her curls away from her uncomfortably sweaty scalp. Just the thought of being caught on camera makes her stomach turn. "No, I like to deliver my words with a good bit of distance between me and anyone encountering them."

"But you'd look so cute with the shoulder pads."

"I'm pretty sure shoulder pads belonged to our mothers' generation."

He falls silent after the crosswalk, eyeing the larger number of people on the sidewalk, and stays that way through ordering and finding an isolated table for two tucked behind the bottled-drinks fridge. Definitely not a date destination.

She looks at the table, the boxes of supplies stacked up just on the other side, and turns back to him. "If the conversation is sensitive, we could just go back and eat on the grass," she says.

"I guess this might be a bit much." He winces as the fridge lets out a squeal and a groaning huff. "Right. Picnic it is."

Back on the south side of the road, Rebecca leads him over to one of the long concrete-and-brick signs announcing the school. It's tall enough to offer some shade for anyone sitting on the grass just behind it. She spreads her hoodie out to protect their clothes from the grass, then blushes when she realizes how closely they'll need to sit to both make use of it.

Det Corby doesn't seem to notice, though, so she folds down next to him and unwraps her sub, incredibly aware of the warmth of him along her side.

"The other night," he begins, "when I told you about my meeting: Have you mentioned that to anyone else?"

"What, that you don't think it's accidental? No, no one. However, I do feel I should tell you that the whole floor was buzzing about the possibility this morning when we ran out of things to say about the Coopers."

"The Coo—" He chokes on a bite of his sandwich, and she politely looks away so he can spit it out. "Does everyone know?"

"So it really is them?" She translates his resigned look into a yes. "Some of the girls on my floor know them. One of them recognized the car."

"When you say *know* them . . ."

"One of their victims is among them, yes."

"Alleged victims," he corrects automatically. She shifts uncomfortably. With a sigh, he shoves his sunglasses to the top of his head and leans against the back of the sign.

"Six-something this morning, she told an entire floor of mostly strangers what they did to her," she says quietly. "I'm not calling it alleged, especially not after how many other stories I've heard through the morning. But I understand why you have to."

He bumps shoulders with her. "I don't suppose you know her name?"

"No, but the campus cops should have filed an incident report. They found her drugged and naked on Fletcher."

"The boys were never arrested."

"You know better than that."

He nods and inhales what seems like half his sandwich. "My captain still isn't convinced that these deaths are anything more than coincidence and encroachment, but the sheriff and the state trooper captain see it more my way, so he's authorized an investigation."

"Should you be telling me that?"

"It's going to be announced tonight when they release the names. Four white male college students in three weeks, all of them alligator bait. We can't afford not to properly investigate."

She nods thoughtfully. "So you want to know who might be anticipating it."

"Exactly. You didn't even tell Hafsah or Ellie?"

Rebecca grimaces and shakes her head. "I don't think any of us want Ellie out there trying to reward the alligators."

The detective barks a startled laugh, his knee knocking into his drink and nearly spilling it over. "Are you serious?"

"This surprises you?"

"She doesn't hate *all* men, surely."

"All men," she confirms, "but even if she didn't . . . well. Keep in mind this is not anything in the way of proof . . ."

"Understood."

"There are a lot of stories going around campus about the boys. Not just the Coopers—all of them, including what's his name in Lake Alice. The kinds of stories girls tell each other in bathrooms because they don't get to tell them in courtrooms." She watches the entertainment drain from his face, replaced by something solemn and wary. "There's a memorial in front of one of the buildings. The Lake Alice floater, not the one at the hooker stop."

He twitches but refrains from correcting her, she's amused to see.

"The poster board around the picture is an interesting read, if it hasn't been replaced."

"You mean the picture that says, 'Rapist and Scumbag'?"

Shrugging, Rebecca pops a chip in her mouth.

"Why haven't the officers doing notifications been told of any of this?"

"Because they're doing notifications, not conducting an investigation," she answers, giving him a strange look. "They're talking to loved ones and chosen community who've just received terrible news. They're not looking for information."

"Have you known any of the boys?"

Rebecca shakes her head. "Not that I know of."

"That you know of?"

"You know what some of the freshie classes are like; there can be more than a hundred students in some of those lecture halls. There's no way to know everyone's name."

"And you're not going to say something definitively that could be disproven later."

"Gee, I wonder who taught me that."

He grins and polishes off his sub; she's only just finished half of hers. "So what kind of things have you heard about them?"

Rebecca takes her time to think about that, aware that there's a line between her friend Det Corby and Detective Patrick Corby. The tone may sound like her friend, but it's the detective who's listening now. She mentally filters out the stories that feel more like gossip, the things that have been likely distorted as they've passed from person to person. Which things had names or faces attached to them, rather than "I heard that" or "said they had a friend who knew that" or all the other indicators that a story is several degrees removed from the person telling it?

Slowly, taking care with her overheard details, she tells him the ones that have weight to them, the ones that feel some kind of real. She wonders if there's a way to warn the girl on her floor that everything will come up again for her, but she knows there isn't, not really. At best she could try to drag everyone back to the lounge for tonight's press conference and hope the girl connects the dots from the investigation to her door.

He listens intently, tapping shorthand notes into his phone. When she's done, he scrolls up to skim earlier notes. "To the best of your knowledge . . . ," he says eventually, and she groans.

"You're about to ask me something I have absolutely no way to know."

"Do you think they did what they're accused of?"

"It makes your job easier if they did," she points out.

"How do you figure?"

"Any additional factors that link them to each other is also a link to the killer, isn't it? Or have my professors just been blowing smoke up my skirt for three years?"

He shakes his head, smiling slightly. "The problem is *what* they have in common. White male college students who've hurt women. Even just at UF, there are over fifty thousand students; how many of them do you think fit that description?"

"Too many."

"Well, this is cozy," a voice calls out, and they look up to see Ellie striding toward them. "I was starting to think Det Corby had turned into a vampire."

"If you two can't manage *Patrick*, couldn't you at least use *Corby*?" he asks, his long-suffering tone balanced against his growing smile. "I'm not interrupting a date or anything, am I?"

Rebecca contemplates kicking her as soon as she's close enough but decides that lack of subtlety would prove the point more than refute it. "We're talking about the news this morning," she says, figuring that's neutral enough.

Snorting, Ellie drops to the grass near Rebecca's feet. "Those little bastards left a trail of blood, tears, and semen behind them, but now that everyone thinks they're the ones out at the farm, suddenly people are trying to eulogize them."

"No one likes to speak ill of the dead."

"Bullshit," she retorts. "Everyone likes to speak ill of the dead; they just don't want to be remembered for doing it."

"You don't seem to have that problem," Det Corby says mildly.

Ellie bares her teeth in what might be generously called a smile. Det Corby is one of the few men she seems to like, after all, or at least not outright detest. One of the semi-mythical good ones. "I speak of people as I find them. If they were useless, destructive little shit stains in life, that's how I'll talk about them once they're dead too."

"And with such tact and delicacy too."

"Please. You're not their family or their friend. The fuck do you care?"

He's got a pretty good reason to care how people talk about the dead, Rebecca thinks, but she's not about to share that. "Aren't you supposed to be sleeping through a class right now?" she asks instead.

"It got canceled. The professor didn't feel like dealing with a riled-up classroom, I guess. And you're one to talk, ditching your own class for a date with a hot cop."

Rebecca fights back a reflexive blush and very carefully doesn't look at the man beside her. "We were only supposed to turn in papers today," she says. "I turned mine in this morning because I was already in the building."

"Suck-up."

"It's called *efficiency*."

"So do the police have anything interesting on the Cooper cousins?" Ellie asks, nudging the detective's polished shoes with the pink Doc Martens she's absolutely not supposed to borrow from Rebecca.

"The names of the most recent deaths have not yet been released," he replies diplomatically.

"Some bleeding hearts on the Row are painting a panel on the wall with the names of everyone who's died this past month. Think it would be tacky to go after dark and paint a giant alligator with its mouth open?"

"Yes," they both answer.

Rebecca sighs. She's not sure yet what to think of Ellie-the-maybe-murderer. As Hafsah keeps saying, there's no proof, which is probably as good a reason as any to hide your head in the sand and try not to think about it overmuch. Still . . . even without wondering about the missing hate preacher, Rebecca has to admit that if she were a detective investigating the recent deaths—like, oh, the man beside her—she'd be looking very hard at Ellie. Not because there's proof, or even suggestive evidence as far as she knows, but because damn near every word out of Ellie's mouth makes it impossible not to suspect her of a wide range of sins.

Oblivious to the direction of Rebecca's pained musings, Ellie shrugs. "They're putting it right next to the permanent one, which feels a little premature." The concrete wall along Thirty-Fourth Street has been getting painted for decades, and only one panel is considered sacrosanct: it commemorates the five students murdered in August of 1990. Where the rest of the wall is painted constantly, with everything from advertisements to marriage proposals to birthday and graduation celebrations, that one panel stays protected and preserved to honor the memory of those slain students.

Rebecca hadn't really thought of the wall yet. "Premature?"

"Sure. I mean, are they going to leave space? Or just repaint it when more rapists end up dead?"

Det Corby shifts to one side so he can put his phone back in his pocket. It only mostly hides the thoughtful look he gives the redhead.

Rebecca's stomach sinks.

13

Despite Ellie's exhortations to go out with her and the others, Rebecca stays in, setting up comfortably at her desk with snacks and soda within easy reach. There's a part of her that agrees that staying in to do class-work on a Friday night probably is kind of lame, but the larger part of her is aware that the end of the semester is approaching, along with a hurricane of due dates, and she'd rather be able to study for final exams in peace without having to panic over finishing all her other work.

She grins and picks up her phone to text her dad. *You were right. I was born old.*

Always knew it, he replies a few minutes later. *Grateful for it now. Harder for crocs to get into a dorm than to chomp on drunk students wandering around.*

Alligators, Dad.

I thought that was just the mascot.

No, it's the animal too. We've got the alligators.

So I should see you later rather in a while?

Dad.

Oh sure, blame the instiGATOR.

DAD.

A new text comes in, this time from her mother. *Do I want to know what you said to make him laugh this hard?*

It's not my fault. He's very pleased with himself.

Oh Lord.

She chats with her parents for a while as she skims back through the articles she's supposed to be analyzing for one of her journalism classes. She's close with her parents, but they get twitchy if she checks in more than once or twice a week, start worrying that she's homesick or not taking advantage of her freedom to have a good time. Lately, though, with the alligator attacks making the news so often—plus, you know, the whole Mountebanks thing—they haven't minded daily check-ins. Hello, still alive, how are you?

The past four days, since the announcement of the investigation Monday night, one of her uncles on night shift has taken to texting her every morning at 6:37. *Remember to zigzag!* The humor masks the general worry; a number of cousins have complained about the dinner table talks being nothing but alligator trivia anymore. It's almost always a comfort to know her family is so invested in her well-being.

And then there's Gemma, who's taken to emailing her photos of gator-skin boots, purses, and suitcases and sent her a pair of scrimshawed alligator-tooth earrings that Rebecca promptly buried at the bottom of her trinket box before Ellie could see them. *Almost* always a comfort.

The article analysis is a weekly project, which means she has to write less than a thousand words total about them. She gets that out of the way, reads back through a paper due next week in Law and Ethics of Social Media to make any final changes, and annotates her outline for the Research Methods in Criminology term paper. The pages are full of notes and revisions and changes as she's added things since midterms, and she'd love to go ahead and start writing it to get it out of the way, but she's pretty sure what they do in class next week is going to have a significant impact on the direction of the paper.

Which just seems mean on the part of the professor, but what does Rebecca know?

She leaves her Victimology work for Sunday. The actual professor is out of town for a conference, and his grad student gave them a frankly tasteless assignment. Rebecca's reasonably certain she's one of many who emailed the professor to protest. The investigation into the deaths by alligators has just opened; it's beyond inappropriate to ask the class to profile fellow students—students who've very recently died—to make predictions about those in risk categories. She's hoping the professor will send out a message negating or changing the assignment before she has to choose between her grade and her principles.

Given the circumstances, she's reasonably confident that her parents would understand her taking a zero. Effort means more than grades, but standing for what you believe is important too.

It would be nice if she could do some of this work during her bouts of insomnia, but even aside from not wanting to disturb Hafsah, Susanna, and Delia, she gets too antsy to sit and study. The walks and bike rides don't always clear her mind, but at least they let her move through the restlessness.

From the next desk she can hear Hafsah muttering from time to time. She's not sure who her friend is arguing with, precisely. Knowing her, it could be the textbook, the TA, or someone in one of the discussion boards. Hafsah has about as much patience for idiots as Ellie does. Unlike Ellie, she gets it out of her system before she puts on a nicer face and explains in minute detail why the other person is wrong.

On the way back to her desk from the bathroom, Rebecca leans over Hafsah to see what she's working on. She groans at the sight on the laptop screen, dropping her forehead to her friend's shoulder. "Why are you reading the comments on a climate change article?"

"Because they're wrong!"

"They're always wrong! They're anonymous comments on the internet!"

"But they're arguing with the people who are right!"

Laughing helplessly, Rebecca wraps her arms around her roommate and sways, making the rolling chair move with her. "Oh my God, Hafsah. Never change. I mean, please change, because you're going to give yourself a heart attack. But never change."

"We're killing the world, and there are people who seem to honestly believe that it's all a hoax."

"There are people who honestly believe that the world is flat. There will always be idiots in the world, and posting rebuttals in the comments sections is not going to convince them of anything."

"I'm not even posting," she sighs. "Just arguing."

"So you're ruining your blood pressure without even the possibility of gain?"

"Something like that." Hafsah leans back against Rebecca and rubs at her eyes. They stay like that a minute or two in comfortable silence. It's remarkable to think that a friendship like theirs grew out of the essentially random draw known as the housing coordinator's database of incoming resident freshmen. "What time is it?" Hafsah asks eventually.

"A little before one."

"I need food."

"Pizza bagels?"

"Bless you."

As Rebecca pulls away to dig through the mini-fridge, Hafsah stretches and shakes herself out. Even knowing they'll likely be up a few more hours, Rebecca pours them each a cup of milk rather than soda. They don't need the caffeine this late. Plus, hopefully the milk will offset any heartburn from the cheap tomato sauce. At the ding of the microwave, she pulls out the mini-bagels and burns her fingers sorting them onto two of the plastic character plates they picked up in the party aisle of the dollar store.

Hafsah accepts her plate with a smile and immediately sets it aside to cool, giving Rebecca a pointed look. She smiles back and sucks on the pad of her middle finger, knowing it won't actually make it feel better but not really having anything else to do for it either. "Have the others checked in at all?" Hafsah asks.

Rebecca glances at her phone to be sure. "Not since ten. They left the bar for Eight Seconds."

"Isn't that the country bar? With line dancing and such?"

"Yep."

"Why on earth are they going there?"

"Because Ellie grew up line dancing and gets nostalgic?"

"Seriously?"

"She's got pictures. Hafsah, she won awards." Rebecca laughs and scoots the bagels around on her plate but doesn't try to pick one up yet. "Little Ellie, her hair in two curly pigtails, bright-red cowboy hat and boots, yellow gingham shirt, and blue jean skirt, holding up ribbons and trophies. It's adorable."

Hafsah looks charmed in spite of herself. "I have a hard time believing she willingly showed you these pictures."

"She didn't." She pokes at one of the bagels to see if it's cool enough yet and hisses when the cheese burns her fingertip. "Last year, when she tried to steal my green dress because she fell in love with it and decided she looked better in it than I did and that should be reason enough? Remember that?"

"I will never be lucky enough to forget it. Likely, neither will anyone else on the floor."

"So when she mailed it home to her mother so I couldn't take it back, I wrote her mother. Her mother sent it back, along with a number of adorable and sometimes embarrassing photos to use as ammunition or retribution, whichever felt more appropriate." Of course, her mother also mentioned that Ellie stopped competing when she started filling out. Or rather, when one of the male judges kept coming into the area the girls were using for a dressing room, and Ellie got disqualified for kicking him in the balls.

Even adorable and pigtailed, Ellie was still apparently Ellie.

"Line dancing," Hafsah says, shaking her head.

"Hey, line dancing is fun. We used to do it in school during PE."

"Sure, but at least you look the part. That kind of crowd doesn't tend to be too fond of me."

"Fair point." Rebecca pokes at another bagel.

"Will you stop that? When they stop steaming and spitting, they're safe to eat."

"But I'm hungry now!"

"Stop it."

Eventually they get to eat without burning more fingers. Hafsah swaps her laptop for a textbook so she'll stop swearing at strangers online. Rebecca pulls out her notes for the article one of the seniors asked her to write for his crime blog. He gets a decent readership, and she's written for him before, generally resulting in a handful of paid requests from some of the smaller professional outlets that pay attention.

Around two-thirty, her phone rings, an unfamiliar number flashing on the screen. She stares at it, trying to think. The university prefix, maybe? That, or the girls got separated, and someone had to borrow a phone again. She accepts the call with a tap. "Rebecca Sorley."

"Awesome, you're awake," says a voice she knows. "This is Kerry; I'm down on desk duty."

"Oh, God," she groans. "Are they too drunk to get up the stairs again? Dammit. I'll be right down."

"It's not about the girls," Kerry says quickly. "Or maybe. I don't know. But you're in the dorm?"

"Yes, I'm just upstairs. Kerry, what's going on?"

"You should get dressed and come down. There are a couple of police officers here who say they need to talk to you."

Rebecca freezes, her heart thumping painfully in her chest. Over the roaring in her ears, she can dimly hear Hafsah asking if she's all right.

Oh, God, the last time Kerry woke them up for the police, it was because Kacey . . .

She swallows hard. "It's two-thirty in the morning," she says finally.

"I know. I'm sorry."

Which means whatever this is, it's important. "I'll be right down."

14

Rebecca looks down at her comfortable cotton shorts and the long-sleeved tee from her high school yearbook staff and decides that's dressed enough. Fear prickles down her spine. What if one of the girls got hurt? What if Ellie got taken down to the station again? What if it's something worse? Kerry didn't tell her to bring anyone else who might be around; the police asked for her specifically. Why?

"Rebecca? What is it?"

"I don't know. There are cops downstairs wanting to speak to me."

Rather than asking questions, Hafsah nods and pushes away from her desk. "I'll join you as soon as I'm dressed," she says.

"Thanks."

Barely remembering to grab her keys, Rebecca hurries down the hall to the stairwell, bounding down three and four steps at a time. When she spills out onto the ground floor, she can see Kerry standing behind the reception desk, arms crossed over her chest, frowning at the pair of uniformed officers in front of her. GPD, Rebecca notes; it was GPD who came to ask them questions about Kacey.

A few feet away from the uniformed pair, an exhausted-looking Det Corby paces between the desk and the mailbox wall. He looks up sharply at the sound of her hurried footsteps and holds up a hand. "The girls are fine—we're not here about them," he says immediately.

She skids to a stop, hands on her knees as she tries to breathe through the rush of relief. "Okay," she manages eventually. The fear isn't gone, exactly, but it's at least less visceral. "Okay. So what's going on?"

"We should sit."

It's polite, almost welcoming, but the tone and the guarded look in his eyes tell her stronger than anything that she's dealing with Detective Corby, not her friend. She feels a brief pang at that; whatever this is, she has a feeling she could use her friend here. She nods, thanks Kerry for calling her—worrying about her—and walks over to the cluster of bright-blue couches near the vending machines. Maybe she should have taken the time to put pants on after all, she thinks, reminding herself to keep her knees together as she sits in a corner against the armrest.

Detective Corby sits on the adjacent couch, the female officer joining him there. The other uniform stands at the end of the couch, watching them and the door in equal measure. The detective pulls a printed picture from his pocket and holds it out. "We need to ask you about him."

She looks at it. It looks like a Facebook photo, a shirtless young man with a fluff of blond hair, a red Solo cup in each hand. She shakes her head, confused. "I'm not sure . . . wait." She takes the photo and rests it on the arm of the couch, pressing her thumbs around the boy's head to change how she sees his hair. If she can imagine it slicked back à la Draco Malfoy . . . her stomach knots. "This is Mountebanks, isn't it?" Mountebanks the Asshole, she almost says, but thinks better of it.

Corby nods. "Mountebanks Pennington-Cabot III."

"Mountebanks is his *first* name?" She claps a hand over her mouth, feeling more than a little mortified. She can see the female officer's lips twitch with a would-be smile.

A muscle jumps in Corby's jaw, something she recognizes as him wanting to smile but knowing he shouldn't. She saw it a lot when he taught the workshop. "He was found dead tonight."

"Oh, God." She stares down at the photo in shock, at the boy who left bruises on her chest, who made yet one more place feel unsafe. "Was it . . . was it another alligator?"

"No."

And now she knows why they're talking to her in the dark of morning. She takes one last look at the photo and hands it back with trembling hands. She doesn't feel bad about not immediately recognizing him, not when the light outside the bar was so uneven, not when his face was so distorted with rage. "What do you need to know?" she asks quietly. Her heart races.

"Keep in mind," says the female officer, "this is just asking some questions. You're not under arrest. You are free to refuse answering or even talking to us at all, and you can call a lawyer if you wish."

If she called her aunts, they could point her to someone in town. Maybe even someone who wouldn't mind a call at this god-awful hour. But she shakes her head again. "It's okay."

Corby said Mountebanks was found tonight; was he killed tonight? Her phone is up on her desk where she dropped it to hurry down, but she has the fierce urge to text Ellie for a check-in. Please, oh please, let Ellie have been picking a very public fight somewhere far away from the body.

"Okay. If that changes at any point in the conversation, just let us know."

Rebecca nods. She's studied how this is supposed to work, heard stories from her uncles and cousins, but this . . . this is a first for her. She never expected the sickly thrum of adrenaline, that taut sensation of every nerve sparking frantically.

Pulling out his phone and opening a notes app, Corby leans forward, his hands hanging between his knees. "Can you tell us where you've been this evening?"

"Upstairs."

"Since when?"

She and Ellie met Luz and Keiko at the dining hall for an earlyish dinner. It was on the walk back to Sledd that Ellie began her campaign to go out for the night. "I think we got back a little before six? I don't know the exact time."

"And after that?"

"Most of the girls in the suite started getting ready to go out. Hafsah and I decided to stay in."

"Hafsah?"

"My roommate. We've been working on assignments all night."

"You two were together the whole time?"

"Except for bathroom breaks, but the bathroom is right off the study space," she answers. "Never more than a few minutes." Her hands are still shaking, she notes, and she slides them down between her thighs and the cushion. She wonders how he died. Probably not in a car accident, if they're talking to her about it.

"So there was no time either of you were out of each other's sight for longer than that?"

"Not until I came down here at Kerry's call." Speaking of whom, she can see Kerry standing and watching, attentive and protective, from the desk, with Hafsah beside her, a silent but visible support. She feels better for having them there. Just the sight of them is reassuring; she's not alone.

The female officer—Rebecca can't see the nameplate, blocked by Corby's shoulder—leans back into the couch, her posture open and welcoming. Inviting confidence, Rebecca thinks and tries not to laugh because this really, really isn't funny, and she would like her brain to please stop treating this as a textbook exercise. "I know the detective knows a bit more about Mountebanks, but could you tell me about him? I understand you two knew each other."

Oh, that's a clever little trap, she thinks, admiring it in spite of herself. Force someone on the defensive, or force them to accept a degree of closeness that wasn't there. Either way, easy enough to put someone off balance with it later. Rebecca shakes her head slightly. "As far as I know, I've only met him the once, outside Tom and Tabby's last week." God, was it really only a week ago?

"Can you tell us about that meeting?"

"My friends were inside," she says. "I went outside to get some air. A guy came up, got offended when I wasn't interested in being hit on, and grabbed me." She rubs absently at where the bruises were. They're not there anymore, too quickly faded, but now that she's talking about the incident, she can almost feel them again. "I kicked him to try to get away; he tore my dress to the waist, and that's when Detective Corby and UPD officer Kevin came upon us."

"When you say you kicked him . . ."

"Once," she confirms. She glances up at the male officer. "Between the legs."

He winces.

The female officer smiles. "Effective."

"Not as much as I'd hoped it would be, I admit. It was the detective and officer who forced him to let go of me."

"Had you been drinking?"

"No."

"You're sure?" she presses.

"I don't drink when we go out." After a moment's hesitation, she tells them about getting roofied in high school and how she checks even her nonalcoholic drinks at bars and clubs. She tells them about Daphne. If Rebecca is drinking, she's safely tucked away with people she trusts and brand-new, clearly untampered-with bottles. Corby's knuckles go white around his phone, but he continues tapping in notes.

"What happened next?"

"Officer Kevin pulled the guy some distance away, and Detective Corby stayed with me while I called my friends. They came outside. The detective offered us a ride back here, given . . . well. My dress was flapping open, and none of us had sweaters or anything. So he drove us back while Officer Kevin stayed with Mountebanks."

"When did you learn his name?"

"When the detective said it after checking his license." She leaves out that they all made fun of it. That's not a useful detail and certainly not a helpful one.

"And after?"

"We came back to the dorm. Some of the girls wanted to go back out, but all I wanted was to shower and stay in, and they decided to stay as well."

"You didn't file a report?"

She can't answer this woman the way she would Det Corby, someone she knows well enough for flippancy. Honesty, even. "It wouldn't have accomplished anything. Aside from shallow bruising and the torn dress, there wasn't enough damage for anyone to take seriously. It just wouldn't have done anything."

"And have you seen him since?"

"Not that I know of."

"That you know of?"

Despite everything, Rebecca can see Corby rub a hand against his mouth to hide his smile, and it gives her spirits a small boost. "There are a lot of students, and I wouldn't necessarily recognize him. It's possible we crossed paths over the week, but I honestly couldn't tell you if we did."

"No phone calls? No texts or emails? Anything?"

Rebecca shakes her head, curling her toes under the edge of the couch and wishing she'd put on socks. "No. I don't know how he would have gotten my name, much less my number or email."

"The other girls in your suite," the officer continues, "are they the ones who were with you that night?"

"Mostly," she answers. "Hafsah had stayed behind that night, but the others were there."

"And where are they tonight?"

"Out?" She gives a tight shrug. "I'm sorry—I don't know where. They said they were probably going to a bar, and then they texted around ten to say they were going to Eight Seconds, but I haven't heard from them other than that." Which, come to think of it, is a little strange. Pretty much everything closed more than thirty minutes ago. They should be back by now, unless they went somewhere by rideshare.

"Were any of them angry about the encounter?"

"We're girls," she says simply. "All of us were angry. All of us were scared. We kind of have to be, you know?"

The male officer gives her a sideways look, but his partner just nods. Whether that's because she actually understands or because she's building rapport, it's impossible to know. "Did any of them talk about trying to find Mountebanks?"

Rebecca winces as her fingernails dig into the underside of her thigh, and she can tell all three of them see it. She knows they have to ask that; it's an obvious question, and they're doing their jobs. She also knows that a thing can be true, ultimately innocent, and still look really, really bad. She takes a deep breath and lets it out slowly. "The dress I was wearing," she says carefully, desperate not to look like she's constructing a narrative. "It was my friend Ellie's. She lives on the other side of the suite. We're the same size, so we borrow clothing back and forth, and she wanted me to wear it that night. So it was actually her dress that got ruined. She stayed with me and Hafsah that night and joked about asking Mountebanks's father to pay for it."

"She knows his father?"

"No, but with a name like Mountebanks . . ." She bites her lower lip at the look of polite incomprehension. "It's a pretty rich sounding name. Could probably afford to replace the dress he ripped, that's all."

"Has she—or any of the others—mentioned him since?"

"In passing. Hafsah and I have talked about it a little, and the others have been checking in a little more regularly. Just making sure I'm okay. And then it came up with Officer Kevin the next day."

"You saw Officer Kevin?"

"He was on his bike on campus when Hafsah and I were walking back from dinner. He asked if I was doing okay, if the guy had given me any more problems, and then insisted on walking us back to the building."

A burst of sound, loud but indecipherable, explodes just outside the main door, out of sight from where Rebecca is sitting. She looks instead at Kerry and Hafsah, both in line to the windows beside the door. They sigh and look resigned.

Must be their suitemates. Who, from the sounds of it, are too drunk to scan into the dorm. One of them finally manages it, and they spill into the room in a torrent of laughter, insults, and Keiko's stress sobs. Ellie skips across the entry to twirl under an AC vent, and oh, God, her dress. Rebecca's shoulders hunch.

Hafsah tilts her head, studying Ellie. "Were you wearing that when you left?"

"Nope!" their redheaded friend announces. It's the dress from a week ago, with two long strips of duct tape holding the bodice closed in place of actual repairs, and she was absolutely not wearing it when she left, or Rebecca would have blocked her in her room until she agreed to change. "I had it in my bag in case we went back to Tom and Tabby's so maybe Mountebanks the Asshole could see what he did!"

The detective and both officers all turn to stare at Ellie.

Rebecca closes her eyes.

15

It's the start to a very long morning. The officers speak to each of the girls. All five who went out are drunk as skunks, which makes getting direct answers rather difficult. Sitting next to Hafsah and listening to the other interviews, Rebecca's not sure if they're just confused or if they honestly kept losing each other for hours at a time in various combinations.

Hafsah, at least, is calm. She thinks about each question before she answers, admitting freely that she wasn't there that night and didn't know anything about it until Rebecca got home. Keiko keeps bursting into tears, which prompts Luz to lean in and reassure the officers that it's just a stress response, and she does this all the time. Delia is falling asleep, and after one too many elbows from Susanna to wake her up to answer, the two of them get into a squirming slap fight on the coffee table.

Rebecca's not too surprised to see the male officer walk away so he can laugh in private. She's more surprised that the other two don't.

And then there's Ellie. Ellie, who cheers when she's told that Mountebanks is dead and then asks for his father's contact information so she can see about getting the dress replaced. The dress she specifically brought out with her tonight in the hopes of seeing Mountebanks again. Rebecca would like to think that sober Ellie will regret that kind of candor.

She knows, however, that Ellie rarely has any regrets, drunk or sober.

It's still the female officer asking the bulk of the questions, Corby offering his own only rarely. That makes sense, she supposes. After all, he knows them. He's friends with them. Very likely he's only here because he was the detective available, and he'll recuse himself as soon as someone else can be assigned to it. Letting the officer lead the conversations removes most of the risk of favoritism.

Every now and then, the door opens for another student coming back. One of the third-floor seniors sees the officers and stops cold, her underwear dangling from one hand and a bottle of vodka in the other. The officers politely turn away to express their disinterest—they're not campus cops, and for all they know she's twenty-one—and the girl races for the stairwell, face crimson.

"So where was he?" Ellie asks, sitting with the front of her dress around her waist. She peeled away the duct tape strips at some point in the conversation so they could see the damage to the dress, and now she seems perfectly comfortable with the entire right cup of her polka-dot bra hanging out for everyone to see.

"We're not prepared to release that information yet," the female officer says with a bland smile.

"Okay, then how did he die? Ooh, was it painful? I hope it was painful."

"Ellie," murmurs Rebecca.

"What? Oh, you can't tell me you're not curious."

"Of course I am, but you've got to realize how that looks to be asking."

Her friend bursts out laughing, and yes, this is definitely drunk Ellie.

It's almost five o'clock before the officer decides—and Corby doesn't argue—that they can leave this for now, but they will come back to it once the hangovers are medicated. The officer stands up, holding out her hand to Rebecca, but before she can shake it, the front door opens again to reveal a girl in jeans and a sports bra, helping another girl in a club dress into the hall. The girl in the dress, one of Rebecca's friends from half a dozen journalism classes, looks shaky, half her makeup cried off, and there's an ER band around one wrist.

Rebecca lurches to her feet and braces herself against the back of the couch, near Corby's head. "Jules? Are you okay?"

Jules opens her mouth to answer, sees the officers, and dissolves into tears.

Her friend pulls her in close, swaying gently in place for comfort. She gives the officers a wary look, then focuses back on Rebecca. "She, um . . . she's had a bad night. But she was in the ER for shock, not for, um . . . it was for shock."

Rebecca stares at Jules's bare feet, her tired mind trying to connect the things she knows are linked. The look at the officers. "You found Mountebanks. His body, I mean."

The female officer coughs over the increased volume of the sobs. "How did you decide that?"

"Shock, not injury or illness. And her shoes are missing."

The officer looks over at Corby, who looks rather more resigned than surprised. "You notice things like that, huh?"

"I have a couple of uncles who are detectives," she replies. "They play observation games with all the kids."

"Huh."

Which Rebecca translates as yes, Jules found Mountebanks. She means to say something—she's just not sure what yet—when from the corner of her eye, she sees Ellie perk up and open her mouth. She twists and tackles Ellie down onto the cushions, plastering a hand across her mouth. "Don't," she says sharply.

Ellie's response is muffled, but to those who know her, the meaning is clear.

Rebecca gives her a little shake. "Don't," she says again. "She's had a shock, and your curiosity does not outweigh her well-being. Leave her alone." And goddamn, but the officers were letting them go, and Ellie seems determined to make them arrest her on suspicion alone.

Ellie argues. Of course she does. Ellie always argues. But Rebecca sits up to straddle her waist, keeping her hand in place, until Jules's roommate ushers her to the stairwell. And then for a bit longer, just to be on the safe side. Rebecca doesn't want to think yet, not yet. She just wants to get to the end of the conversation.

Keiko is crying again, or maybe still, which sets Luz to explaining that Keiko's not just a stress crier; she's also a sympathy crier, and she really is okay—don't mind her.

A shadow falls over Ellie's face, and Rebecca looks up to see Kerry standing over them. "Let's get you upstairs, Ellie, so you can stop bothering the nice people."

"I'm nice," Ellie mutters once Rebecca pulls her hand away.

Even Keiko stops crying long enough to snort at that.

Rebecca eases away, perching on the arm of the couch so Kerry can haul Ellie up. They both groan and sway until they find an equilibrium. "Can we stop by Jules's room?" Ellie asks.

"No."

"Rude." They stumble their way toward the stairwell. "What if I say please?"

"I'd appreciate it."

"Then can we please stop by Jules's room?"

"Still no."

"Fuck."

Shaking her head, Hafsah helps the other girls stand. Delia starts tilting a little too far to the left, and Rebecca lunges to catch her before she tips over into the coffee table. "Thanks," Delia says with a beatific smile. "You really should have been there tonight. Things are much more sane when you're around."

Rebecca stares at her. "Delia, that's terrifying."

"I know, right?"

Hafsah starts ushering the other four to the stairwell. "Come on, everyone will have a nice big bottle of water before going to sleep."

"Can I have orange juice?" Susanna asks.

"As long as you have a full bottle of water before and another one after."

"That's a lot of water."

"You drank a lot of alcohol."

"Yes, I did!" Susanna's cheer trails off into hiccupping giggles, and Rebecca takes a moment to be grateful for the pragmatism of the Gainesville Police Department. They're there about murder; therefore they kindly pretend not to notice what at least one of them knows is underage drinking. And if that lets them think that Ellie's only incriminating herself because she's drunk and riled, that's to Ellie's benefit, isn't it?

Once the sounds of the others have faded from distance, the female officer turns back to Rebecca. "You never argued about me being the one to ask the questions."

Rebecca shakes her head. "It wouldn't have been appropriate for him to take the lead on it."

"Thank you for recognizing that."

"I would like to ask one question, if I could?" At her nod, Rebecca swallows back her caution. "I'm not asking for details, but Jules is not exactly squeamish; her intended focus is epidemic research and coverage. She's got a pretty strong stomach. It was a bad scene, wasn't it?"

"It certainly wasn't pretty," she allowed. "Without putting too fine a point on it, this was an act committed with prejudice."

Rebecca nods, mulling on that. Unlike Ellie, she's perfectly fine without seeing pictures. She doesn't actually have a problem with gore. Too many documentaries, maybe, or the inevitable result of having a nurse for a mother. She's not fazed by it under normal circumstances. But this is . . . this is personal, isn't it? It doesn't matter that Mountebanks wasn't a friend, that he attacked her; he's still someone she personally encountered, and he is now dead in an apparently messy and possibly vindictive fashion. On her behalf?

God, she hopes not.

She wonders when the officers will remember that Ellie changed clothes at some point during the night and ask after the previous outfit. The dress can fold and roll and squish enough to fit into a small purse, but the jeans and spangly top she left in would prove a little harder, if not impossible. But Ellie is her friend, and Mountebanks is in fact the asshole who attacked her, so she doesn't mention it. They'll think of it or not, and it's not her responsibility to do their job for them. Especially not if it points them at her friend.

Corby taps her calf with his phone, drawing her attention. "You okay?"

"I'm . . ." She looks down at her toes, the orange and blue polish chipping and peeling away because Luz has been too busy to paint everyone's nails as she likes to do. "I guess? I mean, I'm not the one who's dead?" She winces at saying it so baldly, but really, is there any other way to say something like that? "I don't know. Just . . ." She gropes for the right word, then cringes at the only one she finds. "Unexpected."

He nods, and she appreciates that he's simply accepting it rather than asking for clarity, because right now almost any question will feel like it's part of the interview. "Once the case is transferred, the new detective will probably want to speak to you again."

"Yeah, I figured."

"If you need anything . . ."

"I'll let you know after there's a new detective assigned."

He laughs, as do the two officers. "Try to get some sleep," he says. "Keep your phone nearby."

Right, sleep is absolutely a thing that can happen this morning. But the officers have been polite and kind, so she returns the favor and doesn't laugh at him.

When they're out the door, she jogs back upstairs to the suite. She should help Kerry and Hafsah deal with putting the tipsy terrors to bed—she can hear Ellie arguing and the first warbling notes of Susanna's rendition of "Signore, ascolta!"—but she wants . . . she needs . . .

She grabs her phone from the desk and goes to the stairwell. Maybe it's selfish, but she wants more time. Time before she has to wonder if Ellie did this, if she should say something. If that something should be to Ellie or to the cops. Time before she has to ask Ellie what happened to the jeans she borrowed from Rebecca's closet after dinner, a consolation prize for Rebecca's refusing to go out.

Tugging on her shorts so that sitting down won't put her ass on the cold tile, Rebecca settles onto the bottom step leading up to the fourth floor, a safe distance from the door. She scrolls through her recent calls, selects one, and taps *call*. Her knee bounces as she listens to the rings.

"What in the hell are you doing awake this early on a Saturday?"

The sound of Gemma's voice, rough and warm and full of exasperated affection, makes her blink back sudden tears. She swallows hard but still has to clear her throat before she can speak. "The boy who attacked me outside the bar? He's dead. Someone murdered him last night."

It's so quiet in the stairwell that Rebecca can hear Gemma pouring her coffee in the long silence that follows.

"You're scared," Gemma says finally. "For you or that angry friend of yours?"

"Yes."

"Tell me."

With a deep breath and one eye on the door, Rebecca starts talking.

16

Mountebanks is a problem.

Not just was, but is. As in, still a problem despite being dead.

Because of being dead, I suppose.

He's a problem, is the point.

Each death becomes riskier, makes things harder. People pay more attention, ask more questions, notice who doesn't belong or who isn't there. I have to be prepared for each victim to be the last in case the attention gets to be too much. That's fine; that's part of the calculus of murder, but Mountebanks . . .

He wasn't part of the plan.

Mountebanks is a wrench.

I move through the party, carrying a beer but not drinking it. It's more for camouflage than anything, especially with how cheap it is. I'd as soon drink horse piss than try to finish the bottle. Although it's nowhere near Halloween, the fraternity hosting the party in their yard declared a superhero theme. Anyone who didn't come in costume can take a cheap plastic mask from the twenty-gallon tubs lining the front walk. Guests can choose from the Joker, Batman, Superman, the Joker, Wonder Woman, Aquaman, the Joker, the Flash, the Green Lantern, Catwoman, or, for something new and unique, the Joker.

Is it worth the risk? People are definitely paying attention, after all, which wasn't the point but isn't necessarily a problem as long as I'm not a fucking moron.

And then I see the reason I came out, the reason I'm wearing a Catwoman mask so cheap I'm somewhat worried about getting high off the fumes. He stands on the rail of the porch, his shorts cut off at the knee to show the tattoo that wraps around his shin and calf just a couple inches down. The letters are large, almost illegibly ornate, and faintly green in the way of cheap ink, spelling out his pledge name. With a ululating cry, he throws himself off the rail into the arms of the boys clustered in front of the porch. They catch him—pity—and prop him against a waiting keg, keeping him vertical as he fits the hose into his mouth.

I watch him and swirl the beer in my bottle. Thunder rumbles overhead, mosquitoes and lightning bugs fighting for space in the close press of ozone-heavy air. In some ways this boy is the reason the others have died. The top of the list, as it were, but far too suspicious if he's the only one who dies.

He's choking and sputtering on the beer, but he doesn't drop the hose or try to move away. It spills into his nose and past his closed eyes into his hair as he laughs and keeps trying. If his brothers dropped him, could the hose lodge in his throat and kill him before anyone noticed? It'd be fitting. Just an accident; oh, what a shame.

A car stops in front of the house, and three boys spill out of the back seat. One of them waves a pair of ladies underwear, torn at the gusset. There's something written on it, I think, stark and black against the delicate gray and rainbows of the fabric, but I can't make it out. The members of the fraternity quickly identify themselves by dropping whatever they're doing and standing to either side of the front walk, chanting, "Pantie! Pantie! Pantie!" as the pantie bearer makes a ceremonial run up the walk and into the house.

I look back at the car as it's pulling away, but there's no sign of a girl in there.

I find him in the line, his Joker mask still shoved up in his hair from his failed keg stand. He's got his arm around one of his brothers,

139

both of them laughing uproariously. With a great crack of thunder, the rain starts to fall. "Wet T-shirt contest!" he yells. He and several of the boys take off running through the party, grabbing full cups of beer and throwing them on any girl in a light-colored shirt just in case the rain isn't enough.

If I were sensible, if I were careful, I'd leave him alone. Keep my head down. Don't attract more attention. Give in, and acknowledge that I can't take out everyone who deserves it.

Fuck being careful.

It's worth the risk to hear him torn to pieces.

Taking the beer and the mask with me to dispose of elsewhere, I start back across campus in the rain. I've been watching him off and on for months, never quite enough to be noticeable. I know at least as much about him as his own mother, maybe even more. I know his habits, his routines. I know where he goes when he wants more privacy than living in a frat house affords him.

I know what he did.

Mountebanks is still a problem, but this boy . . . I can't keep walking away with him still alive behind me.

17

Rebecca sits on the folding counter of the laundry room, cello and piano spilling softly out of the small speaker beside her. She brought her laptop down with her initially, reading through her subscriptions to see what papers and blogs are saying about the alligator deaths. It didn't take her long at all to head back to the room and trade it out for her crochet. It keeps her hands busy while her mind spins in circles.

"Rebecca?"

"Hang on." Muttering the count under her breath, she finishes the row before she looks up. Jules stands in the doorway with a mesh bag of clothing over one shoulder, wearing an oversize T-shirt, leggings, and fuzzy socks. "Hey."

"Mind some company?"

"You're good."

They don't speak as Jules sets about preparing two of the washing machines, splitting her laundry out with a practiced hand. Once the machines have rumbled to life, she clambers up onto the folding table. She's a little too short to make it in any way graceful, but she manages. She pulls her phone out of the waistband of her leggings, mutes it, and starts a game of Candy Crush.

Rebecca doesn't try to fill the silence. She focuses on her hands and the yarn slowly taking shape into a tiny blanket for a cousin's forthcoming baby. Word got around, probably because of Ellie, that Jules found Mountebanks's body. Most of a day later, the details are still sparse, and

Jules has been close lipped about it; that hasn't stopped others from pressing her for information.

She's not sure how much time passes. Her wash cycle isn't done, anyway. The yarn is much lighter than what she usually uses, frustratingly airy, and she loses track of time beyond the regular swivel of her hook and the feel of yarn gradually drying out her fingers. It's enough time that she flinches and drops the hook when Jules suddenly clears her throat.

"Sorry," the other girl mumbles.

"I think I can pick it up." It takes some effort, and she's not sure it won't show, but it's good enough. She gets to a place where she can pause and gives Jules her attention. "What's up?"

"You haven't asked me." Jules looks back at her phone, thumb absently sweeping across the screen to make the matches in the game.

"I figured you had enough people asking."

"Ellie says he attacked you."

"Ellie was fishing for information." When Jules doesn't respond, Rebecca sighs and tells her about the altercation with Mountebanks outside the bar. She wouldn't say Jules has the right to know, precisely, but she did find the body. If the two events are connected—and she hopes to God they're not—then her curiosity isn't unfounded. Rebecca's own curiosity isn't unfounded, either, but with so many people hounding Jules with questions, Rebecca doesn't want to be one more on the pile.

Even if she really, really wants to know.

Jules nods along, absorbing the story. Rebecca's seen that look on her face in their classes, like she's listening with every pore to soak the words in. "You were okay after?" she asks once Rebecca falls silent.

"Well enough. Shaken, sure, and a little bruised, but . . . I mean, it's nothing new, right? Just a little more up front than usual."

"It wasn't at Tom and Tabby's. The body."

That's one of the few details Rebecca already knows, but she doesn't say that. If Jules is ready to talk, if she *wants* to talk, she doesn't need the reminder. Campus has been buzzing about the body found in the Durty Nelly's parking lot. Rebecca's had her own share of people asking questions as stories swirl around classes and the greens.

She's learned that she was far from the only girl Mountebanks felt entitled to, but she is one of the few who had fortuitously timed intervention.

"I'd only had one drink," Jules continues eventually. "I was out with friends, but I told my boyfriend I was going over to his place after. I was perfectly safe to drive."

Rebecca nods, not to agree, because she has no idea how Jules is on one drink, but to show that she's listening.

"I was walking between cars, keys in hand, and I was so busy looking for anyone jumping out that I didn't look down. I tripped over him. Can you believe that? A guy's sprawled out dead on the ground, and I just trip over him?"

"You didn't see him," Rebecca murmurs.

"At least I didn't land on him, right? I caught myself against the cars on either side. Almost took the side mirror off one of them. And I took a deep breath, you know, the way you do when you have to remind yourself that disaster almost happened but didn't? And that's when I smelled it."

"Blood?"

"So much blood. And I opened my eyes and . . . I've been at autopsies. I interned for the CDC. I've read and watched just about everything I can find about horrific diseases and epidemics, and I've been fine. But I opened my eyes, saw him, and screamed. I felt like I was never going to stop screaming."

There's something closed off about her expression, not dull but distant, that makes Rebecca think a hug or blatant form of comfort might not be welcome. She gently bumps their shoulders together instead.

Jules gives her a brief smile. "He was a mess. I mean, I didn't check, but I'm pretty sure his groin area was trashed. I couldn't even move. I just stood there like an idiot, screaming and trying not to hurl."

"That seems like a pretty reasonable reaction."

"He wasn't my first body."

"He was your first accidental body," Rebecca points out. "The others were planned; you could prepare yourself for them. You walked into the autopsy suite expecting them. You didn't randomly happen upon them on a night out."

"I guess that's true." She stares at her screen, the game waiting between levels. "People keep asking."

"People are ghouls."

"Ellie keeps asking."

"Ellie is also a ghoul. You should know this by now."

That gets a laugh out of the other girl, and by unspoken agreement they leave the grisly week to one side and start comparing notes on their final project for their social media course. Jules has spent most of the semester tracking viral tweets and charting their spread through the lens of traditional disease vectors. In conjunction with her own second major, Rebecca has been researching the evidentiary provenance of social media posts and the pros and cons of submitting them in a court of law. It's been interesting, but it's hardly new territory, as her heap of papers to cite will attest; their professor was intrigued by the proposal, though, so she's stuck with it.

"It's two in the morning, and you two nerds are talking about homework?"

They both turn to look at the doorway, and at the sight of Ellie, Rebecca can feel Jules tense beside her. "What's wrong with that?" Rebecca asks calmly, despite her racing heart. She still hasn't asked what happened to the jeans Ellie borrowed. She still isn't sure she wants to know.

"Ugh, you're so boring." Soaking wet from the latest storm, Ellie saunters up to the table, a cloud of scent wafting around her.

Rebecca wrinkles her nose, trying not to sneeze. "You reek of weed."

"I was at a party." Ellie leans against the table and reaches up to flick one of Rebecca's curls. "Why are you all wet?"

"Couldn't sleep, so I thought a cool shower would help. It didn't, so I came down here." She bats her suitemate's hand away before it can drip onto her lapful of yarn. "It's almost dry."

"I can't believe you're talking about class projects when you could be asking Jules about Mountebanks the Asshole."

Rebecca closes her eyes. They've all met the detective assigned to the case, a woman of medium height and stern features who introduced herself as Detective Gratton. Ellie was, well . . . Ellie through the entire second round of interviews, and Luz told Rebecca the detective seemed especially interested in how they often lost track of each other for long periods that night. If there was proof, she'd have been arrested already. So maybe she didn't . . .

Even in the safety of her own mind, Rebecca can't finish that sentence with any kind of sincerity. Not admitting it is one thing, but she's not in the habit of out and out lying to herself.

Everyone's curious about the murder, something that feels . . . almost normal? It seems strange to say, but it's easier for the students to understand an old-fashioned murder than the spate of alligator attacks that are looking less and less like accidents. People want the distraction, the thrill temporarily chasing away the fear.

"Jules doesn't need to tell anyone but the police about Mountebanks the Asshole," she says finally, "and would be best served by continuing her silence. I'm sure there are details the cops don't want to become public knowledge yet."

Jules doesn't say anything. She does, however, lean into Rebecca's shoulder.

"Lame." Ellie strips off her shirt, eyeing the operating machines.

"Don't you dare," Rebecca says. "They're nearly done with their cycles."

"Fine." With a huff, Ellie drops her shirt into an empty machine, following it with her jeans, bra, and socks. "I'm using your detergent, though."

"Detergent, yes. Laundry card, no, because it only has enough for the dryers."

Flapping a hand dismissively, Ellie walks out of the room in just her underwear. Rebecca would really like to be surprised that her friend is so comfortable walking basically naked through the entirety of Sledd Hall. It's almost like she's daring anyone to touch her, just so she can punish them for it.

Jules, on the other hand, is not so used to Ellie. She stares at the vacated doorway, mouth agape. "Is she really—"

"Yes."

"But she didn't even—"

"She'll bring more clothes down with her when she comes down with her laundry card."

Jules shakes her head. "You know there's a rumor that she killed Mountebanks?" she asks quietly.

Rebecca sighs and looks down at the baby blanket. "Did Ellie start the rumor?"

"Uh . . ."

She shakes her head to indicate it wasn't a serious question. Or at least not one she expects Jules can answer.

"A girl in my Russian history class was assaulted by Mountebanks," says Jules, her thumbs rubbing along the sides of her phone. "Then he realized she was on her period and got grossed out, so he smacked her around a bit and left her in a corner with her clothes torn. She never reported it because she'd been drinking. 'Maybe if I hadn't been drunk.'" Jules snorts. "Being drunk may make it easier sometimes, but it never makes it right. Still. I get why she didn't report. I didn't."

"Neither did I. He wouldn't lose, and I couldn't win. Why put myself through that?"

"Exactly. But she bought Ellie a drink today at Starbucks."

Rebecca frowns, twisting on the table to look at Jules directly. "Seriously?"

"Told her thank you."

Oh, God, please don't let that get back to Detective Gratton. "How many people believe she did it?"

"Is that really the important question?"

Rebecca studies Jules's expression: solemn, concerned, and . . . expectant? They've shared a number of journalism classes, and while they have different instincts, they've been taught the same rhythms and patterns. "What do you think is?"

"Did she do it?"

But Rebecca shakes her head again. "That may be other people's question, Jules, but it isn't yours."

They look at each other in silence until Rebecca's washing machines stop with loud clunks. They both slide off the table and go over, transferring the loads to a pair of dryers. Rebecca starts the first one, then hands her laundry card to Jules to start the second. Jules runs it through and promptly hands it back. "What's your question, Jules?" she asks under the dull roar of the machines.

Jules leans in close, bracing her hands against the dryer. "Would it be the worst thing if she did?"

Cursing under her breath, Rebecca automatically starts reaching for Daphne's anklet, until she remembers that she's standing. Instead, she taps the card anxiously against the top of the machine.

"From a moral perspective," Jules continues, "is it any different than punching Nazis?"

"Is there a difference between punching and murdering?" Rebecca asks scathingly.

"I just mean . . ." Jules winces and shakes her head. "Okay, bad example. But I still mean the question."

"Aside from the fact that it's illegal—"

"It's legal to not vaccinate your kids. The law isn't always right."

"—do you really want anyone making life-or-death decisions by the campus rumor mill?" she asks as if Jules hadn't interrupted.

"There's a difference between a rumor mill and a whisper network."

"Enough of one? Would you stake your own life on that?"

Jules slumps against the dryer, chin on her crossed forearms. "Not if you put it like that."

"Whoever killed Mountebanks, maybe they had a good reason. That doesn't make the *action* good. You're still talking about the murder of another human being. It can be understood—it can even be justified—but it cannot be inherently good." Rebecca runs her fingers through her hair, tugging on the ends of the curls where the splits tell her she needs a trim as soon as she's home. "Something like this . . . I worry about its effect on others."

"In what way?"

"It's not always a good thing to be inspired by events."

"Isn't it? This person is angry. We should all be angry."

"We *are* all angry," Rebecca corrects dryly, "but where does that anger go? The pink hats and marches haven't worked. The protests haven't worked. And now someone's decided murder is the thing that could work."

"It could have been self-defense."

Rebecca gives her a long look. Jules blushes and squirms. "You were the one who saw the body; did it look like self-defense?"

"No," she says and sighs. "I just want it to mean something. To *do* something."

"Does it mean more if it was Ellie?"

"Maybe? Or maybe I just want it to." Jules fidgets with the hem of her sweater. Her black nail polish is cracked and peeling, streaky and thin in places where it looks like she used a Sharpie to color in chipped spots. "Do you feel safer? With him dead?"

"No. I don't feel particularly vindicated either." In fact, she hasn't really boiled down how she does feel about all of it. She's such a tangle inside, and talking through it with Gemma did not provide the hoped-for clarity. "We talk about him in terms of the girls he hurt," she continues eventually. "That's not how he'll be remembered. A young life tragically cut short or some such bullshit. We're not even footnotes. When men are the murderers, people remember them, not their victims. But when men are the victims, people still remember them. We can't win. Even in a microphone before the Senate, we can't ever say our stories loud enough to change the status quo. Now someone's screaming, and what if it makes others want to scream too? We can't form packs and go around slaughtering people who've hurt us. Society would collapse."

"Maybe it should."

"And that's why you want it to be Ellie. Because it's hard to think of your own anger as unreasonable if you're around someone who's so much angrier. It's not about whether or not she did it; it's that she could have. It makes us feel better about our snarling, seething cores of rage. It says we could accomplish something wonderful if we would just let ourselves explode with that full fury."

"Couldn't we?"

"You ever seen pictures of Krakatoa?" Rebecca shakes her head. "That kind of rage isn't what it promises. It can only be destructive."

"You're afraid it's Ellie."

"About as much as you hope it is. What kind of people does that make us?"

Jules doesn't seem to have an answer for that. Probably for the best, though, as a minute or two later Ellie comes swanning in, thankfully clothed, lugging a laundry basket.

Rebecca returns to the folding table and her crochet, grateful it's a familiar pattern despite the lightness of the yarn. She wants to think that something good can come of Mountebanks's death. Hell, she wants to believe that genuinely well-intentioned vigilantism can work, that it can effect a change for the better in society as a whole. She grew up on stories of Robin Hood and similar heroes, the lessons distilled for the whole horde of cousins: do the right thing, even when you're told not to.

It was easier, she thinks, when the right thing was obvious. Nowadays it's a lot harder to see.

She notes that her missing jeans aren't in Ellie's laundry basket. She is afraid it's Ellie. She can admit that. But there's a new worry along with it: What if it isn't? What effect will this simultaneous support and suspicion have on her volatile friend?

If Ellie isn't already a killer, is there anything in the world that could keep her from becoming one if she thinks she'll be fucking thanked for it?

18

The storm heralded the arrival of a cold front that brings the temperatures to a balmy low seventies, which in turn brings most of the students spilling out to the green spaces to eat and study in the lovely weather. It's sunny but breezy, the kind of beautiful day that's so rare as the long Florida summer progresses.

The only lingering sign of the recent deaths is the dearth of sunbathers and joggers around Lake Alice. Only one body has been found there, but the gators are still very much present.

Rebecca and her suitemates sprawl across a pair of blankets in the grass. Delia is up on her knees, arms spread wide to catch the breeze, her eyes closed and face tilted back into the sun. Keiko sketches her, leaning back against Luz's knees for support.

The boys with the alligator pool float are back, running at girls to startle them, but they get laughter instead of shrieks this time. To what Rebecca is sure will be Det Corby's chagrin, the students have made the connection between the gator victims. Most of the campus population has felt much safer since the rumors started swirling. For those who don't? Well, if they have a reason to be nervous, they should be scared for once. The more immediate violence of Mountebanks's death proved a temporary wrench at best in the prevailing atmosphere.

Ellie lies flat on her back, her hair a river of flame around her. Her legs are wrapped around Rebecca's waist, feet on either side of the other girl's hips, and one of Rebecca's books rests on Ellie's lower legs. It's more comfortable than it probably should be. Ellie nudges her friend with her heel. "Hey, did you hear Det Corby got a new title?"

"What, really?"

"Yeah, now he's the investi-*gator*."

Rebecca closes her eyes and fights back a sigh.

"What kind of flooring do alligators have in their homes?"

"Please stop."

"*Rep*-tiles!"

Susanna giggles.

Rebecca opens one eye and glares at her. "Do not encourage her."

"What do you call an alligator with GPS?" Ellie asks.

"Oh my God."

"A navi-*gator*!"

"What did you do, look them up?"

"A sophomore printed up little booklets and is selling them for a buck," she replies placidly. "What do you get if you cross an alligator with a flower?"

"I don't know, but I'm not going to smell it," mutters Rebecca.

"What do alligators drink before a race?"

"*Gator*-ade," everyone else choruses.

Ellie huffs. "I guess that one was a bit obvious."

"Here at the University of Florida, where the drink was invented for the Gator football team? Shocking," Hafsah says deadpan.

From Susanna's gasp and giggle, Rebecca thinks it's probably safe to assume that Ellie made a rude gesture in response. She's also not going to ask.

A group of boys, one of them wearing a frat shirt, walks by on the sidewalk. From the grass three girls stand up and start pelting them with mini plastic alligators. "You're next, Tom!" one of them yells. "Was it worth it?"

The other boys cluster closer around their friend to shield him. They all look shaken, Rebecca notes, and she wonders if it's because of the alligator attacks or because people are brave enough to accuse them in public. And when did that start?

On top of one of the bulkier signs, someone has set a carnival-size alligator plush on top of the concrete, a Burger King cardstock crown taped to its head. A collection of flowers, tea light candles, and Post-it Notes has grown through the day. Susanna went over and read several of them earlier, when her back was protesting her long nap on the ground. She came back to report that mixed through the congratulations and well-wishes were names, some of which had stories attached to them. Almost in spite of her unease for the general mood of celebration, Rebecca took several pictures to study later.

There's a story in there, she thinks. An offering of past pain to vengeful alligator gods. Her parents were both at UF during the 1990 student murders, and they've talked about the tension on campus during and even for a time after the short terrifying spree. She would have thought that learning the city probably had a new serial killer would have been more alarming.

Instead, it's like a great weight has lifted from most. Many of the girls seem downright giddy. For once they're not the expected targets. The school has sent out several reminder emails that the mere presence of the alligators is still a danger, and everyone needs to continue exercising appropriate caution. Anyone who's had to walk past one of the lakes at night is well aware of that particular truth. Still, the pervading fear that was starting to gather over the campus has largely dissipated. It's a strange feeling.

And the genuine celebrations are probably not making Det Corby's job any easier.

"Did you know alligators can grow up to fifteen feet?" asks Ellie.

"Really? I thought they only had four." Rebecca wheezes as Ellie's legs tighten around her waist.

"How many arms has an alligator got?"

"She just answered that," Hafsah says, giving Ellie a small push that makes Rebecca sway.

"It depends how far he's gotten with eating his dinner."

There's not even a groan with that one, but rather a thoughtful and somewhat repulsed silence as they all consider that image. Ellie looks pleased as punch.

"What do you call an alligator who wears Crocs?" calls a girl from another group a few feet away.

"A sellout!" Ellie crows.

Laughter ripples around the grassy area, and now others are clustering to share their worst alligator jokes. This must be a version of hell for Det Corby. How do you separate intent from this generalized joy? There's something wrong with all of them, Rebecca decides.

And with her as well, because when they all turn to look at her, she sighs and offers, "What do you call an alligator who manages a food shop?" After a number of grins and guesses, she shrugs. "A deli-*gator*."

The group dissolves into laughter, and the jokes come thick and fast.

Eventually, however, she really does have to study. She's pretty sure her professor isn't going to reschedule the test because of beautiful days and questionably good news. She and Hafsah extricate themselves from their friends, gather their things, and head off toward the library. As much as she'd love to stay outside, she knows she'll be more productive without the distractions and the sleepy warmth of the sunlight. She and Jules stayed up most of the night talking, their topics varying widely depending on whether or not Ellie was in the room with them. The idea of a nap is incredibly appealing.

One of the girls from their floor stops them on the sidewalk. "Hey, have you guys registered in the dead pool?"

Rebecca and Hafsah both blink at her. "The what?" Rebecca asks eventually.

"For who you think will get fed to the gators next. There's a sheet up in the lounge if you get the urge."

Rebecca's pretty sure she's going to have no such urges, but she thanks her politely and keeps walking, Hafsah at her side. "That is disgusting, right?" she asks in an undertone. "Happily anticipating more deaths?"

"Entirely disgusting," she agrees. "Betting on death? Murder," she corrects herself. "I get being happy that it's terrible people being victimized for once, but really."

"Kerry will probably take it down."

"That just means it goes up in a room instead, and who knows how many there are across campus. If I were Detective Corby, I'd be exhausted trying to run around and see them all."

"What, you think the murderer would sign up to make bank on someone unexpected?"

"Or just take advantage of putting suspicion on others."

Rebecca laughs in spite of herself. "And here I thought Ellie and I were the only ones to think that way."

"You've quite ruined me. Happy?"

"Blissfully."

They have their pick of tables in the painfully cold library, most people out enjoying the respite from the heat. They settle into one out of the way of pretty much everything, where they won't be bothered by people with betting books or collections of terrible jokes.

Rebecca loves doing research and pulling information together. She loathes studying. Mostly, she admits, because she isn't any good at it. She's tried a number of methods, and none of them seem to be particularly helpful. She also knows that trying to skate by on memory alone may be fine in undergrad but won't help her later in life.

At some point she decides that she's learned as much as she's going to before tomorrow and closes her textbook and notebook with a sigh. Hafsah follows suit, collapsing in on herself so she can rest her cheek on the peeling surface of her book.

"I don't think it's Ellie," Hafsah says abruptly.

"What?"

"The alligator murders. I don't think it's Ellie."

"Okay," Rebecca says slowly. "Any particular reason? Not just that you think that but why you're bringing it up?"

"I'm bringing it up because we've sort of already talked about it."

"That was about whether or not she'd murder people someday, not about these specific deaths."

"I know, but . . ." Hafsah runs a finger under the exposed edge of the cotton cap under her hijab, absently scratching at an itch. She sits up, glances around, and then leans in over the table as far as she can without standing up. Rebecca obediently follows suit to keep the conversation as private as possible. "Mountebanks. He was different."

"He was personal," Rebecca says, thinking back on what Jules told her. "Fast, messy, public."

"Which I can totally see Ellie doing."

Rebecca winces but nods. That is precisely the kind of slaughter she can picture Ellie committing—and one an unknown number of people on campus already believe she did.

"But the alligators. That's a weird way to kill someone. In addition to all the practical factors that have to be considered, it all depends rather a lot on chance, right? I mean, what if the alligators aren't hungry? What if they want both the victim and the murderer? What if the victim isn't killed, but just sort of . . ."

"Chew-toyed?"

It's Hafsah's turn to cringe. "Sure. Ellie decides to do something; she does it. She might wait on it—she can be patient when she really puts her mind to it—but she's straightforward. Can you really see her relying on pure luck to accomplish something?"

"All murders depend on luck," Rebecca murmurs, quoting one of her professors. It offended a number of people in the class, mostly male, who all seemed to believe that if *they* ever decided to murder someone, *they'd* do it all perfectly.

"But that's luck in not being discovered. This is luck of doing the thing at all."

"Can we go back to where you think she killed Mountebanks?"

"I didn't say that."

"Yes, you did. I speak fluent Hafsah."

Hafsah shoves her things to the other side of the table and walks around to plop down next to Rebecca, sitting so close their knees knock together. They could be discussing anything, Rebecca thinks, crushes or gossip or sexcapades. Or murder. As you do. "She wasn't wearing the dress when she left the dorm."

"Right. She said she had it in her bag."

"So what happened to her jeans and top?"

"My jeans, so I was really hoping they were In her purse."

"I looked when I helped them upstairs. They weren't and wouldn't have both fit anyway. None of us have a car, and they weren't out with anyone with a car, and Ellie is absolutely the kind of person who will simply carry clothing around if she needs to and give an insult to anyone who asks her about it. She's done it before."

Many times before, in fact, on the rare occasions they've gone straight from one kind of activity to another that needs different clothing. She once walked around a bar wearing a pair of rolled-up jeans like a denim shrug because they'd gone directly there from a protest with classmates, and when someone laughed at her, she threw a drink in the woman's face.

"So where are the clothes?" Hafsah continues.

Studying her friend's earnest expression, Rebecca gives in. Obviously there's no escaping the topic. Maybe Hafsah, who knows Ellie in person rather than through Rebecca's stories, can offer assistance Gemma couldn't. "So you think she . . . what?" she asks. "Snuck away from the others, somehow tracked down Mountebanks, lured him out to a parking lot, murdered him, changed clothes, and made it back to the others before anyone noticed she was gone?"

"They kept losing track of each other, don't you remember? The group kept splitting and wandering off and reconnecting, and not always in the same dynamics. She easily could have split off. As for tracking him . . ." She pulls out her phone and opens Instagram, typing in Mountebanks's name and then handing it to Rebecca. There are a ton of memorial posts tagged to him, and she assumes a friend or family member must be moderating pretty heavily because most of them look positive. When she scrolls down to the night of the murder, there's a picture of him and several friends with the Durty Nelly's sign visible in the frame.

"Here all night," Rebecca reads aloud. "Come drink with us if you're not a bunch of pussies." She makes a face and hands the phone back. "Charming."

"He announced his location and his intention to be there until closing," Hafsah says. "And it's not like Ellie's shy about Insta-stalking."

No, that's certainly true. She's lost count of how often Ellie has spammed people's posts with rude comments after they've harassed someone within sight of her. It's only gotten worse since Kacey's attack, rude ratcheting up to bitchy, aggressive, and not particularly veiled levels of threatening. Rebecca rubs her thumb against the bridge of her nose, trying to think. "He's in streetlight, not sunlight; he posted the picture after the girls left the dorm," she says eventually. "She took the dress with her before she had any idea where he was."

"And what she told the officers may really have been her intent when they first went out. She took it with her in case they bumped into him again at Tom and Tabby's. And then she saw where he was and decided to be a little more proactive."

"With what, though? Ellie keeps mace in her purse, but she doesn't have a knife or even a pocketknife. She doesn't even own a pair of scissors. Or have you forgotten the Singer shears incident?"

Hafsah winces. No one in the suite will forget that night. They'll also never again use Keiko's fabric shears on paper. "She could have bought a knife?"

"Sure," she agrees, mulling through possibilities. "Of course, it couldn't have been recently, or the police would know about it. At least if it was through a legitimate source. So she bought it a while ago, or she bought it off market. Where's she keeping it?"

"In her room, I assume."

"I guarantee that if Ellie, of all people, had a big fuck-off knife there, the police would have found that very interesting when they searched our rooms."

"Wait, what?"

"When the RAs crammed us all down in the lobby for the mandatory safety lecture? You didn't realize?" Rebecca shrugs as Hafsah shakes her head, looking perturbed. "They did a good job of covering their tracks, but someone was wearing pretty heavy cologne, and my snack drawer wasn't in order anymore."

Hafsah makes a face.

"Hey, if I go in to grab a study snack, I don't want to have to pay attention to do it. Sweet, salty, chocolaty, and gummy are not interchangeable. So, yes, as we head toward finals, I notice when the contents were suddenly mixed together while we were all downstairs. And there were some other things out of place, like the lid of the miscellany box being off kilter."

"How could they search our rooms without telling us?" her roommate asks. "Don't they need a warrant for that?"

"Nope. By living on campus, we grant the housing office the authority to conduct inspections whenever they see fit. If they wish to allow the police to search, they can. It's why I tell the RAs each year about my knife."

Her grandfather gave her the knife at her graduation party. It's not that long, or rather, it's just short enough to be legal without a permit. His intention was that she carry it with her everywhere. After some reflection, that didn't seem like the wisest course. It's one thing to know an event is self-defense—entirely another to prove it, and more and more these days it seems the courts are determined to punish the victims for surviving rather than the perpetrators for attacking. If something ever happens, she doesn't want to stake her life and freedom on nuance. So the knife has stayed in its sheath, taped to the back of her nightstand in each dorm room, where she can easily grab it in case of an intruder. She's never had to use it, though she came close when someone was stupid enough to let in one of the frats for a three a.m. pantie raid.

Seeing them scream and run from Ellie's baseball bat was far more satisfying, if she's honest.

She checked on the knife once she realized there'd been people through the suite during the lecture. Sure enough, the dust on the grip and sheath had been disturbed. Knife was still there, though. She knew from Jules's description that they were probably looking for a larger, longer knife. Preferably one that didn't have most of a semester's dust on it. Just to be thorough, she also checked the box cutters in the tool bag they kept behind the bikes and the not-really-a-knife-but-could-probably-be-used-as-one-if-you-were-pissed-off-enough inch-long straight razor in the miscellany box beside the tool bag.

They use it to scrape adhesive from stickers off the doors and desks.

Ellie wasn't summoned out of the lecture, and so far, police haven't returned with more questions for her, which makes Rebecca reasonably confident nothing alarming was found on that side of the suite, even with the various sharp instruments that are part of Luz's and Keiko's artistic paraphernalia.

"Truth be told," Rebecca continues eventually, "I'm less interested in where she's keeping the knife she may or may not have than I am in the fact that you're convinced she murdered at least two people but *still haven't said so to the police.*"

19

"I don't have proof," Hafsah tells her, chin set stubbornly. Rebecca knows that look; it's the one she sees right before Hafsah starts arguing with strangers online. It's the look she sometimes imagines must have been on the musicians' faces right before they started playing as the *Titanic* sank. The one that says, "This stance we have chosen cannot win, but we will stay even unto death if we must."

It's more polite than Ellie's various expressions of pigheadedness but every bit as unassailable.

"But you have reasonable suspicion and specific information that could help them in the investigation. Hafsah."

"I am not going to the police to sell out a friend on 'reasonable suspicion,' Rebecca. What if I'm wrong? What if she's innocent? Not only is she our friend—she lives with us; how do you think the rest of the semester would go?"

"You can ask the police to protect your anonymity," Rebecca says weakly. She's grasping at straws, and she knows it but still feels obliged to point it out. She's supposed to have more faith in law enforcement than friends. She doesn't, but she's supposed to. Any system, any hierarchy, any authority is inherently flawed, corrupted by the insurmountable gap between ideal and reality. What's important is that they try their best, and Hafsah doesn't have much reason to expect that they will.

"That doesn't mean they actually will, and besides, that's the kind of thing that spills around. Oh, and, also also, some of that information would necessarily come from someone living with her. Specifically, someone with access to check her purse that night and sober enough to remember it with clarity. You stayed down talking to the officers and Kerry long enough that everything was put away before you came up. Which means she would know, absolutely and completely, that it was me."

"Kerry was the one to take Ellie up," Rebecca corrects her. "So she could have checked before coming back down to me."

"And your knife? Does Kerry know about that?"

"Yes."

Hafsah blinks, startled, but quickly regroups. "I'm just saying, I'm not going to report someone unless I know for a fact they're guilty. No matter what I believe."

"It's not your job to determine guilt or innocence. That's up to the court."

"Yes, and they do that so very well."

Rebecca winces. Leaning back against her chair, she laces her fingers together and presses her thumbs against each other at the pads, like if she can just get the perfect balance in that, it will somehow magically spill over to everything else. Bad acts for good reasons . . . it's not really something the judicial system is prepared to handle. Judges can exercise discretionary powers, juries can temper verdicts, but on the whole, nuance can be hard to highlight without getting into showmanship, and those same things that can be attempted in mercy can be used for punishment as well.

They've had this conversation before, she and Hafsah. That was before Mountebanks turned up dead, of course, but somehow that particular event, despite seeming like elegant proof, hasn't changed Hafsah's stance. So what next?

There are a lot of reasons the old hate preacher could have disappeared from Turlington Plaza. First being that he was, well, old. Perhaps it was simply too hard on his body to keep it up. Maybe a family emergency called him elsewhere. There could have been a Christmas miracle that prompted him to turn into a decent human being and stop pissing vitriol and condemnation at students passing by. Even if he did die, he was, again, old. There are any number of natural causes or accidents or things that don't indicate murder.

So, okay, it makes sense not to go to the police on suspicions that are really nothing more than a lingering confluence of coincidence and uneasy feeling. But then Mountebanks. She wishes she could remember his last name—names?—but her brain insists on supplying Mountebanks the Asshole, like that's any kind of helpful. He attacks Rebecca, someone attacks him, and Ellie is missing clothing and getting thank-you drinks from other girls he hurt.

Well, one girl, anyway. She hasn't heard of any others buying gifts, though she knows there are others. From what she's been hearing, Mountebanks had plenty of hateful intent but less ability to follow through. He attempted a number of rapes that always seemed to go cockeyed for one reason or another—a period or nearby police or a fortuitously timed call from his mother—and none of them were ever reported. As impossible as it is to bring successful rapists to any sort of justice, how much harder when it's just attempted?

Rebecca sat with Daphne in her hospital room between surgeries as the police walked her through the night of the party, as they told her that her parents had given consent for the rape kit while she was unconscious in pre-op. Rebecca was there when the doctors fumblingly explained why the attack had necessitated a hysterectomy and menopause at fifteen, that the series of surgeries on her back could stabilize her spine but not repair it. The officers and doctors were women, friends of the family and genuinely sympathetic, trying to be as gentle as humanly possible. It was still an awkward, humiliating, and horrifyingly invasive experience.

We spend so much time, she thinks, teaching girls how not to get raped, and then we attack them for it. If you drink, it's your fault, but if you don't drink, you're a killjoy. If you show too much of your body, you're asking for it, but if you cover up, you're a prude, and you're asking for it. You're too loud; you're not loud enough. You're too paranoid; you're not paranoid enough. It's your fault. It's your fault. It's your fault. It's impossible not to internalize that to some degree or another.

This is how he hurt me, says the statement.

But what were you doing? ask the police, asks society. What were you wearing? Were you drinking? Were you alone? Were you flirting with him? I bet you were flirting with him. Girls like you—it's like breathing, right? You were leading him on? Are you sure you said no? But did you mean it? Are you sure you want to ruin his life because of a few minutes of harmless fun?

And if you somehow get through it all and still want to move forward, you do it again and again and again and again. You do it with lawyers in offices and conference rooms, and then you take the stand and watch your parents as the defense attorney implies that you're a vengeful, lying whore out to destroy the reputation and prospects of this promising young student/ athlete/entrepreneur/*man*. You relive it again and again and then: not guilty. Or guilty of a lesser charge. Here's his too-brief sentence, but he's such a fine young man, so the judge is going to reduce that to almost nothing, and isn't it a shame about his scholarship, but don't worry, his admission somewhere else will get crowdfunded.

Keeping it secret doesn't lessen the trauma, but at least it hides it. No wonder so many never report. Provided you can even wade through all the bullshit pressed on you from such a young age—that shirt shows her collarbone/shoulder/midriff; it's distracting the boys, but she's *five*—and understand that it's not your fault, *it was never your fault*, there's row after row of people waiting to tell you why it is.

Rebecca was outside, alone, at night, at a bar. Her dress was short and showed a hint of cleavage, so what did she expect? Standing there like advertising—she's just lucky it wasn't worse. And she *was* lucky, is the real kicker, but she sure as hell doesn't need anyone else to tell her that.

She glances at Hafsah, something about that thought tickling the back of her mind. She waits for it, letting it drift toward collision with whatever will bring it into greater clarity. Trying to stomp on it will just scatter the pieces. Why has Hafsah not reported her suspicions?

Why has *Rebecca* not done it?

Why do most women never report their rapes?

"You don't want to report your suspicions because you agree with what she's doing."

A long silence fills the scant space between them, long enough to notice the stressed hum of the air-conditioning and the occasional clunk of the pipes. "Everybody has a line," Hafsah says finally.

"Between capable and likely, yes."

"Maybe there's a line somewhere in the middle, where you're willing to support it but not to do it yourself."

"That's not a line with any moral high ground."

"No. But maybe there isn't such a thing."

Rebecca's thumb pops, loudly and painfully, and she realizes with some surprise that she was still pressing her thumbs together. She shakes out her hands, rubbing at the muscles in the meat of her palm. "You understand you're also relying on me not having any moral high ground," she notes. "Because you're telling me all this with the clear expectation that I won't report it either."

"I'm not telling you not to."

"Except that you wouldn't be saying most of this if you thought I would."

"Reporters get to preserve anonymous sources, right?"

"This is . . . that is not the same thing." She sighs, feeling a tension headache building at the base of her skull.

"But you're not going to tell anyone."

Despite the confidence in her tone, Hafsah visibly holds her breath while Rebecca thinks about her answer. "No," Rebecca says eventually and watches her friend deflate with an explosive exhalation. "For now. You're right in that some of the information would necessarily come from us, and that . . . complicates things. But there are other lines you need to start thinking about."

"Such as?"

"What if more people die? Do we bear the moral weight for that? The legal weight? Keep in mind that even on just what we suspect now, a decent lawyer could probably argue for accessory after the fact, for not coming forward. If you're willing to keep things from the police, are you also willing to lie to them? Are you willing to stand before a judge and swear on the Qur'an and then lie?"

"No," Hafsah says. She somehow makes the word two syllables, each part dripping with reluctance. "I won't lie. That doesn't mean I have to reward police for not asking the right questions."

"Are you prepared to go to prison on that distinction?"

Hafsah scowls, folding her arms against the table and resting her cheek on them, angled to still look squarely at Rebecca. "How many women have to get hurt or killed before people seriously try to change the way things are? Why do we have to suffer and be constantly afraid when they exist in ignorance and privilege? Is it the right way to try to effect change? No, probably not, not in the sense of morally right. But is it effective? Maybe. Maybe if the terrible things happen to them for a while, they'll finally start self-policing so they can all be safer."

"That isn't really how the world works."

"Maybe it should be."

"You also don't have any suggestive evidence that the murderer is trying to effect a change," she points out. "That's just the general interpretation this week. Punishment and revenge aren't the same thing as justice, and they're certainly not reform. What is this person actually accomplishing beyond murder?"

"These boys can't hurt anyone else ever again. That's not a small thing, Rebecca."

"No," she says softly. "I suppose not."

They sit in silence. The conversation doesn't feel done, but it also doesn't feel like there's a way forward. It's just sort of there, hanging around them in heavy folds, preventing the possibility of any other conversation to lighten the tension.

20

It's probably best to give up the hope of accomplishing anything productive. Without discussing it, they pack up their supplies, refill their water bottles, and leave the library, heading out in the deepening dusk. Rather than dig out her keys so early, Rebecca hooks her finger through the loop on her water bottle. It's a heavy thing, steel and solid and eminently suited to bludgeoning someone in the event of assault. Her father bought it for her once he realized she wasn't going to carry her grandfather's knife.

So many ways to tell girls they should protect themselves, she muses, but what are they telling the boys? Her mother and aunts have taken the boy cousins well in hand over the years, telling them over and over that there isn't a single thing a person can do that invites rape, but she also knows that they're in a relative minority. A subset of her high school baseball team wore T-shirts to a school event that said, "No means No except when it doesn't" and didn't even get lectured about it by administration.

She can't remember what it's like to live without the ever-present awareness of possible harm, and yet she knows she has it easier than others. She's often in fear for her safety and well-being but not generally for her life. There are many who don't have even that much reassurance.

"Dammit," Hafsah mutters at her side.

"What?"

"There's a bike approaching. I'm not sure I'm up for Officer Kevin's brand of chivalry today."

Rebecca follows the direction of her friend's nod and sees the flickering bike light coming closer. "He is a bit of a chauvinist, isn't he? But maybe it's not Officer Kevin; there are a lot of cyclists on campus."

"Are we that lucky?"

"We live with a potential murderer and haven't died yet."

"That would be more impressive if we identified as male and were therefore on her list of potential victims."

"I'm kind of curious how she prioritizes that list. How does she rank them?" Rebecca asks impishly. "Vicinity? Immediacy of offense? Opportunity? Are there certain things that piss her off more than others? The color of their hair? Do they get extra points if they're in a fraternity?"

Hafsah giggles into her free hand. "I dare you to ask her."

"Weren't you the one telling me how awful it would be to live with her if she knew we thought she was killing people?"

"No, that was if we told the police we thought she was killing people."

"Yes, I can see how that makes a difference." She feels a little bad for making light of it—it's really not anything to laugh about—but she also doesn't feel like hearing a man tell her to smile, and if it is Officer Kevin approaching, he seems like the kind of man to do that. It's difficult to appreciate intent in the best of moods, at least with that tired, infuriating instruction. She's not sure she's in the mood to be generous tonight.

The cyclist comes closer, into a patch of streetlight. It's Officer Kevin. She studies his approach, eyes narrowed. "His body cam is off."

"How do you know?"

"Because there's no little red light. The department specifically ordered ones with signal lights on them so there'd be no question about it recording or not. Sherriff's office was all atwitter about it when I was interning last summer—and whether or not a department could reasonably order more than one kind of body cam for times when a discreet approach is necessary."

"Interesting, but we may have a problem."

"The fact that he thinks we live in Thomas?" asks Rebecca. "Where we do not in fact live?"

"Right."

"You know, from when you lied to a police officer."

Hafsah gives her a dirty look. She probably deserves it.

"So . . . ideas?"

"I'll work on it," her friend grumbles.

"Work quickly; we're not *that* far away." When the man on the bicycle slows to a stop a few feet from them, Rebecca lifts a hand in acknowledgment. "Officer Kevin."

"Becky, right?" the officer says in greeting.

"Rebecca," she corrects.

"Right, right." He glances at Hafsah under the anemic glow of the streetlight but, perhaps remembering their last encounter, doesn't ask her name. "How are you ladies this evening?"

"We're fine."

"Do you always spend so much time wandering around after dark?" he asks.

"Not wandering—we have a destination in mind."

"Good, good." He waits for her to elaborate.

She doesn't. She wants to give Hafsah time to think of something or at least not to contradict herself if she later says they're going to find dinner.

His friendly smile starts to look a bit strained. "Can I escort you ladies somewhere?"

"If we say no, are you going to follow us again?"

He doesn't look as abashed as she'd like; apparently his sheepishness is only for the first time he gets caught at it. "College is a time when you're all learning to stretch your wings. Sometimes you young ladies are more interested in being independent than in being safe."

Rebecca's fingernails dig into her palm as her fist clenches. The problem is, any response she makes to that he can shoot back with a reminder of Mountebanks the Asshole bothering her outside the bar.

Hafsah holds up her water bottle, which is less solid than Rebecca's but has two rings of spikes on either side of the grip. Sharp enough to startle—not large enough to effectively draw blood. "We've got each other, plus protection, and we're not taking any detours," she says politely.

"That isn't always enough. Besides, Becky here is one of Corby's old students. He'd be pissed if anything happened to you. Should have heard him swearing after that boy bothered you."

As much as she'd love to focus on the warm thrill at the thought of Det Corby's concerns, the larger part of Rebecca's brain latches onto the way Officer Kevin calls them *ladies* and *young ladies*, but Mountebanks is simply a *boy*. It's not just dismissive; it's predatory. It simultaneously flatters them with a semblance of maturity—oh, you're not just girls; you're *ladies*—while also reinforcing the sense of youth and inexperience. One of the aunts walked all the cousins through warning signs and phrases when a barely eighteen-year-old cousin brought her thirty-six-year-old boyfriend home to meet the family.

She also cautioned the teenage horde that, especially here in the South, men can be so steeped in the ideal of genteel chauvinism they don't realize when it crosses into predation. They can't just make the assumption; context is important.

Rebecca wonders if Officer Kevin is one of those men. He's not a Gainesville native; his voice is deeper South, without the college-town dilution. Panhandle, maybe, or Alabama. In that region, anyway.

"I hope you're offering the boys escorts too," she says mildly. "I know it's not normally needed, but they seem awfully nervous of late. I'm sure they'd feel safer for a police escort."

"We're here for all the students," he replies. "All they have to do is ask."

And all the girls have to do is breathe, apparently, but she's not sure there's a benefit to saying that right now.

Hafsah's phone buzzes, still on vibrate from being in the library. "Ellie says we should hurry back, or she's eating our dinner," she announces.

"She ordered for us?"

"Susanna and Delia ordered for us. Ellie's just a pig who suggests we jog."

"Then by all means, let's get you ladies home," says Officer Kevin. He swings off his bike and turns it to face the opposite direction, then looks at them expectantly. "Thomas Hall?"

"You remember," Hafsah says.

"Campus cops are here for the students. It's hard to do our job if we don't know the students."

Hafsah smiles, a fierce, sharp thing that bares her teeth like a snarl. It's Ellie's smile in Hafsah's face, and it's incredibly disturbing. To Rebecca, anyway; Officer Kevin doesn't seem to notice. "And we're just so grateful."

He preens a little, thin shoulders giving a sort of jaunty shimmy as he squares them in response.

They walk quickly. Rebecca doesn't really have anything against Officer Kevin, aside from spikes of irritation at his insistence in providing unneeded escort, but the conversation with Hafsah—and the questions it's forcing her to ask herself—has her on edge, and she doesn't particularly want to be around police right now . . . or men . . . and especially not policemen. In this mood, even Det Corby might not be his usual exception.

They're within sight of Thomas—and the problem of the card-locked door—when a voice calls out through the well-lit approach. "Rebecca! There you are!"

She doesn't actually know the voice, but Hafsah squeezes her hand twice in quick succession, so she smiles and waves back toward the voice. "Sorry, we lost track of time!"

Four girls converge on the trio, one wearing a beautiful bronze-and-indigo batik-dyed hijab. She's the one who spoke and who now speaks again. "We relocated to the lounge so the smell won't linger in the rooms," she says with a grin. They finish the walk up to the door in a mass, with Officer Kevin lingering at the back, and the girl slides her ID through the lockbox. The door opens with a click. "Thanks so much for walking them back!" she says cheerfully.

"Anytime," he replies. He gives one last assessing look to Rebecca and Hafsah, then turns his bike, mounts it, and rides off.

Once they're inside, the door closed securely behind them, Hafsah lets out an explosive breath. "Yasmin, you're a hero."

"I owed you for keeping my wallet safe."

A genuine smile starting to creep across her face, Rebecca takes the phone from Hafsah to read the most recent texts. "You definitely get credit for working quickly."

"Thank you."

They stay in Thomas for a little bit, chatting with Yasmin and her friends, but Rebecca's audibly growling stomach prompts a round of cheerful farewells. She and Hafsah make their way next door without trouble, nodding to the RA on duty. The third-floor lounge is an unexpected hive of activity, mostly girls but with a handful of others, centered on the pair of posters on the wall in one corner. The dead pool, Rebecca assumes. One of them, anyway; the other seems to be a collection of all publicly available information on the deaths and victims, annotated by increasingly ubiquitous Post-it Notes. A number of students are engaged in a lively discussion of whether or not Mountebanks should be counted because he wasn't alligator bait.

Rebecca leaves Hafsah listening intently and returns to their suite, dropping her stuff on her desk. There's a note on Susanna and Delia's door explaining that they're having dinner with a study group to prepare for an upcoming field trip for their lab. She passes through the bathroom and assumes, from the avalanche of clothing visible through Luz and Keiko's open door, that they got off to their gallery showing okay. They don't have anything up—it's only for the graduating seniors—but they go every year to show support and get a preview for their own eventual showing.

Somewhat to her surprise she finds Ellie home, curled up with her head near the foot of her bed, hugging a throw pillow and staring at the massive photo of Kacey on the wall. All around her, the printed articles flutter and crackle in the wake of an oscillating fan. Rebecca sits on the edge of Kacey's bed and pulls one of the other pillows onto her lap. "You okay?" she asks quietly, studying the pained, open expression on her friend's face.

Ellie shakes her head. "I miss Kacey," she whispers, barely audible over the whining whir of the fan.

Looking up at the photo, Rebecca takes a deep breath and lets it out as a sigh. "Yeah," she says. "Me too."

"She was the best of us." Ellie blinks glassy eyes, and a tear slides down the side of her face to join a small damp stain on the bedsheet. "Hafsah is brave, and you're understanding, and Delia is sweet . . . I'm the only one that's terrible. But Kacey was . . . she was . . ."

"Kacey was good," Rebecca finishes softly.

There are stories, she thinks, where the whole world is in peril from a supervillain or an evil god or whatever, and most of the time the Chosen One prevails through a sword and quippy repartee, possibly with a woman's sacrifice to inspire him. There are other stories, though, maybe harder to believe, where the hero can't use a sword or magic, where at every step of the journey, their genuine goodness and kindness create small changes all along the way, and somehow that returns a thousandfold in the face of a great evil. The world is saved, yes, but it's also made fundamentally better.

Kacey was the second kind of hero. She made the world better just by being in it, but she never demanded that of others. She never lectured, never made ostentatious examples, never tried to shame or belittle her lesser fellow mortals. She never consciously drew attention to her goodness; it just sort of blazed out of her, an almost tangible radiance. Rebecca knows the temptation to mythologize her, but she felt the same way when Kacey was with them every day, full of laughter and light and a bone-deep sweetness. Her honest optimism made life feel more manageable, even on the rotten days.

It's impossible to reconcile her vibrant friend with the girl condemned to the hospital bed, trapped between unresponsiveness and brain death. There's no chance of recovery for that girl. She'll never wake up, never know her family and friends, but there's no death for her either. Whatever made her Kacey, Rebecca hopes it's gone rather than buried. She can't stand the thought that some deep part of her friend is suffering. Bad enough the pain her loved ones will carry for the rest of their lives; some days, especially last semester, the prayer for that mercy was the only thing keeping Rebecca from drowning in sharp, aching grief.

She's learned to live with it, which didn't seem possible last semester. Keeping busy helps somewhat. Time—and Gemma's reminder that Kacey would want her friends to live their best lives—has carried her the rest of the way.

Anger has carried Ellie through. No, not anger—rage. Words have meaning, and Kacey—who read the dictionary for fun because she loved learning interesting new words; her favorite was *effervescence*— would find the distinction important.

"I can't go see her," Ellie says. "I try, and I get to the care center, and once I even got all the way to her door, but I can't . . ."

"It hurts," admits Rebecca. "Seeing her like that, seeing what it's doing to her parents; it's . . . well. Not being able to do it doesn't make you a bad person."

"You do it."

"Penance."

Sniffling, Ellie pushes herself up on one elbow and shoves her hair out of her face. A small pile of clips and pins sits on the floor next to the foot of the bed. Ellie, Rebecca, and Kacey—the Titian Trio, as their first-year RA called them, but each of them with such dramatically different kinds of red. "What do you mean?"

"Kacey invited me to that party," she says quietly. "It was held by a bunch of her high school friends, remember? One of them was in journalism, and I couldn't stand her. We were paired for a project sophomore year, and I spent the whole time fantasizing about shoving her in front of a bus." Rebecca smiles at Ellie's startled laugh. "It was entirely mutual. Linsey Travers, that absolute bitch. I didn't want to ruin the party for Kacey by making her keep the peace all night, so I told her I had homework to do. She wished me good luck and said she'd see me in the morning; she was planning to just crash with the high school friends."

"What happened to Kacey wasn't your fault."

"I know." And she does. That's the strange thing; she *knows* it's not her fault, just like what happened to Daphne wasn't her fault, but that leaden knot of guilt that lives in her chest doesn't give a shit about logic. She toes off her shoes and pulls her legs up on the bed, tangling her fingers through the anklet. "It wasn't your fault either."

"I was at a different party," Ellie mumbles. "I was dancing and drinking and laughing when . . ."

"You had absolutely no way to know that halfway across town, something terrible was about to happen. Carry the guilt if you have to, Ellie, but not the fault."

Her friend crumples back onto the bed, suddenly sobbing, and Rebecca lurches across the gap between the beds. Her fingers snag in the anklet before she snatches them free. She climbs over Ellie so she can press along the girl's back, arms around her and face pressed against her shoulder. "I've got you," Rebecca murmurs. "I've got you."

Ellie weeps, occasionally breaking off into wheezing, mostly incoherent rants about Kacey's high school friends, about the boys who hurt her, about burning the world because there's nothing worth saving. Then the words run dry, leaving behind a keening wail.

Hafsah comes running, one hand clutched to her chest as she appears in the doorway and takes in the scene. She pants and flicks her hand at Rebecca.

Obligingly, Rebecca scoots closer to the wall, bringing Ellie with her, and Hafsah eases onto the edge of a bed really not meant for three people. They secure Ellie between them, even as she shakes from the violence of her grief and rage.

This is why, Rebecca realizes. This is why, despite everything, despite every sensible reason, she and Hafsah haven't gone to the police with their suspicions. Why they won't for as long as possible. Because this is Ellie, and she's theirs, all of her, even her recklessness and the broken edges sharp enough to bleed. She meets Hafsah's eyes, sees the same thought reflected there, and gives a slow blink in place of a nod.

They'll never be able to protect Ellie from herself, but they can damn well try.

21

Someday, when I'm safely and comfortably settled in a nonextradition country, I should write a book about all this. *Thinking with Your Dick: How Men Walk Willingly to Their Deaths Because It Could Never Happen to Them.* A brief bubble of fear that bursts so quickly, and then they're back on their bullshit, ignoring those who've already died.

It isn't just stupidity; it's arrogance. As if they're somehow superior specimens, and nothing can harm them.

Gee, college boys with a history of hurting women have been turning up dead after being torqued to bits by alligators. You're damn right that I, a college boy with a history of hurting women, will absolutely take you to my grandparents' secluded house on the river now that they've returned north for the summer.

Dillon McFarley—Dillweed Dillon, as his frat brothers call him—stands out for his imbecility even in a horde of other candidates.

The cold front has ended, bringing back thick swarms of mosquitoes and a sweltering heat. Even now, long after sundown, heat bakes up from the packed earth and stone leading down to the McFarleys' private dock. Dillon stands at the very edge of the dock, toes curling over the corner of the final plank, legs spread wide, pissing into the river. Classy.

Of more interest are the red gleams in the mostly darkness. One of the neighbors has an old-fashioned lamppost on their back patio, wrought iron and frosted glass. The red gleams come in pairs, and there are a lot of them. Alligators really do look like demons when you catch them at night.

When Dillon wobbles his way around to face me, he hasn't tucked himself back in. It's a less than inspiring sight. "Never fucked a redhead before," he slurs.

He's not going to now either.

"Sure you have," I tell him, teeth bared in a snarl. "What about Kacey?"

"Who?"

"Kacey Montrose. Short, pretty—long, long hair the color of a blood orange?"

He stares at me blankly. I can see the thoughts trying to spin together behind his eyes, striving to push through the haze of alcohol and party pills. Maybe I'm slipping. It's not like I really took the time to tell the others why they were dying. I knew why they were condemned, and it wasn't that long before other people realized why they'd died. The fuckheads didn't need to know. They'd already shown they didn't care.

Kacey demands more, though. Kacey is personal. Kacey is bright and vivacious, full of compassion and forgiveness. Now she's a frail shell on a hospital bed, her brain so damaged by asphyxiation she'll never wake up.

Because of Dillon.

She wouldn't understand this, would never approve of it, especially not for her sake. She'd still forgive me. She would have forgiven the devil if he'd said sorry or no. She even would have forgiven Dillon.

I'm not Kacey. I'm not interested in forgiveness.

I smile at him, sliding off the rail of the deck to stand on the house-side end of the dock. The McFarleys have a shepherd's hook mounted horizontally along the outside of their dock, in case they notice anyone drowning behind their house, I suppose.

Drowning is a kind of asphyxiation. But the McFarleys don't really care about that. If someone drowns in their backyard, they'll be held liable.

They managed to avoid any liability after Dillon drugged Kacey at a party. After he wrapped duct tape around her wrists and ankles, even around her neck so she struggled to breathe. After he shoved his dick down her throat and kept it there, even though she was choking, even though she passed out, even though he buried her face in his groin so her desperate body couldn't even try to breathe through her nose instead. His friends were too busy filming and laughing to help her. He peeled away the tape after, but he didn't clean up the residue on her skin. He just left her there in a room at a party, letting people think she'd passed out from drink, and it wasn't until the hosts tried to wake her up hours later that they realized there was a problem.

But Kacey was underage, and the hosts were scared, so they took her to the hospital and propped her up on a smoking bench close to the entrance of the ER. They left her there for someone else to find, after who knows how many hours, when every single second mattered to try to save whatever brain function they could. She never even woke up.

They were her fucking friends, and they just left her there.

She'll never wake up.

All that joy and light and kindness, snuffed out in an instant because he decided his dick was more important than her life. His friends deleted the recordings, but not before word of them got around. The county declined to press charges because, as they claimed, there was no way to know Kacey hadn't consented; maybe she just hadn't taken her asthma into account, and really, it was a tragedy, but there was no reason to ruin a young man's life over a simple accident. The incredibly expensive lawyer his family retained may have had something to do with that. Her family is so strapped paying for her medical care, they'll never be able to afford an attorney to go after him in civil court.

"I'm going to be kinder to you than you were to Kacey," I tell him gently, pulling the shepherd's hook off its posts. I loop the cord around one of his wrists—just one—and twist it to loop it again, the way it would look if you got caught in it while flailing. Not suspicious. Not murder. Just a drunk-ass fool stupid enough to poke at alligators with a long stick still attached to him. He stares at the cord around his wrist and tries to pull it away, but the alcohol has his brain so befuddled that he can't seem to figure out how to get it past the widest part of his hand. We stopped twice on the way here so he could hurl, any benefit from throwing up immediately lost as he kept drinking; he's got to be in the realm of alcohol poisoning by now. "You're going to be in pain, yes, but it will be over quickly. That's more than anyone can say about Kacey."

"Who are you?" he asks, eyes wide and face pale. Spooked, but not scared. Not really.

Not yet.

"Someone who's tired of letting boys be boys, when the girls never get to be anything." I push the pole toward him, and his hands curl around it by reflex, letting me lean him out farther and farther over the water. He clutches the pole for balance, teetering at the edge of the dock. Those red gleams are getting closer, congregating. "I wish I could do to you what you did to her so you'd know it exactly. So you'd suffer it exactly. But I can't. This will have to do."

He gapes at me. He doesn't understand, clearly. I don't have time for him to sober up enough to make him understand.

I take several steps back, then pivot to one side and snap my right leg up in a midkick against the pole. He flails back with a startled curse, followed by a splash. Adjusting my thin leather gloves, I walk back up onto the deck, then turn to watch. It's not precisely a safe distance. The alligators can easily get onto the deck. It might even be why his grandparents decided to return north a bit early this year.

Dillon flails briefly, mouth already full of water. Alcohol makes it hard to be coordinated, though, and the pole is heavier than it looks. It's hard to maneuver it when you're clawing at the surface of the water, too panicked or distracted or drunk to realize you could just lean back and float.

But drowning isn't often as it is in the movies. The flailing doesn't last for long, replaced by a dazed lassitude as the oxygen deprivation begins, and soon Dillon slips below the surface and doesn't come back up. In the light of the neighbor's lamp, the red gleams converge, and the water suddenly thrashes and boils with movement.

I put my bike to rights on the deck, where I can see the alligators if they decide to crawl up for a second course. I'm done before the water settles, the dull roars and bellows of the gators abruptly silencing the frogs and crickets along the river. I shrug into my bag, carry the bike around to the front of the house, and throw my leg over, kicking off smoothly.

I don't look back.

It's not enough.

Goddammit, it's not nearly enough. Not enough time, not enough pain, not enough shame. It was supposed to be enough, but it's not. It's over so fast, and then he's dead, and why should he have it so much easier than Kacey?

Why do we allow any of those assholes less pain than they inflict on others?

The fury and resentment don't ease through the long ride back to town, not the way it has before. Because it was personal? They're all personal.

It's always personal.

22

Shoving her sweat-damp sheet down to the foot of the bed, Rebecca groans and sits up, hair clinging to her unpleasantly. The Sledd Hall air conditioner, never in the best shape to begin with, sputtered out and died yesterday afternoon. Now, despite being not quite five in the morning, heat and humidity curl heavily through the halls and suites. Even without the constant hum of questions and anxieties in her mind, she wouldn't be able to sleep in this.

She doesn't tiptoe or try to move quietly to avoid waking Hafsah. After nearly three years of sharing a room, she's learned that almost nothing wakes Hafsah except Hafsah and her specifically chosen alarm. She's heard the stories of how long it took Hafsah and her mother to train her body into responding to that alarm, and it apparently involved a lot of buckets of ice water.

She supposes that counts as a form of aversion therapy. If you wake up to the alarm, you don't get drenched.

Not bothering with any lights, Rebecca changes into shorts and a sports bra, pulling on a tank top that belongs to Ellie but hasn't been returned because she hasn't washed it yet. She tucks her keys, phone, and wallet into her small cross-body purse and then, on a whim, ducks into the strap for her camera bag. She has to bite back a groan as she stretches to ease her bike bag down from the top shelf in the study space, her other hand shoved against the miscellany box to keep it from toppling onto her. Whoever invented folding bikes deserves a special space in heaven, she thinks; hers has certainly made her life easier, and Ellie, Luz, Keiko, and Susanna all have them as well. Delia is not allowed on a bike, given the number of bones she broke as a child trying and failing to learn, and Hafsah doesn't particularly like them.

Most of the time they walk around campus because it's easier than dealing with the bikes, but when they need to get farther off campus than the bars across University Avenue, the bikes are a godsend.

The dorm is quiet as she heads out into the hall and down the stairs. She can hear the buzzing of plug-in fans and a handful of snores and reminds herself that this, this is why she'll never have a hookup in a dorm room. She doesn't want to become one of the many greeted with reenactments of the sounds they make during sex.

Stepping outside is . . . not the relief she wanted it to be. It's already muggy and close, with the faint unpleasant smell of car oil burning off the roads. It makes her think of last year, when the smoke from the Sawgrass fire down in the Everglades drifted north along the interstate. Every now and then her parents and their siblings like to tell stories of the wildfire summer of 1997, when it felt like three-quarters of the state was aflame. A number of her family members were already in law enforcement by that point, and they all remember the piled-on shifts of volunteer firefighting as well as of directing traffic around newly closed roads or areas.

Her knee pops when she drops to a crouch, more sound than pain, as startling as it is. She winces and stretches it out. She gets so achy when she tries and fails to sleep, always holding herself too tensely, as if she can will sleep to take her if she just thinks hard enough. Because that can work. Shaking her head, she unfolds the bike and checks to make sure everything locks properly into place, then mounts and sets off.

She doesn't really have a destination in mind. She almost never does in this mood; she just has to get her body in motion to match her frantically spinning brain. She rides slowly in the gray morning, savoring what little breeze there is. She likes when the campus is busy and full of life, but there's something to this, she thinks. The gray light of earliest sunrise softens the edges of the newer buildings, fills out the shadows between the crumble-cornered bricks in the older ones. The history is easier to see when everything else is still.

A family of raccoons looks up from busily pillaging a cluster of trash cans behind one building. From the narrow steps near the door, a stray cat watches them, fur fluffed but not hissing. When she reaches the edge of campus, she keeps going and eventually turns out along Thirty-Fourth Street, riding along the graffiti wall. One of the panels makes her stop and pull her bike over to the grass so she can look without being in anyone's way.

The wall gets used for any number of things. Birthday greetings, PRIDE, graduation announcements, proposals, memorials, sports encouragements, even advertisements. Political messages tend to get painted over fairly quickly, as does anything offensive. So either these panels are new, or no one has felt the need to cover them up.

One of them has the famous pantie board shown, and each painted pair of panties has a girl's name on it. She frowns, wondering if the girls consented to that or if this is a violation all over again—and far more public. The boys' names are there, too, in a tall column framed by alligators. Another panel shows a cartoon gator sitting at a table, holding a fork and a knife, with a napkin tied around its throat. On the plate before it is another stack of names. **BON APPETIT** curves above the gator's head. She recognizes a couple of the names, but not because they've been gator bait. Near the center of the wall, not immediately next to the permanent panel but close to it, there's a section that looks to have been started as a memorial for Mountebanks. It's still visible under the words spray-painted over it and decidedly at odds with the hot-pink **THANK YOU** over his poorly painted face. Running across the bottom are yet more names.

Rebecca realizes with some shock that her name is among them. Maybe it was too much to hope for that his attack on her wouldn't make it into the general rumor mill, but somehow it's still unexpected.

She stares at it, the careful letters that shape her name—first name only, thank God—and the muscles in her chest throb with the memory of his fingers. Is there still catharsis if someone else names you?

Maybe it's just lost in the welter of emotions.

Toeing down the kickstand, she looks for oncoming cars before jogging across to the median for a better perspective. The damp grass tickles her shin as she kneels to carefully pull her camera out of its bag. Several of her journalism classes were heavily photography based and required them to get decent equipment. Those were a painful few weeks before the check for the excess scholarship money for the semester cleared and she had a little breathing room in her bank account again. Checking her settings, she takes several pictures of each panel connected to the recent deaths. This early in the morning there's no glare on them yet, no heat distortion rising from the road.

With that literal distance, it's easier to see the distinct styles across the panels. She can see the differences within each panel that show they were group efforts, but they were also done by different groups. Not just one angry girl but a fleet of them.

She looks through the viewfinder, wishing the distance offered some metaphorical clarity as well. As immersive as the contents of a picture can be, the nature of a photograph inherently places you outside of things. It removes some of the immediacy because it's a medium that spreads far beyond that moment.

The theory might be failing her.

What sends a group of girls spilling out in the middle of the night to paint rage and accusations on a wall? When there are still so many dangers all around, why is this worth the risk? She doesn't spend much time on this stretch of road, but the panels feel new, like angry tears still falling. Did it feel different for the first ones out, the courage and strength to scream in Technicolor, than it did for the ones who came after, the ones who could see proof that it wasn't just them? Or did they overlap, shoulder to shoulder in the streetlights?

Cradling the camera in her hands, she lowers it so she can look at the wall without a barrier. Without the distance. There are so many names. There are so many stories here.

She has digital subscriptions to a number of national newspapers and magazines, and she's read what they've been saying about the recent events. The involvement of the alligators makes it sensational, so they've spent a fair bit of time on that, where it often derails into diatribes about urbanization and habitat encroachment in ways that make it hard to know if they're rooting for the alligators or the developers; either way, they view the boys as unfortunate collateral. She usually forwards those articles to Susanna and Delia.

The others have focused on the boys as victims. So-and-so was studying this and wanted to be that. They came from this place, and here's their family. Here are their friends. Here are their hobbies and achievements and all their potential. Few of the articles have mentioned the stories swirling around campus. Even the ones that have only made oblique references to them, hesitating even to use the word *alleged* in order to state the accusations and reputations. Instead, they became "possibly controversial figures."

The pantie board is Jordan Pierce's most enduring legacy, a spur in the scars of countless girls, but she hasn't seen a single mention of it. Because the papers are afraid of getting sued? Or because the reporters don't think there's anything to it? Just harmless fun. Youthful energy. After all, they had such potential.

Once the camera is settled back in its bag, she returns to her bike and resumes her ride, heading back to campus, specifically to the concrete sign with its reigning alligator plush and collection of notes and trinkets. The university sent maintenance to take it down, and maybe five minutes passed before a new one was in its place. There are others, she knows, scattered around campus in a macabre parody of the sponsorship alligator statues decorated by local businesses and placed around the city. The wall may be bigger, but it's also easier to ignore, the panels changing so often the eye can just slide past. These are different—loud and out of place and impossible not to notice.

Someone has strung up a clothesline since the last time she looked at the display. Plastic pins hold a cluster of underwear with names and stories written in Sharpie, a confessional version of the fraternity's pantie board. A small plastic tub at the base of the sign holds markers, pins, and brand-new packs of underwear for anyone wanting to follow suit. She takes a breath, steadies herself, and brings her camera back out.

She's more careful with these pictures than with the ones she took on her phone the other day, stepping back to get the full image before narrowing in on individual notes. There are photos taped up there, too, which she doesn't remember seeing before. Girls at parties—or worse, in the ER or their rooms afterward, bruised and crying. She snaps a picture of one set that's been printed out as a before and after before she really notices the content.

She lowers the camera, holding it protectively against her belly, and stares at the paper taped to the concrete. There's shiny silver duct tape bordering all four sides to make sure it can't get blown off or easily torn away. The girl in the first half of the picture is beaming, wearing a pair of cat ears and a T-shirt for a local cat rescue promoting their semi-annual spay-and-neuter marathon. The second half shows the same girl, dull and faded in a hospital bed, eyes closed.

"Kacey Montrose," says a male voice a respectful distance away from her. She still flinches, even as she identifies the voice as Det Corby. "What happened to her was terrible."

Rebecca nods, even though it feels inadequate. She can still remember going to the hospital with flowers and copies of all of her class notes, so Kacey would have help catching up once she was released, and the feeling of shattering when Kacey's mother tearfully told her that the doctors didn't think that was ever going to happen. She remembers leaving the hospital and calling her father, sobbing, and how he drove two hours then and there to come pick her up and take her home for a few days so she could be with her family. She remembers spending the rest of the semester drowning, trying to support Kacey's parents.

The day it got around that there would be no charges, no trial—no justice—Det Corby met her at Steak 'n Shake, sitting with her all night in the cracked vinyl booth, holding her hand as she sobbed and raged. And suddenly she thinks of Ellie, safely sandwiched between her and Hafsah, just as helpless in that flood of emotions.

"What are you doing up so early?" Rebecca clears her throat again, still a little choked up from the reminder of her friend. Someday she'll be able to speak of Kacey without feeling the threat of tears. She's not sure that's actually a good thing.

"Couldn't sleep," he answers. "Thought I'd get a start to the day and examine this while no one was around."

"Need me to leave?"

"No, you're fine. It's not that kind of examination." He looks at her curiously but doesn't ask, even though she did.

So she offers. "Dorm's too hot to sleep. Riding along Thirty-Fourth made me think of this again."

He cringes, running a hand through his auburn hair. "The new sections."

"They're really something."

"I noticed one of them has your name on it."

She grimaces. "Wish you'd told me. I have no idea how long it's been there."

"You didn't give permission?"

"I have no idea who did it or how they heard the story." But it makes her wonder again about all those other names. Who'll feel relieved? Or betrayed? Does it offer healing or more harm?

He leans forward to read a turquoise Post-it laminated with lengths of clear tape because the writing tore through the paper in several places. "I can honestly say I've never had a case like this."

"Used to interviewing Gators rather than *gators*?"

"When's your next class?"

"Not till ten, but I'll need to be by the room to change and get my bag."

He looks at her as if just now noticing what she's wearing, his eyes lingering briefly on the shorts that are a bit shorter than anything she usually wears out of the dorm. When he flushes and looks away, she hides a smile. "Can I treat you to breakfast, then?"

"You keep feeding me," she notes, putting her camera away. "Is this a Hades and Persephone thing, or do you just think I'm too skinny?"

It's impossible to keep a straight face through his flurry of flustered protests, but she does try. When the grin finally breaks through, he stops, stares at her, and blushes again. "That was mean," he says.

"Maybe." She makes quick work of folding the bike up and zipping it into its bag. It's not light by any means, but it's not uncomfortable, either, as long as she remembers which way to sling it over her back.

It's comfortable walking beside him, she thinks. They have about the same stride, and he doesn't try to speed up and lengthen his steps as some men do. His hand brushes against hers between them several times, and she thinks that if she were a little braver, she might slide her palm against his and lace their fingers together and see how he reacts. Then again, maybe not. No matter how close her birthday is, she's still twenty, she's still an undergrad, and she's still tangentially connected to a murder case. Even if he does like her like that, he has to be careful.

She lets herself mourn that thought for a moment, then lets it go. She values his friendship and company, and she's not going to let wishing for more ruin what they already have.

"I was surprised not to get a second visit from Detective Gratton," she tells him as they walk. "When she said she'd be in touch, I thought she meant imminently."

He laughs and shakes his head. "Gratton is very protective of time—her own and other people's. If she contacts you again, it's because

191

she has specific things to ask you, not to check in. She's been all right, though?"

"She was perfectly polite and professional. Perhaps a little spooked from some of her previous interviews."

"I know the feeling."

"She hadn't talked to Ellie yet."

The involuntary snort has him covering his mouth, his shoulders shaking with laughter that's not silent as he would probably wish. "Wasn't actually what I meant, but fair enough."

"So what did you mean?"

"The city's in a strange mood right now; have you noticed?" he asks.

"I haven't been going out as much, but I know campus is fairly off the walls."

"More of the same, probably, if more visceral on campus. People have all sorts of reactions to death. I know that. Vindication or satisfaction is certainly one possible reaction, and I've encountered that before. But I've never worked a case with such a tide of . . . of . . . of public celebration, if that makes sense. I've certainly never worked a case with altars of suggested victims."

"Naming their sufferings to a universe that finally feels like it's listening," she murmurs. She thinks of the girls pelting a boy with tiny plastic alligators. It's more temporary than even the wall—but the same impulse.

His step stutters. He gives her a thoughtful look as he settles back into rhythm. "How are you doing?" he asks after a moment. "After Mountebanks?"

She absently rubs her chest, then slowly drops her hand back to her side when she sees his brow furrow with concern. "Physically I'm okay," she says honestly. Beyond that . . . "I guess all this has me thinking a lot about social contracts."

"Social contracts," he echoes, sounding nonplussed.

She's not sure if he's intrigued or simply being attentive, but she nods anyway. "All those unspoken agreements about how we're supposed to interact with each other, what is and isn't good manners, that kind of thing. Except a lot of those contracts are used to prop up, oh, not the status quo exactly, but . . . actually, yes," she decides. "Exactly the status quo. It props up sexism and racism and classism and mountains of other isms that are inherently flawed systems. The continued dominance of the status quo is dependent on the social contracts that reinforce some behaviors and discourage others."

"Okay, I'm with you so far."

"Social contracts are often contradictory," she continues. "A lot of them are designed to only benefit the people already in power. So, for example, if a man tells a woman she's pretty, one set of contracts insists she say thank you, while another insists she modestly demur. Neither allows for the possibility that she's uncomfortable or busy or at work. Neither allows for the attention being unwanted. 'Thank you' or 'Who, me?' Those are the acceptable answers, and there's absolutely no way to know which contract the man is invoking, so either one you choose, you could still be punished for it. Or you can refuse the contract as a whole, reject the attention, and also be punished." This time she notices her hand floating up toward her chest and catches herself before it can get there.

He nods, eyes flickering between her and the handful of cars moving past them on the road. He looks tired, she thinks, stretched too thin.

"You see them all the time," she says quietly. "When a man insists on buying a woman a drink she doesn't want, but somehow *she's* the rude one for declining. It's used to coerce dances and dates and sex because we're made to feel like we're failing societal expectation." She thinks of Ellie that night after the bar, spitting nails at being raised to be *polite*. "You see it when people with legitimate criticism and complaints are remonstrated for not being civil or nice, in the demands 'to elevate the discourse' or otherwise police the tone because policing the content is a losing game. If you try to convince people that there's no correct way to say a thing, maybe you can keep them from saying it."

"And you broke the social contract when you rejected Mountebanks."

"I never agreed to a contract that makes my wishes subordinate to any entitled asshole who comes along," she says. "We're victimized for our good manners, and we're punished for our bad manners, but now . . ." She waves a hand behind her in the general direction of the altar. "They're breaking the contracts, saying all the things society tells them they're supposed to be properly ashamed of, bringing it out into the open, and not apologizing for it. They're not minimizing their trauma to abide by arbitrary demands for tone. And that's amazing, but . . ."

"But?" he prompts.

"What happens next?"

"Something good, surely."

"You think?" She shrugs. "Maybe. Maybe the contracts can be overturned. Maybe the conversation can change. It's not something people are especially good at. Mostly I wonder if the effort is self-sustaining."

"Self-sustaining." He shakes his head, shifting to walk closer. The backs of their hands rub against each other as they walk. "Now I'm a little lost."

"This is happening because of the deaths," she points out. "Whoever's doing this, why they're doing this—only they know that. But the actions create a story, intentional or not, that this is revenge. This is warning. For the first time ever it's the rapists and scumbags who need to be afraid, not the girls, and that gives the girls the courage to step up and scream. To break the contracts and know that just this once, the boys might be too afraid to punish them for it. Do you think it has enough momentum to continue without more death?"

He looks stricken, and she almost regrets saying it. Only almost, because he did ask, but he's one of the good ones.

"I hadn't really thought of it like that," he admits.

"What's your captain think?"

He snorts, some of the color coming back to his face. "He's come around to the notion that these aren't accidents. There's coincidence, and then there's our victim pool. He went from loudly declaring that I was wasting my time trying to investigate something that wasn't a case to loudly declaring that I needed to hurry up and solve it before any more fine young men die."

"Fine young men?" she echoes incredulously. "Has he read up on the victims?"

"He has. He was also instrumental in the lack of consequences for a couple of them," he says. She appreciates that he's trying to be delicate or professional or something, but she's shocked breathless by the snap of fury in her gut. "I'll be honest; I care less about these 'fine young men' than I do about catching whoever this is before they get someone innocent by mistake or before they unravel entirely and go on a spree."

"Aren't they already on a spree?"

"Right now they have a type. What happens when they lose sight of that?"

They stop short of the crosswalk, staring at the light post ahead of them. Or, more important, the real live alligator on its back legs, plastered along the thick pole like it's climbing a fence or tree, the crosswalk sign digging into the underside of its jaw. Its tail curves through the corner. Not a coil like a cat's, she notes in the back of her mind, just a curve. The rest of her mind is urging her to slowly back away.

"Maybe not Starbucks," Det Corby says, far too calm.

"Maybe call animal control?"

"That too."

She keeps an eye on the alligator as the detective makes the call. She's not thrilled to be this close to it, but at the same time she's a little bit grateful that its appearance brought a halt to the conversation. It's one thing to talk things through with Hafsah, bouncing around partially formed ideas to refine them into something that holds the meaning she wants them to. When she does it with anyone else, she has a lamentable tendency to trip over her words and end up with her foot in her mouth.

Honestly. Can the girls be brave if the boys stop dying . . . ? That was not at all what she meant.

Was it?

Well. At the very least, it's probably not the best thought to share with the investigating detective. To do his job, he can't doubt whether solving the crime will do more harm than good.

She glances at him. He's scowling at the alligator, his foot tapping and his phone to his ear. He lifts his other hand and extends his middle finger in the reptile's direction.

She stifles a giggle. He'll be fine.

23

There are bits of a story swirling through Rebecca's head; she hasn't managed to thread them onto a spindle yet. It's frustrating, but she also knows if she tries to force a story before it's ready, not only will nothing useful come of it, but she probably won't be able to go back and rework it into anything better. Unfortunately, it's also left her too unfocused to try to do anything else just yet.

Restless and irritable, she pokes around the dorm room. Crochet is out; she can't sit still long enough. She can't study, can't read, can't nap. Can she eat?

No, because they've left off grocery shopping too long, and there's very little in the mini-fridge or the cabinet above it.

Now there's a thought.

God, she hates when her brain has a squirrel day.

She runs down the list of her suitemates to see if she should invite anyone along or ask them if they need anything. Hafsah is in class, Susanna and Delia are out at one of the rivers for a lab, but she's not sure about the other three. Rather than texting them, she heads into the bathroom between their suites and stops dead at the sight of Ellie perched across the sides of neighboring sinks, clad in bra and underwear and reading something off her phone.

"Hi?"

"Need something?"

Okay, then. "I was going to head to the store. Need anything or want to come?"

"Oh, thank fuck, yes."

"Why are you hanging out in the bathroom?" she can't help but ask, walking up to Ellie's side. "It's not noticeably cooler in here."

"Luz and Keiko are having sex, and the wall is too thin to stay in the room without hearing it," Ellie replies. "I didn't want to hear it."

"Okay, but the bathroom?"

"I also didn't want to get dressed."

It's on the tip of Rebecca's tongue that she could have just come through and hung out in Rebecca's room or study space, but she doesn't say it. Ellie does things Ellie's way, and that's fine. "Well, you will need to get dressed if you want to come to Publix. They have rules about that." She reaches out and gently touches a welt on Ellie's thigh. "We can get you some oatmeal lotion or something for all those mosquito bites."

Ellie whines and pushes her head against Rebecca's shoulder like a cat. "Thank you. They just won't leave me alone at night. Are we walking or biking?"

"Biking. Bring your cooler bag?"

"Meet you downstairs."

Leaving the bathroom, Rebecca grabs socks and shoes to put on, then finds her purse, her bike bag, and her grocery bag. All the girls in their suite have one, a gift from Susanna's mother when they came back from winter break first year. Meant to be worn like a backpack, it has a firm-sided cooler as the base and a sizable bag on top. When Susanna's mom dropped her off and handed out the bags, she watched her daughter bemusedly as Susanna went on and on about how eco-responsible it was and how it was using so much less plastic and they could reuse it constantly. When she finally ran out of steam, her mother looked around and said she thought it would just be easier than carrying bags the normal way.

Rebecca's still not sure if she was serious or if she was teasing her daughter.

Outside, she settles into a patch of shade to set up her bike. Perhaps it's just a leftover something from the pictures she took this morning or the conversation with Det Corby over coffee, but she's unsettled by the number of girls walking around with small gators painted on their cheeks. Usually that's just for football season, maybe basketball season. It's not an everyday sort of thing. She's heard stories of an enterprising graphic design student with a screen press; she sees the results now, as a group of girls passes her wearing shirts that feature a cartoon alligator framed by text that reads **FOR A GOOD MEAL CALL**, followed by different names. The names, she notes, are handwritten in Sharpie. Some of the shirts have more than one name.

It makes her think of the conversation with Hafsah, with the assumption—or hope, maybe—that the murderer is genuinely trying to effect a change with their actions. Punish rapists for their actions, make them afraid as everyone else always has to be, maybe even force a shift in how everyone else regards them. She wonders who's naive enough to think it could work.

One of her uncles is still texting her at 6:37 every morning, *Remember to zigzag!* But now his wife texts her at 6:38 with *Or just shove the nearest boy in the gator's direction and saunter away.* She knows her aunt well enough to know that it's still an expression of concern for her safety, couched in the sharp humor that makes her the best to sit beside at weddings, christenings, funerals, and other serious occasions, but it certainly got a strange look from Det Corby when this morning's repetition arrived.

What would the reactions be if the deaths had nothing to do with alligators? Or if the victims were young women? Or, well, anyone but white men, really. White straight men expect to feel safe in the world, whether they consciously think that way or not. What would the reactions be if the victims weren't complete and utter assholes?

She remembers the fear that lurked through campus after the first few deaths, the ones that felt like accidents. When everyone thought it was just encroachment, and there were no talks yet of a serial killer or a vigilante or whatever they're calling the murderer on Twitter. She's been more interested in what the news is covering than what they're calling it, and so many competing hashtags have sprung up that it's impossible to skim them all and have time for anything else.

"All right, bitch, let's do this!"

She sighs and rolls her eyes. "Really?"

Ellie just grins and mounts her bike. "I'll buy you a cookie."

"Promise?"

"Promise."

The grocery store isn't far, thankfully. They don't see any surprise alligators at the intersections either. This morning Rebecca was actually the one to get the coffee, as Det Corby had to keep the gator in sight until animal control could come get it. They sat on a low section of the brick-and-concrete corner sign, watching and talking and wincing whenever a passing car nearly lost control at the sight of the beast. She's still grateful that the alligator seemed more interested in hugging the pole—or, more likely, trying to climb the unnatural tree—than in crossing the road, or it could have been a complicated morning.

She knows hitting a deer can royally fuck up a car. She's pretty happy not knowing what hitting an alligator will do.

When they get to the store, she makes Ellie buy her the cookie right off so she can eat it while they wander the aisles. She doesn't really have a list in mind. It's probably not quite as bad as shopping hungry, but it does mean they tend to backtrack as they think of things. It's the type of chaos that usually pisses Ellie off. Today, however, perhaps in light of Rebecca's obviously squirrely brain, it cracks her up, and they place bets on how many times they'll cross the store before they get everything they can think of.

As they draw near the pharmacy for the eighth or ninth time, Rebecca ducks down one of the shorter aisles and grabs a tube of ointment to throw into their cart.

Ellie reads the label and looks up at her. "Will this help with the itches?"

"Between that and some Benadryl, it should help some with the eight million mosquito bites on you," Rebecca says.

"Oh, like you've never been covered in bites."

"Mosquitoes tend to leave me alone. Apparently I don't taste good, so no one tries to eat me."

The words are out of her mouth just as she understands how they can sound, and sure enough, that's how Ellie takes them, laughing so hard she loses her balance on the cart and falls to the ground. The cart shoots forward, and Rebecca barely manages to grab it before it can crash into the shelves. She blushes at the looks from other shoppers, some of them merely curious, some judgmental and disapproving.

It could be worse, she thinks. They could be standing in front of the condoms and K-Y. Or Det Corby could have heard it. She can still feel the heat in her cheeks and chest, but she leans against the cart and smiles down at Ellie, who's now wheezing and clutching her side. Even if it's at her expense, she's happy to see Ellie enjoying something that doesn't involve violence.

It's early evening as they ride back to Sledd, everything tucked neatly away except for one brown plastic bag swaying from Ellie's handlebar because they couldn't fit the two bags of chips without crushing them. Each of them also has a two-liter bottle tucked into their shorts, the caps nestled safely under the front joint of their bras to keep them from dropping. They left their bikes chained outside while they were in the store; now they're both wearing gloves to keep a thin shield between themselves and the painfully hot metal beside the handlebar grips. Welcome to Florida, where you can get second-degree burns opening a door.

Rebecca sends Ellie upstairs with the grocery bags to put the cold things and the sodas away as quickly as possible—there are limits to the miracles the coolers can perform—and crouches down to fold away both bikes. They need to be washed, she thinks absently, trying not to get covered in grass from her bike or dried mud and dust from Ellie's. One of the car washes might be bicycle friendly; she'll have to ask around.

With both bikes put away in their bags, she straightens up and reaches for her purse to get her ID out. The faint call of her name stops her. Turning around, she doesn't immediately see anyone. That's not unusual, though. She's fairly tall and carrottopped, so people tend to see her before she sees them.

After a crowd on the sidewalk passes, she sees Det Corby walking toward her, but it was definitely not his voice she heard, unless someone messed with his jockstrap. Then she sees a female sheriff's deputy behind him, one arm across Delia's back, Susanna on Delia's other side. Both Susanna and Delia look spooked as hell.

Rebecca grabs the bike bags and runs toward her friends. "Are you okay? What happened?"

As soon as she's close enough, Delia bursts into tears and throws herself against Rebecca, hugging her for dear life. "I didn't sign up for this!" she wails into Rebecca's chest. "If I'd wanted to touch dead people, I would have gone premed! I just wanted to get a water sample to check for tannins! I didn't want to find a dead body!"

"Part of a dead body," Susanna says helpfully.

With another wail, Delia trails off into sobs that quickly spread a wet patch across the front of Rebecca's shirt. Shooting Susanna a stern look, Rebecca eases the bike bags down so she doesn't disrupt Delia, then gently wraps her arms around her friend and sways her back and forth in wordless comfort. She glances between Det Corby and the deputy. "Am I allowed to ask for clarification?"

"Delia braced herself between a handful of cypress knees so she could get a water sample from between them," Susanna tells her without waiting for the officers to answer. "Her hand bumped into something. She thought it was just vegetation, but when she pulled her hand away, it bobbed up to the surface. It was a leg. Part of a leg. Like, from the knee down. Ish."

Susanna looks like she's about to shake apart. She's carrying her own bags as well as Delia's, backpacks and sacks of lab equipment to bring back samples, but Rebecca holds out one arm anyway, and Susanna crashes into the two of them, burrowing her face into Delia's hair. Susanna's been strong this far for Delia's sake; it doesn't mean she was any less shocked by the event.

She looks up at the detectives, feeling queasy. "Have you, um . . . found more?" she asks.

Det Corby wobbles one hand. No, not Det Corby, she thinks—Detective Corby. If there was a body, he's on duty now. "More? Yes. All of it? Not so much. We'll be trawling the river for a while."

Rebecca closes her eyes. "Well. That makes it official: we are not tubing down the Ichetucknee for my birthday this year."

Delia and Susanna both nod and cling more tightly. Given everything else going on, no one in the suite had gotten on top of their usual plans. They missed their usual fall back-to-school trip because it had been scheduled for the weekend after Kacey was attacked. They always timed their spring trip to celebrate both Rebecca's birthday and the end of the semester, but this year . . . they could wait, she thought. They could reschedule to sometime after alligator-courting season.

"This was the Santa Fe, away from where the Ichetucknee flows in, so you should be fine. But, ah . . ." He hesitates, which is enough to make her open her eyes and look at him. "It wouldn't be the worst thing if you went to one of the springs instead."

"Because they're colder?"

"Right."

"I am not going anywhere near water ever again in my life," Delia mutters, muffled by the shirt.

That's probably fair. Extreme, certainly, and unlikely to stick, but fair.

She wonders if they found the right parts to identify the person, the way they struggled with the Lake Alice body, but she doesn't ask. Besides the problem of it being macabre to ask, they can't tell her who it is even if they think they know. They need to verify identity, then notify the family. One thought overrides the rest: What happens to the investigation if it's one of the names on the wall? Or on a shirt or one of the offering clusters? She frowns, trying to spin that out into something more coherent.

"Finals start next week," Susanna says quietly. "Most of the school will be gone after that."

Rebecca glances at Detective Corby, who nods grimly. Everyone's been so focused on what happens after courting season is done, no one's been asking what happens to an investigation when both your victim pool and suspect pool scatter for the summer. What will that mean for Detective Corby?

"Come on, you two," she tells her suitemates. "Let's get you upstairs and cleaned up. Ellie just put away brand-new ice cream, and we'll lock the hall doors so no one can get in to bother you with questions once the news gets around."

The deputy clears her throat, her dark-blonde hair scraped back into a severe bun. "Miss—"

"We won't spread it around," Rebecca says immediately. "But it was a class trip. They drove out with someone. And . . . I mean. Everyone's really invested in what's going on."

"We don't know for sure yet that it's connected to the ongoing situation."

Delia snorts.

Detective Corby grimaces. "A toddler died this afternoon in Broward County," he says, voice soft. "Every county is on notice to share information about alligator-related incidents."

"What happened?" she asks, trying not to picture any of her baby cousins in place of this other child.

"Her grandmother left her in the backyard in a kiddie pool for a few minutes while she went inside to get them a snack and something to drink. Next thing she knows, the child is screaming. She raced back with a shotgun that didn't do much but piss the gator off. A neighbor saw what was happening and called 911. The girl died en route; the grandmother is in critical condition. She's lost the one leg for sure, might yet lose the other."

Delia starts crying again. Right, she found a leg. Rebecca rubs circles into her friend's back and resolves to hug all the youngest cousins at least three times each as soon as she gets home. She can't even imagine losing any of them.

"We can't assume," Detective Corby finishes awkwardly.

Rebecca nods. "Do you need anything more from them?"

"Not at the moment. We wanted to make sure they got safely home."

"And you're off back to the river." To look for the missing parts, she doesn't say, and search for evidence. How do you even start with something like that, when you have everything upriver to worry about? Downriver, too, really; there's no reason to expect that the alligators wouldn't move things about.

He shrugs, fidgeting with his tie.

"Put some sunscreen on."

He gives her an astonished look that slowly shifts to a reluctant smile. "Take care of them, Rebecca."

"I will." She gives her suitemates a squeeze and returns the smile. "Thank you for bringing them back. Both of you."

The deputy glances between the girls and Detective Corby but gives a friendly nod that doesn't say much of what she's thinking. No one in the suite has been questioned about the alligator incidents, Rebecca reminds herself, and he isn't the detective on Mountebanks's case; there's no reason for the deputy to make a report of unprofessionalism.

Taking a deep breath, Rebecca pulls away from Delia so she can grab the bike bags and rearrange her support of her friend. Susanna sticks to Delia's other side. "Let's get you two inside."

24

It takes hours to truly settle Delia and Susanna, and Rebecca's pretty sure the only reason they ultimately manage it is because the two girls finally have no energy left to freak out. Hafsah, Luz, and Keiko are still in the room with them, a massive puppy pile on a bed too small to hold five grown women. They kicked Ellie out in under half an hour when her good mood, made even brighter by the news of another gator bait, led her to rattle off long lists of possible identities; both Keiko and Delia started crying. Rebecca hasn't seen Ellie since.

For her part, Rebecca still has a story swirling through her mind. She slides a notebook between her laptop and camera and takes them out to the third-floor lounge, where she can spread out and possibly talk to herself without waking her traumatized and finally sleeping friends. The coffee table pushes aside easily, and a search of the couches turns up a grand total of two throw pillows to put under her. It's not necessarily comfortable, but it's enough.

The laptop dings when it recognizes the plugged-in camera, bringing up the day's pictures. She scrolls through them slowly, reading each note on what she can only think of as the altar anymore. To a vengeful god? Or a healing one? One of the pictures grabs her attention, and she zooms in carefully, letting the image settle. What is it about this one? Why does it feel familiar? She pulls her knees up to her chest, clasping her hands at her ankles, and studies it.

It's the handwriting. Tall and thin, with dainty little loops and curves anywhere a loop or curve is feasible; she knows she's seen that handwriting before. When she sat down, in fact: it's up on the dead-pool poster that Kerry elected not to remove, because if it stays some-where public, she can at least keep an eye on things. This is an offering from someone here on Rebecca's floor.

"What are you doing?"

Her focus narrowed on the screen, she flinches at the sudden sound, nails digging into her ankles, and looks up. Jules stands there, her dark-brown hair in a tangled mess down her back. "You startled me."

"I see that." Grinning, Jules clambers over the back of the closest couch and flops onto the cushions. "So what are you doing?"

After a moment's thought, she turns the laptop so Jules can see the screen. "Whoever wrote this lives on our floor."

"Yeah." When Jules is debating with herself, she doesn't bite her lower lip like most people; she bites the upper, which makes her look, depending on the rest of her mood, like a pissed-off shih tzu or a slow bulldog. "It's Lori's handwriting."

"Lori, the one who always wears sweatshirts no matter how badly everyone else is dying?"

"That's the one. We were suitemates last year, but we all got jum-bled up for this year."

Rebecca looks back at the screen. *He told me I deserved it,* the note says, the script delicate and almost fragile. *He said what did I expect, dressing like a whore. I was wearing a T-shirt and jeans. Now they call me prude. We never win. We never can.*

There isn't a name on there, not hers, not even his. She doesn't wonder that it's anonymous; almost all of them are. But she doesn't name him. Isn't that part of it? The shaming, the accusation? She flips through several more pictures and realizes that a good half of them don't have the names of the perpetrators.

"You have that face."

"What face?" she asks, glancing over at Jules.

"The one you get in classes when you're about to tear someone's argument to shreds. If you were a cat, your ass would be up in the air and wiggling. What are you about to pounce on?"

"Why do girls tell each other stories in bathrooms?"

"To keep each other safe when we can," Jules answers promptly, "and to show they're not alone when we can't."

"So why are we now telling stories out loud?"

"Because . . . holy shit." Jules laughs, hands pressed against her cheeks. "Because we know someone is listening. We don't know who it is, but it's obviously someone. Someone is listening, for once, finally, and . . . and . . ."

"How many times have we seen articles where a cop or a lawyer or a judge says we can't let 'one night of fun' ruin a fine young man's life?"

"Too many." Sliding down to the floor next to Rebecca, Jules leans against her and clicks to the next picture. "Their scholarships, their degrees, their futures . . . we never factor in. They don't want to hear our stories because they've already decided on their own."

He was dating my roommate, another note says. *He kept trying to sleep with me, too, or creep on me in the shower. When I complained to her, he told her I was coming on to him and she kicked me out.*

"We don't report because no one's listening," says Rebecca. "No one cares. We don't report because the optimistic outcome is that we get ignored. Too often we're punished for it, in ways they never are. Now we know someone's listening. Someone cares. It's so much easier to be brave when there's the chance something good can come of it."

"Crocodile courage?"

"Something like."

Greg Samuels offered me a ride home from class because it was raining. Then he said if I didn't give him a blowjob, he'd dump me off on the side of the road. I had to walk six miles in a thunderstorm to get home, but he still told all his friends I'd blown him. Now his friends won't stop texting because they think I'm easy.

"They're not just talking to the murderer," Rebecca says slowly, still piecing it all together. "They're talking to each other. It's the bathroom stories—but finally out in public. Warning each other, commiserating with each other. We're not in this alone. And more . . ." She bites her lip, testing the new ground. "You read the papers for classes; how many have mentioned the boys as predator? None," she answers herself, even as Jules shakes her head with a frown. "But people across the country are looking at Gainesville because of the deaths, and whoever started these altars, the panels on the wall, they're giving everyone something else to see. They're speaking and demanding people listen."

"We took our voices back."

She nods, thinking on the word *we*. It is a group effort, she realizes, not only in the literal sense. Without other girls coming forward, without that whisper becoming a roar, who would notice? "That's why all of this feels so different. It's not just that the boys are finally the ones scared; it's that we're finally the ones talking."

"God." Resting her head on Rebecca's shoulder, Jules lets out an explosive breath. "So how do you make that into a story?"

"By talking to some of the people who left offerings, if they'll agree. Complete anonymity if they want it. Let's see if we can give megaphones to students at other universities." Her fingers itch and twitch until she pulls her pen out of the spiral binding of her notebook, flipping the book open to a blank page. She can't care about how wretched her handwriting is right now, skipping letters and even whole words as she scrambles to get down everything they just said.

"My phone's in my room," Jules says, pushing to her feet. "Let me get it and send out some texts."

"Jules." She waits until she's got the thought finished on the page, then looks up at her patient friend. "Don't push anyone if they don't want to, but if they're at all interested, promise them I'll be respectful. Tell them about Mountebanks if you think it will help. I'm not interested in exploiting them or in splashing their pain all over the place."

"If they wrote one of the notes, Rebecca, they've already taken the extra step of talking out loud. Telling you in private is just another story from the bathrooms."

She nods, mulling on that, and keeps writing as Jules jogs off to her room.

Lori comes to the lounge just a few minutes later, wearing a massive hoodie that half drowns her and a pair of baggy cotton pajama pants. She brings with her another girl, petite and brunette. Rebecca recognizes the second girl; she was the one who talked about the Cooper cousins that morning around the televisions. Rebecca wants to ask for her name, feels bad not knowing it, but also knows that this isn't the right context. If she's promising anonymity, that means from her, too, if that's what's desired.

"Do you really think it will help?" Lori asks instead of a greeting.

"I think that help or not, we have about half a second to try."

"And you're going to do this instead of studying for finals?"

"If I don't know it by now, I'm not going to," Rebecca says with a shrug. "This is more important."

Lori doesn't look entirely convinced, but the other girl walks around to sit on the couch, hands pressed between her knees. "Can we read it when you're done? Before you do anything with it?"

"Absolutely."

"Okay." She takes a deep breath, then meets Rebecca's eyes. "I left one of the candles. I printed off a picture of the Coopers to tape behind it and wrote *Thank You* across the top of the paper. I felt like I could breathe for the first time in forever. I'll always have my scars, but now I don't have to be afraid of seeing the two of them on campus. I don't have to have panic attacks the first two weeks of a new semester at the thought of possibly sharing classes with them. It's a gift."

Rebecca spends nearly ten minutes speaking with her, watching the girl's shoulders gradually relax when there's no pushing for details. Rebecca doesn't have a picture of the candle—it was cleared away with the first installment—but the girl knows someone who does, and she promises to get it to her. Lori, too, slowly unwinds as she watches the interview, and by the time they've run out of things to say, she agrees to tell her own story. She's crying when she's done, but she also looks like a weight's been lifted.

Rebecca takes Lori's hands and holds them, not sure if a hug would be welcome but wanting to give her some kind of comfort for her strength. Lori gives her a watery smile in return.

After Lori comes a girl from Thomas Hall, bringing with her a pair of girls from Murphree. Others follow them, always in at least a pair if they come from outside Sledd, even if their companion doesn't have a story of their own to share. An entire gaggle of girls comes from one of the sorority houses on the Row, every single one of them wearing tank tops or T-shirts with their letters. Rebecca remembers them; they're the same ones who told her about Jordan Pierce. Only two of them share personal stories, their sisters wrapped around them for support, but they all talk about painting one of the panels on the Thirty-Fourth Street wall. Rebecca's not entirely surprised to learn it's the pantie-board shaming. They promise that every girl's name on the panel was painted with full consent, and one of the knots in Rebecca's belly vanishes.

There are excellent, healthy Greek houses. She does know that. But—they have much quieter reputations than the terrible ones. It's hard not to think of the entire system as being corrupt. Those who pledge, even if they follow the best behaviors, have to reckon with the reflexive response of someone else learning they're in a house. For those who love their chapters, who work to make it something to be proud of, the stains on the Row are a blow to the heart. These girls love their sisterhood and take it seriously, she can see that. What Pierce and his friends do offends them not just as women but as fellow Greeks.

They offer her a picture of the wall with the whole sorority posed around the edges in pride, but Rebecca declines. She has a good photo of the panel itself, and she really does want to do this without naming or displaying any of the women involved. It's stronger, she thinks, when it can literally be anyone. Every now and then she can hear Jules talking to someone in the hall, the world's strangest social secretary as she holds some people back so that others can have privacy in talking to Rebecca. Not everyone wants or cares about the privacy, but they're good about respecting the ones who do.

No one seems to care that it's the middle of the night or that finals start on Monday or that most of them don't know Rebecca or her personal ethics. Someone's promising to listen, to let them be as angry as they need to be, and then share that with the world.

Her brain is spinning with all their stories, and no matter how many notes she takes, her fingers still itch with the need to write. She has a feeling she's not sleeping until this is done, whatever that might mean for her exams.

She hears someone come in, and she holds up one finger so she can finish scrawling notes from the group that just left. A paper cup is set on the floor in front of her, warmth radiating out against her knee, and she looks up to see a girl sinking onto the very edge of the couch, like she expects to jump up and race off at any second.

Linsey Travers.

Rebecca blinks, her brain still half in the previous story. She finishes her notes, tucks her pen behind one ear, and studies the girl who was one of Kacey's friends from high school. She hasn't actually seen Linsey since a couple of weeks after Kacey was attacked. Suddenly she just wasn't in classes anymore, and a few people who knew her said she'd withdrawn and gone home for the semester. At that point, Rebecca wasn't in much of a position to care, entirely focused on Kacey and her family and her own raging grief.

Linsey clears her throat. "Hot chocolate, right? You always got that when we met to work on that project."

Nodding slowly, Rebecca reaches for the drink and inhales the steam. Part of her, the part that spent a good measure of her sophomore fall wanting to shove the girl in front of a bus out of sheer annoyance, says not to trust it, but isn't that what all of this is? Girls trusting each other? She takes a sip and tastes vanilla, caramel, and cinnamon. When she takes a longer drink, something releases in Linsey, and Linsey settles back into the couch. Rebecca tries not to make too clear a comparison to the girl who bought Ellie the thank-you drink. "I didn't know you were back at school," she says finally.

Linsey nods, fingers lacing and unlacing around her own cup. "I came back, but I, um . . . I left the journalism program. Went over to social work instead."

Thinking of Daphne, Rebecca wonders how many social workers go into the field because of trauma.

"I wasn't at the party," Linsey says abruptly, the words spilling over each other in a rush. "That party. I wasn't there."

Rebecca doesn't really know what to say to that.

Then again, maybe Linsey doesn't need her to say anything just yet, because after a fraction of a second, she continues. "Kacey told me she'd invited you, and I . . . I really did not want to spend any time with you. I spent most of that project wanting to stab you through the eye with a pencil."

Choking on her drink, Rebecca desperately tries to swallow before she spews it out over the papers and computer. She covers her mouth with a hand, shoulders shaking with laughter, and meets Linsey's eyes.

The other girl gives her a rueful smile. "Yeah, it always seemed mutual. I didn't want to spend time with you, and I didn't want to put Kacey in the middle, so I didn't go. And then . . ." The amusement fades. "I put up her picture," she admits. "I felt so damn guilty that I wasn't there that night. Which is stupid—I know it's stupid; a whole lot of therapy has told me again and again that that's stupid."

"I'm reasonably sure your therapist didn't tell you that you were stupid."

"That's what it boiled down to. I could barely function, which is why my parents brought me home. When I heard what happened, I was so angry I couldn't see straight. How could they . . ." She shakes her head, visibly pulling herself together. "Our friends left her outside the hospital. How could they do that? How could they be so selfish? And then my parents told me you were with the Montroses, helping them, and I felt guilty all over again because I practically grew up at the Montroses' house. We had parties and sleepovers and homework sessions and Girl Scout meetings *all the time*, and I joked about calling her parents Mom and Dad, and I couldn't . . . I didn't . . . I couldn't go to the hospital." She stares down at her drink. Hazelnut mocha, if Rebecca remembers correctly. They traded off buying each other fancy drinks during the project because it was the only way to make things bearable. "I couldn't go to the hospital and see Kacey like that or see her parents so distraught, so I went to their house instead. I cleaned, did laundry, made meals to pack away. Threw away the meals when they went bad because her parents were hardly ever home. Took care of the dogs and cats. Checked the mail."

"They appreciated that," Rebecca murmurs. They did; she remembers them talking about it, how much easier it made things on the occasions Rebecca could convince them to go home for a few hours.

"I hated you even more for a while. You were doing what I couldn't."

"But you were doing what you could."

Brown eyes tear bright, Linsey nods. "It took time. It . . . it's still taking time. I'm still in therapy. Settling into the new program, making new friends. And tonight, Jules texted me."

Rebecca glances beyond the couch to the hall. Jules looks her in the eyes and lifts an eyebrow. Rebecca resists the urge to roll her eyes, because she knows it wouldn't be well received (or correctly interpreted), but really. She made a promise to listen, to not judge. That wasn't predicated on who she does or does not like.

"I wasn't sure if I should come," says Linsey, "but . . . I thought Kacey would like it. If, I mean, you know . . ."

If she had a way to know about it, yes, Kacey would like it. Rebecca smiles to show she understands. "People should remember her," she says.

"Kacey helped people. It meant a lot to her that she could. It's why I changed majors. I want to help people in her name."

Rebecca holds out her hand, and after a moment Linsey takes it. "I wish you all the best with that," Rebecca says sincerely.

"Thanks. You too. With this, I mean." Getting to her feet, Linsey lifts her cup in an awkward salute and hurries around the couch and down the hall.

Jules leans against the wall, arms crossed over her chest, with her phone still in one hand. "Did it help any?"

"I didn't blame her, Jules," she says softly, in case anyone else is coming down the hall. "I already knew she wasn't at the party."

Jules opens her mouth, closes it, and scowls. "You did?"

"I did. If she needed to tell me that, then I'm glad she got the chance. But I never blamed her for it." She smiles wryly and takes another sip of hot chocolate. "I do recognize the irony in neither of us being there for Kacey because we didn't want to see each other, but that's . . . that's not our fault."

"You're doing a lot of emotional labor tonight," notes Jules. "Are you okay to keep going? Or do you want me to send people home?"

"Don't send anyone home." She takes a deep breath, shakes herself out, and pulls her pen from behind her ear. "I'll listen to anyone who wants to speak."

"Okay. But I'm giving you five minutes to pee and stretch. Go."

Grinning, Rebecca obeys. She checks on Delia and Susanna while she's in the suite, but they're still fast asleep on the bed with Hafsah, Luz, and Keiko curled around them. She has no idea where Ellie is. Just for tonight, when she has so many other stories crowding into her mind, she's going to choose not to worry about that. When she gets back, there's already a trio of girls sitting on the couch, leaning into each other. She recognizes the girl in the middle, not because she knows her but because there was a picture of her on the altar, dancing in shorts and a checked shirt tied under her bust, a sash across her chest that read "Bridesmaid." She has the sash in her lap now, torn and stained. Rebecca sits down and prepares to listen.

As soon as it's light, she checks with Jules to make sure no one else is on their way, then scrambles to get ready for the day. It's still painfully early when she rides her bike away from Sledd, aiming for the library and one of the private study rooms, where she'll be left alone with her thoughts and the voices of all the girls who came to speak to her. Papers cover the surface of the table, pages and pages of notes, lists of the dead men and their dates of discovery, a sheet with the photos she wants to use and how. She settles into the chair before her laptop, puts on her headphones without music to block out everything but the sound of her own heartbeat, and sets to work.

She's vaguely aware of a visit from Jules, bringing her coffee and a couple of donuts, so hot and fresh that the sugar glaze is still oozing down the sides. Hafsah brings her lunch and eats with her and extracts a promise that she won't walk back to the dorm alone if she's still here after dark. She writes and rewrites furiously, balancing voice and structure, desperately trying to ensure that the story on the page is the one she wants to tell and not yet one more piece of drivel that extolls the supposed virtues of the dead. She's talking about the living.

Ellie brings dinner, and eventually she's going to wonder why no one cares that so much food has been brought into the library today, because it is not her experience that finals week causes the librarians to relax their rules. As Rebecca wolfs down a quesadilla and chips, Ellie reads the current draft of the article. If she were the slightest bit less hungry, she'd be concerned at the way that Ellie silently goes back to the top to start reading again as soon as she's finished, without showing any hint of her reaction. But there are carbs and proteins and a soda to give her brain back some of the sugars it's now craving.

"It needs a few edits," Ellie says eventually, "but I think this may be the best thing you've ever written."

Rebecca blushes. Actual compliments from Ellie are rare, especially about work. "You think?"

"I do. You've captured something important. Elusive. I don't know how you did it, but you manage to portray everyone as vindicated without tipping over into saying the assholes needed to die, which is probably a pretty good line to tiptoe if you want it to be taken seriously. Are you submitting this somewhere or giving it to the senior with the crime blog?"

"I thought I'd run it past a couple of profs tonight, see if they have thoughts. Strike while the iron is hot and all that; there's a limited window for pieces about these events. The news will move on quickly enough."

"Even if people keep dying?" Ellie asks idly.

Because that's not a concerning thought at all. "People get used to things," she says quietly. "Even terrible things. There's only so long the media is willing to pay attention before it becomes a footnote or a page forty-six article."

The page of email addresses for the participants is folded over and taped for the sake of privacy, but she scribbled more addresses on the exposed back as she thought of them. Ellie runs down the list, stopping at one of the names and tapping it. "You're sending it to Det Corby?"

"He's the detective on the case. I know he's getting a lot of attention because of it—"

"You mean because there are no leads?"

"—and it's not a bad idea to give him a heads-up that I'm contributing to the current media frenzy. I mean, not that this will spark a fresh deluge, but . . ."

"Get this to the right outlet, and there might be." Ellie taps on his name again. "I know you've been reading tweets and articles, because you're you. Florida Man has been a running joke around the country for, shit, decades? How old is social media? But people are seriously weirded out by the campus's reaction to all of . . . this." She makes a vague gesture that somehow encapsulates both the deaths and the altars. "This gives them an explanation that makes sense and doesn't belittle two very different dominant feelings of fear and justification. Unless you have substantive changes to make, send out this draft for critique. You can do the small edits later as you fold in responses."

"Okay. Thanks."

It takes her a little while to stick the format correctly, making sure the photos will be precisely where she wants them. She's got software for that, but she has to make her own specifications this time, not abide by professor-assigned specifications. Finally she sends out a flurry of emails, each one separate despite how many names there are. She made promises, and she intends to keep them.

"All done?" Ellie asks when Rebecca closes her laptop.

"For now. I just need to pack up, and then I can tell Hafsah that you're here and I'm not walking home alone, as I promised."

"She just texted a little while ago, actually. Her study group ran late, so she was just leaving."

"On her own?"

"She didn't say."

Rebecca stands, wincing at the sudden stretch of muscles too long inactive, and piles everything into a folder for safekeeping. Reorganization will come later. "Let's go find her partway, then, just in case. There are still assholes and dillweeds in the world, after all."

"Give it time."

Ducking into the straps for her bag, Rebecca shakes her head. "Please don't say shit like that out loud. Not when there are so many murder investigations going on."

Ellie just laughs and gathers the trash. "Exactly! Who's going to notice one more?"

Whoever's dead, their friends, their family, the police . . . "You've been really lucky," Rebecca says quietly, moving to the door. She doesn't open it yet, and she can feel the electricity of Ellie's full attention like a building storm. "As many times as the police have taken you to the closest station, as many times as you've assaulted people, even in a good cause, you've never been arrested, and you've never been charged. For your sake, I hope that continues to be true."

"But?" Ellie asks, voice flinty with challenge. Her eyes are just as hard.

Except . . . Rebecca knows her better than most. She can see the other things lurking behind that hardness, the confusion and suspicion and a little shred of something that seems almost like hope. "But. You're not untouchable, and one of these days, if you're not really careful, you're going to get caught in a way that you can't laugh off."

"So . . . you're saying . . ."

Rebecca licks her lips, then worries the lower one between her teeth for a long moment. Neither she nor Ellie break eye contact. Finally, Rebecca takes a deep breath. "I am asking you to please be careful." She opens the door and holds it so that Ellie can walk out first.

25

Walking around campus after dark with Ellie is a different experience than it is with just about anyone else. It isn't that anything astonishing happens or that people see them and run in the opposite direction. It's just that Ellie radiates such a powerful aura of "Danger: Fuck Off" that it almost feels like nothing *can* happen. Like if anyone were going to think about attacking them, they would instead measure the risk to their own life and limb and decline to pursue.

It is not as relaxing as it should be. Maybe if she hadn't just said "Hey, I think you're a murderer, but I've got your back." That would have been an excellent thing for her exhausted brain *not to say*. Fortunately, Ellie seems absorbed with processing that particular thing that shouldn't have been said, and she doesn't try to continue the conversation. Thank God.

With finals just days away, there are more people out than usual, desperate for the last-minute study sessions. Still, there are large pockets where Ellie and Rebecca are the only people in sight. If there are others around, they're blocked by buildings or stands of trees.

They get all the way to McCarty Hall without seeing Hafsah. Which would be fine and would probably indicate that the study group is still inside, except . . . the doors are locked, and the lobby lights are out. That doesn't necessarily mean she's not in there, but it does mean they can't go in to check.

Rebecca pulls out her phone and taps a text to Hafsah, asking where she is. She doesn't get a response, nor does it show as read. "The most sensible ways to Sledd all intersect with the path we took."

"If she got nervous, she might have ducked over to a less sensible route," Ellie points out. She bounces her water bottle against her thigh. Like Hafsah's, it's heavy, made of steel, and has two wide rubber bands affixing spikes in place on either side of the grip. Her eyes dart around the open spaces.

"Or someone could have dragged her off."

"Cynic."

"Let's just go look, all right?" Rebecca is tired; she knows that, and she's feeling raw and drained, which makes her twitchy, but she wants eyes on her friends. She wants to find Hafsah, head back to the dorm, check on the others, and fall asleep listening to them talk so she can know all her people are safe and sound in one place. It makes her feel a little like a dragon protecting its horde, but it's at least a familiar feeling. Once Daphne came home from the hospital, Rebecca walked between their yards every night before bed, because she just couldn't sleep without knowing that her cousin was safe and watched over.

As they set off, she intermittently sends more texts to see if Hafsah will answer. Still no response. She pulls up a map of the campus on her phone. She doesn't have any classes at McCarty, but it's just a stone's throw from both the stadium and the dorm, so there's not a lot of room to get lost.

"Maybe we should check the stadium," she says. "Lots of nooks and crannies along the outside."

"Is there a specific reason you're so worried about Hafsah today?"

Rebecca can still feel all those stories swirling through her mind, lending her urgency she might not otherwise feel so keenly. "My head's still in the article," she says, and because Ellie knows her in return, her friend nods. "Also, my lizard brain wants us all nesting."

"God forbid we disappoint your lizard brain."

They keep walking, and Rebecca mutters savagely under her breath about promises and hypocrites and putting Hafsah on a child leash for a day just for worrying her.

Ellie reaches out and smacks her arm. "I hear voices," she whispers.

They slow, taking more care with their steps. She can hear them now, too, two voices, one male and one female, coming from under one of the large looped walkways to the upper levels of the stadium. The shadows are thick under the walk, making it hard to see until they get closer. They lean up against the wall separating the broad sidewalk from the grassy insert and the open court beyond.

Hafsah is backed up against one of the supports, hands held up before her, palms out. In front of her, looming over her, the man has one hand bunched in her hijab, the other on her shoulder. He looks smug, sure of himself. She looks terrified.

It's Officer Kevin.

Rebecca stares, feeling her stomach knot up anxiously. Officer Kevin, who's a bit of a chauvinist and utterly paternalistic but is always so keen to walk the girls home.

Oh fuck.

Beside her, Ellie seems just as flummoxed, her mouth hanging open.

"I need to get back to the road," Hafsah says, her voice shaking. She's speaking as loudly as she can without shouting, trying to project; except for the fear, it's the voice Rebecca's heard countless times as she practices presentations. "I'm meeting friends to walk the rest of the way home."

"You'll get home, sweetheart," he tells her. He has the nerve to laugh. "You're just going to earn it first. Everything we do to keep you young ladies safe, we deserve a little consideration from time to time."

Rebecca grabs Ellie and yanks her back as her friend tries to charge in. "Are you trying to get her shot?" she whispers fiercely. "Or yourself? The man has a gun!"

"You're just going to—"

"Of course not, but let's pretend we know how to think!" She calls Hafsah's number instead of texting, praying the other girl doesn't have it on silent.

She doesn't. There's a flinch as the sound echoes off the concrete overhead, but then Hafsah looks a little stronger, more sure. "That's my friends," she says. "They're looking for me."

"They can look a little longer." He lets go of her shoulder to grab her phone out of her pocket, hurling it over the wall. Ellie jumps up to catch it, then purposefully drops her water bottle with a clatter so that it sounds like the phone landed. "A polite little thing like you, you don't want to be rude now, do you?"

Shit.

Ducking down behind the wall, Rebecca tugs Ellie down with her. "Go to the roadside end of the sidewalk," she whispers. "I'll go to the glass front. We'll start calling her name like we're looking for her. We can meet in the middle where they are. Quickly."

Ellie looks mutinous, but she nods and grabs her water bottle, holding it like a club as she stalks off. Rebecca hurries through the stand of trees to one side of the stadium's fancier entrance, reaching the large glass-and-metal arch between two tall sections of brick. She can barely hear Hafsah now. "Hafsah!" she yells. "Where are you?"

There's a startled exclamation from the shadows, followed by a thump and a muffled cry of pain.

Her blood boils, and she's about ready to fuck the plan, even if it was her idea.

Then she hears Ellie. "Hafsah! Come on, bitch, answer your phone!"

Officer Kevin curses and lets go of Hafsah's hijab as Rebecca jogs closer, using her phone as a flashlight. "Hafsah! Hafsah, where are— oh!" She shines the light directly at the scumbag. "There you are! Are you okay?"

The light gleams off the tear tracks on her friend's face.

"She had a little scare, that's all," the officer says with a charming smile. He hooks his thumbs through his belt.

"Ellie's looking too," Rebecca says, one eye on the officer. Specifically on how close his left hand is to his holster. "Let me let her know." And before the officer can decide if he wants to try silencing two girls instead of just one, she bellows in the direction of Ellie's voice. "She's under the loop!"

"Coming!"

There's a scrabbling sound, and then Ellie clambers over the wall and drops to the grass. "Hey, this is your phone, isn't it?" She holds it up. "Did you see a gator or something?"

"Or something," Hafsah answers hoarsely. "I'm glad you found it."

Ellie doesn't move to hand it back to her. Instead she keeps it upright in her hand, the camera facing the two under the walkway. She's recording it, Rebecca realizes, and she feels a stab of gratitude for her volatile friend. "And aren't we *lucky* you were found by such an upstanding citizen as friendly officer Kevin."

"You know, sir, you should really get IT to check out your body cam," Rebecca adds, trying and probably failing to sound innocent. "It seems like it's off more often than it's on."

His hand goes to cover the cam, not that it matters. They've all seen that there's no little red light.

"Come on, Hafsah. I'm thinking of treating everyone to Cold Stone delivery. A last hurrah before finals, seeing as we can't go tubing next week." Ellie bares her teeth in an unmistakable snarl. "Did you hear, Officer Kevin? They found another body yesterday. Yet another dillweed who hurt the girls on campus. I guess the gators got sick of the Lady Gators being treated that way."

The Lady Gators certainly did.

Rebecca edges forward, holding a hand out to Hafsah. Her friend takes it with a punishingly strong grip, tremors racing under her skin. "Where's your bag?"

225

"She dropped it here," says the officer, still pretending there's nothing wrong. She notices he keeps a careful eye on Ellie, though it's hard to tell if it's actually on her or on the phone she's still holding up.

Rebecca clips her water bottle to the strap of her backpack and grabs Hafsah's bag, backing away with the other girl in tow. "We'll let you get back to your patrol, Officer. We'll get her home safe."

"Let me get my bike; I can walk—"

"Yeah, you can fuck all the way off with that," Ellie says lazily.

Hafsah and Rebecca both flinch, watching his hand near the gun on his left hip. Rebecca shoves Hafsah behind her.

"Didn't you hear me, Officer Kevin?" With a snicker, Ellie walks slowly toward the other girls, careful to keep facing him. "The Lady Gators are protected on campus now. I'm sure the assholes and rapists would be grateful for the continued protection, though. Have a good night, now, y'hear?"

The girls keep backing away until they're in the broad cone of a light. Rebecca hands Hafsah's backpack to Ellie, as she only has her bike bag to manage. "You okay to jog?" she whispers.

"Can we run?" Hafsah asks with a whimper.

"Yes. We're not far."

They break into a full run, the other two keeping Hafsah between them. Rebecca watches the area in front of them while Ellie throws regular looks behind. With three of them, the officer is unlikely to actually assault them, but he could still follow to threaten them into silence or just to watch them go into their dorm. It's a risk to go straight to Sledd, but Rebecca's not going to delay long enough to find someone in Thomas to let them in.

Ellie slams her ID through the lock and nearly shoves them through the door as soon as it's open. With the door closed behind, that little extra bit of safety, Hafsah nearly collapses onto Rebecca. She steers them over toward the couches, and they drop down onto the cushions, Hafsah breaking into sobs.

Behind the reception desk, Kerry stands with a look of alarm. "Is she okay?"

"Hang on." Ellie frowns down at Hafsah's phone. Hafsah uses a passcode rather than a thumb or face lock, so she can't be forced to open it, but everyone in the suite knows the code in case of emergencies. A moment later Ellie's phone beeps with an incoming text. "I'm sending the video out."

"Please don't," gasps Hafsah. "It won't do anything."

"Yes, it will." Kneeling down in front of her friends, the redhead folds her arms across Hafsah's knees. "This isn't just 'he said, she said' this time. We actually have video proof. This will make a difference."

"Does it ever?" she asks bitterly.

Rebecca rubs her hand in slow circles along Hafsah's back. "Hafsah got cornered by Officer Kevin," she tells Kerry, who's left the desk to hover worriedly beside the couch. "He tried to make her . . ." She presses her lips together firmly, but that kind of silence is its own explanation.

The senior drops down onto the arm of the couch, looking worried. "Do you need a ride to a clinic or the ER?"

Hafsah shakes her head. "Just some bruises. Ellie and Rebecca got there in time."

"I should have asked you if there was someone in the study group to walk with, or who could give you a ride," Rebecca mutters. "You made me promise, but I didn't do the same for you, and you got hurt."

"Not very hurt," Hafsah says with a shaky smile. Weak as it is, it's diminished further by the steady track of tears down her cheeks. "I knew better."

"We shouldn't have to." But she lets it go. For now. Hafsah is distressed enough; she doesn't need to deal with Rebecca feeling guilty on top of that. There are better ways to make it right. "We'll go through your exam schedule up in the room, compare it across the whole suite. If we can't guarantee an escort to and from each one, we'll farm out assistance."

"I'll be fine during the day. He patrols at night."

"Do you really want to bank on that?" she asks quietly.

". . . no."

Ellie sits back on her ankles, tapping out message after message on her phone. "This will get that bastard fired. Rebecca's right; we should make sure you have an honor guard until it happens, but this is going to work."

Rebecca shares a glance with Kerry, who looks as doubtful as she feels. The worst she can see happening is that he gets a warning or possibly a suspension for turning his body cam off. She doesn't see any actual discipline happening. Even if Ellie started recording as soon as she caught Hafsah's phone, she can't imagine that she captured anything truly damning.

Ellie sees them and scowls. "What? We have him—on camera—assaulting her."

"Let's see the video," suggests Kerry, "and that will give you a better idea of what you actually have."

Thank God for Kerry. She's been an amazing RA this year, especially after everything with Kacey. Rebecca's going to miss her calm sensibility and her unwillingness to take anyone's shit. Even Ellie seems to respect her, or at least she does when she's not screaming down fury road.

The video is . . .

Perhaps there would be more to it on a larger screen, but from what they can see clustered around the phone—Hafsah leaning into Rebecca with her eyes closed—it's too dark to make much of anything out clearly. You can see the shadows move a little and hear Hafsah's yelp, but other than that, it's just Officer Kevin letting go of the hijab and standing too close. To be honest, it looks worse for Ellie than for the officer.

Kerry shakes her head. "I'm sorry, Ellie, but that isn't going to do anything."

Seeing Hafsah scrub her hand against her hijab—against the place Officer Kevin grabbed—Rebecca shakes her head. "Let's get upstairs. You'll feel better for a change of clothes."

Hafsah gives her a look of naked gratitude, but Ellie snorts. "Sure. New clothes, that makes it all better."

"Of the three of us, who has been attacked this month and therefore knows the sorts of things that actually make you feel better?" Rebecca and Hafsah raise their hands.

Ellie glowers. "And justice? That isn't going to make you feel better?"

"What justice do you think is going to happen?" demands Rebecca. "Cops protect their own; you know this. Whether they are clearly in the wrong or not, there's a solid blue wall between you and any justice you think that video can achieve. You *know* this."

"There are limits to that!"

"Not for this," she says, despite how it pains her. "Not for an attempted sexual assault. Not for a successful sexual assault. Most of the time not even for murder. Cops stand with each other whether it's the right thing to do or not because the way they're trained is them against the world, and standing against that can get good officers frozen off the force. Don't let adrenaline fool you into thinking one video of half an attempted assault is going to change the state of the state."

Kerry gently pokes Hafsah in the shoulder. "How in the hell do you live with these two?"

"By keeping them on opposite ends of the suite." Her smile looks a little stronger now, as if seeing Ellie and Rebecca arguing has restored some of the natural order.

Ellie ignores them. "And what, you think you're going to change the world with your articles? Here's what the police did well, but oh dear, they just murdered someone in cold blood, so that's an area they may need to improve?"

"Because law enforcement is going to be keen to enact reforms suggested by someone with a byline of 'Fuck the Police,'" Rebecca says

229

with a sigh. "Ellie, I'm not saying not to report him. I'm just saying it's not going to do nearly as much as you're hoping it will. You can bet that if GPD knows there are issues with Officer Kevin, UPD definitely does, but he's still biking around with a uniform and a badge. This is not going to be the tipping point you want it to be."

"Then maybe we should just kill him!" With a shout, Ellie shoves to her feet and starts pacing around the couches like a caged animal. "If we can't hold him to account, we kill the bastard before he can hurt anyone else! A fucking public service!"

Kerry looks alarmed. Hafsah just looks tired. Rebecca shakes her head and sighs. "Ellie."

"I'm sure the gators would be thrilled. He might be a bit gristly from all the biking, but a meal's a meal, right? Especially during courting season?"

"Ellie."

"Why limit it to students when there are so many assholes in the world who need killing?" Her hair whips around her with the force of her movements, a one-woman hurricane of rage and fury. "It's still cleaning up campus if it's UPD."

"Ellie!" When she finally turns to look back at the couch, Rebecca glares at her. "Have you really never fucking heard of plausible deniability?"

Ellie blinks at her, stares, then bursts out laughing, mercurial as ever. "Jesus Christ, Rebecca, you'd think you want me to murder him or something."

"If you're going to get arrested and questioned for anything, I would prefer for it to be after finals," Rebecca says, voice prim enough to make Hafsah snicker. "It's hard to crowdsource bail when everyone is focused on exams."

Flopping down onto one of the other couches, Ellie clutches her belly and laughs. "I'm still going to kill him."

"For fuck's sake." She glares at her friend. This is *not* being careful.

A ding from her phone makes Ellie glance down at the screen. "Det Corby says he'll be here in ten."

Rebecca sits back and stares at her. "Why?"

"Because I sent him the video."

That doesn't actually explain why he's coming to talk to them about it, unless Ellie said something particularly incendiary along with the video. There's not much a detective from GPD can do about a UPD officer's transgressions, especially if his captain is likely to block any efforts he does make. But why is he coming? Surely he's swamped investigating the boy in the river.

"Do you want to go change before he gets here?" she asks Hafsah.

Hafsah shakes her head. "I probably shouldn't. And honestly, once I'm in the room, I don't really want to leave it again."

Rebecca squeezes her in a sideways hug. "I know how that feels."

The phone rings at the desk, making Kerry flinch. "Crap. All right, back to work for me. If you need anything . . ."

"We'll let you know," promises Rebecca. "Thanks."

Now that Hafsah's stopped shaking, even if she's still intermittently sniffling, Rebecca stands and picks up their water bottles, grabbing Ellie's from beside her bag. "I'll be right back." If the AC is dead and making everyone else want to die, at least there's still cold water. She fills all three bottles at the fountain, standing there for a moment longer to let the water splash the inside of her wrist. Her grandmother has always told her that when she's feeling overheated, she should focus on her pulse points first, that it'll help cool down the rest of her faster. She honestly has no idea if it's true or not, but she always does it anyway.

After sitting back on the couch and redistributing the bottles, she places her partially numb wrist across Hafsah's forehead. The other girl groans and leans into it. "That feels amazing," she mumbles.

Ellie guzzles her water, then winces and clutches a hand against her stomach. Rebecca shakes her head. A Florida girl like Ellie should know better than to drink water that cold that quickly; of course it's going to make her stomach cramp.

"How's Delia doing?" Rebecca asks.

Ellie snorts. "She's buried in her books and refusing to share details. She found part of a body, but she won't talk about it at all."

"The police probably instructed her not to talk about it," Rebecca points out, "so stop nagging her. She's traumatized and needs to study."

"Yeah, I'm sure she's very focused on her final lab analyzing the tannic structure of her murder water."

"Her professor gave her a new sample today," says Hafsah. "Said she'd witnessed Delia's proper collection and that it wasn't fair for her grade to suffer just because the sheriff's office confiscated the original sample."

"Why?" Rebecca frowns, trying to think through the science in that, which is not, she can admit, her strongest suit. Still. "There's a whole river of water; what can they possibly learn from Delia's sample that they wouldn't learn from taking their own?"

"I didn't ask."

Ellie shrugs. "We can ask Det Corby when he gets here."

26

They don't have long to wait. He knocks on the door when he arrives, and Kerry waves at the girls to keep their seats while she lets him in. His forearms and hands are tanned, but his face and the back of his neck are burned a tender-looking pink. It could be worse, Rebecca knows—both she and Ellie spend more on sunscreen than on shampoo—but it looks painful enough as it is.

The first words out of his mouth are, "Hafsah, are you okay?"

"Ish?" she answers with a shaky smile. "I'll have some bruises on my shoulders and back, but otherwise, well enough, I guess."

"Your back?"

"Too dark to see in the video," Rebecca murmurs to Hafsah. "You just hear the yelp."

She nods. "When the girls first yelled for me, he shoved me back against a concrete column."

He sits on the arm of Ellie's couch so he's not looming over Hafsah. He looks exhausted, Rebecca realizes with a pang. She has no doubt his captain is on his ass to find the murderer. Fine young men and all that. He scrubs his hands against his face and promptly winces at the contact with his sunburn. With a long sigh, he drops his hands to his thighs and looks solemnly at Hafsah. "I really wish I had anything good to tell you."

Hafsah and Rebecca nod, not surprised in the least. Ellie squawks and punches him just above his knee. "What the shit, Det Corby?"

"Let me start by saying that, Hafsah, I am very grateful he wasn't able to do more than he did."

"But there isn't enough to be damaging," she says. "Yeah."

"Hafsah!"

"It's what Rebecca was trying to tell you, Ellie. Even if you'd recorded everything from the moment he saw me, it'd be what, a warning?"

"It's your choice if you want to report this to UPD," Det Corby continues before Ellie can protest. "You absolutely have the right to do so."

Glancing at Rebecca, who shrugs, Hafsah considers that for a moment, twisting her thumbs through the cuffs on her long sleeves. "How likely is the rest of the department to retaliate?" she asks finally.

"Mixed bag," he answers. "The female officers will be sympathetic; they hate him but haven't been able to get him kicked off the force. Male officers are more of a gamble. There are plenty who don't like Kevin or what he does, but that doesn't mean they won't protect him until it's out of their hands."

Rebecca sighs. Solidarity is a hell of a drug. She'd like to say her family members are immune to it, but there are bad seeds on the force back home who get defended. The officers might disagree and protest in private, but to the public they're an impenetrable wall of support.

"And GPD doesn't have any jurisdiction, does it?"

"*If* UPD decided to open an investigation, and *if* they decided to recuse themselves to avoid bias, they could ask GPD or ACSO to take it over. Short of that, no."

The honesty is what she expects of Det Corby, but Rebecca finds she's still grateful for it. He doesn't try to sugarcoat his answers, but he's also not making them unnecessarily harsh to try to scare or influence Hafsah. He's just answering, as matter-of-factly as if he were discussing the weather, despite the terrible weight of what he's saying. She can see Hafsah calming further in response, sitting up straighter, the hitch in her breathing gradually evening out. Logic is soothing to Hafsah.

"So aside from another nondamning mark on a no-doubt extensive record, will reporting it to UPD accomplish anything good?" Hafsah asks.

"I don't know."

"Then—and please don't get me wrong; I'm grateful you're here—but why are you here?"

"I wanted to make sure you were all right," he says, giving her a sheepish smile. "Also, to be a stand-in if you wanted to scream and yell at someone."

"I think you have me confused for Ellie."

"Only if your foot is flying toward my . . ." His cheeks turn a little pink, and he doesn't finish the statement.

He doesn't have to. Hafsah and Rebecca both snort. Ellie can't seem to decide if she should be flattered or offended.

"And also to tell you to be careful," he continues more seriously. "I admit that being male, I'm offered a different side of Kevin, but I trust you, and I trust the others who've told me similar things about him. What they tell me is that once he decides he's entitled to something, he's patient and relentless."

Rebecca startles; if he had any reservations about Officer Kevin, why didn't he warn them?

"Persistence hunting," murmurs Hafsah. "It's how ancient man became an apex predator. If you can't catch something running, you just keep walking after it and outlast it."

"His response to being told no is always going to be to regroup and keep working at it." Det Corby holds his hand out to Hafsah, palm out, not demanding but letting her decide if that's contact she wants. When she gives him her hand in return, he curls his fingers into hers, a hold she can easily break. "For the next week, if you're walking anywhere, even with a group, keep your phone recording. Even if it's just in your pocket. It's easy to delete a video if nothing happens."

"Easy to ignore a video when something does happen," retorts Ellie, folding her arms over her chest.

"The footage you took shows that he's a creep, not a predator," Det Corby answers, mostly patiently. He's starting to fray a little around the edges. It's a common reaction to conversations with Ellie. "Yes, there are probably other people who can identify him as a predator. It's not what the video shows. Might I remind you that you made some not-so-veiled threats that would make submission of the video officially more of a problem for you than for him?"

Ellie glares at Rebecca. "Should have let me charge ahead, but no, you had to try to be *smart.*"

"And *careful*," she retorts.

"Thank God, because otherwise you could all have been arrested for assaulting an officer." Det Corby gives Ellie a glare of his own. Rebecca wonders if it hurts to scowl like that, given how tight sunburned skin can get. "Charging ahead would have made it his word against yours, which is pretty much always going to go in the officer's favor in a courtroom. Right now, given the strange atmosphere on campus, it would definitely go his way. All he has to do is say that the girls on campus are enacting a witch hunt based on nothing more than hurtful rumors. It dismisses the stories about him as unimportant and makes you look bloodthirsty and murder minded, without a care for a man's reputation."

"She is bloodthirsty and murder minded, without a care for a man's reputation," Rebecca and Hafsah chorus. It's the expected response, really; it would look strange if they didn't make their cue. They grin across at Ellie, who looks grumpy but pleased with herself.

Hafsah squeezes the detective's hand and pulls away, and he immediately lets her go. "I'm not going to start a grudge match with UPD when there's no hope of a good resolution," she announces, "and if I won't be reporting it, then I would very much like to go upstairs and shower. Thank you, Detective, for coming to check on me. I appreciate it."

"I wish I could promise you a good solution."

"I wish you could too. I don't blame you that you can't." With Rebecca's help, she pushes herself off the couch and picks up her backpack. "Good night, Detective. Ellie, don't snarl at him too much. He's one of the good ones."

"Which means he should be helping to clean up the terrible ones," she replies but flaps a hand dismissively at Hafsah. "So does Delia's body part have a name yet?"

"It's called a leg," he informs her, waving at Hafsah as she rolls her eyes and walks to the stairwell.

"Cheeky bastard."

"In the video, you told Kevin that the discovery was another dillweed who hurt girls. How do you know that?"

Rebecca blinks, startled at the swift subject change.

In a dazzling show of maturity, Ellie blows a raspberry at him. "It was a guess. Jesus, Det, loosen up."

"*Dillweed* isn't usually in your insult pool."

Rebecca gives him a sharp look. This isn't their friend right now, not with that tone in his voice, not if he's asking about specific word choice in a completely different conversation. She doesn't say anything, though, too curious about what's bothering him.

Ellie just shrugs. Being about as subtle as a brick to the face herself, she's not good at picking up on it in others. "A bunch of frat boys were going around campus, asking if anyone had seen their dillweed. Must have gotten stuck in my head."

"Do you remember which fraternity?"

"What's with the third degree, *Detective*?" she asks, tossing her hair behind her. "Of course I don't remember which frat. Who can tell them apart? They're all 'Beta Who Gives a Shit' and 'Alpha Chi Look at My Cock.' They are the only ones who care."

Which is . . . strange for Ellie to say, because she's the one who spent the first few weeks of freshman year memorizing every fraternity and sorority on campus so she would recognize the letters by sight. She said she wanted to know where she should go to bitch people out for the behavior of their brothers and sisters. Rebecca shifts uncomfortably on the couch. Diverting questions is nothing new for Ellie, but flat-out lying? That might be a first; usually her problem is being excruciatingly honest.

Then again, she thinks before she can squirrel off in a deep dive, Ellie could also just be punishing Det Corby for not being able to do more for Hafsah.

Ellie pushes to her feet and grabs her bag and both of Rebecca's, swinging them up in such a wide circle that Det Corby has to duck to one side to avoid getting hit. "If you're going to be boring with this, I'm going to go see if Delia is feeling more cooperative."

"Or you could try studying," Rebecca says. "I've heard that's a thing."

"It's a boring thing," Ellie retorts. "You didn't let me take out Officer Kevin, so now I have too much energy. I need entertainment."

"So go punch someone."

"Officer Kevin?"

"No." It's hard to tell who manages to infuse the word with more resignation, Rebecca or Det Corby.

Sticking her tongue out at them, Ellie flounces off to the stairs.

With a bone-deep groan, Det Corby stands and flops onto the couch next to Rebecca, letting his head fall back as far as his sunburn will comfortably allow. His knee bumps against hers. "She is one of the most exhausting people I have ever met," he confides in a whisper. "And I actually like her."

"I think she's only exhausting to the people who like her; no one else really bothers trying to weather her." Rebecca shifts sideways on the cushion, folding one leg in front of her. Her fingers twist through her anklet, and she looks down. She worried clear through her last one, rubbing the threads so much they broke, so Daphne spent part of Christmas break making her a new one in colors to represent Kacey: electric blue and sunset orange and a cream with the barest hint of orange. Some of the twisted threads where the ends are tied together are starting to fray and snap. Will Daphne be concerned if she asks for another new one?

Well, it's been a hell of a month, even if Daphne doesn't know all of it. Maybe it wouldn't be *that* surprising.

A warm hand covers hers, stopping her fidgets. Her cheeks warm. "Are you okay?" the detective asks gently.

She shrugs and shifts her fidgeting from her anklet to his fingers, tracing the calluses. She's worried about Hafsah and Officer Kevin, yes, what has happened and what may yet, but it's more Ellie on her mind at the moment. She's not sure how to articulate that, though. She's also not sure she wants to. It's safe, or safe enough, to swap theories and fears with Hafsah, both of them intent on protecting their friend. Saying it to a detective rather defeats that. "You have an identity already for the boy in the river, don't you?"

He blinks, then gives a bare nod. "Too obvious?"

"Probably not for Ellie. But you've laughed before at how she's a magpie for new insults; you've never shown that kind of interest in them."

"Don't tell Ellie?"

She raises an eyebrow. "Do I ever?"

"His nickname in his fraternity was Dillweed. He had it as a tattoo a little below his knee. It meant we had his last x-rays from his dentist before we even found his head."

Lips pressed together, Rebecca clears her throat, as if that will clear the image from her head. She remembers a video making its way around

Twitter a while back, one of those things that goes viral for no apparent reason, of an alligator slowly cruising through a tank with a giant watermelon in its jaws. She'd be happier if her brain did not correlate those images. "Lovely."

"Sorry."

"No, I . . . I did ask."

"We're releasing his name in the morning."

"Seems safe to assume he has a record."

"Your friend Kacey, among others."

It feels like a punch to the chest, the memory of Kacey so like an open nerve after talking to Linsey Travers in the morning, and her fingers drop back to the anklet, twisting painfully as she tries to breathe. She can feel his hand still warm over hers, the other lightly touching her cheek, just the barest brush of fingertips.

"I've got you, Rebecca," he whispers. "Just breathe in. Can you do that?"

After an uncomfortably long moment, she's able to suck in a breath. Her cheeks flame with painful heat, probably rivaling his sunburn. Rather than lose herself to mortification, though, she continues following his prompts until she's breathing easily again. Her head aches with the unexpected flare of emotion after the long day and longer night. She can hear him shifting position in front of her, but she closed her eyes at some point and doesn't want to open them, not yet. Then she feels fabric against her forehead. His shirt, she realizes, and with a sigh she drapes against him, face buried in his collar. His arms slide around her back, comforting but still somehow respectful. She spent all night listening to other girls share their traumas, spent all day immersing herself in them again, and then with Hafsah . . . the world isn't safe.

But she feels safe with him.

"I'm sorry," he says eventually. "I should have done that better."

She shakes her head but doesn't feel up to speaking just yet.

"After his family was told, I went to the Montrose house and told them in person," he continues. "They're not going to have to find out through a press release. They get tonight to process it a little before they get bombarded."

"Thank you," she mumbles into his shirt. He smells like sunscreen and sweat and cypress and a little like swamp water. It's sort of unpleasant, if she's honest, but she also doesn't feel like pulling away from him.

"On a completely different note, I read your article."

She still doesn't feel like pulling away from him, but she thinks seeing his face might be more important now. Reluctantly she sits back and brings up her other leg, settling cross-legged and folding her hands in her lap. "How?" she asks. "I just sent it, what, like an hour ago?"

"We left the river around sundown; no one was keen on tramping around alligator-infested waters in the dark. I came back to town and started checking emails over dinner. Read it on my phone." He drapes an arm across the back of the couch, shifting to face her better. "I've enjoyed and admired most of your stuff that I've read, Rebecca, but this one was really something else."

"In a good way?" she asks when he takes too long to continue.

"In a very good way," he says with a laugh. "It . . . it encapsulates the very strange feeling around the school right now. You achieved a good balance too. You don't ignore the dead, but you also make it clear that they're part of a bigger story, and *that's* the one you're telling. Hopefully this comes out the right way," he adds with a grimace, "but I don't think it's a story a man could have written."

She nods. "That makes sense."

"I've been getting a deluge of media requests since the news first broke. With your permission, I'd like to email you a couple of those contacts. They're interested in a lot more than I can give them; while they spin their wheels between official updates, I think your story is exactly what some of them will be interested in."

Her smile grows, but then a thought occurs to her. She bites her lip. "Would publishing this—in whatever venue—create a problem for you or the investigation?"

He shakes his head, giving her a soft smile. "Doubtful. You don't have any privileged information in there, and it isn't really talking about the investigation. You never even mention me directly."

"Feeling neglected?" she teases.

"Positively pining." He leans forward and taps the end of her nose, making her cross-eyed. "It's a good piece, and if people have an explanation for what's freaking them out, my department will have to field fewer panicked calls that all the men on campus are being slaughtered."

"Not all of them, surely. I'd say thirty percent or so should be safe."

"Ouch."

"I'm reasonably sure you'd be one of the safe ones."

"Still a little painful that the number is so low."

"On a night like tonight, I'm stunned it's that high," she says solemnly.

He nods and rubs a thumb against her cheek; she reminds herself to keep breathing. "I should go. Let you study, rest, check on Hafsah. I'll send you those media contacts tonight."

"Sounds good." She slides off the couch and offers him a hand in standing, forcing herself not to blush when he doesn't immediately drop it. "I'm waiting to hear back from a couple of professors with their thoughts as well as the girls who spoke to me. Hopefully even with finals they'll be prompt."

"Given the topic, I'm sure they will be. Good night, Rebecca. Please stay safe."

"You too." She watches him until the door closes behind him and then, because she might be a bit pathetic, a little longer.

Kerry's sudden cackle makes her flinch. Oh, God, she'd forgotten Kerry was at the desk. How did she forget someone else was in the room? The RA is half-collapsed on the work counter, laughing herself breathless. There's a pained wheeze to the sound, like she's hurting herself.

Or that she hurt herself containing it for this long.

"Oh, Rebecca," she says eventually, wiping tears from her eyes. She's still laughing. "Girl, you have got it *bad*."

Face flaming, Rebecca decides there's nothing ignominious about a strategic retreat, and she quickly grabs her bags and flees up the stairs.

27

Back in the old days, when *executioner* was a living rather than an epithet, there used to be something of a ritual. You paid them—possibly your coin, possibly the Crown's, depending on the orders of the court—and they asked, "Do you forgive me?" It's always caught my attention, that little detail. *It is my job and not my wish to kill you, for the court has decided you are condemned to die. Do you forgive me?*

In other words, it's not personal.

But there is something personal about death, about being the one to deliver it. It doesn't matter the method used. Whether it's up close or from a distance or, you know, by alligator, it is intensely personal. Even if you don't stick around to see the life leave their eyes, you are the vehicle by which they have departed. An entire person, ended, and by your will.

Finals week always feels like the whole town is holding its breath. The permanent residents can't wait for most of us to be gone for the summer, and the students, of course, are losing their fucking minds. Construction projects explode during the summer, as jobs get assigned that are easier to do with lighter road traffic. The local schools won't be out for another month, so the exams aren't a countywide insanity, and even the AP exams for the high schoolers won't be starting for another week.

This is an older neighborhood off Thirty-Ninth Street, the houses comfortably spaced on lots that are maintained but not obsessively. Everything sags a little, from the roofs to the cars to the women in bathrobes who shuffle down to the ends of their driveways each morning to pick up the papers. It's not country, by any stretch of the imagination, but it's not uncommon to hear a random gunshot from time to time as people shoot to scare off raccoons.

I wonder if any of them have tried scaring off alligators with gunshots. Seems more likely to piss off the gator than deter it.

Reconnaissance is always a part of what I do. It has to be. Alligators aren't the most predictable of creatures, and despite suggestive evidence to the contrary, neither are college boys. Stupid, sure, especially with some booze in them. The boys, that is. But if you're going to do something without getting noticed—without getting caught—you have to make sure you don't stand out.

Hence, reconnaissance. Learn their patterns and habits. Where are they most vulnerable? What weaknesses can you exploit? Where are the cameras, the people paying attention, the blind spots? It's served me well thus far.

There are rules too. You have to set yourself rules, or you're just a monster. That's also part of the research: What did these assholes do? What have they gotten away with? Who have they hurt? No one is completely innocent, of course, but when I decided to satisfy that familiar itch, I gave myself strict parameters: They have to have earned it. No one dies because of hearsay. No one dies if they seem to be genuinely making amends.

What can I say, I'm a soft touch.

Once the rules are obeyed, once the research is done and the preparations are made, it's time to act. You can't hesitate; that's important. Either do it or fuck off, but anything in between is only going to make you screw up.

The whole neighborhood is quiet, mostly asleep, I think. There aren't generally people holding all-night keggers on Tuesdays. Not this far from the college, anyway. The community college is just a stone's throw away on this side of town, but there are no residences on the campus. The nearby apartment complexes geared toward students are bookended by retirement communities and assisted-living facilities—like Kacey's—so too much noise too late at night tends to get shut down quickly and with prejudice. It means the neighborhood settles down fairly early on weeknights.

The house at the end of the cul-de-sac has vacant properties on either side. To the west, a **FOR RENT** sign sags to one side in rain-soft ground. To the east, the house is boarded up for a long sleep, the snowbirds having flown north for a hopefully cooler summer. That one confuses me somewhat. I get the whole snowbird thing, and if you're well heeled enough to afford two residences, why not? But why Gainesville? Maybe they have grandkids here or something, but that's about the only reason that makes any sense. Whatever their strange love for Gainesville, they pay the neighbor on their far side to take care of the yard and occasionally poke into the house through the summer and fall to make sure disaster isn't blooming.

Or at least, they did. According to the newspaper two weeks ago, the neighbor's oldest kid borrowed the keys in order to throw a party when his parents weren't home, and the fire department got called when the group of drunk high schoolers decided to start a bonfire in the back-yard. The article said the kids are grounded until they go to college, but if I were their neighbors, I might be rethinking my choice of caretaker.

The house in the middle is just a little bit shabbier than the others. It's maintained well enough, but it isn't loved, and there's no pride. It's the house of someone who does the bare minimum and calls it done. It's also easy to spy on from the roof of that boarded house. The backyard abuts a field, the property line marked by natural growth on one side and a clean-cut lawn on the other, no fence to separate them. From there, the wooden ladder left outside by the caretaker gets you up to the roof, where you can tuck up behind the front-porch gable, several feet higher than the area immediately around it.

I've spent a lot of time the past few nights curled up there, watching. Verifying what the charming folks on the neighborhood app have had to say about that house in the middle. Some of the more general information there also proved helpful.

Like the number of complaints about the garages; unless, the residents say, you go through all the hassle and expense of replacing the original garage door, three opener frequencies can get access to more than half the neighborhood. I didn't test all of them, of course, but I tested a number of them with cheap openers from a couple of home-improvement stores. With self-checkouts so popular now, as long as you pay cash and keep your head down, there's no reason for anyone to notice you.

The house in the middle opens to the third frequency. Obliging of it. I got rid of the other two openers—separately, of course.

With the occupant of the middle house not home yet and the neighboring houses vacant, there's no one close enough to be bothered by the sound of the garage door rising and falling. Even if there were, they'd be used to the occupant coming home at this dark hour of the morning.

Although, if the neighborhood app is to be believed, they're also used to him drunkenly shooting at nothing in particular on occasion, but hey, what's a broken window between friends? (It's a blistering tirade on the busybody app, apparently.)

Officer Kevin Frasier of the University of Florida Police Department is a man of habits. Wear down his potential victims until it's almost impossible for them to stick the *no*. Change out of his uniform at the station when his shift is done. Drink most of a bottle of gasoline-grade vodka as he drives home in his worn-out, older-model station wagon. There's a gap between when the garage door comes down and when a light comes on in the kitchen, closest to the garage; I'm fairly sure he stays in his car to finish the bottle. Once he heads inside, he walks past a stack of dirty dishes in the sink to settle in a recliner surrounded by faded, peeling wallpaper from the seventies and knock back a few beers in front of the television until he falls asleep, screen still flickering and talking.

I love creatures of habit. Predictable people make things so much easier.

Closing the garage door behind me, I settle into a patch of shadow beside a broken fridge; the door hangs off, and the shelves are stacked high with more bottles of his drinkable lighter fluid. Last night while waiting for him to come home, I left a few extra bottles of the same brand carefully stacked with the others on the top shelf. Officer Kevin is too tall for it to be precisely eye level, but it's human nature to take what we can see most clearly. A couple of taps with a hammer and one of Luz's felting needles created holes in the thin cheap metal of the bottles' caps, tiny holes just large enough for a syringe to push in more vodka mixed with some of the crushed-up date-rape pills I took from Forrest's car. Thin round stickers almost the same shade of red as the rest of the cap cover the holes. In the shadows of the garage, it's impossible to tell the difference from the undoctored bottles if you're not actively looking for it. Now I count the stickers, and sure enough, one of my bottles is missing.

When he comes home from running errands, he takes care to back into the garage, ready to peel out for action if summoned. After his shifts, though, he's tired and drunk, and getting it in facing forward is enough of a trial. There are dents and dings on the fridge, giant toolbox, and folded-up treadmill that show he isn't always successful.

There's about a twenty-minute window for his usual return from work; the garage door screeches upward thirteen minutes in. He's a fairly steady drunk—all the practice, no doubt—but this morning his driving is erratic. He narrowly avoids sideswiping someone's mailbox, comes even closer to fishtailing into his own before he manages to steer the car into the garage at an angle that would make pulling out later in the day difficult.

He leaves the car on after he parks, the radio cranked up high. He's already finished the bottle of vodka, it looks like, judging from the tall boy in his hand. It's easy to be angry—harder not to be—but Jesus fucking Christ, what a goddamn hypocrite. The missing bottle sits on the front passenger seat, the neck bumping up against the gearshift.

If Officer Kevin drank down the whole bottle, roofies and all, it definitely explains why his driving is worse than usual.

I walk out of the shadows and lean against the driver's side door. He's left his windows down, safe enough from rain in a garage, though I wouldn't trust it against bugs. There's nothing between the two of us. It takes a long minute for him to notice me.

"What?" is all he manages to get out.

"You've been a very bad man, Officer Kevin," I tell him.

His eyes cross with the effort to focus on me. "What?" he asks again, his speech slurred.

"Well, I'm not an alligator." Double-checking my thin gloves, I reach across him for the empty bottle, replacing it with one from the recycling bin. There's no benefit in leaving behind evidence. With the doctored bottle safely in the bag at my feet with the others I retrieved from the fridge, I lean in again to turn off the car and retrieve his gun from the cup holder. I get that it's probably not comfortable to drive with a gun strapped to your hip, but the fact that he actually drives with it in the cup holder like that is both laughable and disturbing.

He moans, his eyes blinking slowly.

"You dishonor the shield you wear," I inform him, nearly shaking from fury. *Hold it together.* I can let it out later. "You hurt those you're supposed to be protecting and then endanger other lives with your habits. You are one of the reasons so many people have trouble trusting the very people who are supposed to help us. You are part of the problem. I won't pretend to be part of the solution, but I'm certainly *a* solution, and we're taking care of this tonight."

"You can't . . ." His mouth keeps moving, but the words are so far past slurred they're mush.

"Don't worry, Officer Kevin; there's going to be good that comes of your death. So much more good than you've managed in life. See, it's not just that the girls on campus are going to be a little bit safer with you gone. You're also going to help your brothers and sisters in blue." Gently rearranging his left hand properly around the gun, I hold it up to his temple. Fear crests on his face through the haze of alcohol and drugs, but it's an impotent kind of fear, helpless against the body-numbing chemical dissent. "Cops have alarming suicide rates. The pressures of the work they do and the things they see. And sometimes the trouble they cause. Cops and soldiers. Too often they take their loved ones with them. But you aren't burdened by loved ones, are you, Officer Kevin? All alone in the world; thank fuck for that."

His right hand flops against the stained seat, trying to reach for something. His phone, maybe.

"You're going to do your brothers and sisters in law enforcement a great service, Officer Kevin, by raising awareness of suicide. It's a better death than you deserve, but I've got a good thing going with the alligators, and I'd hate to throw off the pattern. You don't fit, you see, except in the ways that you do. This will be fast, and when you're found, people will mourn. Imagine that. People will actually mourn you. They'll think it was all just too much, and they'll gather together to talk about counseling and support for police, and who knows? One of your fellow officers may be saved by those services. Your death will be the best thing you've ever done with your life."

He makes a sound deep in his throat, a cry he can't control his mouth enough to form. Clearly Forrest Cooper had some good shit.

"But right here and now," I continue, "you and I know the truth. We both know you're a scum-sucking son of a bitch who preys on vulnerable girls, who gets off on abusing your authority and forcing others to do things they don't want to. You and I both know you're every bit as

250

bad as the assholes feeding the gators. You should never have hurt any of the young women you swore to protect, but your final mistake was in hurting one of mine. That, I will not overlook or forget. If there's a hell, I sincerely hope you burn in it. This is for Hafsah and every other girl you hurt."

The gunshot shrieks loud in the garage, and before my ears have finished making sense of the sound, blood and brain matter are spattered across the passenger side. His hand, one finger still looped across the trigger, falls into the car, tangling in the steering wheel as his body slumps deeper into the seat, listing to the right.

A much better death than he deserves.

I check around me to make sure I haven't caught any spray. More important, that I haven't *blocked* any spray. His death loses half its good if it doesn't look convincingly like a suicide.

Satisfied with my appearance and the dead asshole in the car, I lift the garage door one last time and close it behind me. There's a good rain coming tonight; I doubt I'll get back without a thorough soaking. It'll be enough to wash out any tracks I leave across the driveway. Retrieving my bike from the shadows of the neighbor's house, I head out into the early, still-dark morning.

The next two days are Officer Kevin's regularly scheduled days off, and after that? Well. It's unlikely the department isn't aware that he has a drinking problem. I don't know if they've made concessions for him in the past, but they must be aware, and things have been rather frosty for him on campus since the video went out. Unlike the UPD, the girls on campus don't care that the actions on video can be explained away. They care about what they know came before it. What some of them know would have come after, if the encounter hadn't been interrupted.

Given the number of eggs that have been thrown at Officer Kevin as he rides his patrols, perhaps the department will even be grateful he apparently decided to take some extra time. Who knows how long it'll take for someone to come look for him?

I ride off, back in the direction of campus, as thunder rumbles overhead. The bottles clink in my bag like a reminder. Once I'm a good distance away, I'll empty them out and toss the bottles, find somewhere else to toss the garage door opener. By the time I get back, I might well be wet, but I'll also be devoid of evidence.

Reconnaissance is so important.

28

There should be a rule, Rebecca thinks, that if a professor assigns a massive term paper due finals week, they aren't allowed to also have a comprehensive final exam. She's aware that it doesn't fall under any legal definition of cruel and unusual punishment, but it still sucks.

It certainly isn't helped by Ellie sitting at the desk behind her, incessantly tapping out theme songs with her pen or pencil, whichever her other hand isn't using to write her answers. The sound is obnoxious enough on its own, but the way Rebecca's mind starts automatically trying to identify each new theme is distracting.

And infuriating.

It's *The Addams Family* now.

She yawns and tries to focus back on her exam packet for History of Criminal Justice in America. She really loved the class, despite its workload, and the professor wasn't afraid to challenge students and make them question their viewpoints. He didn't back away from sensitive topics either. The present, he told them on the first day of class, is history that's being written, and we study it the same way.

Now if she can just synthesize a semester of classes into 120 multiple-choice questions, 40 short answers, and 2 essays. The suggestion at the front of the packet was to budget one hour for each section.

She's pretty sure the professor qualifies as a sadist.

In the front corner of the room, one of the desks suddenly tips over to clatter onto the floor. The senior who was sitting there slumps against the wall, breaking out in noisy, gasping sobs. Rebecca grimaces and looks back to her test as the professor heads over. He isn't going to give them all extra time just because one person had a meltdown.

Rebecca finishes ten minutes early and spends the rest of the time reading back through her essays as she massages her cramping writing hand. There's not much she can do if she finds something she doesn't like; the Scantron was in pencil, but the written answers had to be in blue pen, and there's only so far she can adjust what's already down. She feels hesitantly proud of herself and her answers, especially as most of her study time this week has been dedicated to filtering through emails responding to her article inquiries.

She yawns again, hiding it behind her hand. It's not that she regrets the string of incredibly late nights—not precisely—but the classroom is, aside from Ellie and the continued whimpers of the one senior, so quiet and the scratch of pens on paper so soporific that she just wants to curl up and nap.

Two minutes to time, Ellie ends her latest performance—*Mission Impossible*—and closes her blue book and exam packet with a long groan. She kicks the base of Rebecca's desk with her stretch. Just in case Rebecca was inclined to think it was an accident, she does it again a few seconds later.

Rebecca ignores her. This professor has strict opinions regarding cheating; she is not about to get her entire exam invalidated for turning around to see what her friend wants.

The call of time causes a loud chorus of complaints through the room, at least half the students complaining that they didn't get to finish. Professor Inglesbee leans against the table at the front of the room and shrugs. "Every test this semester has been designed to teach you to prioritize the things you know," he tells them. "If you don't know something, if you're not sure about something, move on to the things you do know, and come back to the ones that need more time. If you haven't learned that this semester, you probably haven't learned much else from me, and your exams will reflect that."

Ellie snickers and gathers her backpack and water bottle, clutching her test materials in her other hand. "Come on, Rebecca, Mama needs to eat."

Rebecca makes a face. "Please don't call yourself Mama. It's creepy."

"In a minute my stomach is going to be calling you a stupid cow if you don't come on."

Rebecca puts away her writing utensils before shrugging into her bag, then walks up with her suitemate to hand in the materials.

"Ah, the Carrottop Caucus," he says with a smile. "How do you think you did?"

"Well, that's a loaded question!" laughs Rebecca.

Ellie gives him a sharklike grin. "How many of them got to the back thirty of the multiple choice and freaked out that they got too easy?"

"I reward intelligent test takers. Rebecca, have you heard back from the *Washington Post* yet?"

"Seeing as my phone was in my pocket through the exam, I do not have a different answer for you since you asked me three hours ago." She does, however, dig her phone out of her pocket to check her email. "Holy shit."

Ellie's jaw clacks painfully against hers as her friend gloms on to her, straining to read it herself. "Holy shit what? Is this a good holy shit or a bad holy shit?"

"This is an amazing holy shit. They want to run it on Friday!"

Giggling and giddy, Ellie dances her around in a madcap loop. "You're going to be published in the *Post!* You awesome bitch!"

"Congratulations, Rebecca," says Professor Inglesbee. "It's an impressive piece; I'm glad it's finding a market."

"Thanks for your suggested edits," Rebecca replies, her cheeks starting to hurt from a no-doubt goofy smile. "They really tightened up the last section."

"Have a good summer, ladies. I expect to see you both in the fall for Contemporary Issues."

"Have a good summer, Professor," they chorus. They get a few nasty looks from other students, but whether that's because of the celebration or because of what Ellie said about the exam is anyone's guess.

Rebecca skims back through the email as they walk out of the classroom. "They have a few notes and edits, and they're checking with legal about naming the fraternities, but on the whole they think it's a clean piece, and they're excited to run it. Holy shit."

"Is that about your exam?"

Startled, they both look up at the voice. "Det Corby?" they say in unison. Rebecca's heart leaps.

He looks pale and strained, lifting one hand in acknowledgment. Next to him, one of the senior detectives glances pensively between him and the pair. Not Det Corby, then—Detective.

A sinking feeling in the pit of her stomach, Rebecca sends her screen to sleep and lowers the phone. "This isn't just to wish us well on finals, is it?"

"No." He clears his throat and looks to the older detective. "Either of you know the name Dillon McFarley?"

Rebecca frowns and shakes her head, but Ellie snarls. "Hell yes, I know that fucker. He's the asshole who hurt Kacey."

Feeling her stomach swoop, Rebecca looks between Ellie and the grim-faced detectives. "He's dead, isn't he?" she asks reluctantly, mostly for Ellie's benefit. She didn't pass on what Det Corby told her after the attack on Hafsah, nor does she want to get him in trouble for sharing reserved information.

"We identified the boy in the river."

"Hot damn!" crows Ellie. "And Delia found the fucker? And she didn't breathe a word, the sneaky bitch."

Rebecca narrowly avoids slamming her phone in her face as she thumps her hand against her forehead.

"Ellie, we need to take you down to the station for some questions," Detective Corby says gravely. "Given our friendship, I'll be present, but it'll be Detective Washington asking the questions."

Rebecca sucks in a breath. She can feel her heart racing madly, an almost painful thump in her chest.

And then there's Ellie. "Are you serious?" With a put-upon sigh, Ellie flips her hair over her shoulder and nudges Rebecca again. "Hey, so that lawyer you found me after the pantie-raid thing, can you call him?"

She gestures vaguely. "I'll call, but I don't know if he does, um . . ."

"Murder?" she offers baldly.

Rebecca winces, darting anxious looks between her friend and the officers. "I'll call his office and find out. If not, I'll call my aunt and see who she recommends."

"Awesome. Go work on those edits now."

Right. That is absolutely her highest priority in the moment. Not like her friend is being taken into custody or anything. Sure.

Both men give Rebecca a nod. Detective Washington, who may be one of the tallest men she's ever seen, gives her a card with his name, number, and email and the address of the station written on it. "We may have some questions for you as well," he says. "I assume Detective Corby has your contact information?"

She stares at him. "Ah, yes, sir, he does. Um, should I . . . she has another exam in the morning; should I email her professor?"

"If you could email me instead, with the schedule and professor's info, I'd appreciate it. Include yours as well, if you please."

"Yes, sir," she says and swallows hard. She feels three feet tall and five years old, trying to explain a bit of trouble to her stern great-aunt Cloris.

They walk off with Ellie between them, neither of them touching her, neither moving to put her in cuffs. They didn't say she was under arrest, Rebecca reminds herself. They just have questions. And they have questions for Rebecca at some point.

The lawyer's name and number are still in her phone; it seemed like a good idea given that she lives with Ellie. A call to his office yields an apologetic secretary explaining that he's out of state for a family medical emergency. She offers to put Rebecca through to the other partner, but she remembers meeting him, a gruff older man who hates college students in general and Ellie in particular, and she's not going to trust her friend's well-being to the hope that he'll be professional.

So as she heads to McCarty to wait for Hafsah to get out of her current exam, she calls her aunt Becky, who married into the family a few months after Rebecca was born and joked that she was named after the baby. Her aunt is the reason she won't consider going by Becky—the family doesn't need two—but the other nicknames for *Rebecca* just never felt right. Her mother laughed and said it was just one more sign of Rebecca being born old.

"Hey, kiddo, excited to come home for a couple weeks?"

Her heart skips and settles at the sound of her aunt's voice. Her aunt oozes cheerful confidence, even over the phone. "Just one week, Aunt Becky, but that's not why I'm calling."

"Uh-oh. Hang on." There's a muffled murmur, like her aunt put her hand over the microphone, and then the background sounds drop away with the closing of a door. "Okay, this sounds serious."

"Ellie just got taken in for questioning about the gator baiting."

"The baiting or the murdering?"

"I mean, in this case they're really the same thing."

"Did she do it?"

She takes a deep breath. "I have no idea."

Her aunt's sharp exhalation whistles in the speaker. "Comforting. She's one of your best friends; you can't manage an emphatic 'of course she's innocent'?"

"You've met Ellie. Could you manage it?"

"Did you try Grable?"

"Out of state for an indeterminate amount of time. Also," she continues, her voice shaking slightly, "the detectives said they may have questions for me later."

"Because of Ellie or because you may also be a suspect?"

"Um . . . they didn't say, but I'm guessing because of Ellie. If they suspected me, too, wouldn't they take me in now?"

"Possibly. Okay, two lawyers, coming up. Did the detective give you a location?"

She gives her aunt the information from the card, then Ellie's contact info as well. After a moment's thought, she also gives her the name and number for Ellie's mother. Becky promises to dispatch the first likely candidate to the station for Ellie. What she doesn't say, what Rebecca knows her well enough to hear anyway, is that she'll take considerable more care vetting representation for her niece should it prove necessary.

"Keep me informed, kiddo, and I'll filter it through to the rest of the family. If they need you to stay in Gainesville past the break, we'll come get your things and find you a hotel room."

"Thanks, Aunt Becky."

"Love you, kiddo."

"Love you too."

Half an hour later she gets a text with an attorney's name, phone number, and email for Ellie. She forwards it on, not expecting a response, and gets back a *yeah bitch, thanks.* It can't be too terrible if they're letting her use her phone, she thinks.

She settles into the edits the *Post* requested, finishing them quickly and sending them off. She also sends out emails to everyone on her previous list, giving them the final text and apprising them of the run date. If anyone changes her mind about being included, it's probably not too late to amend it. She hopes. She wouldn't say it keeps her mind off Ellie. Ellie, having drinks bought for her in gratitude. Ellie, who always knows the rumors of what any given boy has done. Ellie, who can't take two seconds to be shocked before she celebrates.

Hafsah joins her sooner than expected, looking tired but pleased. "How'd it go?" asks Rebecca, putting her things away.

"I think I did pretty well, actually. I doubt I'm breaking the curve, but I think I'll be pleased when the grades come out. You?"

"I did okay. I think. My article got accepted by the *Post*, and Ellie got taken in for questioning."

She can see Hafsah twitch, trying to take in the very different pieces of information. "Mountebanks?" she asks eventually.

"Alligators."

"Really?" Shaking her head, she holds open the door, and they walk out into the blasting heat. "Wonder what they have solid enough to question her?"

"Besides her general attitude and her specific knowledge of why each person probably died?"

"Ah. She okay?"

"Pleased as punch. My aunt found her a lawyer. She'll probably make them cry."

"The lawyer or the police?"

"Yes?"

"How are we friends with her?"

"Exposure therapy."

Laughing, Hafsah hooks her elbow through Rebecca's. They manage maybe ten feet before they remember why they don't walk that way, with more than half a foot's difference in their heights. "She'll be fine, right?" Hafsah asks as she pulls away so they can walk normally. Despite the attempt at a breezy tone, she sounds anxious. "I mean, if anyone can brazen it out, it's Ellie."

"I guess we'll find out," Rebecca murmurs. "Det Corby looks gutted."

"How likely is it to reflect poorly on him that one of his former students is a murderer?"

"Might be a murderer," she corrects with a grimace.

"Is probably a murderer," counters Hafsah. "Alligators or not, I'm not convinced her hands are clean."

"And yet here we are."

"It's a public service."

"We keep having this conversation."

"A few times, yes. So your article is getting published? That's amazing!"

Rebecca shakes her head. She knows Hafsah is trying to lighten the mood, keep spirits up, but Ellie is sitting in a room in a police station, a walking exclamation point of fury and tactlessness, and how can she not worry? "Smooth," she says dryly.

Hafsah pats her arm. "She'll be okay. She's Ellie."

Will that be enough this time?

"And I really am proud that your article's getting published," Hafsah continues. "That's an incredible accomplishment. I'm glad all those girls had you to listen to them."

"Thanks." Rebecca smiles, some of that giddy celebration fizzing back through her veins. She barely had two minutes to just be pleased about it before.

When they get back to the dorm, Susanna and Delia are still in a final, but Luz and Keiko are home. Keiko sobs through saying hello, so they look to Luz. "Relief," she translates for them. "Her portfolio presentation went beautifully, and the only exam she has left is a walk in the park."

"Good to know. Well done, Keiko." Rebecca pokes her head into Ellie's room. Unlike the rest of them, who've at least made an effort to start packing up, everything is still in its place. She studies it, trying to decide if distraction could be helpful. "Hey, if Ellie's getting questioned, should I sort my stuff out from hers or just leave it?"

"Ellie's getting questioned?"

She explains everything to Luz and Keiko as she tries to eyeball just how much of her clothing has made its way into Ellie's room. She returned all of Ellie's clothing two days ago, clean and neatly folded in a tote bag. Packing would be a good activity right about now, not only necessary but an excellent way to work through all the nervous energy buzzing through her.

After spending entirely too long dithering about it, she texts her uncles so they can debate among themselves whether or not she should reclaim her clothes from Ellie's room or if that will compromise a possible search by police. She works on packing the rest of her things, all thoughts of studying blown out the window by the news that spreads rapidly through the dorm. Some of it has to do with Dillon McFarley and his death, but the rest is about Ellie. Someone's already started crowdsourcing for her legal fees. Rebecca and the other girls take turn guarding the doors and explaining to people that no, they cannot go into Ellie's room and leave gifts. More gently, she explains to a handful who want to leave something at Kacey's picture that the gesture is appreciated but ill timed. When there's every possibility that police may want to come inspect the room again, it's best not to complicate things.

Finally, the energy dissipates, and the exhaustion overrides her anxieties, at least for a while. A little past three in the morning, Rebecca wakes up to the slam of her bedroom door against the wall. Trying desperately to blink the sleep from her eyes, she swivels up to her knees and gropes for the knife still taped behind the nightstand. She's met with peals of laughter from Ellie. "Bitch," grumbles Rebecca, dropping back down. Hafsah hasn't so much as twitched. She rubs at her eyes, and slowly Ellie comes into focus. "You're back?"

"I'm back," Ellie replies gaily. She flops down onto the bed, half-draped over Rebecca. "Lots and lots and lots of questions, but they let me go once I told them where I'd be once school let out and how to get in touch with me. Also, lawyer lady wants to talk to me again after finals are done. Thank your aunt for me? She's awesome."

"My aunt or the lawyer lady?"

"Both." Kicking off her shoes, Ellie squirms up the bed until she can spoon behind her friend. "I think I might be their only likely suspect."

"Does this excite you?" Rebecca asks around a yawn. Something in her eases to have Ellie back in the suite, her lizard brain counting its people and resting now that they're all safe and sound. She'll ponder the dearth of likely suspects later, when she's more awake.

"I feel a little bad for Det Corby."

"Only a little?"

"You were right; his captain is really riding his ass to find the master baiter."

"Oh my God." Rebecca squirms away from Ellie's snorting laughter. "That's gross."

"I don't think his captain cares if whoever they arrest is innocent," Ellie continues once she's gotten control of herself. "Corby cares."

"Yes, he does," says Rebecca.

"But maybe, since I'm a suspect, they'll hand the case over to Washington completely. Then he won't have to worry about it."

"Yes, I'm sure that he won't worry at all that someone he counts as a friend is the only current suspect in multiple murders."

". . . he considers me a friend?"

"You thought he didn't?"

"Huh. I always figured he just tolerated me because he liked you, and we're sometimes a package deal." She snuggles into her friend, burying her face against the back of Rebecca's neck. "That's kind of sweet."

Rebecca pats her arm. They slept like this the night Mountebanks attacked her, but Ellie's in a good mood this time, positively cheerful despite the danger of the detectives' suspicions. How can Ellie not feel that like a noose around her neck? Rebecca sighs and pats her friend's arm again.

"There's a thing we haven't talked about," Ellie whispers, suddenly solemn.

And they're not going to talk about it at three in the morning either. Or at all, if Rebecca has her way. Whatever Ellie's fears, her theories, her suspicions—she doesn't want to know. Not definitively. She wants the plausible deniability that Ellie doesn't seem to find important. "Go to sleep," she says. "I've got a final at nine."

Ellie's quiet and still for a long time. Then she slumps bonelessly against Rebecca and smiles. "We're still partying on Friday night, right?"

"Yes, but first we have to get through the rest of Thursday and the first parts of Friday."

"Killjoy."

"Say good night, Ellie."

"Good night, Ellie."

Rebecca kicks back, connecting with Ellie's shin and eliciting a shocked yelp.

29

Thursday evening following her afternoon final, Rebecca gets called to the police station and meets Natalie McKinney, the lawyer her aunt engaged on her behalf. She's a tall, bone-pale woman with silky white hair in a tidy braid and extremely dark sunglasses she wears even indoors. She's reserved but not unkind; her calm, steady presence eases Rebecca's twanging nerves as they talk with Detective Washington. Detective Corby sits to one side, listening and watching but not engaging beyond a greeting.

As Detective Washington asks her questions, Rebecca gets the feeling that they don't really have anything on Ellie. They're suspicious because she's suspicious, and at least Detective Washington is trying to find out if that's unfounded or reasonable. Partway through the interview, they take a short break to use the restroom and get some water, and Rebecca texts Hafsah to check in. She gets back an irritated message that their rooms are being searched—again—and officers are collecting every piece of paper from Ellie's walls.

Given that Hafsah intended to start packing, she's surprised it isn't more than irritated. They have to be cleared out of the dorms no later than noon on Saturday, and neither of them wants to repeat the enormous clusterfuck of last semester's move-out with Ellie, Delia, and Luz frantically trying to find everything and shove it into tote bags to carry down to their impatiently waiting relatives while Keiko sobs through arranging the more delicate art supplies into cases and realizing they don't fit. Rebecca's parents had arrived at six that morning; the three of them got her things tucked tidily into the back of the car, and then they laughed at her and went to breakfast with some Gainesville friends while she helped the others. When she met them for lunch, her mother took one look at her, patted her hand, and promised her a mudslide when they got home.

If her mom was giving her a boozy milkshake, she had to look *really* bad.

The rest of the interview is less nerve racking once she has the feel of it. The detective isn't trying to scare her or trick her into anything, and he asks his questions with a calm courtesy that doesn't feel patronizing. When he asks for additional information or double-checks something she says, it doesn't feel like he's trying to trap her or go for the cheap *aha!* She doesn't relax, precisely, but her hands aren't shaking anymore.

They confirm her contact information and where she'll be for the next week before returning to campus for her summer classes and internship, and then they let her go. Ms. McKinney tells her she did well and to keep her apprised of any further developments before wishing her good luck on her last final.

Now it's Friday, and that last final is finished—she walked into the room to see her professor reading her article in the *Washington Post*— but there are still several hours before most of the girls will be back. Rebecca and Hafsah both have rules that birthday parties can't start without everyone present, so no, Ellie, the others can't just catch up later. She bullies Ellie into getting her packing done save for anything she'll need that night.

Ellie grumps and starts stacking things into piles on her bed. Rebecca hands her clothes, using the opportunity to remove the things that have migrated from her closet to Ellie's. "Oh!" Ellie says suddenly. "That reminds me." She crouches down and pulls a bag out from under the bed, holding it out to Rebecca.

"Presents are tonight, remember?"

"This isn't a present."

Frowning in confusion, Rebecca takes the bag and examines the contents. It's a brand-new pair of jeans, the tag still clipped to the waistband. It's the same name brand as her missing ones, close enough to the same style. They're a darker blue than before, rhinestones on the back pockets form skulls and crossbones rather than the decorative swirls of her old pair, but she can see the size and fit should be the same.

She blows out a breath and sinks down onto the edge of Kacey's bed, the jeans puddled in her lap. Ellie watches her from over one shoulder, her eyes hard like a challenge. Rebecca's not sure what the challenge is supposed to mean, exactly. Is Ellie daring her to say something? Or daring her to stay silent?

"The skulls might be a bit on the nose," Rebecca says finally.

With a huff of laughter, Ellie twists to flop on the tile floor, her back against the bed. She shakes her head. "I don't understand you at all, Sunnybrook Farm."

"Orange Blossom Ranch," she corrects. "We raise horses, you know."

Ellie stares at her.

Rebecca grins. It's so rare to catch her mercurial friend genuinely speechless. "Look," she says after a moment, the amusement fading. "This conversation that you inexplicably want to have? We're not having it."

"Why not?"

"Because I don't need an explanation from you. We all have lines, and we all have different reactions when people cross them. We do what we have to do. But also . . ." She takes a deep breath, anxiously licking her lips. "I can't protect you if I know the truth," she whispers, conscious of the open door and missing suitemates. "It doesn't matter if I suspect it. But I can't *know it* and lie about it. You do a lot to protect us, more than Delia, Susanna, Luz, and Keiko will ever know; can you protect us a little further by maintaining our ignorance?"

The redhead worries at one thumbnail. The skin around it is raw and peeled, Rebecca notices; when did Ellie start doing that? "So Hafsah . . . ?"

"Suspects," she admits, "but also shouldn't know for sure. Her faith means a lot to her; please don't ever put her in the position of having to choose between your friendship and what it'll do to her to put her hand on a holy book and lie."

"You're not freaking out."

"It's been a hell of a month," she says with feeling, and Ellie laughs. Rebecca traces one of the rhinestone skulls with a fingertip. "We're not looking for reasons to make your life hell. If you want to return the favor, then please don't force the point."

"Ignorance as a shield."

"If you'll let us."

Rebecca and Ellie study each other, the moment stretching taut between them. Then Ellie flaps a hand behind her at all of her stuff. "I don't see why this can't wait until tomorrow."

"Because the winter move-out took literally years off of my life." She bundles the jeans back into the bag and stands. "I'm going to take these to my room, then come back and pack up the pillows. You are going to pack your things. And when you are done, provided you do it quickly and there's enough time before the others get back, we are going to do something, just the two of us."

"Really?"

"Really really."

Ellie smiles at the blatant bribery and goes back to her sorting, rather more cheerful about it now.

A few hours later there are still things unpacked, but they've accomplished enough that Rebecca feels comfortable leaving it for now. The others still have time to finish their finals, come back, and pack for a bit before the gathering is supposed to start.

Despite Ellie's laughing protests, Rebecca doesn't tell her where they're headed. They ride out on their bikes, making one brief stop at a florist so Rebecca can pick up her special order. She sets the box carefully in her nearly empty backpack and tucks tissue paper around it just in case. Ellie's having too much fun playing the nagging child to realize where they are when they turn off the road. Then they stop the bikes, and Ellie looks up at the doors and pales.

"You said you couldn't see her," Rebecca says quietly, weaving a chain through her bike and around a narrow post. "You don't have to go in if you don't want to or if you're not ready, but I thought . . ." She stands and dusts off her hands and knees. "I thought maybe if you don't have to face doing it alone, it might be easier."

Ellie swallows and stares at the door.

Letting her think it through, Rebecca locks up Ellie's bike as well, then walks over to the double doors and waits, looking back over her shoulder. After several minutes, Ellie hesitantly joins her, and they head into the cool air of the long-term care facility. The receptionist smiles and waves, the phone cradled between her ear and her shoulder. Rebecca guides her friend up the stairs and through the halls, then stops in front of one of the doors. It doesn't look different than any other door on the floor, really. If you don't know what's behind it, there is nothing particularly ominous about it.

They stand in front of the door for a time. Rebecca reaches out for Ellie's hand; it's shaking. She squeezes it gently, then laces their fingers together and stands, letting Ellie have as much time as she needs.

"I've always figured there's a part of her that must hate me," Ellie whispers.

"Why's that?"

"Because I never came."

But Rebecca shakes her head. "If there's enough of Kacey left in her to feel anything, the last thing she'd feel is hate. I think she'd understand that some things are just too hard. It's . . . it's painful to have this image of her," she admits. "Especially now that it so often superimposes over the bouncy, bubbly Kacey we knew. She'd understand that you couldn't do it before, and she'd understand if you can't do it now."

"My mom doesn't want me to bring Kacey's pillows next semester. She thinks I should donate them. Let Housing give me a roommate next year."

There was nothing wrong with the girl Housing moved into their suite when they came back from winter break. Or the three girls after that. Or the two girls they moved in last fall, after Kacey's parents had to withdraw her from school. Nothing wrong with them at all except that they weren't Kacey, and not even Keiko or Delia protested when Ellie drove them off. Rebecca honestly cannot imagine any of them being fine with a new eighth person next year, nor can she imagine that eighth person being any kind of happy when the rest of them are so close. *Isolated* would probably be the kindest word for how they'd feel.

"I'd maybe leave the poster picture at home," she says finally. "Just put a normal-sized picture of her on the nightstand. Leave half the pillows at home, so instead of burying the entire bed, you make it more like a couch, with the pillows along the wall and headboard. Still not a bed, still not someone else's space, but . . ."

"Compromise."

"Yeah. Or healing, a little."

Ellie sucks in a deep shuddering breath and nods. "Okay. I think I can do that. And maybe Mom will think it's a good step."

Nearly ten minutes more pass in front of the door. Eventually Ellie brushes her fingers against the cool metal handle. "How do you reconcile missing her so badly when she's right in front of you?"

"Because she isn't. This is just her body, Ellie. Kacey isn't in there anymore." She hopes.

Ellie opens the door.

There's no escaping the slightly clinical aspect of the room; Kacey can't take care of herself, and so there are discreet reminders of that. Still, they've done their best to make this place look welcoming, not quite a home but at least hers. The pictures that used to plaster her side of the dorm room are up on the walls, mixed through posters and prints. The walls themselves are painted a deep rose, with paler-pink curtains over the windows and in front of the tiny nurse's alcove for supplies. The bed is very clearly a hospital bed, but it's made up with linens from home, including her great-grandmother's handmade Tumbling Blocks quilt.

Small stacks of books and CDs show how much time her parents spend here. A rocking chair sits near the head of the bed, a sewing basket and a knitting tote on the floor beside it, and a recliner stands near the window with a lap desk leaned against the side. Things are softer, less crisp than they were when they first moved her in last November. It looks less foreboding for being lived in.

Kacey's vivid hair is duller now, not flying about her face and shoulders with the force of her gesticulations but braided tidily to one side and more than a foot shorter than it used to be. It's easier to take care of when it's shorter, but her parents couldn't bear to take all its length away. Kacey loved her hair; as far as Rebecca could tell, she never went through the traditional carrottop phase of discomfort with its color. Her face is rounder than it used to be, a side effect of the steroids helping her lungs. Her arms rest atop the quilt, palms up and fingers lightly curled.

Rebecca moves away from the door to set her backpack in the rocking chair. Pulling out the florist's box, she carefully undoes the ribbon and tape to open it, setting a blue glass vase on the nightstand. Carefully trimmed sprays of hothouse orange blossoms emerge from the mouth, interspersed with peach and rust roses. She asked the florist about it months ago, knowing that blossom season would be long over before the end of the semester. It was worth the effort it took to find a hothouse that could provide the off-season blooms to the florist. Gemma gave her the money for it, as it went somewhat past what she'd budgeted.

Kacey loved orange blossoms. Her mother's family owned wide sweeps of orange groves, and Kacey regularly brought in crates of oranges for the suite, or fresh orange juice. It was her grandfather who would weave the orange blossom crowns, resting the bands of cream-colored flowers on her hair.

Aware of Ellie standing frozen in the doorway, Rebecca sits on the very edge of the rocking chair and takes Kacey's hand. Her friend's hand is cool, the skin dry. She thinks about finding some lotion and rubbing it on for her, then decides that might be a bit too much for Ellie to see. Clearing her throat, she starts to speak quietly, telling Kacey what's happened since she saw her last. The Montroses made her promise that she would visit less as finals approached so that her grades wouldn't suffer. Rebecca saw the wisdom in it; more important, she saw the relief it brought Kacey's parents when she agreed.

She tells Kacey about the alligators, yes, but also about how Hafsah's off to Houston for the summer for an internship with NASA, how Luz and Keiko are planning a road trip to New York to spend entire days in the art museums. She tells her about the morning Delia woke up early and put oVertone in Susanna's conditioner, turning her blonde hair bright green, and how Susanna got revenge by putting superfine glitter in all of Delia's lotion bottles.

As Rebecca speaks, Ellie gradually comes closer until finally she's standing opposite Rebecca. Her hands are visibly shaking, but she wraps both of them around Kacey's still hand, bending over to press her forehead against Kacey's fingers. After a while Ellie clears her throat and stands straight, blinking the tears out of her eyes. "Rebecca is being sneaky," she tells Kacey. "She isn't telling you about Det Corby."

"Oh, God."

"So here's the scoop . . ."

Rebecca shakes her head but doesn't interrupt or try to stop her. It's only the three of them in the room; she can live with the embarrassment.

They spend nearly an hour with Kacey, teasing each other as they give more and more ridiculous updates to their friend. Eventually, though, a look at her watch tells Rebecca that it's almost time for a nursing assistant to come through and give Kacey her bath. "We should head back," she says. "The others should be done with their exams by now."

"And their packing?"

"The party doesn't start until the packing is done."

"Hard-ass." Ellie leans down and kisses Kacey's cheek. "I miss you," she whispers.

Rebecca reaches into her backpack. With the flowers on the nightstand, the bag is empty except for a single folder, which yields an article cut out from the *Gainesville Sun*. It's laminated in strips of clear packing tape rather than a proper single sheet, but she had to work with what she had. She studies it for a moment, then tucks it under Kacey's hand. Dillweed Dillon's face stares out from between her fingers.

Unlike many of the earlier articles about the various victims, this one is written by someone who knew Kacey, one of her cousins by marriage who cares less about the possibility of being sued than about getting the truth about Dillon McFarley out to the general population. It came out this morning; on her way to her final, Rebecca found a copy of this article and one of her own on the alligator altar closest to her dorm.

Ellie watches her and scowls at the sight of Dillon's face. "I'm glad he's dead."

"Me too."

Still looking at the black-and-white photo, Ellie shakes her head. "Just wish I knew who did it so I can shake their hand."

Rebecca blinks, opens her mouth, and changes her mind. Some things are best left unsaid. She understands that, even if Ellie doesn't.

Outside, as Ellie frees their bikes, Rebecca takes out her phone and turns the ringer back on, scrolling down an unexpected stream of messages, at least half of them from numbers she doesn't know. Frowning, she pulls up a thread from Jules, hoping to find some clarity there. Unfortunately, it's mostly exclamation points and gibberish. She taps the contact info and calls her rather than text.

"Where the hell are you?" Jules says in greeting. "You've got to see this!"

The last time Rebecca heard that, it was someone pounding on doors at six in the morning to summon everyone to the lounge; that was the morning they learned about the Cooper cousins at the gator farm. "See what?"

"Are you on campus?"

"Coming back to it. Why?"

"Then get to the Row. I promise, the detour will be worth it. Hurry!"

Rebecca pulls her phone away from her ear and stares at the screen with its blinking notification that the call has ended. "How do you feel about swinging by the Row on the way home?"

Ellie growls. "Why?"

"I don't know. But everyone and their mother apparently wants me to go there."

"Then who are we to disappoint them?" Shrugging, Ellie winds the lock chains and stuffs them back in her bag.

They can't claim to race back to campus given all the lights and crosswalks, but they go as fast as they can. Half the campus is leaving today, ahead of the Saturday congestion; therefore traffic is worse than ever. They pass Sledd Hall, and from there they can just follow the cheers and sounds of celebration. They exchange confused looks and keep going.

A massive crowd is gathered outside one of the houses on Fraternity Row, so dense that Rebecca and Ellie can't see what they're actually gathered for. Rebecca looks around and spots a familiar clutch of sorority girls, holding each other and bouncing in place as they giggle madly.

She swiftly folds down her bike, replaces it in its bag, and squeezes her way through to the gaggle. "What's going on?" she asks.

"There you are!" shrieks one of the blondes. "You made it! Come on!" She and her sisters grab Rebecca by the arms and bull their way through the crowd, Ellie following in their wake, until they get to the concrete sign for the fraternity. Jules is standing on top of it with her camera, alongside someone in the film track of the journalism program with a hefty camera rig balanced on one shoulder. "Here she is!" the sorority girl announces. "Oh, don't worry; we'll stay right here and guard your bags."

Bemused but willing to go along with it, Rebecca lets herself be pushed up to the sign. She and Ellie climb it and take a second to find their balance, looking down into the yard, where a rusting green dumpster sits on the grass. The fraternity brothers are all wearing shirts with the letters stitched several inches high and DC superhero masks covering their faces. She looks for the Jokers—the frats love the Joker for deeply disturbing reasons—but she doesn't see a single one.

"What are they doing?" she asks Jules.

"Watch."

The front doors of the house are propped open, two of the burlier boys standing guard to keep anyone from entering. Others stand around the dumpster, watching the crowds. Yet more parade back and forth between the house and the dumpster, carrying logs and tossing them into the dumpster. A few of the logs make the metal clang as they land, but mostly there are thunks as they collide with the logs already in there. Then a ceremonial trumpet flourish plays over speakers on the porch, and a new procession of boys begins, marching out of the house in pairs with pieces of painted plywood held between them. Scraps of fabric cling to the boards around nails and industrial-sized staples.

Rebecca startles as a hand grips her arm hard enough to bruise. Once she's got her balance back, she looks over at Ellie, who's watching the boys with laser focus even as she clings to Rebecca's arm. "What is it?" she whispers.

"That's the pantie board," Ellie answers. "They're taking apart the scoreboard."

"Not just taking it apart!" Jules adds, twirling a giddy circle on her tiptoes. "Watch!"

The boys hurl the boards into the dumpster, a cheer meeting each one. Rebecca's somewhat stunned by the number of boards. Just how large was the scoreboard? Empty handed, the boys move to either side of the dumpster to line the path to the door. A new boy comes out of the house, holding a large cardboard box. He stops in front of the bin and opens the box, holding it out upside down over the woodpile. Photos spill out in a flood.

By now, the crowd is so big they're pushing out into the road and obstructing traffic.

Three more boys come out of the house, walking slowly and carefully, carrying laundry baskets piled high with ladies' underwear. The cheers crescendo as the baskets are emptied into the dumpster with everything else. One of the boys climbs up onto the edge of the dumpster and holds his hands up for silence. Miraculously, he gets it.

He pulls off his Green Lantern mask, and a shocked gasp ripples through the crowd. The anonymity made sense, even if every member of the fraternity can be named with a little crowdsourcing. This, though . . . this might be even more of a statement than the burning. "My name is Thomas Wyatt," he says, pitching his voice to carry. "I'm the chapter president."

Boos roar back at him.

He accepts them stoically. "I should have spoken up against the scoreboard when it was first proposed three years ago," he continues once the insults die away. "I should have spoken up against it at every opportunity since then. When my brothers voted me chapter president, I should have dismantled the board myself if I had to. It was a disgrace and a failure of character. I'm sorry." He waits through the murmurs. "To everyone who was violated by the boys of this fraternity, to everyone who was harmed and humiliated by initial actions and being put up on the board after, I apologize. We can never undo that or make it up to you. But today, the board burns."

Rebecca's ears ring with the force of the cheers and screams.

"Today, our chapter agreed to a new code of conduct for all brothers moving forward," he says when the crowd allows. "The past few years, that board and the behavior that created it have defined our reputation. We were stupid enough to think that was a good thing. From now on, there are no second chances. Anyone who commits assault or rape, anyone who tries to bring back the board, anyone who uses drugs or force or fear—they will be kicked out without appeal. We've hurt a lot of people, and it's not going to happen anymore. We're going to do better. We're going to be better. It starts with this."

One of his brothers hands him a lit torch; other torches get handed out to the boys surrounding the dumpster. Two other brothers pour lighter fluid over the wood and fabric. "Ten!" yells Thomas. At the next count, half the crowd bellows it along with him. By *eight*, it seems like half the city is saying it. Rebecca glances down at the sorority girls, who are laughing and crying and dancing in place as they chant the numbers with everyone else. "One!" shrieks the crowd, and the boys hurl the torches into the dumpster. Thomas backflips off the rim as the lighter fluid ignites with a soft *thwump* and a billow of smoke.

Under the screams and cheers, Rebecca can hear the steady click of Jules's camera to her right. To her left, Ellie watches the rising flames, her eyes wide and gleaming bright. "You're crying," Rebecca murmurs.

"It's the smoke."

The smoke is mostly going straight up; what is drifting to the side is going away from them. Rather than argue, though, Rebecca wraps her arm around Ellie's waist, leans her head against Ellie's, and they watch the pantie board burn.

30

Rebecca and Ellie make their way back to the dorms, smelling of smoke, faces aching from smiling and laughing. The gathering at the fraternity has turned into a party, complete with massive pyramids of twenty-four-packs, not of beer but of off-brand soda. It's by no means the answer to world peace, but it's something. They just have something else waiting for them back at Sledd Hall.

They detour around a parking lot crowded with students packing cars and blocking each other in. Two girls rage at each other, surrounded by opened boxes and tubs with belongings strewn all around them. "Guess they won't be living together again," Ellie says.

"Hopefully not."

Passing the most familiar alligator altar, Rebecca reaches out and brushes her fingers against her laminated article. It wasn't by any stretch the point, but it's really nice to be appreciated.

Their suitemates are waiting impatiently for them and are only marginally appeased by their explanation until Ellie strikes a dramatic declamatory pose and tells "The Burning of the Board" with all the pomp and circumstance of an Edda. It has the other girls in stitches, and even Rebecca, who was there to witness it, laughs so hard she's almost crying.

She takes a quick shower while the others finish the very last of their packing; she doesn't want to go into her birthday party smelling of smoke, even if she loves the reason. The pantie board is gone, and an entire fraternity was so scared by all the attention that they made a public commitment to shape up. It's anyone's bet whether or not they'll actually follow through with it, of course; Thomas Wyatt is the graduating chapter president, not next year's leadership. Who knows what the fraternity of the fall will choose to do? But it's *something*—something beautiful and unexpected and absolutely bizarre.

"So where are we going?" Hafsah asks once Rebecca is back in their room, wrapped in towels and poking through her overnight bag. "No one has any idea what to wear."

"We are getting dinner, buying booze, and coming back to the lounge."

"Boo, you whore!" cries Ellie, sprawled across Hafsah's bed. "We're supposed to go clubbing! Dancing! Drinking!"

"Except for the clubbing, we can do those here, and I will only do the drinking here," Rebecca replies. "And not just for safety; Jules said a lot of the girls who talked to me for the article want to come say hi. Besides, I want to be comfortable, and it's my birthday, so I get to choose."

Ellie scowls but doesn't argue further. Birthday Girl always gets to choose, and she can't demand it on her birthday if she's not willing to abide by it on others'.

They're all in jeans and tank tops when they head out, except for Hafsah, who wears a long-sleeved tee. Dinner is a run through Moe's followed by a power walk to the closest liquor store, where they spend a good half hour entertaining the cashier with their arguments about what to get. Rebecca flat-out refuses to let anyone buy Ellie's rotgut vodka. Drinking gasoline would give the same buzz with less poison. Ellie keeps trying to sneak the bottles into the basket; Rebecca keeps taking them out and putting them back in their proper place on the shelf, and at the end, none of the terrible stuff is on the counter when the chuckling cashier gives them a twenty percent discount on everything just because.

Delia meeps and goes back to grab another couple of bottles of rum with the discount.

The bottles clink unambiguously in the tote bags as they walk back to Sledd, sending them all off into gales of laughter. Rebecca hasn't had a single drop of alcohol but already feels half-drunk from the whirlwind emotions of the day. Keiko and Delia try to dance to the rhythmic clinking, which goes a little better once Delia takes off her flip-flops. Hafsah and Susanna giggle and walk on the edges of the sidewalk to be living bumpers for the pinball girls, keeping them from spinning off or falling down.

They scan into Sledd, troop up the stairs, and make a brief stop in their suite to change into even more comfortable clothes. Rebecca swaps her jeans—the jeans Ellie bought her, with the skulls on the back pockets—for plain leggings, and even though she'll be overwarm within minutes, she pulls on the Royals hoodie she still hasn't returned to Det Corby. Even Hafsah laughs at her for that.

When they make their way out of the suite and down to the lounge, a massive yell of "Surprise!" startles Rebecca so badly she almost drops the bottles she's carrying. The lounge is packed with girls, most of whom don't even live in Sledd, but Rebecca recognizes probably eighty percent from that long night of listening to stories. Some of them, including the knot of sorority girls she really is going to have to learn the names of at some point, have streaks of ash on their cheeks in a weird marrying of eye black and Ash Wednesday. She doesn't have to ask to know the ash is from the literal dumpster fire of the pantie board.

A large sheet cake sits on the battered coffee table, with a frosting gator on most of the top. Just above the gator in as close to a newsprint font as you can get with a piping bag, a "headline" reads "Lady Gators Snapping Back" and, in a smaller cursive below it, "by Rebecca Sorley."

"That's not my headline," she says, laughing.

"We had to put the order in a few days ago," Jules replies. "We had to wing it."

Bags and bowls of snacks are stacked over the rest of the coffee table and the counters of the small kitchen beyond, and there are green alligator decorations everywhere. It's ridiculous and amazing, and Rebecca can't stop laughing as she takes it all in. Linsey Travers walks up to her and plops a silver plastic dollar-store tiara on Rebecca's head, the jewels painted green. For a moment, Rebecca considers going back to her room to dig out the alligator tooth earrings Gemma sent her. Only for a moment, though; she quickly decides she doesn't want to spend the rest of the night defending them from Ellie.

In addition to their gifts of food, the girls all brought their own drinks of whatever variety. Alcoholic or not, everyone has her own bottle or can. There's still a lot of sharing as girls sample each other's drinks, but there's no actual common source for anyone to drug. Safe among friends and people who trust her, with doors and stairs between her and the outside world, Rebecca drinks, and the party swings into full blast when someone plugs their iPod into portable speakers.

The actual number of attendees shifts constantly as girls leave to finish packing or join other parties, and new girls arrive. Rebecca perches on the back of one of the long couches, her back to the hall, and smiles whenever she notices someone new making their way to the cake.

Ellie twists the cap off a brand-new bottle of whiskey and passes it up to Rebecca. "Drink!" she commands. "Your article reached a national audience today! Drink!"

The lounge fills with cheers, and everyone with a drink in their hand lifts it in a toast. Rebecca obliges, coughing as she tries to swallow what is definitely more than a shot's worth. "To Ellie!" she replies. "For somehow not getting arrested!" Everyone laughs as she passes the bottle back to Ellie, who takes a swig.

"To Keiko!" Ellie cries, holding out the bottle. "For never getting dehydrated no matter how much you cried!"

They pass the whiskey to a new suitemate with each toast, each one more ridiculous than the last. Even Hafsah plays along, though she drinks from her bottle of Gatorade. "To Jules!" announces Rebecca, and the girl lifts her much-smaller bottle of fizzy flavored vodka. "For knowing half the goddamn world!"

Jules grins and drinks.

"And to Kerry!" Rebecca continues. The senior looks startled but lifts her beer. "For being the best damn RA in Sledd Hall!" A roar of cheers follows, at least half of them from girls who don't even live there.

After a couple of hours, the party has mostly wound down to a handful of groups chatting on couches and finishing up bags of chips. Rebecca isn't disappointed by that; the large surprise was nice but so is just sitting with her suitemates and giggling over three years of inside jokes and stories. She blinks at a strange sound. "Does anyone else hear 'Cell Block Tango'?" she asks.

"That's your cell phone, you drunk bitch."

"I am not drunk," she corrects primly and sticks her tongue out at Ellie. She manages to dig her phone out of the kangaroo pocket of the hoodie without falling off the back of the couch, which she thinks she can be rather proud of, and yelps at the name on the screen. "It's our Corby!"

The masculine laughter coming out of the speaker informs her that she accidentally accepted the call. Cautiously, she hits the speakerphone button so everyone can hear. "Our Corby, huh? At least you didn't call me *Detective* this time."

"But you are a detective," she points out. "Hi."

"Hi." He's laughing at her still, but that's okay. She can ride out the shame at home, where only Gemma knows about her silly crush. "If I wanted to talk to you and your roommates, where should I go?"

"Did you see someone put my story up on the altar?"

"Altar? You getting married now?"

"Not a wedding altar, an aggilator altar," she tells him earnestly.

Hafsah leans over and tells the man that they're in the third-floor lounge in their dorm, and Kerry offers to go down and let him in. She has to go to bed soon anyway because she'll be out of her mind in the morning trying to help everyone with the move-out. "When will you be here?" Kerry asks, eyeing the level of beer left in her bottle.

"Just a few minutes," he answers, his voice distorted. "Last night of finals week; there are a lot of us out here. Lots of extra patrols tonight."

"Oh, no!" cries Susanna. "What about Officer Kevin? We're not sober enough to protect Hafsah if he decides to be a dickhead!"

There's a pained silence from the phone. "I'll see you soon," Det Corby says.

"To Det Corby!" says Ellie as the call ends. "The best fucking cop in the whole damn city!"

Susanna hiccups and starts warbling "Tanto amore segreto." Delia hits her in the face with a throw pillow to make her stop.

When steady footsteps come down the hall in their direction, Rebecca twists around to see Det Corby walking toward them. He's in a vest again. She likes how he looks in vests. Keiko pops her head up over the top of the couch, eyes wide. "You didn't bring Officer Kevin with you, did you?" she asks anxiously.

"I did not," he tells her. "That's actually why I needed to come up." He glances curiously at the bottle of vanilla vodka in Rebecca's hand, which she's been drinking from whenever the whiskey bottle is with someone else. "Officer Kevin was found dead at home this afternoon after missing work. Looks like he committed suicide."

"Shame," Ellie says cheerfully and takes a slug of whiskey. Rebecca follows suit with the vodka. The drink, not the cheer. She probably shouldn't cheer, even if she kind of wants to.

"Can't even pretend, Ellie?"

"A predator is dead. Only ones mourning are other predators. A drink! For all the girls safe from Officer Kevin."

The others look a little sheepish as the bottle gets passed around. Ellie reaches between Rebecca and Det Corby to take the bottle back from Luz. "You can't have any; you're too young," she tells the detective.

"*I'm* too young?" he mutters. He shakes his head and smiles at Rebecca. "Congratulations," he says warmly. "*Washington Post*, that's pretty big."

"Only on Sundays," she says. "Otherwise it's a normal newspaper size."

"Just how drunk are you?"

"I am not drunk. I am tipsy! Wanna know how I know?" She lifts her legs and spins on the top of the couch to face him but misjudges the force needed and topples off the back. Hafsah rescues the bottle of booze, and Det Corby rescues Rebecca, laughing and holding her close to keep her from falling. "I'm a sleepy drunk," she whispers loudly. She buries her face in his collar and takes a deep breath. "You smell much better without the swamp water."

"River water," corrects Delia.

Det Corby's hands are large and warm against her sides, where the hoodie has twisted up from her movement, his fingers curving around her ribs. If she forgets that she's tipsy—and she's pretty good at that when she's tipsy—it's almost like he's hugging her, only there's nothing sad this time. "You're not going to get in trouble for being here, are you? What with Ellie being a murderer and all?"

"Hey! Suspected murderer, thank you!"

"I was taken off the case as a precautionary measure," he says. "But yes, let's call it for the best that Ellie is going home for the summer."

Susanna nods along with him. "Betcha the dying stops," she says sagely.

Ellie hits her again with the throw pillow.

Rebecca looks down at the hoodie and blinks. "Oh! This is your hoodie! I should give it back to you." She reaches for the hem, but his hands lightly squeeze her sides.

"Keep it," he tells her. "It suits you."

She beams, even as Ellie fake gags behind her. "It's too hot for outside," she confides, probably louder than she intends. "But earlier, when we were, you know . . ."

"Outside?"

"Yes! There were fireflies, and they were beautiful." *Beautiful* becomes at least five syllables and ten seconds long. "That means it's going to storm tonight. Lightning bugs come out before lightning storms; that's what my grandmother says."

"I don't know if that's true, but The Weather Channel agrees with her for the forecast," Hafsah informs her.

"Drink for your grandmother!" Ellie cries and tries to pass the bottle again.

"Any chance you could wait to do that until you're not in front of law enforcement that knows you're underage?"

Rebecca laughs so hard she loses her balance, and his arms around her are suddenly the only things holding her up. "It's my birthday! Twenty-one years ago today, Gemma became my grandmother, so we have to drink to Gemma! Give the bottle to Corby Detective I mean Corby Det."

"How about Patrick?" he asks, leaning forward so his nose is nearly touching hers.

"Now that I'm legal?"

He blushes and puts a couple of inches between them, making Ellie cackle. He does not accept the bottle from Luz.

Rebecca does and then passes it back to Ellie.

Det Corby clears his throat. "Happy birthday, Rebecca."

"You too."

"I think she means *thank you*," Hafsah says dryly.

"That too."

Draping herself across the back of the couch, her flaming hair wild around her, Ellie grins up at the detective. "Do you have a present for her?"

"He didn't know it was her birthday!"

As Susanna and Ellie start arguing over whether or not that's any excuse, and Keiko anxiously retrieves the throw pillow before it can hit

Susanna again, Rebecca yawns and wraps her arms around Det Corby's neck, nestling into him. The problem with silly and tipsy is that it can turn into sleepy and drunk—and without much warning if she doesn't keep a steady intake. "This is my present," she whispers. "It's the best present."

She can feel more than hear his laughter. One hand leaves her side, and she mourns it for a moment until it returns to cup the right side of her face. He leans forward again, and this time he presses a soft kiss to the corner of her mouth. "Happy birthday," he says again. "I hope it's been everything wonderful."

She plants a kiss on his cheek, less soft and less graceful. "It is now."

Ellie gives a loud wolf whistle, and Susanna tries to copy her but ends up sputtering all over Delia, who protests and shoves her into Keiko, who starts crying because she's Keiko, and Luz darts over to comfort her, dropping an open bottle that starts spilling all over the floor, and Hafsah rolls her eyes, and Rebecca just laughs and snuggles into Det Corby's shoulder and neck.

The pantie board is burned, and Officer Kevin is dead, and girls on campus got to tell their stories for a major national newspaper, and she just feels so damn proud of everything she's done. It has been everything wonderful, she thinks.

31

I didn't kill Mountebanks the Asshole.

I feel like that should be said.

As many people as I killed in the past month and change, Mountebanks Fuckface-Whogivesashit III was not one of them. There's a difference between taking something personally and making it personal, and unlike Ellie, I respect both that difference and the importance of it.

I take it personally that so many assholes make the world unsafe for women.

I don't make it personal; I don't attack the ones who attack me, because that would draw suspicion. Officer Kevin is the closest I've ever come to that line, but my lizard brain is strong, and he attacked Hafsah, so he was worth the risk to satisfy the rage. Dillon hurt Kacey, but it was months ago, long enough that he'd already hurt others, long enough that most people won't immediately connect him to our group and retaliation.

Two days into my week home, I get a call from Ellie that she's being taken in for questioning again, this time for Mountebanks. It's a short conversation, one I suspect is taking place from the back of a police car, but she doesn't seem at all worried or afraid. I don't think it's because she's innocent but rather that she's so good at blazing her way through obstacles she's stopped seeing them as problems.

The rocking chair creaks as my grandmother sits down, joining me on the back porch. I'm perched on the rail, back against a post, looking out over the land. It's still technically all one massive ranch, but my family has gradually and unofficially portioned off parts for wedding gifts as various generations of children have gotten married, letting them build houses of their own. Now we surround the lake, family as far as the eye can see.

A drift of smoke wafts past me. Gemma usually has her first cigarette lit as she's walking out the door. Some people call their grandmothers Grandma, or Nana, or Gram. Thanks to one of the oldest cousins consistently mispronouncing Grandma back when he was a toddler, we all call the grand dame Gemma. We sit together for a while in silence save for the steady rhythmic creak of her rocking chair.

"I've got a question for you, girl."

I shift to better look at her without losing my balance or straining my neck.

"What are you going to do if your friend gets pinned for things you did?"

It's habit to check for other family members, but it's the middle of the day, and most everyone's at work, and the few who aren't are sleeping because they'll be at work tonight. The younger cousins and the handful of older cousins who still have summer break are God knows where, but they're not in the house I share with my parents and Gemma, and they're not in sight. Safe enough. "Probably nothing," I admit. "It was never my intention to frame Ellie or even to cast suspicion on her. She does that all on her own."

"But?"

"But," I agree. "I'm not about to look a gift horse in the mouth. It's not my fault that people think murder and go straight to her."

She blows out another plume of smoke. There's a ridge on both her upper and lower lip where the tissue has literally reshaped itself for the frequency of her cigarettes. Elaine Sorley, for whom I was given my middle name, used to be a beautiful woman. She's a handsome one still, despite the heavy lines from years of smoking. Her red hair is mostly white now, bound in a heavy braid down her back, but her blue-gray eyes are still sharp. She was a true redhead in her prime, not a ginger like me. She once told me, when I was complaining about my universe of freckles, that she has exactly three freckles, and they're all on her ass, and I should be grateful to have so many that no one ever asks to see them.

I love everyone in my family, and genuinely like almost all of them, but my grandmother is special. She taught me about lightning bugs and pulse points and which drugs keep breaking down in the body after death and are therefore safe to use in a murder.

I'm a lot like my grandmother.

She flicks the ash off the butt of one cigarette and uses the butt to light the next. "I was surprised to see the article. You think it's safe to write about your own murders?"

"I wasn't writing about them, though. I was writing about the other girls on campus."

She thinks her way through that, careful and deliberate, then nods. Near my feet, the railing has a large box for the giant glass jars of brewing sun tea. A glass of ice and the finished product sweats under my bent knees. "Courting season lasts the rest of the month," she says eventually. "Are you going to keep going once you get back?"

"No. If I stopped for a week and then started again, it would make it really obvious that it was one of the summer students. Best to leave it, I think, and leave the possibility that it was one of the graduating seniors."

"Did it scratch the itch?"

I lift one hand and wobble it back and forth. "It did at first." I lean my head back against the post and try to gather my feelings into some semblance of sense. The itch is what Gemma always called her own urge to kill, and she introduced it to me the summer between junior and senior year of high school, when the attack on Daphne left me a snarling, seething creature made of rage. I'd always been the one most like Gemma; it wasn't until she taught me how to parse rumor and hearsay for fact to track down which soccer players were responsible for the actual assault that I realized just how deep that went. She was with me as we figured out the boys' habits. Over the next two years, together or separately, we brought revenge to the assholes who hurt my cousin so badly.

It also taught me that straight-up revenge is a dangerous thing, addictive as hell, and prone to making you fuck up. Officer Kevin was personal. Dillon McFarley was personal. That rage is so seductive, so welcoming, it's hard to pull back far enough from it to not be stupid. To be careful, as I keep telling Ellie she needs to be. The laundry list of people I could kill without mourning them is . . . long. That doesn't mean I can go about killing all of them.

That's why Gemma calls it an itch. It's an impulse, one that we can choose to satisfy or not. Bugbites itch, chicken pox itch, healing wounds itch. You still shouldn't scratch them. Or as Gemma put it, "Just because a man's balls itch doesn't mean he should scratch them in public, and one day your fool uncle Gabe'll finally learn that." Gabe married into the family; it's why Gemma feels comfortable insulting his upbringing.

At the end of the day, I'm not made of any less rage than Ellie. I'm just much, much better at focusing it, at understanding when it's okay to let it out and when it's best not to act. To wait. It's tempting to constantly give in to that fury, but the more you give in to it, the more you become a slave to it. That's how you get caught.

"I wasn't looking to become a folk hero," I say wryly.

She barks a laugh and gives me a crooked smile. "Oh, sweetheart. That's the thing about being a vigilante: if everyone knows why the dead ones are dying, more than a few are going to be grateful to the one doing the killing. You picked a good reason. Did you really think no one was going to put it together?"

"I did not expect the altars. I'm used to girls whispering their stories, not blasting them out for everyone."

"But that's a good thing, isn't it? That they're sharing them publicly?"

"For now." I sigh and pick up my glass so I can straighten my legs, crossing them at the ankle so Daphne's thread anklet shows on top. She's not back from Pennsylvania yet, but she's promised the new one is already done. She won't tell me the colors. "People forget things, Gemma. They move on and forget, and the smart girls are going to realize that and go back to whispering in the bathrooms. I worry about the ones who don't understand that and try to keep being loud."

"This world's always going to hurt women, Rebecca. You can't change the world."

"I know. I guess everyone else had me half-convinced it was possible."

"And that's the trouble with folk heroes. You can't fall for your own legend, sweetheart."

"It's probably for the best that I'm stopping for a while."

"Probably."

I sigh and lean my head back against the post. "I didn't intend for it to be a warning," I admit. "I wasn't trying to scare anyone into changing their behavior; I wasn't trying to inspire the girls. I was just trying to stop the boys. They hurt people, viciously and deeply, and I didn't want them to be able to keep hurting new victims. That was it. It wasn't about social change or being a champion or any of that. All I wanted to do was stop them. And then . . ."

"You don't get to choose how people interpret your work," she reminds me. "Maybe they read into it too far, saw what they wanted to see, but that's human nature, orange blossom. You can't change that. You can't protect yourself from it either. You do your work the best you can. The rest is out of your hands."

"I know."

She flicks the ash of her new cigarette, giving me a long considering look. "You planted a kiss on that detective yet?"

"Gemma!"

"Oh, my girl. Going out and getting what you want isn't just about murder, you know?"

There's something, I think, some foolishness or absurdity, in being more embarrassed by a crush than by murder. I'm proud of what I've done. I don't think it's good or right or even justified, but it's satisfying in a way that feels important, and as long as I have that itch to kill that I inherited from my grandmother along with her eyes and nose and the heart-shaped birthmark near my navel, I can choose to aim it in a better direction than undiscriminating slaughter. The actions are not good, but if good comes of them, that's a reason to keep on doing them, isn't it?

Intermittently, anyway. I still don't want to get caught.

I think Hafsah is right about Ellie killing that damned hate preacher who used to stalk about in front of the buildings and abuse the students passing by. I think she's right about Ellie killing Mountebanks. It's vindictive and messy and strangely smug—and satisfying in a more immediate way. Despite playing devil's advocate with Hafsah, I've really never doubted that Ellie is a murderer. Like calls to like, maybe.

What I have wondered is whether or not Ellie recognizes that same element in me.

I still don't have an answer for that. I don't know if I ever will.

At least it keeps things interesting.

ABOUT THE AUTHOR

Dot Hutchison is the author of the Collector series (*The Butterfly Garden*, *The Roses of May*, *The Summer Children*, and *The Vanishing Season*) as well as *A Wounded Name*, a young adult novel based on Shakespeare's *Hamlet*. Hutchison loves thunderstorms, mythology, history, and movies that can and should be watched on repeat. She has a background in theater, Renaissance-festival living chessboards, and free falls. She likes to think that Saint George regretted killing that dragon for the rest of his days. For more information on her current projects, visit www.dothutchison.com.